THE BELOVED ENEMY

BOOKS BY GILBERT MORRIS

THE HOUSE OF WINSLOW SERIES

The Honorable Imposter
The Captive Bride
The Indentured Heart
The Gentle Rebel
The Saintly Buccaneer
The Holy Warrior
The Reluctant Bridegroom
The Last Confederate
The Dixie Widow
The Wounded Yankee
The Union Belle
The Final Adversary
The Crossed Sabres
The Valiant Gunman
The Gallant Outlaw
The Jeweled Spur
The Yukon Queen
The Rough Rider
The Iron Lady
The Silver Star

The Shadow Portrait
The White Hunter
The Flying Cavalier
The Glorious Prodigal
The Amazon Quest
The Golden Angel
The Heavenly Fugitive
The Fiery Ring
The Pilgrim Song
The Beloved Enemy
The Shining Badge
The Royal Handmaid
The Silent Harp
The Virtuous Woman
The Gypsy Moon
The Unlikely Allies
The High Calling
The Hesitant Hero
The Widow's Choice
The White Knight

CHENEY DUVALL, M.D.[1]

1. The Stars for a Light
2. Shadow of the Mountains
3. A City Not Forsaken
4. Toward the Sunrising
5. Secret Place of Thunder
6. In the Twilight, in the Evening
7. Island of the Innocent
8. Driven With the Wind

CHENEY AND SHILOH: THE INHERITANCE[1]

1. Where Two Seas Met
2. The Moon by Night
3. There Is a Season

THE SPIRIT OF APPALACHIA[2]

1. Over the Misty Mountains
2. Beyond the Quiet Hills
3. Among the King's Soldiers
4. Beneath the Mockingbird's Wings
5. Around the River's Bend

LIONS OF JUDAH

1. Heart of a Lion
2. No Woman So Fair
3. The Gate of Heaven
4. Till Shiloh Comes
5. By Way of the Wilderness
6. Daughter of Deliverance

[1]with Lynn Morris   [2]with Aaron McCarver

GILBERT MORRIS

the BELOVED ENEMY

BETHANYHOUSE
Minneapolis, Minnesota

The Beloved Enemy
Copyright © 2003
Gilbert Morris

Cover illustration by William Graf
Cover design by Josh Madison

Scripture quotations are from the King James Version of the Bible.

Published by Bethany House Publishers
11400 Hampshire Avenue South
Bloomington, Minnesota 55438

Bethany House Publishers is a division of
Baker Publishing Group, Grand Rapids, Michigan.

Printed in the United States of America

ISBN-13: 978-0-7642-2974-9
ISBN-10: 0-7642-2974-5

The Library of Congress has cataloged the original edition as follows:

Morris, Gilbert.
    The beloved enemy / by Gilbert Morris.
        p.   cm. — (The house of Winslow ; bk. 30)
    ISBN 0-7642-2704-1
    1. Winslow family (Fictitious characters)—Fiction. 2. Americans—Egypt—Fiction. 3. New York (N.Y.)—Fiction. 4. Archaeologists—Fiction. 5. Jewish women—Fiction. 6. Ex-convicts—Fiction. 7. Egypt—Fiction.
I. Title. II. Series: Morris, Gilbert. House of Winslow ; bk. 30.
    PS3563.O8742B45   2003
    813'.54—dc21
                                                                    2003002572

Dedication

TO MARY MOYE
How wonderful it is to meet those who are loving,
cheerful, honest—and love my books!

Johnnie and I have found a friend in you, one who
brings some light into our lives.

Gil and Johnnie Morris

GILBERT MORRIS spent ten years as a pastor before becoming Professor of English at Ouachita Baptist University in Arkansas and earning a Ph.D. at the University of Arkansas. A prolific writer, he has had over 25 scholarly articles and 200 poems published in various periodicals, and over the past years has had more than 180 novels published. His family includes three grown children. He and his wife live in Gulf Shores, Alabama.

CONTENTS

PART FOUR
The Prize

THE HOUSE OF WINSLOW

★ ★ ★ ★

THE HOUSE OF WINSLOW

★　★　★

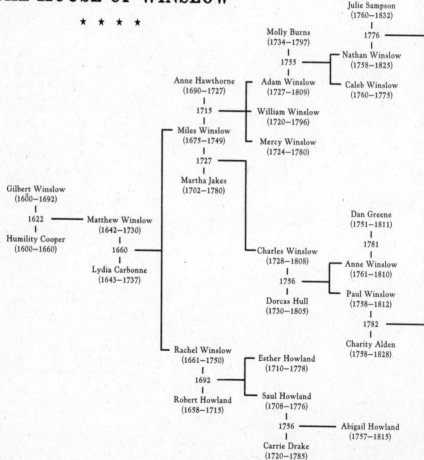

Julie Sampson
(1760–1832)
|
1776 ————
|
Nathan Winslow
(1758–1825)

Molly Burns
(1734–1797)
|
1755
|
Adam Winslow
(1727–1809)

Caleb Winslow
(1760–1775)

Anne Hawthorne
(1690–1727)
|
1715 ————
|
Miles Winslow
(1675–1749)

William Winslow
(1720–1796)

Mercy Winslow
(1724–1780)
|
1727 ————
|
Martha Jakes
(1702–1780)

Gilbert Winslow
(1600–1692)
|
1622 ———— Matthew Winslow
(1642–1730)
|
1660
|
Lydia Carbonne
(1643–1737)

Humility Cooper
(1600–1660)

Dan Greene
(1751–1811)
|
1781
|
Anne Winslow
(1761–1810)

Charles Winslow
(1728–1808)
|
1756
|
Dorcas Hull
(1730–1805)

Paul Winslow
(1758–1812)
|
1782 ————
|
Charity Alden
(1758–1828)

Rachel Winslow
(1661–1750)
|
1692
|
Robert Howland
(1658–1715)

Esther Howland
(1710–1778)

Saul Howland
(1708–1776)
|
1756 ———— Abigail Howland
(1757–1815)
|
Carrie Drake
(1720–1785)

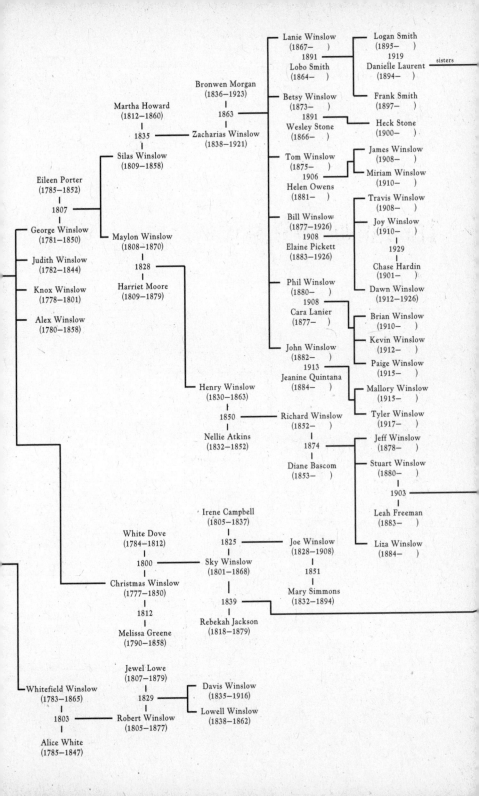

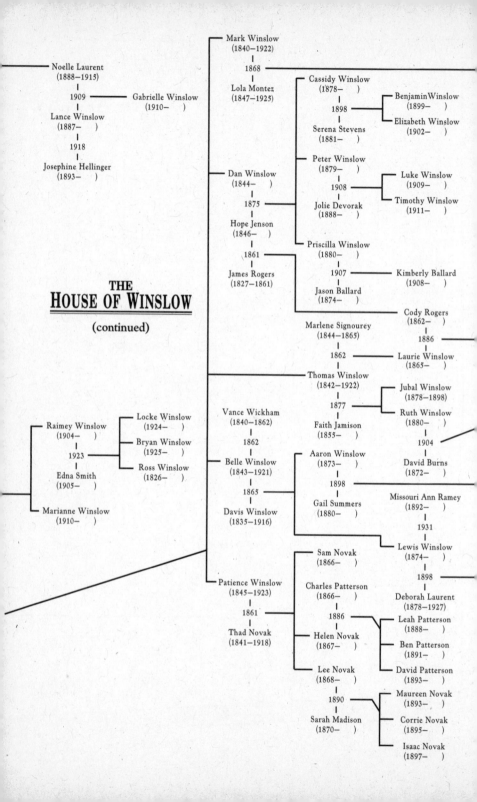

**THE
HOUSE OF WINSLOW**

(continued)

Noelle Laurent
(1888–1915)

1909 ———— Gabrielle Winslow
(1910–)

Lance Winslow
(1887–)

1918

Josephine Hellinger
(1893–)

Mark Winslow
(1840–1922)

1868

Lola Montez
(1847–1925)

Cassidy Winslow
(1878–)

1898

Serena Stevens
(1881–)

BenjaminWinslow
(1899–)

Elizabeth Winslow
(1902–)

Dan Winslow
(1844–)

1875

Hope Jenson
(1846–)

Peter Winslow
(1879–)

1908

Jolie Devorak
(1888–)

Luke Winslow
(1909–)

Timothy Winslow
(1911–)

James Rogers
(1827–1861)

1861

Priscilla Winslow
(1880–)

1907 ———— Kimberly Ballard
(1908–)

Jason Ballard
(1874–)

Marlene Signourey
(1844–1865)

1862

Cody Rogers
(1862–)

1886

Laurie Winslow
(1865–)

Thomas Winslow
(1842–1922)

1877

Faith Jamison
(1855–)

Jubal Winslow
(1878–1898)

Ruth Winslow
(1880–)

1904

David Burns
(1872–)

Vance Wickham
(1840–1862)

1862

Belle Winslow
(1843–1921)

1865

Davis Winslow
(1835–1916)

Aaron Winslow
(1873–)

1898

Gail Summers
(1880–)

Missouri Ann Ramey
(1892–)

1931

Lewis Winslow
(1874–)

1898

Deborah Laurent
(1878–1927)

Raimey Winslow
(1904–)

1923

Edna Smith
(1905–)

Locke Winslow
(1924–)

Bryan Winslow
(1925–)

Ross Winslow
(1826–)

Marianne Winslow
(1910–)

Patience Winslow
(1845–1923)

1861

Thad Novak
(1841–1918)

Sam Novak
(1866–)

Charles Patterson
(1866–)

1886

Helen Novak
(1867–)

Leah Patterson
(1888–)

Ben Patterson
(1891–)

David Patterson
(1893–)

Lee Novak
(1868–)

1890

Sarah Madison
(1870–)

Maureen Novak
(1893–)

Corrie Novak
(1895–)

Isaac Novak
(1897–)

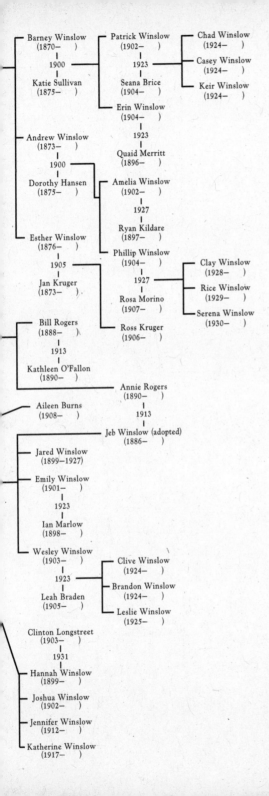

PART ONE

Kefira

★ ★ ★

CHAPTER ONE

DREAMS

★ ★ ★ ★

High overhead, huge billowy clouds drifted across the light blue sky, driven along by a soft summer wind. The clouds looked like giant pillows, whiter than anything Kefira had ever seen. Even the pure blue in the sky was unlike any other color, without blemish as it spread its ethereal canopy over the horizon. It was, Kefira thought, like a great round bowl set over the earth and illuminated by the glowing sun, which threw its beams upon the fertile ground beneath.

On her left, fields stretched all the way to where the mountains, low and humpbacked, scored the blue of the sky. On her right, the fields stretched to a verdant forest, a brighter green than the mountains, so colorful it almost hurt her eyes. Far off she could see cows grazing on the emerald grass, and overhead a bird was circling slowly and majestically.

The pungent smell of the rich, loamy earth tickled her senses. Her nostrils tingled at a sweetness she couldn't identify, perhaps the fragrance of the red, yellow, and orange blooms that lined the roadside and spotted the landscape like fiery sparks.

She sauntered along, her senses fully engaged with the enticing smells and sights and sounds. The road bent in a dogleg, and she picked up her pace, anticipating a new vision beyond the turn—at once wonderful, beautiful, exotic. As she passed a stand of trees around the bend, her eyes were drawn to a lone house straight ahead, with tall, stately oaks lining the road up to it. This was strange to her. In her world, houses were always crowded together, side by side, but this one stood alone, rising two stories with four columns along the front porch and chimneys on either end. The house was as fresh and white as the clouds, and puffs of pearly white smoke rose from its chimneys. A picket fence surrounded the yard, where a woman was hanging clothes on a line stretched between two trees. In the front of the house, a large bluish dog with floppy ears was reared up on a tree, barking shrilly toward the upper branches.

Kefira had never seen such a house, but somehow she knew it was filled with people who loved each other. She broke into a run, her arms outstretched, longing to embrace the vision before her—but even as she did, the house faded from view. She looked wildly around, and the colors were fading also. The vibrant yellows, blues, and greens sank into a dull, monotonous gray. She choked out a cry as it all disappeared. . . .

Kefira awoke with a start and opened her eyes to the darkness, fragments of the dream still more real than the hard, narrow bed in which she lay. She could still smell the flowers, the loam-scented earth, the enticing greenery that had filled her dreamland.

But gradually the real smells of her life assaulted her, even in her closetlike room—the sewage-filled drains, the sweat of human beings crowded closely together, the rotting stench of old cabbage, and the foul odor of leaky gas lines. She sat up in bed, throwing back the thin, moth-eaten blankets, then stopped as the damp chill of the room engulfed her. She did not move as a sense of loss came over her.

"It was so beautiful," she whispered aloud. "So very beautiful!" For an instant, she could still feel the earth under her feet as she moved down that road—and she knew she would never be able to forget the vivid dream of the inviting house, the woman hanging up her freshly washed laundry, and the dog barking up the tree.

With no window in her dreary bedroom to admit the morning sun, Kefira had to depend upon her inner clock to know when to get up. Somehow she always knew the time, within a few minutes, but she could never explain why. Even throughout the day when someone asked what time it was, she could tell instinctively. It was an intuition that was not in other people. Although it was pitch black in her room, she knew with certainty that outside those brick walls, the gray January dawn was creeping up over the streets of New York City, and there was no more time for dreams.

Climbing out of bed, she winced as her feet hit the icy floor, and when she reached up and turned on the light, the room seemed uglier to her than it had ever been. There was nothing pretty about it. A few pictures clipped from old calendars and magazines were pasted to the walls, but compared to her dream, their colors seemed faded and tired. A single bed was covered with threadbare sheets and blankets; an old chest of drawers sagged to one side, propped up by a brick. A few tattered clothes hung from pegs on the walls. A glass of artificial flowers offered its bit of color, a sad reminder of the vivid freshness of the flowers along the wayside and scattered about the fields in her dream. She at once pushed all such vain imaginings out of her mind.

Quickly she shucked off her flannel gown and shivered as she pulled on the warmest underwear she had. It needed washing, but that would have to wait. Kefira loved the touch and smell of clean clothes, but washing was a luxury in her home, so she pulled on three pair of dirty woolen stockings, faded and worn thin, then a pair of awkward black shoes stiff with the cold.

Leaving the bedroom, she passed into the main living area of the apartment. At one end was the gas stove, a cabinet nailed to the wall, and a kitchen table with four mismatched chairs. At one time they had all been painted blue, but the color had become chipped and faded, exposing the assorted layers of paint and raw wood beneath. The floor was a leprous gray, patchily covered with remnants of rugs salvaged from previous tenants. A window on the east wall admitted the first pale light of the morning sun, and Kefira noted the dust motes dancing almost merrily in the beams. Feeling no such gaiety, she turned and left the room, heading downstairs and out the back door to a smelly outhouse located in the bare and junk-filled backyard. Closing her eyes to the sights and her nose to the smell, she took care of her necessary business as hastily as she could, shivering in the icy cold, then ran back up the stairs and down the hall to the bathroom she shared with other tenants on the floor. With a sigh of relief that no one was there, she stepped inside and shut the door, bolted it, then turned to look at the bathtub. She choked back the impulse to gag at the grime that clung to its surface. She was by nature a young woman who liked cleanliness, but in this New York tenement she had to fight a daily war to salvage some bit of it for herself. Most people simply gave up and sank back into the filth that fell from skies choked with coal smoke from thousands of chimneys and that accumulated from the habits of human beings herded closely together.

She did not have time to clean the tub now, so she quickly splashed cold water on her face from the faucet at the equally grimy sink, dried her face and hands, and took a few swipes at her thick hair with a comb. The mirror was spotted and streaked, but she stopped a moment to examine her face. Staring back at her from vacant eyes was a young woman of seventeen years with black hair dulled by the ravages of her unhealthy living conditions but still framing her face softly with its natural curl as it cascaded about her shoulders and down her back. She pinned it up quickly, looking into her own eyes as she did. In the dim light, they looked almost black, but depending on the outfit she wore, they could appear a dark blue. Over her eyes, black eyebrows arched in a way that usually only great artists could invent, but hers were natural. The eyes themselves were almond shaped, overshadowed by thick black lashes. Her mouth was wide and mobile—too wide, she thought. The fashion plates she saw in the few magazines that came her way showed women with pouty, tiny mouths. She tightened her lips to imitate a tiny pout, but the look was comical and made her smile.

"Too late to try to have a little mouth," she murmured, laughing at her own foolishness. Her face was oval, and her skin smooth, though her sallow complexion revealed the hard living conditions she suffered. She pinched her cheeks in an effort to make them rosy and bit her lips slightly to redden them. Despite the toll that tenement life had taken on her appearance, she knew she was still pretty. Men's heads turned her way as she walked down the street, and ever since she had begun to blossom into a young woman at the age of twelve or thirteen, men had told her how beautiful she was—some in ways she did not want to think about now. She finished pinning up her rebellious hair, opened the door, and turned out the light, promising herself a hot bath in a freshly scrubbed tub when she came home after work.

Going back to her bedroom, she shut and latched the door behind her. She glanced around the room, feeling a touch of despair at how ugly it was. It gave her no comfort to know that the other rooms and apartments in the tenement were no more attractive. Survival was of paramount importance on the Lower East Side of New York in the early weeks of 1931. In this world there was little time and no money for fresh frilly curtains, new rugs, and fine furniture. Any neighbor who stepped into this room would not feel out of place, for theirs looked much the same.

Moving back into the living area, she glanced at the closed door of her mother's bedroom, then quickly at the clock. As she had guessed, it was only a few minutes past five, and she hurried to the larder to examine its scanty contents.

Years ago her father had managed to procure a pie safe with a pierced tin door to keep out the flies and insects. Opening it, she took out a deep covered bowl and saw with satisfaction that there was plenty of kugel left. She had made the bread, suet, and raisin pudding the day before, and she and her mother had dined on it the previous night, but there was plenty left for breakfast and for another supper. Grabbing a kitchen knife, she pulled out what was left of a loaf of dark bread and sliced off two thin portions, making a sandwich for her lunch with a few slices of dried beef and some horseradish. She wrapped it in brown paper and put it in a sack.

A door creaked open behind her, and Kefira quickly turned. "Good morning, Mother." She walked over and kissed her mother, then said, "Come and sit down. I'll heat up some kugel for your breakfast and make you some tea. In the meantime, you can have the last of the milk."

Kefira's mother, Rachel Reis, was only forty-nine, but she looked much older. She too had been a beauty in her day, but now her hair was gray and brittle. Her face was lined with weariness and fatigue, and her eyes seemed sunk too far back in her head. She smiled faintly and sat down. When Kefira put the glass of milk before her, Rachel said, "You have some too, dear."

"Oh, I've already had mine," Kefira said, feeling no compunction about telling this untruth. She did not want to worry her mother and often invented fanciful lies to keep her from doing so.

Kefira took out two saucers, spooned a small serving of kugel into each, and heated them over the stove. She made tea, using the last of it and reminding herself she would have to bring some more home. Kefira sat down and, as always, bowed her head while her mother whispered a brief prayer, continuing the family tradition that had been the role of her father when he was alive. As her mother began her prayer with the usual words "Eternal God," Kefira looked up at the daguerreotype over on the wall. The old photograph showed a young man and woman bundled up in ill-fitting clothing, yet with handsome faces filled with hope. These were her parents the day they had arrived at Ellis Island. They had been excited at coming to the New World, where they'd expected to find a better life, and for a time they had, because Samuel Reis had been a skilled watchmaker. Kefira could remember living in a better apartment as a child with plenty to eat and good schooling—but since her father's death three years ago, there had been no money.

Her only sibling, Chaim, was twenty-five now and serving a five-year sentence in Sing Sing Prison, not too far north of the city. He had been found guilty of stealing from his employer—though Chaim maintained that his boss paid Jews less for the same work and that he had only taken the money he had coming. Chaim's picture was on the wall also, and Kefira knew that her mother went to it every day and prayed that God would protect him in prison and deliver him. He had another year and a half to go, and Rachel Reis lived for the day when he would be free.

Kefira leaned over to pat her mother on the arm. "I'll be going to visit Chaim tomorrow. Do you have a letter written?"

"Oh yes—it's a long one. I've been working on it for over a week now."

"He'll be so glad to get it. He misses you so much, Mother."

"I keep thinking," Rachel said wistfully, "that I ought to go see him myself."

"Perhaps when spring comes. You'll be feeling better then. We can both go. Won't that be a good thing?"

Even as Kefira said this, a dark cloud of doubt settled over her. Her mother was not getting better. She was getting worse, it seemed, almost daily. Twice Kefira had taken her to the doctor. The doctor had prescribed a tonic to ease the symptoms but offered little hope for recovery. He had said quietly, when Rachel was out of hearing, "You must prepare yourself, my dear. I'm afraid she won't live too much longer."

Fiercely Kefira had denied the doctor's words, and she tried every way she knew to make life as pleasant for her mother as she could. Her mother's well-being was the central focus of her life now, and she knew that Sing Sing Prison was no place for a sick woman.

Hastily she arose, put on the heavy coat that had belonged to her father, and pulled an attractive shawl over her head, tying it under her chin. It was the one pretty garment she owned—a gift from Chaim for her thirteenth birthday, and now she treasured it.

"You rest today, Mother, and when I come home I'll bring you a surprise."

"Try to get off early, dear."

Kefira didn't remind her mother that she had to work long hours to earn enough money for doctors and medicine. "I'll try, Mother, but we're very busy at this time of the year."

Kefira kissed her mother and left the tenement. Descending rapidly from the third floor, she realized her mother would never be able to climb back up those steps in her condition. It was a thought she had had before, but she tried to shove it away as she stepped out onto the street. As she turned and headed toward the shop where she worked, she was struck by the lack of color around her, and her dream appeared again in her mind's eye, as vividly as when she had dreamed it. She had a gift for remembering dreams in this way. But instead of a blue sky, white clouds, and green fields, the street before her remained a monotonous gray; concrete and steel and faded brownstone buildings rose high on each side like canyon walls. There was so little color, she had almost ceased to look for it in this world. She did, however, turn to look into one particular window—almost a morning ritual. On the windowsill sat a red pot with a brilliant blue flower nestled in bright green leaves. Another pot the same size burst with white blossoms, and Kefira stopped for a moment, wistfully admiring, drinking in the color, and finding it impossible to believe at that moment that she could ever be surrounded by such things as flowers and grass. She had been out in the country only rarely as a small child. She could find grass and flowers in Central Park, but it was a long way from her apartment, and she worked so constantly, she had no opportunity for luxuries like a walk in the park.

She turned the corner and headed down River Street, along the murky East River. When she got to the building with a sign reading McCauley Mission, she saw that the food line was even longer than usual, snaking all the way down the block and around the corner. Kefira had heard that the mission fed the homeless men who roamed the streets of New York during these dark days of the Depression. She saw no women in line and wondered why. As she made her way down the other side of the street, she kept glancing at the men in line. They were bundled up in old torn and patched clothes, with dark hats pulled low over their heads and rough shoes or boots. They all looked more or less alike—some taller than others but all pale and thin and without hope. Some turned to look at her, but none called out. She wondered again why there were no women, but then the Christians, like the ones who ran the mission, were a mystery to her. She did not like any of them, for when she was only a little girl, she had been chased by boys who had called her "Christ killer." She was often struck with a strong curiosity to look inside the mission, but she was afraid and kept her distance from the place.

Ten minutes later, when she was almost at the shop where she worked, she passed a man standing in front of a wooden box. On it were four apples, three of them rather large and edible and one past its best day. The hand-painted sign blazoned the price of five cents. She started to pass by, for there were many such stands like this in New York City and, from what she had heard, all across the United States. Men were starving, trying to get enough money to stay alive. She wondered what a man would feel when he had a family he could not feed.

Inadvertently she met the eyes of the old man at this apple stand. White hair stuck out of his hat, and his face was wrinkled, especially around the eyes. He had no teeth, and his mouth was puckered. His entire face was blue with the cold. He wore a pair of worn gloves with most of his fingertips exposed.

Kefira looked into his eyes and wondered what had brought him here. *He once had a mother who loved him*, she thought, *and a father. They dreamed great things for him, as all parents do for their babies. Perhaps they saw him as a successful lawyer or a doctor. Maybe a politician or a teacher. And now here he is old and wrung out and starving. Would they have brought him into this world if they had known it would come to this?*

Impulsively Kefira reached into her pocket and pulled out the few coins there. She handed the man a nickel. He smiled at her, more with his eyes than with his lips, and said, "Thank you, daughter."

"You're very welcome."

He handed her the apple, then said, "May the Lord God bless you a thousandfold."

The words surprised Kefira. She paused for a moment, then returned his smile. "Thank you," she said quietly. "I hope you have a good day."

The old man reached up and clasped his hands together for a moment, then nodded. The smile in his faded eyes was genuine. "Jesus will take care of me."

Kefira stared at him, and a thought rushed into her mind. *Jesus isn't doing such a good job for you.* But instead she merely nodded and turned away. For some reason his words troubled her. She put them out of her mind but knew she would not forget the man. She seemed unable to forget anyone she met. It was almost startling how she could see a person only one time, then six months later see them again and remember them vividly, usually even remembering the circumstances under which she had first seen them.

She came to the three-story smoke-stained building where she worked and entered, climbing up to the second floor. About fifteen women in all worked in the manufacturing shop of Adolph Kurtz. The German immigrant managed to stay in business during the Depression by charging less for his goods. He was able to do this because he paid lower wages for his workers, a considerable feat considering the already low pay scale in New York City. Many came here to work, but few could withstand the long hours, low pay, and grim setting.

Kefira stepped over to some pegs on the wall, where she hung her coat, keeping her shawl in place about her shoulders in the chilly workroom. She was making her way to her work station when a large hand landed on her shoulder. Startled, she turned to see Adolph Kurtz, a big man with a broad, brutal face and a pair of small blue eyes. He had a thick German accent, and now he said, "You are early dis morning. Gut for you." He did not remove his hand but squeezed her shoulder, and only when Kefira pulled away and nodded did he remove his hand. As she moved toward the bench where she worked, she could feel his eyes on her. He was a known womanizer, a fact she knew well from the other workers, especially the young, pretty ones. He had touched her before, seemingly by accident, but this was no accident. She seated herself at her workbench and at once began to work. She was paid by piecework, and her job was simply to make stacks of cloth, pin a pattern to them, and cut them to fit. She clipped these pieces together with a pin and laid them on a table where a putty-faced young boy came by and picked them up. He took them, she knew, to another place, a larger factory where the pieces were sewn together.

She worked steadily, hardly ever lifting her eyes. There was little to lift one's eyes for. The building was cold and cheerless and dirty. Working methodically, she could isolate her mind. While her hands were busy cutting out the pieces, her mind was going over something she loved to think about. Usually it was a book she had read, for she was an avid reader. Or she would think of the pleasant times she and Chaim had spent with their father, watching the ducks in the park on a sunny summer day. Those were the good days of her life, and now as her fingers flew rapidly, she reveled in the imagery.

She worked steadily, speaking from time to time with one of the women who came by, and at lunchtime she joined Agatha Swartz and Millie Johnson, the two women in the shop she knew the best. They sat by a grimy window in the back where they could look outside, although there was nothing too exciting to see. But at least they could glimpse a patch of blue sky, and they enjoyed watching the pigeons huddled on the outer windowsill waiting for handouts. When Mr. Kurtz wasn't watching, they'd push the window open slightly and slide a few crumbs out to the shivering birds.

As Kefira shut the window she winced at the pain in her back, then realized her right hand ached as well. She flexed her hand and said, "You know I've heard of people who can work equally well with either hand. I sure wish I could do that."

"So do I," Agatha agreed. "But I can't keep my cuts straight with my other hand." She was a thin, pale young woman who lacked any attractiveness. She'd had a succession of boyfriends, but none serious, it seemed. Millie Johnson had traces of beauty, though the weariness of the work had drained most of it from her. She was silent now, which was unusual for her. Normally she was the most talkative of the three. When they had eaten their sandwiches, Kefira brought out the apple. She fetched a knife and said, "I know how to cut an apple in two, but how do you cut it in three?"

"Oh, don't do that!" Millie said quickly.

"It's nice and fresh," Kefira said, "and I'd like to share it with you. I bought it from a sad-looking old man on the street corner." She cut the apple into three roughly shaped pieces and the women bit into them, quietly enjoying their portions. "I'm going to see my brother tomorrow," Kefira said.

"Aren't you afraid to go in there with all those criminals?" Aggie exclaimed.

"Of course not! I go to a visitors' room, and they bring my brother in. And there's always a guard standing close by."

"When will he get out?" Aggie asked.

"He has another year and a half to go. That'll be the happiest day of my life."

Millie had said nothing, and finally Kefira looked up and saw with surprise that tears were running down her face. Quickly she asked, "What's wrong? Are you sick, Millie?"

Millie shook her head, her thin lips pressed tightly together.

"What is it, then?" Aggie demanded. "Has someone been mean to you?"

"I ... I'm going to have a baby," Millie gasped, her body shaking, and more tears wetting her cheeks. "My father will kill me," she whispered. "He'll kill me."

Kefira and Aggie exchanged glances. Both felt the young woman's sadness, and it was Kefira who said, "No, he won't kill you. He'll understand."

"No, he won't!" Millie sobbed. "He'll throw me out of the house. I'll be on the street. What will I do?" She looked up suddenly and whispered, "I've got to get rid of it. Do you know any-one—?"

Kefira blinked with shock. An abortion was not part of her world. No Jewish girl would think of such a thing!

Aggie, however, put her hand out and took Millie's. "I know someone," she said. "Do you have any money?"

"A little."

"We'll go there after work. You'll probably miss a few days' work. How far along are you?"

"I don't know. Not very."

Kefira listened, and her mind rebelled. She had heard of this many times, but never had it happened to a friend of hers. She longed to beg Millie not to do it, but what did she have to offer instead? She certainly could not take her in. Or perhaps she could. She was toying with the thought when the whistle suddenly blew, and Kurtz came yelling, "Back to verk! Back to verk!"

★ ★ ★ ★

Quitting time came at different times for different women. Needing money to buy medicine and being stronger than most, Kefira worked until she was left alone. She was almost startled when she looked up and saw that the sky was dark. She had been lost in her thoughts of a picnic she and her family had gone on once. Now, however, she put the last bundle of cut pieces on the table, looked at the stack, and went to find Kurtz. At the end of the day, he would come and count each woman's work, carefully recording the numbers in a little book he carried with him at all times. Kefira watched him closely as he counted, knowing that he often shorted them. She leaned over to see what number he was writing in his book, but he snatched it away, turning his back to her as he finished recording her day's work.

Controlling the anger in her voice, she said, "Good night, Mr. Kurtz. Remember I won't be working tomorrow."

She started to leave but found suddenly that he had blocked her way. He reached out, put his beefy arms around her, and ran his hands up and down her back. Panicked at being alone with the man, she broke away from his grasp and screamed at him with her eyes flashing, "Don't do that, Mr. Kurtz!"

Kurtz merely laughed. "Vhat a touch-me-not you are! I don't mean anything by it."

Kefira knew very well that he did, but she simply said, "Good night," and left, yanking her coat from the wall peg on her way out. She ran down the steps, her heart pounding, hoping that he was not following her. Exiting the building onto the street, she relaxed a little seeing that he was not behind her.

She hated walking home after dark, and on the way she noted many homeless people. She knew it was dangerous for her to be alone, but there was no other way. She often had to work late to make enough money for her mother's medical care. She walked as fast as she could, thankful for the streetlights and for the knowledge that at least she had a place to call home—a roof over her head, a little warmth, and a meager supply of food. It was better than nothing.

When she reached the tenement she ran up the stairs, and when she stepped in, she saw that her mother was not up as usual. She quickly went to the bedroom door, opened it, and saw her mother lying in bed. Hurrying over, she put her hand on her head and found she was feverish. "Don't you feel well?"

"No, not very."

"I'll fix you something to eat. You'll feel better."

She prepared a meal and helped her mother to the table. Rachel tried valiantly to eat, but Kefira saw that it was no use. She talked as cheerfully as she could, but finally her mother whispered, "I think I need to lie down again, Kefira."

After she helped her mother back to bed, Kefira went next door and knocked. The door opened at once, and Mrs. Simmons, a heavy middle-aged woman, nodded. "Hello, Kefira."

"Mrs. Simmons, I need to be out of town tomorrow. Would you check on my mother please, at noon? I'll try to be back by dark."

"Of course. Is she worse?"

"She's not very well. Thank you, Mrs. Simmons."

She went back to her apartment and began to heat some water. When the kettle was boiling, she took it to the bathroom down the hall and used it to scrub out the grime. She heated more water, poured it into the clean tub, and tempered it with cold water from the faucet. Making sure the door was locked, she stripped off her clothes and stepped into the shallow, but delightfully warm, water in the big tub. Enjoying the sensation, she leaned back and imagined herself luxuriating in a tub filled to the brim with warm water and fragrant soap bubbles. Her dream wasn't to last long, however. The old man from the other side of the hall was pounding on the door, demanding his turn, so she hastily rinsed with cold water, threw her clothes back on, and returned to her apartment.

Next she tackled the kitchen, cleaning away as much of the coal-smoke grime as she could from the floor and countertops and stove. Every greasy spot attracted the coal dust in the air like a magnet, but, Kefira reasoned, at least it was easier to tell where the grease was. After this last chore of the day, she dropped into bed, completely exhausted. She dreaded her visit tomorrow to

Sing Sing, but she had to see Chaim.

She fell asleep almost at once, and instantly, it seemed, she was having another one of her dreams. This time nothing was familiar. She was in a bleak land with no grass, and the sky overhead looked hard enough to scratch a match on. The barren land stretched off into the distance seemingly forever, and there were strange buildings she did not understand. Dark-skinned people wore odd clothing and spoke in a language she had never heard. Everything was different—even the trees and plants—and she did not like it. She woke up with a start and thought about the dream. She whispered, "I liked the one I had last night better," then closed her eyes and went back to sleep.

CHAPTER TWO

SING SING

★ ★ ★ ★

As the train pulled up to the station platform, it emitted a huge gust of hissing steam, the suddenness of it frightening Kefira. She had ridden on a train before, but only three times, and still its massive power alarmed her. Glancing down she saw a boy, no more than six years old, who was grinning and waving his arms and shouting at the engine. *I guess if he's not afraid of it, I don't have to be,* she told herself.

The huge wheels revolved more slowly, and then there was a series of miniature crashes as the cars slammed against the engine, each one echoing down the track as it was struck from behind. Almost at once a conductor in a black uniform stepped out of one of the cars, placed a moveable step onto the platform, and turned to reach his hand to a woman who came hesitantly down. As the passengers disembarked, Kefira stood back, waiting until the way was clear. After the last one was off, she joined the other passengers who were surging forward to board. The conductor, a tall, gentlemanly sort, offered his hand and she took it, keeping the box she carried securely under her left arm.

"Be twenty minutes before we leave, miss."

"Thank you."

Mounting the steps, she turned and walked into the car,

which was already half full with passengers. She took a seat by the window and watched as the milling crowd moved like ants. Soon the car was three-fourths full, and in a booming voice, the conductor bellowed, "All aboard!" Kefira watched as he swung on board easily, and the train jerked forward roughly, then began to move more smoothly out of the station. Despite her anxiety about the huge machines, it fascinated Kefira to be on a moving train. It appeared to her that the train was standing still and the people and the buildings outside were moving by.

They passed smoke-stained factories and unpainted buildings, gaunt and gray under a bleak winter sun. As the train rumbled through the inner city and into the industrial section, the bleakness of the scenery so struck Kefira that she looked away from the window.

She saw a newspaper on the seat beside her and picked it up and began to read it. Most of the political news items meant little to her, but she did find an interesting story on the inside pages about an elephant stampede in London that had injured fifty people. *What in the world would elephants be doing in London?* she wondered. *They should be in Africa.* With a giggle, she tried to picture elephants stampeding down Fifth Avenue in New York, then felt guilty for laughing when so many people had been hurt.

She turned the page and read with shock that eight thousand people had been killed by rebels in Shanghai. The story had a strong effect on her, and moved by the plight of these poor people, she laid the newspaper down on her lap and stared out the window. They were in open country now with farms and trees, which fascinated her, yet she couldn't stop thinking about the terrible tragedy that had happened all the way around the world. Like many children she'd had the idea when she was very young that if you dug through the earth and reached China, people there would be standing on their heads. Now as she pondered the immensity of eight thousand people dying, her thoughts sobered. *Every one of those people had a life that was precious to them. I'll never know any of their names or what they looked like, but all of them had a childhood with the joy and sorrow that comes with that time of life. Many of them fell in love and married, had children of their own. They all had their dreams and longings, and now they're all dead. Yet it doesn't mean much to me. I can't think of eight thousand people! I have to see one before I can really be involved in hurting for them.*

She shook off this thought and read the story that appeared on the front page. President Hoover had said in a speech that the nation must prevent hunger and cold for those in real trouble. She wondered wryly how he could prevent cold. *I suppose,* she thought, *he means to buy clothes for them.* Hoover had named a committee to draw up plans for combatting unemployment, a terrible problem across the entire country. His proposal had to do with a joint venture of public and private industries collaborating to spur industry. Hoover was very positive about the whole thing. Kefira could not help but think about the toothless old man from whom she had bought the apple and wondered if the president's plan would do anything for him. She did not think so, and finally she read the rest of the paper. Her mind moved ahead to the meeting with her brother, and she both longed for it and dreaded it. She loved Chaim dearly, but visiting him in prison was such a depressing experience she could hardly stand it.

★ ★ ★ ★

The bus that took Kefira, along with eight others, to the prison burned oil badly, and she wondered if it would make the trip. The tires, she had noted, were slick, and the engine backfired several times, making all the passengers jump at the terrific explosions. The road was smooth enough, but with every little bump, the bus seemed to have been struck with a gigantic sledgehammer.

The passengers, five women besides herself and two men, were all silent. Everyone seemed to be under a cloud—every face taut, shoulders slumped in weariness. An elderly woman sat beside Kefira, and after casting several glances at her, said, "My name is Mabel. Who do you have on the inside?"

"My brother. My name is Kefira."

"My, that's a nice name. What does it mean, I wonder? Did your parents just think it was pretty?"

"In Hebrew it means 'lion cub.'" Kefira smiled as she saw the woman's expression. "It's a funny thing to name a baby, but my father was very fond of an aunt with that name, so I inherited it."

"It's very pretty. Have you been here before?"

"Yes, several times. Who do you have inside?"

"My son. His name is Harold. He's my only child now. I had a daughter, but she died."

"Do you live close?"

"No, quite a ways from here. In Troy."

"Oh, that is a long way, ma'am!"

"Yes, it is. I've been coming here for nine years now. I've never missed a visiting day."

Kefira took in the older woman's worn clothing. Her eyes fell on the hands, and she saw that they were callused and chafed with work. "How much longer will your son have to serve?"

"Oh, he's in for life."

Kefira could not think of a reply. She finally said feebly, "I'm sorry to hear that."

"Yes, it's hard," the woman remarked. "But I've tried to give thanks to the Lord. My son's healthy, and I get to see him every visiting day. What about your brother?"

"He only has a year and a half more."

"Oh, won't that be fine!"

"Yes, I live for the day."

The two talked until the bus pulled up in front of the walls of Sing Sing Prison. The passengers disembarked silently, and Kefira walked along with the others, accompanied by two armed guards. Kefira thought it odd that the guards both carried rifles. *Are they guarding the prisoners from us? That can't be.* The guards were hard-looking men, and she wondered what it would be like to be constantly dealing with prisoners who lived with no hope of a better future.

She knew the way by now and followed the others into a large room with a modicum of furniture. A table along one wall held a commercial-sized metal coffeepot, and cups lined a shelf above it. Kefira sat down and waited, and after what seemed like a longer time than usual, the prisoners began arriving. She saw a heavyset man with weary eyes greeting the woman she had spoken with. Mabel reached up and embraced him, and he patted her shoulder. She could hear the man say, "You've never missed a visiting day, Mom. Never once in all these years."

A movement caught Kefira's eye, and she saw Chaim walk through the door. Her heart felt a quick surge of pity as she remembered how handsome and full of life he had been. Now all the life and joy seemed to have been drained out of him, but she let none of this show in her face. She rose quickly, went over to him, put her arms around him, and kissed him. "Hello, Chaim," she said.

"Hello, sis."

"Come over and sit down. I brought you some blintzes."

She pulled him down and opened her box, bringing out a bag on the top. Unwrapping one of the blintzes, she handed it to him, and he downed it in two large bites. "Mmm, that's good," he said. "I wish they served Jewish food in here."

"Are the meals very bad?"

"Monotonous. The same thing all the time. What I wouldn't give for some knishes." It had been his favorite food—round, flat dumplings, filled with potato or other fillings and baked.

"How's Mother?" he asked, reaching into the bag for another blintz.

For a moment Kefira hesitated. "Well, she's not as well as I'd like."

"That means she's worse."

"I'm hoping that when spring comes she'll be better. Maybe she'll be able to get outside some."

"She's not going to live, is she, sis?"

"Oh, don't say that, Chaim! She can get better. It's possible."

To change the subject, she reached into the box again and began bringing out more items, small gifts she had worked extra hours to buy. "I've brought you some things. Just toothpaste and razor blades and some aftershave. It'll make you smell good."

"I don't think it'll help much in here, but thanks, sis."

The conversation was difficult. Chaim almost seemed to be in a trance, and she knew he was depressed. He was older than she by eight years, but she had learned to read him even as a child. Putting her hand on his, she said, "It's only a year and a half, Chaim."

He squeezed her hand so hard it hurt, but he seemed unconscious of it. His eyes grew flat, and he withdrew for a time. Then he shook his head and said, "Eighteen months. That doesn't sound like much to someone on the outside. But every day in here is like a year. I don't think I can make it."

"Of course you can!"

"I have nightmares. You know you were always the one who had dreams, but now I have frightful dreams every night."

"You seem depressed."

"I guess I am. It's my cellmate, Harold McKenzie. He got in trouble and was punished for it."

Despite herself, she asked, "What did they do to him?"

"They gave him the water treatment."

"What . . . what's that?"

"They put you in a shower in a chair and tie your hands down. Your feet and head are locked in place so you can't move. Then they put this trough around your neck that catches the water. It fills up as the shower runs and comes all the way up to your nose. You try to gulp the water, but you can't. Finally it gets in your nose, and you pass out." He shuddered and swiped his hand across his face. "Then they slap your face to bring you back awake . . . and they do it all over again."

It was such a frightening scene, Kefira knew she would have dreams about it. "I hope it never happens to you, Chaim."

"It already has—twice."

There was nothing to say to this, so she quickly changed the subject again. She talked of things that were happening in the world outside, and for a while he seemed mildly interested. Finally he ate another blintz and said, "It's good that you've come to see me. Some men don't have any visitors."

"That must be terrible." She put her hand on his arm and squeezed it. "It'll be hard, but one day you'll be out. God hasn't forgotten you."

Chaim turned to face her, a strange expression twisting his

features. "You still believe in God? I don't."

Actually Kefira had little faith in God, but she would not say so. "Don't talk like that. You remember what Papa always said. 'The Eternal One will help us.' He said that a thousand times."

"Yes, he did." He looked at her and shook his head. "But he was never in a place like this."

The visiting hour was quickly over. When she rose to go, Kefira said, "I'll come back when I can. What can I bring you?"

"I know you're having a hard time making ends meet. Just take care of Mama."

She reached up, put her arms around him, and clung to him fiercely. Her heart smote her as she thought of having to leave him alone, but she could not let him see it. Smiling brightly, she said, "I'll write you. You don't have to write me back."

"Your letters help a lot, sis."

She turned and left the room, and at the door she took one look back and saw Chaim standing there, watching her with an empty expression on his face. He waved and then turned and, with his shoulders slumped, passed through the door back toward the world that was destroying him.

★　★　★　★

As soon as Kefira returned from her visit, her mother wanted to know every detail. Kefira sat down beside her, and the two drank cups of hot tea while Kefira gave her a report. "He looks fine, Mother," she said, smiling. There was no point in telling her the truth. Anything she could do to make her mother feel better she would do, and a lie like this seemed to be the kindest thing.

"I suppose he's all pale and has lost weight."

"Oh, no indeed. He gets to go out in what they call 'the yard.' Of course, during the winter not so much, but when spring comes, he'll be as brown as a berry."

"Do they treat him badly in that place?" Rachel asked in a trembling voice. She had a coughing spasm and covered her mouth with a handkerchief. "I've heard so many horrible tales."

"Oh, those are just newspaper stories," Kefira said quickly.

"He said the food was pretty good, and he has a good friend in his cell. They read the same books, and he has a lot of other friends there."

For some time Rachel sat drinking in her daughter's words, and finally she sighed. "I'm going to see him in the spring if I get better by then."

"Of course you are, and you will be better." Actually Kefira said this to encourage her own heart, but her eyes told her that her mother was not getting better at all. She was so thin now that her legs were like broomsticks, and her eyes were sunk back in her head. Kefira's chest tightened in fear at the thought of losing her mother, and she tried to put it out of her mind. "I'm going to make some teiglach."

"I wish Chaim could have some."

"Next time I go I'll make him some. He liked the blintzes so much."

Rising, she busied herself making the little cakes, which would be dipped in honey, and soon the kitchen was filled with the sweet smell of baking. Afterward she sat down and coaxed her mother to eat three of them, which was the most she had seen her eat in some time.

"Will you read to me a while, daughter, from the Scripture?"

"Of course, Mother."

Moving across the room, Kefira picked up the Yiddish Bible that was on the table. She brought it back and laid her hand flat on it. "How many times," she murmured, "have I seen Papa put his hand on this book? He loved the Scriptures, didn't he, Mama?"

"Yes, he always did. I don't think a day in his life went by that he wouldn't read some part of it, if at all possible. And he had such a marvelous reading voice. I miss it so much."

"So do I. What do you want me to read, Mama?"

"Read me one of the stories in the First Book."

Kefira thumbed through the book and came to the story of Abram. She read very well indeed. She had learned from her father how to put light into the readings. She always said of him, "He could make a telephone book sound interesting."

She read aloud the story of Abram, the first Jew, as her father often pointed out, who was called by God to leave his home and his people and go out into a land he had never seen. She made it sound like an exciting adventure as Abram and his wife, Sarai, left Ur of the Chaldees and settled in Haran, finally traveling to the land of Canaan that God had promised him. She read with vigor, and when she was finished, she smiled and took her mother's hand. "That would take a lot of courage, wouldn't it, Mother, to leave your home and family and go to a place you've never even heard of?"

"Yes, it would. Samuel always said that Abram had more faith than any man in the Scriptures."

"I wonder if Abram heard the voice of God like you're hearing my voice, or if it was just something that went on in his head."

"My Samuel thought he heard the actual voice of God," Rachel said, remembering her husband with great fondness, "and he thought Moses did too. You remember in the next book it says that God spoke to Moses in the same way a man speaks with his friend. Samuel always insisted that it was the real, actual voice of God."

The two spoke quietly, and the presence of Samuel Reis was very real in the room. He had been a devoted husband and father, and after his death Kefira had seen her mother grow silent and lose all taste for life. She felt now, somehow, that even this physical sickness was part of her grief over her husband.

"I like that story so much," Rachel murmured. "We all have to go to a country that we don't know someday."

Startled, Kefira looked up. Her mother had never before referred to death, and now a lump came to her throat. She did not know what to say, and her mother smiled suddenly and said, "I think about that sometimes, daughter, and I believe that I will see my Samuel again."

Tears filled Kefira's eyes, and she could only choke out a few words. "I believe so too, Mama."

Her mother was tired, she saw, and after she got her to bed, Kefira cleaned up the kitchen. Her weariness was especially great this evening, and she knew that part of this, at least, was emotional. She went to her cold bedroom, climbed into bed, and fell asleep almost at once. She dreamed the same pleasant dream that had come to her before—walking down a road with hills and forests in the distance and fields on either side of the road. She could see the white house with its columns, with the oak-lined road leading up to it, but once again, when she moved toward it, it vanished . . . and the vanishing pierced her with a sorrow she could not express.

CHAPTER THREE

"LEARN TO LOVE GOD ..."

★ ★ ★ ★

For a special treat Kefira had packed half a dozen teiglach and a small jar of honey along with her sandwich. Now she sat with Millie at their lunch break and smiled. "I want you to taste some of my cooking."

Millie looked wan. She had been lifeless for some time now, and Kefira and Agatha had spoken of her. Agatha had revealed that she had taken Millie to an abortionist. From that time on, Agatha had tried to cheer the girl up, as had Kefira, but there was a deep sorrow in the young woman that words and sympathy could not heal.

Outside, a small snowstorm had gathered, and pale light filtered through the snowflakes as they fell. They swarmed and fascinated Kefira, but she took her gaze away from the window to say, "Here. Take one of these and dip it into this honey."

"What is it?"

"Just little cakes. We call them teiglach."

Millie dipped one into the honey, took a bite, and chewed, nodding, "These are very good! Are they hard to make?"

"No, very easy. I'll write down the recipe for you if you'd like to try it."

"All right."

The two girls ate all of the pastries and then sat waiting, savoring their brief moment of rest before they had to return to their workbenches.

"How's your mother?" Millie asked.

"Not very well."

"It's this terrible winter. There are people sick everywhere." She looked down at her hands and said, "Do you think she'll live, Kefira?"

"I hope so. I hate to leave her alone, but I have to work."

"It's too bad. I wish I could help."

Kefira reached over and patted the girl's hand. "You would if you could. These are hard times." She was actually very concerned about her mother. Rachel Reis had grown worse the past week, and it was hard for Kefira to leave her. Mrs. Simmons and other neighbors would come periodically to look in on her and make sure she was all right, but Kefira still wished she didn't have to go to work.

"I can't help thinking of my baby."

Kefira looked up, startled. This was the first time Millie had mentioned the operation. Her lips were drawn together in a tight line, and tears rolled down her cheeks. "I can't ever have him, Kefira."

Not knowing how to comfort the girl, Kefira reached over and held her hand. "Don't think about it. It's in the past. You have to start in where you are."

"But it's so awful. I can't have him—I killed him!"

Distressed at this thought, Kefira began to urge Millie to try to forget. "We all make mistakes," she said. "You're not the first girl to get in trouble."

"Getting in trouble is one thing, but killing my baby—that's something else. I'm nothing but a murderer!"

"Millie, don't talk like that! You did what you had to do." In truth this was not what Kefira thought. She had a deep aversion to the very thought of abortion, and she knew she herself would never do such a thing. Still, there was no point in berating the young woman. Millie felt bad enough already. So Kefira began talking about how important it was to put things behind you.

Millie listened, her eyes fixed on Kefira and seeking for some grain of hope, but finally, sadly, she shook her head. "This is different from other sins, Kefira."

"Sins are all alike, aren't they? I always thought so."

"No, they're not," Millie insisted. "Some things that you do wrong will hurt you but nobody else—but other sins hurt other people, so they're twice as wrong. Don't you see?"

Actually this did seem true enough to Kefira. She sat silently, wishing she could think of something to say to comfort her friend, but she could only make sympathetic sounds.

Tears ran down Millie's cheeks, leaving silvery tracks. From far away came the sound of a siren, an eerie wail like the death cry of some fabulous monster. The sound seemed to hurt Millie, and she dropped her face into her hands and began to sob. "This sin was against my own child—and against God." Her shoulders shook convulsively, and she cried out, "God will never forgive me!"

★ ★ ★ ★

After lunch Millie was no longer able to work, and she pleaded for Mr. Kurtz to let her go home. He did so reluctantly, then came by Kefira's work station to demand, "Vhat's de matter vit her?"

"She's sick, Mr. Kurtz."

"Vell, she'd better get over vit it. Dere's plenty folks who vant to verk." Disgusted, he turned on his heel and went away, and Kefira wondered how a man could be so brutal as to feel no compassion. She had watched him cruelly run women out of his shop for no fault at all, knowing they had no place to go and no other work available to them. He seemed to have been created without any sense of pity, or of right and wrong, and she wondered what he had been like as a boy. *Probably just like he is now— only shorter*, she thought as she went sullenly back to her work.

She left early that day, even though it meant less pay, but she was worried about her mother. As she walked down the street she did not see the old man who had sold her the apple, and she wondered if the freezing weather and snow had driven him from the streets. Her own clothing was insufficient, and by the time she got to her building, she was numb with cold. She saw a young girl no more than eight or nine years old shivering, clutching her ragged coat about her, and Kefira thought, *There are rich people in this city who are sitting in warm rooms and eating off china plates, their food being brought to them by servants. They don't have any worries. I wonder if they ever think about anybody like that little girl there who's freezing and starving?* Anger surged through her as she thought of the injustice in the world. She wondered how God could let such things happen. At times God seemed to be her enemy, but she hated to think this. Unable to come to grips with such overwhelming problems, she turned and went upstairs, where she found her mother weaker than she had ever been. Kefira piled more covers on her and turned the gas up to warm the room, not knowing how she was going to pay for it.

Mrs. Simmons came after she had started cooking and said, "She's very bad, Kefira."

"I know. If only this cold spell would pass. . . ."

Mrs. Simmons was a compassionate woman. She lived alone, and no one could understand how she stayed so heavy when she had so little to eat, but she was indeed very fat. Her eyes, however, were kind, and she came to stand closer to Kefira. "I think we'd better send for someone."

"Send for someone. For who?"

"For the rabbi maybe."

Kefira hesitated. She knew her mother had a great deal of confidence in the rabbi, and she nodded. "I think you're right. I'll go get him."

"And maybe a doctor."

Kefira felt a moment of bleak despair. She wanted to scream, *"I don't have any money for a doctor!"* but the situation surely wasn't Mrs. Simmons's fault. "I'll go ask him," she said quietly. "Will you watch Mama while I'm gone?"

"Yes, and you'd better hurry."

Kefira threw on her coat and shawl and hurried from the house. She knew that the rabbi would come, but a doctor had to have money. At the doctor's office, she humbled herself and begged. "I promise to pay as soon as I can," she offered. "You've got to come. You've got to!"

Thankfully the doctor did agree to come. But after examining Rachel, he gave Kefira no hope. With as much kindness as he could muster, he said gruffly, "She can't last more than a day or two, Miss Reis. You must be prepared for it."

The rabbi stayed for over an hour. He sat beside the dying woman and held her hand. He was young and thin, his face planed down almost to the bone, but he had large beautiful brown eyes that reflected the kindness in him. He stayed until Kefira finally said, "You must go now. You have others to see."

"I will be back. At times like this we must look to the Eternal One for strength."

"Yes, rabbi," Kefira whispered.

When he left, the apartment seemed frightfully empty. She sat beside her mother, whose eyes were closed, her light breath scarcely stirring the thin breast. Often Kefira would lean over and stroke the gray hair and whisper loving words, but she never felt that her mother heard them.

She remembered what her mother had said about seeing her Samuel again. And in the silence of that lonely room, Kefira Reis wondered if there was anything to the stories she had heard— that there was a heaven and that people she knew would be there. She knew that Gentiles were much firmer in their beliefs about the afterlife than Jews. She had once asked the former rabbi, who was an old man, if she would see her father again. He had been evasive and had given her little comfort. He had clothed his own doubt with words she did not understand and left her feeling more miserable than she had been before asking the question.

★   ★   ★   ★

When dawn arrived, Kefira knew it without looking outside. As always, a mysterious inner clock had told her that morning had come, and she left her mother's room to stand before the apartment's only window in the living area. The snow was swirling, and the streets outside had been transformed into a beautiful wintry spectacle. They were covered with snow, and the traffic had not yet trodden it into mush. The light posts were sculpted into graceful white crystal forms, and the ugly buildings across the way looked like castles now with snow-capped chimneys and roofs. Someone had left clothes on a line that looked like white ghosts frozen solid. It was strange to see such beauty where the day before had been such ugliness. It struck her then how strange it was that ugliness could be covered over with just a few inches of frozen water, when the snow and the cold were really the enemy, bringing sickness and pain. Still the scene was beautiful. She had always loved to get out in the snow when it first fell. The silence of the streets seemed almost supernatural. Now she stared out at the empty frozen streets and felt only despair.

Kefira went back to her mother's side and held her hand. Time passed, and the rising sun began to filter its pale light through the living room window. She had been sitting there for so long she was startled when she felt the slight pressure of her mother's hand. Quickly she leaned forward and saw that her mother's eyes were open.

"Mama, do you know me?"

"Yes . . . Kefira."

"Mama, don't leave me."

Rachel Reis found strength to squeeze her daughter's hand again. Her eyes fluttered, and she whispered something that Kefira could not understand. Kefira leaned forward and asked, "What, Mama? What are you saying?"

The words came out slowly but firmly. "You have . . . been . . . a good . . . daughter. Learn to love God . . . for He . . . loves you."

These were the last words her mother spoke. She sighed and then seemed to settle in the bed. Her eyes were closed, and the lines of fatigue and pain eased away. Kefira held her mother's hand, kissed it, leaned forward, and kissed the thin cheek. Then she held her mother in her arms, pulling her up and sobbing. She wept wildly at first and then quietly. When the spasm of grief had passed, she laid her mother's still form down and arranged her hands and her hair.

When she stood up, she found two things within her heart. The first was a great sharp, piercing grief, almost like a sword being pushed through her breast at the very thought of losing her mother. The other was anger at God for taking both of her parents away.

CHAPTER FOUR

FLIGHT

★ ★ ★ ★

Slowly Kefira wrote a line, then paused and looked at it. Overhead, the single naked bulb threw harsh light down on the sheet of paper, and she read again the words she had written:

Dear Chaim,
I know you are grieving over Mama, as I am. It's only been two weeks, but every day has been a misery for me—

A knock sounded at the door, and Kefira put the pencil down and rose from the table. When she went to the door, she saw the tenement manager, Mr. Goldman. He took off his hat and said quickly, "I'm sorry about your mama."

"Thank you, Mr. Goldman. She was very ill, but I'm grieved to lose her."

"We all have to go," Goldman said. He was a man of medium height with pale blue eyes and only a fringe of hair on the sides and back of his head. He turned his hat around nervously and said, "I'm sorry to mention this, but I have to have the rent, Miss Reis."

"I don't have it right now, Mr. Goldman, but I'll have it for you very soon."

"It's not me, you understand. I just collect rents. The owner—

he says you have to pay it now or evacuate."

"But, Mr. Goldman—"

"Please don't make this harder on me than it is. I hate this job, but it's all I could get. You think I like telling people they have to move?" Goldman ran his hand around the fringe of hair and shook his head. His lips were drawn into a bitter line, and he said, "He's a rich man. He owns six of these tenements. You think he has any mercy in him? Not a bit! I begged him, Miss Reis, but you're just a name to him. And he told me if I didn't bring this message, he'd get somebody who would." He looked down, and shame marred his face. "I have four children, Miss Reis. I don't have any choice."

Anger flared in Kefira but not at this man. How could she hate a man as ineffectual as this? The rich owner sat somewhere in the midst of luxury throwing people out. She was angry at him, although she had never seen him.

"All right. I'll leave at the end of the week."

"I'm sorry," Goldman said and whirled away, jamming his hat down over his head.

Kefira closed the door and sat back down at the table. She picked up the pencil and finished the letter. There was really nothing she could say, but now she added one postscript:

I will be moving from here soon, and I will send you my new address just as soon as I have it.

> *With love,*
> *Kefira*

She folded the letter, put it in an envelope, and laid it on the table. She stared at it for a moment, then suddenly laid her arms down on the table and rested her forehead on them. The two weeks since her mother's death had been terrible. The funeral had been as inexpensive as she could make it, but there were some things that had to be paid. She had spent what little money she had saved up and promised to pay the rest out by the week, but it had taken all of her cash, and she had been unable to pay her rent. As she hid her face with her eyes closed, she tried to think what to do. She knew she would have to leave, and the only thing cheaper would be to share a room with another girl or maybe two other girls. She valued her privacy, and besides, this place had been a home for her. True her father had never lived in it, nor her brother, but she and her mother had made it a home, and it wrenched her within to think of leaving it.

Tears gathered in her eyes, and she rose and rubbed at them fiercely with the heels of her hands. "I've got to go to work," she muttered.

She had only two apples, a half loaf of bread, and a chunk of hard cheese in her larder. From this, she scraped together a small lunch. Then she put on her coat and shawl. She turned around and looked at the unlovely room, but still her only home, and wished for one moment that she had died with her mother. There seemed to be so little to live for. She turned and left, shutting the door with more force than necessary.

★ ★ ★ ★

Kefira sat at her workbench, mechanically cutting out her patterns, and at lunchtime she joined Millie. Aggie had gone to another job. Millie noticed that Kefira was unusually quiet. "What's the matter? You're not talking."

"I've got to find another place to live, Millie. I couldn't pay my rent. I can't afford to keep the apartment. My mother's funeral expenses took all I had and more. I'll have to pay them."

Millie sat quietly for a time, and finally she spoke up. "You can come stay with me, Kefira."

Kefira looked up quickly. Her friend's kindness touched her, and she blinked quickly, saying, "Do you have room, Millie?"

"Well, I live with my parents, of course, and it's a small room. But at least it's a big bed. You and I'd have to share it."

"I wouldn't mind that. What would it cost?"

"Not much. I'll talk to my father. You can take your meals with us too. Breakfast maybe and supper. We'll work out something."

Kefira felt a sudden warmth. "You are kind, Millie."

"No, you'll be company for me. I'll have to warn you, though, that my dad doesn't like Jews much. If I were you, I wouldn't tell him about your religion."

As the afternoon wore on, the idea of living with Millie's anti-Semitic father seemed less and less appealing, so Kefira took off early to look for another place. She did find a room to share with another working woman, but it was a grubby, filthy place, and the woman drank excessively and let her boyfriends stay overnight.

Confused and not knowing what else to do, Kefira understood that she would have no choice but to stay with Millie, at least until she could find something better. She spent two nights packing up, and Mrs. Simmons agreed to store some of Kefira's treasured items for her.

There were actually many things she wanted to keep. The furniture, of course, was hardly worth selling, but there were pictures and letters, and Mrs. Simmons promised to keep them safe.

On her last night in the apartment, she read a book she had bought at a used book store. It had only cost ten cents and was badly worn. The cover was torn off, but the owner had told her, "The name of it is *Call of the Wild,* written by a guy named Jack London. It's all about a dog, I think."

Kefira did not particularly want to read a book about a dog, but it was cheap, and she had heard others mention the book. It had made London a successful writer.

She got caught up in the story and read until late in the night. The story was simple enough. Buck, a large strong dog from the south, was captured and taken to the north, where he was made into a sled dog. The gold rush was on, and muscular dogs were at a premium. Buck nearly starved to death, for he was basically a gentle animal, but he was not going to survive in the harsh realities of the frozen north. His survival was assured, however, when he learned to steal. He stole a fish from another dog, and from that time on, he lived doing what he had to do to survive.

The story was stark, and the frozen north sounded terribly cruel. The weak did not make it, only the strong who would take from their weaker neighbors. This was true of men as well as dogs.

Finally Kefira closed the book, her eyes gritty with fatigue. It was very late, or rather early in the morning, and she had to get up at dawn to go to work. *What a terrible story,* she thought. She went to sleep and dreamed about the book. She could almost see the big dog Buck fighting to stay alive. She woke up in a fright and lay awake thinking about the book. Her mother's death was still painful to her, and she was still angry with God. *I'll do whatever I have to do to stay alive,* she thought bitterly. *Whatever I have to do—no matter how hard I have to be. I'll stay alive.*

★　★　★　★

The next day was difficult, for Kefira was weary from lack of sleep, and her emotions had been bruised until she could not think straight. She knew she had to have more money and made arrangements to move to Millie's house after work.

"I'll have to stop at the apartment first and pick up the last of my'things. I may be very late."

"That's all right," Millie said. "I'll save something from supper for you to eat. Just come on in. I'll be waiting for you."

"Thank you, Millie. You're so kind."

After Millie left, Kefira thought, *Millie wouldn't make it in the world. She's like that dog Buck stole food from. She's just not hard enough.* She had worked all day thinking about the book and how hard life was, and she resolved to steel her heart. *I can't be sorry. I can't be helping anybody,* she thought. *I can't buy apples from old men. I've got to keep the money for myself.*

All of this was somewhat foreign to Kefira's nature. She was basically a kind person, but hard times and cruel blows had wrought a bitter streak in her.

She worked until almost ten o'clock. Only one other woman was working late, and she finally left. Doggedly Kefira kept on until her hands were aching and her eyes blurry. She had counted her patterns and put the last batch of them on the table, then went to the office. Kurtz was sitting there drinking from a bottle. "I'm all through, Mr. Kurtz."

"Vell, you verked late." Kurtz got up and moved out to the

table with his tally book in his hands. Kefira went with him to watch as he counted.

Announcing the total, he jotted it down and said, "That's a gut day's verk."

"I'd like to be paid now if you don't mind."

"Of course. Come into my office."

The place was deserted, and the quietness seemed more startling than the noise she was accustomed to. When she stepped into the office, he shut the door, for he had a stove in there. *He can stay warm*, she thought, *while the rest of us freeze.*

Kurtz opened his safe, removed a box, took out some money, replaced the box, and slammed the door. He came over and counted out the money, and Kefira said, "Thank you." She put the money in her pocket and turned to go get her coat. She did not make a complete turn, however, for suddenly he seized her arm and swung her around. Before she could even protest, Kurtz's meaty arms were around her, and he was kissing her roughly.

She smelled the reek of alcohol on his breath and struggled to free herself, feeling powerless against his strength. She hit him in the chest, and then in the face with her fist, but it was nothing to him.

"Look," he said, dropping his grip on her arms but still holding her fast. "You don't have to verk so hard. You're having a tough time, leipshen. I know. I am sorry about your mother and I heard about you having to move in vit Millie."

"Let me go!"

"Now, don't be so hard. I'll put you up in a nice room, pay all your bills. We'll have a gut time. Right now ve'll go out and eat and then I'll set you up."

"No, let me go!"

But he did not let her go. He was very drunk and began tearing at her clothes, his hands groping her body. Fiercely, with all her strength, Kefira fought. She knew he was cursing and saying awful things in German, and she knew she had to get free. She reached up and scratched his face, and he bellowed what sounded like an oath and released one hand. She wrenched herself away from him and half fell, but she had only angered him.

His face was bleeding, and he muttered in German again and reached for her.

Kefira lunged away, and he stumbled and fell, but he struggled to his feet again. He was between her and the door, and Kefira began to scream, "Leave me alone!"

"Come here!" he yelled.

Kefira was petrified, knowing what he had in mind for her. Her eyes fell on the poker in front of the coal stove, and she reached out and grabbed it. Holding it with both hands, she said, "Leave me alone or I'll hit you!"

Kurtz paid no attention. He was either too drunk or did not care. He lunged forward, and Kefira swung the poker. It struck him on the forearm, and he yelled with pain, but still he came forward. She swung the poker again, and this time it caught him on the forehead over his left eye. He hesitated, grunting, and she struck him again. This time he fell loosely to the floor as if he had no bones.

Kefira could hardly catch her breath. The scene had terrified her. She dropped the poker and stared down at Kurtz. His face was bleeding, and she wondered if she had killed him. Leaning forward, she saw that there was a twitching in his jaw, and she could tell his chest was heaving.

He's not dead, she thought, *but he'll have me arrested.* She dashed out of the office, grabbed her coat and shawl, and exited the building. She saw a policeman and made herself walk by. "You're working late, miss. I'd get off the streets."

"Yes, sir, I will," Kefira whispered. She moved on by, expecting him to stop her at any moment. When she was out of his sight, she ran like a frightened deer. Her mind was fragmented, but she knew Kurtz would come after her as soon as he could.

She got to her apartment completely out of breath. She had a pain in her side, but she charged up the steps two at a time. Running inside the apartment, she slammed the door behind her and locked it, grabbed her carpetbag, and began stuffing what few clothes she could into it. She had given Mrs. Simmons most of the pictures, but she threw a few remaining things into the bag, including her father's Bible, and then added some scraps from the larder—a puny apple and some thin sandwiches made from the last of her bread and cheese. Going to the door, she stopped and looked around. She knew that she had to get away, but she felt like giving up and just weeping. Kefira straightened up, and her eyes lit on the book that she had read the night before. "If Buck can do it, I can too," she said aloud. "I'll survive no matter what." Her words stirred the silence, and grabbing the book that was her inspiration and shoving it into the bag, she turned and left the apartment.

CHAPTER FIVE

A DESPERATE PRAYER

★ ★ ★ ★

The cold air cut through Kefira like a knife, and from time to time a lone snowflake bit at her face like liquid fire. The weight of the heavy carpetbag dragged her to the side, but she paid little attention to it. Now panic had seized her, filling her so full she had no rational thoughts left. All she knew was that she had to get away.

Once again she passed a policeman, so filled with apprehension that she was certain he would see her pale face and arrest her on the spot. She moved to the other side of the street to avoid him, watching him furtively until he disappeared around the corner. The snow fell intermittently, swirling and dancing in the cone-shaped light of the streetlamps, sifting a thin white glaze upon the city streets.

There was a ghostly atmosphere about New York at this time of the night, especially with the snow drifting down from the opaque heavens. There was no moon, and only the greenish glow of the streetlights illuminated her way as she struggled onward. She knew little of New York City beyond the Lower East Side, but she knew where to find Pennsylvania Station, from where she could get connections south of the city. She knew she wanted to head away from the cold weather. She could see the massive terminal building ahead of her as she suddenly realized that she had in her pocket only the few dollars Adolph Kurtz had just paid her. The thought of Kurtz ran through her, and she saw again in her mind's eye his bloody face as he lay on the floor of his office. *What if he died?* she wailed inwardly. She forced herself to remember the rising and falling of his chest and the blood flowing from his forehead. *Dead men do not bleed, do they?*

Traffic was light, but now and again a lumbering, heavily laden truck or a single automobile would move along the streets, the lights flickering faintly through the darkness, their engines breaking the silence. Almost no one was walking, for which Kefira was deeply thankful.

She reached the station and stepped inside the enormous building. The warmth rushed to meet her as her eyes sought out the ticket sellers' windows. There were numerous windows in a row, but only one of them was open. Three people stood in line, and Kefira moved forward to take her place, pushing the heavy bag along the floor beside her. Even as she stood there, she suddenly asked herself, *Where am I going?* And she realized with a start that she had no idea. She had no friends, no relatives anywhere. The line moved forward until only one person was at the window ahead of her, and her thoughts flickered in her mind like a bat trapped in a closed room. She still had not decided on her destination when the man in front of her took his ticket and stepped away. She hesitated, and the sharp-faced clerk behind the grill said, "Yes, miss, where to?"

Frantically Kefira tried to think, and her eye lit on a board that gave a list of arrivals and departures of the trains. The first one was an incoming train from Florida, and she said, "How much is a ticket to Florida?"

"Coach or Pullman?"

"The cheapest."

"That'll be coach." The clerk opened his book, glanced at it, and looked up at her. "Fourteen dollars and thirty-eight cents."

Kefira counted out her money. She had barely twelve dollars. "How far could I go with seven dollars, sir?" She lowered her eyes while he searched in his book, embarrassed at having to ask the question.

"Washington, D.C., ma'am," the clerk answered curtly. "One way, of course."

"Of course," she mumbled, sliding seven dollars under the window and taking her ticket without meeting his glance. She turned and walked away, feeling the eyes of the clerk boring into her back. She crossed the enormous waiting room and came to a bench, where she sat down and rested her arm. She rubbed it and felt her face begin to grow warm with the heat. Across from her, a couple wearing expensive apparel sat together and seemed to be watching her. It made her nervous, and although there was no reason for them to stare at her, for they could know nothing about her, she got up and made her way to the tracks.

Following the signs down several hallways and sets of stairs, she came to the tracks, read her ticket again, and found track number 15: Newark, Philadelphia, Trenton, Wilmington, Baltimore, Washington. Moving along, she watched until a train pulled in, hissing steam and giving one short blast on its whistle. It eased to a stop, and she heard the sounds of people getting off and the conductor calling out, "Pennsylvania Station!"

She wasn't sure that Washington was where she wanted to go, but one thing she knew for certain was that she wanted to head south. She was tired of freezing weather, and the farther she got away from New York City the better. After the few passengers on this nighttime train emptied out, she boarded it and found a seat. Stowing her heavy bag and settling herself, she suddenly thought of Chaim, and her stomach churned wildly. *I won't be there next visiting day. And if I write him, the police will be able to find where I am.* She struggled with the thought and wondered what she should do. She almost got out of the car with the intention of going back and turning herself in to the police, but instead she remained frozen in her seat as a few passengers took widely scattered seats. Before long, she heard a clanging up ahead and a whistle, and she handed her ticket to a conductor who was making his way up the aisle. Like it or not, she was on her way now. There was no turning back, she thought as the train pulled out of the station, slicing through the dark tunnels under Manhattan and the Hudson River before emerging into the open and heading south. She allowed herself the luxury of leaning her head back and closing her eyes, and before she knew it, the rhythmic swaying of the train had lulled her fast asleep.

★ ★ ★ ★

She awoke hours later with a start as the conductor tapped her on the shoulder and said, "This is your stop, miss. Washington, D.C."

He pulled her bag down from the overhead compartment and helped her off the train onto the platform. She stood looking around, confused, dazed, and wondering, *What now?* There was no point in buying another ticket, for her money was already dangerously low. No, from here, she would have to travel by her wits.

It was daybreak now, and as she stood in the gathering light, she remembered reading a news story of how homeless men had begun to be a real problem for the railroad. They were called hobos, and they hid in the empty boxcars. The article had said, as best as she could remember, that special railroad detectives had been hired to roust the men out.

She moved along the line of tracks, walking parallel with them away from the station itself. As she walked, she saw that there were many trains there and wondered which of them would be headed south. No one seemed to be watching her, and as she moved farther down the line, she spied some trains a few tracks over that appeared to be freight trains. Checking all around to be sure she hadn't been spotted and that no train was coming, she threw her bag down on the tracks, lowered herself onto the tracks, and made her way as quickly as she could toward the waiting freight trains. The closest one consisted of one boxcar after another, and on the side of one, she could barely make out the faded words ATLANTIC COAST FREIGHT. She thought grimly, *I hope you're going south, because if I can get in, I'm going with you.* She moved down the line of cars and checked each of the doors. She was disappointed for a time, for every door was locked shut, but finally she found one that was open about six inches. Putting her bag down, she shoved at the door, and her heart leaped when it opened. She picked up her bag, furtively looked around, then threw it inside. She pulled herself up inside with a grunt and sprawled on the floor.

The smell of the boxcar was rank, and the floor was covered with dirt, but she was inside. She left the door open a crack so she could stare out, then sat down cross-legged. Depressing thoughts came to her and fear mingled with them. She had almost no money. She knew that the world was full of men like Adolph Kurtz and that she would be absolutely at their mercy if one of them found her in this boxcar. She had no way of knowing how she would live, but she could not go back.

Her heart nearly stopped at a clanging sound far up ahead, and then it came closer. Suddenly the car gave a tremendous jolt forward, almost throwing her flat. She grabbed for the door, held on, and stood to her feet. The car moved forward slowly and then picked up speed. She had the urge to jump from the car, for it was still moving slowly enough she didn't think she'd be hurt, but she did not. What would that accomplish? She could not go back now, and finally she sat down with her back against the door. The cold air was whistling through it, so she closed it and sat down in the darkness. For a time the train picked up speed, and soon the wheels were making a *clickety-clack* sound on the rails beneath. She sat there feeling as lost as she had ever felt in her life.

★　★　★　★

Kefira had been almost stiffened by the cold. Shivering in the dark boxcar, she pulled out all three changes of underwear she had brought and put them on, quickly pulling on most of her clothes over them. Bundled up as she was, her hands were still freezing, and she longed for a pair of warm mittens. She had been riding for hours, and she knew it must be midday by now. The train had stopped twice, and once she had heard a man's voice faintly, but no one had disturbed the car door.

Now she stood up and bent over to ease her aching muscles, balancing against the motion of the train. Groping around, she felt for the bag and pulled out her water bottle. By touch alone she located the bag of food, pulled out one of the sandwiches, and ate it slowly. She wanted to bolt it, but she knew it might be a long time between meals, so she savored every bite, chewing carefully until it was almost dissolved. When she had finished one sandwich, she drank a few swallows of water and stowed the water bottle back in the bag.

There was absolutely nothing to do, so she stood to her feet, leaning against the car. The side was not as cold as the floor, and she wished she had brought a blanket with her to wrap up in. As the train made its *clickety-clack, clickety-clack* over the rails, she thought back over the scene in Kurtz's office. She knew she had escaped being violated only by a stroke of fortune. If he had not been drunk, or if she had not been able to get her hands on the poker, she knew she would have been ruined, and she felt a sudden burst of gratitude. Her father and her mother both had taught her, ingrained in her from earliest girlhood, that a woman must keep herself pure for her husband, and although Kefira had little religious faith, she had enough, at least, to be grateful that she was still chaste.

Unlike the passenger train to Washington, this train seemed to stop every few minutes, sometimes backing up to attach more cars, or take on more loads or water. She wasn't sure what was happening at all these stops, but time passed slowly and she realized she was not getting anywhere very fast. When her inner clock told her it must be past noon, she cracked open the door and saw that the train was in open country, passing through a heavily wooded area. She hoped that as the afternoon wore on, the sun would verify that she was indeed heading south. The air did not seem to be quite as cold as when she had boarded in Washington, so that was a good sign.

It won't be long now before I'll be warm, she thought happily. She remembered seeing pictures of people in Florida on the sunny beaches. There had been a story in the paper about how women's bathing suits had grown steadily more daring, and she had seen a picture of the Miss America contest, where bathing beauties competed for a prize. She had never seen a beach, not even Coney Island, but on one rare occasion she had gone to a movie, where she had seen people bathing in the ocean. Even in the black-and-white film, the sands looked as white as sugar, and the dark waves curled softly upward with sparkling white caps. Kefira shivered in the still cold boxcar and longed for the warm breezes, but she had no idea how far away Florida was.

★　★　★　★

The day passed, and the train inched steadily south, continuing to make frequent stops at every small town and intersection, it seemed. Around suppertime, she ate her other sandwich and drank a few sips of water, making sure to leave about half of it. She knew she would have to get off soon and find something to drink, but she hoped she could last until they were in warmer country.

She stood at the slit of the door and stared out at the towns, which fascinated her. Once they passed through a large city, where the train did some complicated maneuvering. She became fearful at the thought that they might leave this car behind as they had others, but it remained linked to the train, and after several hours, she felt the southward journey begin again.

The sun was going down now, and the shadows were lengthening over the earth when the train stopped again. She glanced out and saw far down the line that the engine had halted at a water stop. She could see one of the crew moving about and knew they would soon be on their way again. There was no town that she could see, and no buildings, so she had no apprehension.

Suddenly she heard running footsteps. Alarmed, she grabbed her bag and moved back into the shadows at the end of the car. She held her breath in dread as the door rumbled open. Light flooded the car, and a blanket rolled in a sausage shape came sailing in. A man heaved himself into the car after it and lay flat for a moment. She could hear his raspy breathing and fear assailed her. He sat up with a grunt and stayed there until his breathing became more regular. Mumbling to himself, he reached around and untied the blanket. Kefira watched as he pulled out a bottle, took several swallows, and gasped, "Ahhh!" Then he capped the bottle and stuck it back in the blanket. He did not close the door, so she could see him fairly well in the fading light. He was a large man in a tattered blue coat. A misshapen felt hat was pulled down over his head, but as he turned, the light caught him, and she saw that he was unshaven and had a broad, bulky face.

For a time she sat as quietly as she possibly could, hardly daring to breathe. But then the straw on the floor began to make her nose itch. She felt a sneeze coming on and quickly covered her face with her hands to try to muffle the sound. The man must have had ears like a fox, for he whirled at once and called out roughly, "Who's back there? Who are you?"

Kefira did not answer but tried to push her back farther into the wall. She watched as he advanced, and then he was standing over her. "What's your name, boy?" he said hoarsely.

When she did not answer, he reached down and grabbed her, saying, "Answer me when I talk to you!"

Kefira felt the power of his grip and smelled the raw alcohol. He dragged her to the middle of the car, then suddenly stopped and stared at her with bald surprise. "Wot's this! A woman!" He laughed rawly and said, "Well, lady, I'm glad to meet ya. My name's George. Wot's yours?"

Kefira was terrified. She seemed to be reliving her nightmare in Kurtz's office. "My . . . my name's Kefira."

"Well. Kefira. Ain't that a pretty name?" He reached up and jerked her shawl back so that her black hair spilled free. "Now, ain't you a pretty one. I'll say!" He held her arm with one hand and put his other on her cheek. "Smooth as a baby's tukus," he said, grinning. She tried to get away, but he grabbed her by the hair and said, "Now, don't be shy with old George." He laughed roughly. "I ain't had me a lady friend in some time now. You and me's gonna be real friendly."

And then Kefira knew she had little hope. The train had started moving, and her only escape lay in throwing herself out the door. She made a wild lunge and jerked free from his hand, but before she got to the door, he took a quick step and caught her. The train was picking up speed, and the hobo swayed. He was drunk, and there was a brutality in his features that told Kefira she could expect no mercy. The thought came to her, *Oh, God, why did you let me get away from one man just to let another one get me?* She began to scream, and he cuffed her on the face. "Now then, I likes a little spirit in a gal. You fight all you want. It'll be all right."

Kefira spit in his face, and when he involuntarily released her, she kicked his knee. Letting out a cry, he made a wild grab at her. She dodged, and he came after her. It was a cat-and-mouse game she was bound to lose. Several times he lunged at her, and by this time the train was going full speed and the footing was unsteady. Kefira made a lunge at the other door, but it was locked. She felt his hand graze her shoulder, grabbing at her clothes, and when she pulled away, she heard the material rip. She desperately threw herself toward the right, and when he followed her, she jerked quickly left. She made a run for the door, and when she looked back, he was right behind her. She was only two feet from the door itself but knew he would catch her. She threw herself to one side, and so intent was he on catching her that he shot by. She fell to the floor and saw amazement and fright strike him as he realized he was going over. Off balance, he went through the door, missing his grab at the sides. He uttered a long, terrified yell, turned a somersault, and disappeared. Kefira lay there for a moment, unable to speak or move, and then she got up quickly and stuck her head out the door. She saw him rolling down the embankment. He got up and looked around and shook his fist at her. The train swung around a sweeping curve and she could see him no more.

Kefira's knees buckled, and she sat down abruptly and began to cry. She ground the heels of her hands into her eyes and tried to stem the tears and the sobs but finally gave up. She cried until she had little strength left. Finally she straightened up, and there before her lay the bundle, the blanket roll that the hobo had thrown in. Out of curiosity, she untied the leather shoelaces that bound the end. When she unrolled it she found an extra blanket inside, three cans of soup, half a loaf of bread, and a box of matches, but then her eye fell on the gun that lay at the other end. She stared at it, then reached over and picked it up. She had never held a gun in her life, although she had, of course, seen pictures of them and had seen them in the movies. She stared at it, fascinated, and realized it was loaded. She could see the metallic bases of the bullets. She held it for a moment, feeling its weight, and then her mouth became a determined line. She stuck the pistol in the side pocket of her coat and searched through the rest of the bundle. She found sixteen dollars in cash and four shells that probably fit the gun, but no letters of any kind.

She sat there on the floor of the speeding train and realized how close she had come, twice now, to being ruined. She remembered suddenly how, when she was fleeing from the tramp, certain that she would be destroyed, she had cried out to God. She thought of how miraculously, it seemed to her, she had been saved, and finally Kefira got to her feet. She wrapped one of the blankets around her, then went to the door. She held on and stared out at the moon, which was rising now, and looked up into the dark sky. She did not speak for a long time, but serious thoughts passed through her mind. Finally she whispered, "If you're up there, God, as my father and mother believe, thank you for saving me from that man."

It was not much of a prayer, but Kefira bowed her head and knew, somehow, that she was going to survive.

PART TWO

Josh

★ ★ ★

CHAPTER SIX

THE DOOR OPENS

★ ★ ★ ★

A large black fly buzzed Josh Winslow's face, looking for a possible landing site. As Josh brushed it away for the tenth time, he wondered, *What's a fly doing in here in the middle of February? They all ought to be dead or hibernating.* Looking up from his book, he watched the insect circle, then apparently decide that Josh's companion, stretched out flat on the cot below, was a more appealing victim. The fly disappeared, and Josh heard a slap as Legs Spradlin made an ineffectual attempt to rid himself of the pest. Smiling as Legs grumbled under his breath, Josh looked toward the window, where a pale shaft of morning sunlight penetrated the cell. He watched the tiny dust motes dance in the light, wondering idly how many fragments of dust there were in that single spot. He had a vivid imagination and was interested in everything he saw. His father, Lewis Winslow, had often said with exasperation, *Josh, you're not going to be a poet, I don't suppose, so why don't you concentrate on what's important rather than on how many blades of grass there are in a field or why beans will always climb a pole in a clockwise direction?*

The thought of his father saddened Josh, and a dull sense of despair touched him as he lay flat on his back on the upper bunk. He was twenty-nine years old, and many times he had looked back over the years of his life and realized that he had accomplished nothing. Now in a Georgia state prison he had reached the very bottom of his existence. For years he had been an alcoholic, drinking far too much and breaking off from brilliant beginnings of projects, such as college, when he was defeated by his lust for alcohol. Now, as he lay there, his mind reached out, and he could almost begin to imagine what it would be like to drink again. He had not had a drink for a month. There was no alcohol to be found in prison, and even if there were, he was determined to turn his back on the temptation to drink himself insensible.

Some usual prison noises reached Josh, but he had learned to ignore them. They had become part of the grim world he had inhabited for the last four weeks. From somewhere down the cellblock, Johnny DeFrancis was crying, having one of his bad days. At one time Josh would have been concerned about a grown man crying, but Johnny was just one of the many misfits who had wound up in the Georgia State Penitentiary. One of the black prisoners, Spade Jones, was singing a hymn, and Josh lowered the book onto his stomach and listened. Just as Spade ended his song, Josh heard a slap and a curse come from below. Then the double bunk shifted, and the face of Legs Spradlin appeared to his left.

"What you readin' this time, Josh?"

"A book on archeology."

"Arky-whaty?" Legs Spradlin was a small, wiry man with more scars than any person Josh had ever seen. Someone had tried to separate his head from his body once, leaving a frightful scar from his right ear down to his collarbone. The rough surgery had pulled his neck muscles around, and also his mouth, forcing him to speak in a rather crooked fashion. His nose had been broken innumerable times. It bent sharply to the east just below the bridge and then took an abrupt about-face to the west. This left a nasal cavity so crooked that Legs whistled through his nose with every breath.

Legs reached over and pulled up the book. He glanced at it, then shook his head. "Too many words and not enough pictures." He grinned crookedly and exposed a mouth almost bereft of teeth, giving him the appearance of a smiling jack-o'-lantern. Freckles were epidemic across his face, and he was altogether one of the homeliest men Josh had ever seen. He had been good for Josh, however, for he was optimistic, always looking on the bright side of things. He kept Josh entertained with his stories of his escapades working in the oil fields, and he had told Josh when they first met that an injustice had been done. "I'm innocent," he had proclaimed indignantly. "It was a fair fight, and I won it fair and square."

"What guy were you fighting with?" Josh had asked.

"Wasn't no guy. It was a big old woman from the Purple Lantern. I got to admit she outweighed me by fifty pounds, most of it muscle. She claimed, after the brawl was over, that I pulled a knife on her. But that weren't so. I didn't use nothin' but a little ol' blackjack."

Spradlin studied Josh as if he were some exotic alien creature. "Do you read all the time when you ain't in the slammer?"

"I read quite a bit."

"Well, what's that there book 'bout? What is this here arky-whatever-you-said?"

"Archeology is the study of ancient civilizations. What people did five thousand years ago."

"You readin' a book 'bout dead people?" Spradlin's eyes opened as wide as the scars permitted, and he was the picture of astonishment. He had light green eyes, and now the light danced in them as the wind whistled through his nose. "What 'n tarnation you wanna read about dead people fer?"

"They're interesting."

"I swan, you're a caution, Josh!"

Josh looked over and grinned. "Sometimes I think dead people are easier to get along with than live people."

"Ye're shore as shootin' 'bout that," Spradlin said, nodding. He looked at the book again and shook his head. "Never knew nobody wanna know so much 'bout dead people."

Josh sat up and held the book loosely in his hand. "I wanted to be an archeologist once. Started out to make a career of it." His thoughts went back to his college days, one of the more pleasant memories. "I went on several digs, and I enjoyed it more than anything I ever did."

"A dig! What's a dig?"

"Well, one was in Louisiana. There were some Indian mounds there, and we dug down to see what we would find."

"Well, what did you find?"

"Well, for one thing we found a graveyard. One grave that I dug up had a man and a woman and two children in it. It looked like they'd all died at the same time. Maybe some sort of sickness."

"And you enjoyed diggin' up dead people?"

"Well, it doesn't sound like much fun, but it was to me." Josh closed the book after inserting a slip of paper in it and laid it on the bunk. "I like to think about that family. They'd been dead for hundreds of years, maybe thousands even, and they had names, and they had their sorrows, and they had their joys. They had children. I just like to think about what they were like."

Spradlin shook his head. "I don't like messin' round with no dead people." He looked over to where Josh's few belongings were all laid neatly on the floor beside the bunk. "Well, ye're gettin' out, buddy. An' ya ain't hardly even been here! Ya got you a lady out there waiting fer ya?"

For a moment Josh thought about Dora Skinner. It was primarily her doing that he was in prison. She was the daughter of a local bootlegger and had enticed Josh, not only into her bed but into the moonshine business as well. She had been intoxicating in every way, and he had not known a moment's rest since he had met her. But he shook his head and told Spradlin, "Not really. Don't guess I'll have one either."

"Why not?"

"Because it takes money."

"Shoot, you gotta find yerself one that's *got* money!" Spradlin grinned.

"Maybe I'll do that, but right now all I want to do is help my family get on their feet."

Spradlin reached into his pocket and pulled out a sack of tobacco. Expertly he extracted a cigarette paper with one hand and, with dexterous fingers, held it while he dumped the tobacco in a straight line. He rolled it up, licked it, and stuck it in his mouth, then closed the sack and stuck it back in his pocket. Pulling out a kitchen match, he struck it on one of his few remaining teeth, a trick that fascinated Josh. "Ya got a good family, ya tell me. Me, I ain't got nobody."

"That's too bad, Legs." Josh thought for a minute and added, "My family—they're better than I am. I've been nothing but a grief to them for years."

"Yer sister Hannah. You tell me she's gettin' married?"

"Yes, and that's an amazing thing to me too."

"Why's that? Women get married all the time."

"We all had given up on Hannah. She stuck to her room for years. Wouldn't come out. A real recluse."

"What's a recluse?"

"A hermit. And then a fellow came along called Clint Longstreet. He about saved our bacon." Josh shook his head thinking back over the past.

"How's that?"

"My family lost everything back in the crash of twenty-nine. My father was into stocks. All we had was the clothes on our backs. No place to go. Nothing. But Hannah was going through some family papers and came across a deed to a farm in Georgia that had belonged to my mother's people. When my father checked it out, he found it was still good, even though my mother had died a couple years earlier. We had no idea what we'd do, but Clint had patched an old truck together. He loaded us into it with all we could haul and took us to Georgia."

"He sounds like a decent sort."

"He is. Reminds me of you a bit, Legs. He can do anything. Grew up on a farm just like you grew up on a ranch."

"Well, what about yer pa? He never married after yer ma died?"

"No, he didn't. He was engaged to a fancy socialite. A rich woman in New York, but she dumped him as soon as he lost his money. But he's getting married now pretty soon."

"That's good. D'ya like yer new ma?"

"I sure do! Her name's Missouri Ann. She found my dad when he broke his leg falling into a deep gully and couldn't move. She hauled him out of there, set his leg—" Here Josh laughed with delight. "And she told him that God had sent him to be her husband. Dad nearly had a fit."

Legs grinned. "Well, I admire a woman that knows her mind. What sort of a lady is she?"

"Oh, she's about as Christian as anybody I ever saw. I never thought God spoke to people, but I believe He speaks to Missouri Ann. She's good at healin' people, and she's good for Dad. He needs somebody. He's been lonesome."

"What about yer sisters?"

"I've got three—Hannah, Jenny, and Kat. Kat is just a kid, but Jenny is really something! The most beautiful girl you ever saw."

"She ain't hitched, though?"

"No, not yet."

"Well, one thing about it"—Legs slapped Josh on the knee—"ya shore got religion out of this trip to the poky."

"That's right," Josh said, his face growing sober. When he had been sent to prison, Josh felt as if he had reached absolute bottom, even though his sentence was miraculously light. His first day out in the prison yard, one of the other prisoners, Thad Gilbert, had spoken of his love for Christ, and somehow the simplicity of the man's belief brought a heavy spirit on Josh. He had heard the Gospel in church all of his life, yet he'd always turned from it. But recent events had been softening his heart, and he knew he could no longer run from the truth of it. That night he had cried out to God and accepted the Lord Jesus Christ.

His life had changed drastically in the few weeks since then. He had begun reading his Bible, and somehow the old words that had seemed so dry to him when he'd heard them in church services as a child came alive with a dramatic force and intensity. To his surprise he took pleasure in praying, although he was awkward at it. He gladly joined the prison services held by a local pastor for those prisoners who cared to attend. Life had become different for Josh Winslow, and to his shock and amazement, all craving for alcohol had left him. He had quit drinking before for short periods, but always, every morning, he had awakened thinking of liquor, and his last thought at night had been a craving for a drink. Now somehow he had been delivered and purged and cleansed. It was as if God had given him this gift to show him that his conversion was real and not just "jailhouse religion," as some of the other prisoners had scoffed.

Turning now, he said, "I worry about you, Legs. I'd like to see you find the Lord."

Spradlin shook his head defiantly. "Nope, I got me some wild oats to sow 'fore I hit the Glory Trail."

"That's dangerous, I think. What if you die first?"

Spradlin suddenly grew sober. "I guess I've thought a little bit about that."

"I'll be praying for you, Legs, and I'll write you. And you write me back. You stick with Thad. The world doesn't have anything good to offer you except a beating."

Spradlin stared straight at Josh and said, "I'd appreciate that. Yer writin' to me, I mean."

"Well, you'll be out in seven more months. Tell you what. I don't know where I'll be then, but let's keep in touch. When you get out, we'll get together and celebrate."

"Lots of fellas say that, but not many do it."

"Let's be different." Josh stuck his hand out, and when Legs took it, Josh gripped it firmly. "I'll be praying for you every day, and I'll get Missouri Ann, my new ma, to pray for you too. Sometimes I think she climbs right up into heaven and talks to God personally."

"Well," Legs said slowly, "I reckon I can use all the help I can get. I'll be in Texas, though. Got a longin' to see some longhorn cow critters. Maybe do a little more rodeoin'. But I'd like to see you again, Josh. I shore would like to get a letter from you now and agin."

Josh heard the sound of approaching footsteps, and when a guard named Prentice appeared, he jumped down and said, "Hello. Is it time to go?"

Prentice was a tall, broad man with a round face and a pair of steady gray eyes. "You're all set. Say your good-byes to Spradlin."

Josh shook hands again with Spradlin but resisted the impulse to hug him, for he knew it would embarrass the little Texan. He picked up his few belongings he had packed in a paper sack and stepped outside as the door locked behind him with a metallic clang. "I'll be writing you, Legs," he said.

As he followed Prentice down the cellblock, Josh said good-bye to his fellow prisoners. Some of them called out ribald things to him, giving advice on how to behave. He passed Thad Gilbert and stopped long enough to reach through the cell bars. "I'll be writing you, Thad, and I'll never forget you."

"May the good Lord smile on you. You're in His family now. A child of the king," Gilbert said. He was a tall, dark-haired man with steady, warm brown eyes, reflecting the spirit within.

Josh followed Prentice to a large room where he received the clothes he had worn when he arrived a month earlier. As he stripped off the striped convict's uniform, the inmate who worked behind the counter grinned and said, "I'll be seein' you pretty soon."

"Not me, Taylor."

"Why, that's right, Winslow. You done hit the Glory Road."

"Yes, I have, and I hope you will too."

Taylor, a small, plump man with a dapper mustache, grinned at him. "Maybe you're right. Good luck, Winslow."

"Thanks, Taylor."

"C'mon, Winslow. I got more to do today than just turning you loose." Prentice grinned.

"Sorry to be a trouble to you, Officer," Winslow said. Prentice was one of the more admirable and friendly guards, and he had been a help to Josh during his stay. "I hope your boy gets better. I've been praying for him."

Prentice nodded his head and grew solemn. "I appreciate that, Josh."

They stepped outside and walked to the gate, where Josh found Warden Harlow Jennings waiting. Jennings shook his hand and said, "Good luck to you, Winslow." He handed him an envelope. "There's five dollars, and I've added a little something myself."

"Thanks, Warden. You didn't have to do that."

Warden Jennings shook his head. "Don't come back. That's all I ask."

"You won't see me anymore. Not here. But I appreciate all you've done for me."

Josh shook hands with the warden, then stepped outside the gate. As he walked toward the waiting bus, the cold February wind cut through his thin shirt. He looked back at the prison and prayed aloud, "God, keep me out of this place and others like it forever!"

CHAPTER SEVEN

HOMECOMING

★ ★ ★ ★

Night came early in Georgia during February, and by the time Josh walked the last hundred yards toward the tall two-story house, a sickle moon was already grinning overhead. A dog rose suddenly from the porch and ran toward him, teeth bared and a low rumble in his throat.

Josh tensed. "Steady now, steady!" he ordered. He had forgotten that his family had a dog now. Kat had written to Josh in jail, describing the strange bluish dog she had found and adopted. *But what had she named it?* The enormous dog growled again, baring a mouthful of teeth like a great white shark, and suddenly it came to him. "Down, Stonewall," Josh commanded, then repeated firmly, "Stonewall, down!" The dog's growl softened into a whine and he slunk away. Josh made his way to the house, thinking, *Well, I hope that's not the reception I can expect from the others!*

As Josh climbed the steps to the porch, he noticed that the front of the house had been freshly painted and that the windows wore new curtains. When he'd left they were still getting the old house into shape, and now it looked as though the work was almost complete. He stopped for a moment and listened. He could hear muted voices inside, which he identified easily. His little sister Kat's voice was shriller than the rest as she demanded attention. He grinned and put his hand on the door handle, thinking, *Kat should have been a boy. She's more like one than she is a girl.*

As he opened the door, the sound of merriment spilled out, and he moved down the hall, past the parlor to his left and the stairway to his right. He stepped in front of an open door and paused, a lump rising in his throat as he took in his family. They were gathered around the large oval oak table, which was laden with bowls and dishes and glasses. His eyes went first to his father, Lewis Winslow, and he thought, *He looks good. I think marriage is going to agree with him.* His father was fifty-six now but looked at least ten years younger. He was a few inches shorter than Josh's six-one, and he looked trim and tan even in the winter. He brushed his gray-tinged light brown hair back from his forehead, and his eyes squinted as he laughed at Kat's remark.

Sitting beside Lewis was Missouri Ann. She was taller than Lewis, strongly built and with the clearest eyes Josh had ever seen. He noticed how often her eyes went to his father, and the love she had for him was obvious.

To Missouri Ann's right sat Hannah, Josh's older sister. She was thirty-one now, but like her father, could have passed for much younger. It was hard to believe she had been practically a hermit, for her brown eyes were bright now and danced with laughter, and the overhead lamp caught the reddish glints in her auburn hair. She was not a beautiful woman but had good, strong features and, as Josh well knew, a will as strong as the iron in a railroad track.

Beside Hannah sat her new husband, Clint Longstreet. He was a tall man exactly Josh's height, lean and muscular with sandy hair and gray-green eyes. His nose had been broken, and there was a scar on the right side of his chin. It struck Josh that he was almost as battered as his cellmate, Legs Spradlin. He admired Clint tremendously and knew that if it had not been for him, the family would probably have gone to the poorhouse in New York City. Clint was one of those men who was not highly educated but had "country smarts" and was able to do anything with his hands.

Across from the pair sat Jenny, an eighteen-year-old beauty with dark green eyes and flaming red hair, set off by a perfect complexion. Josh remembered how spoiled she had been in New York, caring only for clothes and good times. But being thrown onto a farm in Georgia, with no resources save what the family could produce, had hewn a strength in his sister that made him proud indeed.

Josh's eyes went to Kat, and he smiled involuntarily. At the age of thirteen she looked more like a boy than a girl, at least from her clothing. She was wearing one of Josh's old shirts, which was far too large, and he suspected she was wearing a pair of faded overalls beneath it. She cared nothing for clothes but loved farming, hunting, fishing, and collecting bird eggs—anything out-of-doors. Josh loved this girl with a special care, and his heart grew full as he saw the goodness and innocence in her fine gray-green eyes, the exact tint as his own.

Josh stood listening another moment, then stepped inside, announcing loudly, "Fine thing starting supper without me!"

Josh's words and sudden appearance electrified the family. They all leaped to their feet and made a wild rush at him. Kat reached him first, nearly bowling him over. He picked her up and hugged her as he felt the others crowding around, thumping him on the shoulders and crying out words of welcome.

"Well, don't beat the poor boy to death!" Missouri Ann scolded. She pushed the others aside, big woman that she was, and took Josh's face between her hands, pulled him forward, and kissed him soundly on the cheek. "Welcome home, son." She and Lewis would be married soon, but she came often to help with the cooking at the Winslow house.

Josh's eyes grew misty at her use of the word "son." It made him feel odd inside, and he reached out and touched her cheek. "Thanks, Ma," he whispered.

"Well, if we'd known you were coming, we would've killed a fatted calf," Lewis said, grinning, "but you'll just have to put up with what we've got." He winked at Josh, adding, "I'm marrying a poor cook indeed, but I'll have to make the best of it."

Josh found himself pulled into a chair that Clint had dragged in. He looked over the table. "I can see you're all starving here," he said with a smile. With pleasure he scanned the platters filled with squirrel and dumplings, pickled okra, butter beans, and corn bread. A pitcher of milk sat at each end of the table, and the smell of fresh-baked bread was rich in his nostrils.

"What was it like in jail, Josh?" Kat demanded. She had eased herself into the chair next to his and now pulled at his sleeve until he turned to look at her. "Were there any murderers in there?"

"Some pretty rough fellows, sweetie. Almost as rough as your dog. He about ate my backside just now."

"Stonewall wouldn't hurt a fly. But what about jail?" Kat insisted. "Were there any murderers?"

"I expect there were one or two."

"What were their names? Who did they kill?"

"Kat, would you please stop asking those questions!" Lewis demanded. "Josh doesn't want to talk about that."

"You're right about that, Dad," Josh said. "Particularly not about murderers, but I do want to tell you a few things."

Missouri Ann commandeered Josh's plate and piled it high until it resembled a miniature Mount Vesuvius. The food was steaming hot, and Josh wolfed it down, talking in between mouthfuls. He finally managed to answer all of Kat's questions, and more than once Hannah reached over and patted his arm, as if to reassure herself that he was really there.

"Well, now, don't eat too much. We've got blackberry cobbler for dessert," Missouri Ann declared.

"And I picked the blackberries myself last summer. Got about ten million chiggers," Kat said, nodding. "You should've seen me. I had welts all over—even on my bottom."

"Don't talk like that," Jenny scolded. "You're getting to be a young lady." But even she could not contain a smile. "I got a few chigger bites myself that day."

Missouri gave him a heaping bowlful of blackberry cobbler, then poured rich, thick cream over it. He took a bite and sighed with ecstasy. "I wish my buddies in jail had some of this."

"Was the food pretty bad?" Clint inquired. "Some of the jails I've been in weren't fit for hogs."

"Oh, the food wasn't too bad. At least there was plenty of it.

But nothing like this, Ma." Josh smiled at Missouri Ann.

While he ate his cobbler, Missouri Ann brought him a cup of steaming black coffee, and he sipped it gratefully. "The best meal I've had in my whole life, I do believe." He reached up and patted Missouri Ann's arm, and she smiled warmly at him.

"You'd think anything was good after what you've been eating," she said.

"Oh no, I wouldn't. I'm a better judge than that." Josh sat quietly for a moment, then went on, "Well, it's been tough, but like I told you in my letters, I found the Lord Jesus in there, so it was all worth it."

Kat blurted out, "Tell us all about it, Josh. How did you get saved?" she demanded. "Did you cry?"

Josh smiled slowly. "Yes, I cried, and I may do it again if I start telling you about it."

Kat stared at him, her gray-green eyes wide. "But men don't cry."

"Sure they do," Clint said. "I do it myself sometimes."

Kat was amazed. She stared at Clint with a shocked expression. "I don't believe you," she said.

"Next time I get ready to cry," Clint remarked, "I'll come and get you. Then you'll see."

Lewis leaned forward. "Some of the greatest heroes who ever lived cried like babies, Kat—men like King David and Beowulf. Nothing wrong with shedding a few tears. As a matter of fact, I've shed a few myself. But tell us more about how you got converted, Josh. We've read your letters, but I'd like to hear it all over again."

"And don't leave anything out!" Kat cried. "I want to hear every bit."

For the next half hour Josh Winslow told how he had found Christ in prison. He ended by saying, "I'm having to learn a little at a time how to follow the Lord, but I'm never turning back."

"That sounds so good," Hannah said. "I knew you'd become a Christian someday, and I'm sorry you had to go to prison to do it, but that's all behind you now."

"Come on, fellas, let's go into the parlor," Lewis said, rising. "Let these pesky females clean up the mess we've made and do the dishes." He winked at Missouri Ann.

"I've got half a mind to make you do them," she said in mock indignation. "You're settin' a bad example for your son." She smiled, however, and nodded. "You go on and bring Josh up to date. Us girls'll be there soon as we can get these here dishes done."

"And I want to hear *Amos 'n Andy* at eight o'clock," Kat chimed in.

"I'd rather listen to Josh than any old radio program," Jenny said firmly.

"So would I," Hannah agreed. "Don't you tell anything, Josh, until we get back. You just listen, you hear?"

Josh joined his father and Clint in the parlor. When Josh sat down, he looked at the wood stove, which glowed with a satisfying cherry color, then said, "I'd like to have had that stove in my cell. We nearly froze to death when the cold hit."

"It was the worst winter we've had in a long time. Wasn't there any heat in those cells?" Lewis asked.

"Not a bit. They did give us an extra blanket or two. It didn't hurt me, though. I didn't get sick." And then Josh said, "Tell me all about the place here. What's been going on?"

Lewis began giving him the latest news, with Clint putting in a few words now and then. The essence of their report was that things were still pretty bad financially. "This depression is tough. People are hungry and men just can't find work."

When the women all came in, Kat climbed up on Josh's lap.

"Hey, you're not a baby anymore!" he hollered. "You're a young lady now."

"It won't hurt me to sit on your lap. Now tell me some more about the criminals in the prison."

Josh laughed and squeezed her. She was filling out, and he could see the promise of beauty in her youthful face. "I'll make up some real horror stories to tell you tomorrow. For now I just want to hear about you. What have *you* been doing?"

He listened as Kat described her hunt for a woodpecker's egg, and then she looked up at the grandfather clock and said, "It's time for *Amos 'n Andy.*"

"I guess we'll have to listen to it," Missouri Ann said, sighing. "She loves that program."

After listening and laughing together over the antics of Amos and Andy, they talked for another hour. Then Jenny played the piano while they sang a few hymns and songs, and Lewis finally said, "It's getting late. I'll bet you're tired; you've had a long day, Josh."

"Yes, I am pretty tired, Dad."

"Well, let's all gather around and give thanks to the good Lord for bringing Josh back. *And* bringing him back as a member of the family of God!"

They all stood in a circle and held hands, Kat and Jenny on either side of Josh. Jenny squeezed his hand after the amen was said. Then she reached up and kissed him. "Good night, Josh. We'll talk tomorrow."

Kat piped up, "Tomorrow you can get up early, and we can go look for eggs."

Josh laughed. "All right—but only if Dad says it's okay. I know there's work to be done."

"Son, I want you to take a week off and do nothing but what you want to do."

"Thanks, Dad. That's like you."

Josh turned and went to his room, accompanied by Missouri Ann. She opened the door and said, "I'm glad you're home, son." She hesitated, and he turned to her, noting the troubled look in her eyes. "What's wrong, Ma?"

"I . . . hope you don't feel bad about me marryin' your pa. I know I ain't the woman your real ma was, but I'm gonna do my best."

Josh reached forward and put his arms around Missouri Ann. He kissed her on the cheek and smiled directly into her eyes. "You *are* my real ma. The Bible says two are better than one, and I've got two fine mothers."

Tears sprang to her eyes, and she reached out and touched Josh timidly on the chest. "You've got to help me, son."

"Help you? How can I help you, Ma?"

"I want to learn how to be genteel."

"Genteel! Why, you are genteel."

"No, I ain't. I don't know how to talk right, and I don't know how to dress. I don't know how to be with fine people. You know I was raised in the woods and never went to school. I want you to help me."

"Dad loves you just the way you are, and so do I."

Josh's words seemed to reassure her. She straightened and laughed. "You go to bed now. I'll come back tomorrow morning and fix you a breakfast that'll set you free."

Josh smiled, and when she closed the door, he at once began to undress. He was weary, but the excitement of his homecoming had kept him going. Now when he climbed into bed and pulled the blankets over him, thoughts of his future ran through his mind, troubling him, for he could not see his way. There were no jobs to be had, and he had no skills. It was too late for him to go back to college—besides, there was no money for such things now. He wrestled with the question of what to do with his life until weariness overtook him. He finally prayed a simple prayer and went to sleep instantly.

★ ★ ★ ★

"I always did like to paint," Jenny said. She dipped her brush into the bucket and carefully applied a layer of gleaming white paint to the clapboards, which had been scraped and sanded until they were as smooth as new wood. "I wish I could make a living painting."

Josh was up on a ladder getting the higher parts beyond Jenny's reach. He looked at the side they had finished and then glanced upward. "We're going to have to get extension ladders to get the upper story."

"Clint painted the front a few weeks ago, but there you could stand on top of the porch. Back here, Clint said we'd have to build scaffolding."

Josh had gone fishing with Kat that morning, but after lunch he had joined Jenny in painting the back of the house. She was wearing a pair of worn overalls, as was Josh himself, and both had succeeded in splattering themselves with the white paint.

"This paint's pretty expensive, isn't it?"

"Dad did some work for Mr. Huntington at the general store. He goes in once in a while and helps him with his accounts. We only buy a few gallons at a time, but it'll all be done when we get the back finished."

Josh climbed down the ladder, set the paint bucket down, and glanced over to where Kat was working with Clint. He had the hood of the truck up, and Kat was right there every time he tried to turn. Josh laughed and said, "Kat's really something."

"She loves Clint," Jenny said, "and he's very partial to her. I think sometimes Kat's jealous of Hannah. She's jealous of anyone you like too."

Josh looked over with a worried expression. "Is that healthy, do you think?"

"She's only thirteen, and you and Dad and Clint are the only men in her life." Jenny suddenly smiled. "That's all that the rest of us have too."

"Don't you have another man in your life?"

Jenny gave him a quick glance. She was a strong-willed girl with a spirit that was not easily quenched. She had not taken the fall from high society well at all, but now she seemed over it. "No, I don't have a beau, if that's what you're asking."

"What about Reverend Crutchfield?"

"Oh, there's nothing to that," Jenny said with a dismissive wave of her hand.

"I thought you and he had something going."

Jenny turned to face Clint, her large, expressive eyes half closed. "I think it's one of those cases where he feels more for me than I do for him."

"That's a tough one. Have you told him so?"

"Yes, I did."

"How did he take it, sis?"

"Surprisingly well."

Josh looked off into the distance where the low hills rose like small gray elephants. They were rounded and smooth, not like the Rockies—sharp and piercing. He liked these gentle mountains, for they seemed more tranquil. "How do you tell someone you don't love them?"

"Well," Jenny said slowly, "there are two ways. You can do it slowly or quickly. I think it's kinder to meet it head-on." She pulled off the soft cap she had worn to protect her hair from the paint and examined it, then said, "I've known some women that did it the slow way. They stopped taking calls. They put the man off. They started being cold to him. I think that's cruel."

"Better to do it all at once, huh?"

"If you had a dog that you wanted to have a bobbed tail, you wouldn't cut off one inch today and another inch tomorrow and a third inch the next day all the way down. You'd just do it all at once."

Josh laughed. "That's a strange way of putting it, but I think you're right."

"You'll have to do the same thing to Dora, you know."

Jenny's blunt words hit Josh like the flat of an ax. "I'm finished with her," he said curtly.

"You may be, but she's not finished with you."

"Have you seen her lately?"

"Yes. She asked me when you were going to get out. She's just waiting for you, Josh. You'd best be careful."

Josh shook his head. "That's all over."

Jenny smiled warmly then, her eyes gleaming with gladness. "I'm glad to hear that. I'm just telling you, she's going to try."

They began painting again, and Josh found a real pleasure in covering the old boards. He so longed to see the old house gleaming and spotless and beautiful, as he imagined it was during his mother's childhood. She had often told them about the lovely home she'd grown up in, but when they'd arrived and seen its dilapidated condition, they'd been very disappointed. Now, with a great deal of work accomplished with very little money, the house was rising up like a phoenix out of its ashes. Finally they finished and began cleaning their brushes with turpentine in a bucket.

"It takes real character to clean out a brush," Josh said. "If I were rich, I'd use it once, then throw it away and get a fresh one."

"I wouldn't think of doing that now!" Jenny said. "They cost too much." She looked up and shook her head. "I never thought about how much things cost back when we lived in New York. Now I count every penny. Do you think I'm becoming a miser?"

"I hardly think so. These are tough times. Everybody has to be careful these days."

"Do you have any idea what you want to do, Josh?"

"You mean for a living? No, I don't. I have no trade, no profession. I'll just have to work at whatever there is until this depression is over. It can't last forever. America's too strong to go down permanently."

"I know what you'd like to do."

"What's that?"

"I never saw you so excited as when you were in college. Every time you came home from one of those digs, you were bubbling over."

"Too late for that. You have to study for years to become an archeologist. It's kind of a closed field."

"You could do it if you wanted to."

"No, not anymore."

Suddenly Jenny said vehemently, "Why, Josh Winslow, I reckon you could do anything you set your mind to!"

Josh looked up at her, astounded. "Where'd you get an idea like that?"

"I've always seen it in you."

"I don't see how. I was so drunk most of the time in college that nobody could see anything but a drunk."

"That's what you did. It's not what you *are*."

Josh smiled sadly. "We all have to put some dreams aside, Jenny. That's one of the penalties I have to pay for the kind of life I led."

Jenny stared at him and said, "Well, you remember what I said."

"Right now I'm thinking more about a job that will pay me any kind of money. Austin Whelock came by yesterday. He told me about a mill in Tennessee that's opening up. He saw in the paper that they'll be hiring two hundred men. I'm going to go there and try to be one of them."

"You're leaving! But you just got here. You haven't even rested up."

"I can rest up on the way there. I need to go to work so I can help Dad out some."

"You know what I think?"

"No, but you're going to tell me, aren't you?"

"I think you're running away from Dora."

Josh stared at the ground for a moment, and when he looked up, his eyes were troubled. "You're too sharp for me, Jenny. I guess I probably am running. I don't know why it is, but I haven't gotten her out of my system yet. I know what she is, and the worst thing in the world would be for me to get mixed up with her again. I'd just as soon not have to be around her."

"That may be a good thing, Josh. You remember Joseph in the Bible when Potiphar's wife took hold of him? He ran like a scared rabbit."

"That's what I'll do," Josh said, grinning. He reached over and pulled Jenny's red hair. "Always keep your red hair, sis," he teased.

"Never mind my hair. You run like a scared rabbit from that woman, you hear me!"

★　★　★　★

The radio held a fascination for the family that Josh could not explain. Every evening they gathered around it to hear their favorite programs, and one evening Lewis complained, "This contraption's going to ruin family life!"

"What do you mean, Dad?" Josh asked.

"I mean we used to sit around and talk to each other. Now we sit around and stare at this box and it talks to us. Sometimes, I want to shove my foot through it and throw it out the window."

"You'd better not!" Josh said in mock horror. "Kat would have your head if you did."

Kat jumped up and came over to stand before her father. "You wouldn't do such a thing, would you, Daddy?"

Lewis put his arm around her. "No, I probably wouldn't, princess, but I don't want you to forget how to read!"

"Oh, Daddy, I could never do that. Can I go to the movies tomorrow?" She changed the subject so abruptly it took her father by surprise.

"For goodness' sake, Kat. If it isn't the radio, then it's the movies!" Lewis said, sighing. "You're always wanting to go to the movies. What is it this time?"

"It's called *Frankenstein*."

"Never heard of it."

"All the kids have seen it. It's about this scientist who makes a monster out of the bodies of a bunch of dead people. He sends his helper out to get a brain, and the helper breaks the bottle containing the good brain and puts an evil brain in it."

Lewis stared at Kat. "That's the most awful thing I've ever heard of!"

"But all my friends have seen it!"

"And if all your friends jumped into the river and drowned, would you do that too?"

"Don't be silly, Daddy. They're not drowning themselves. They're just going to a movie."

"Well, I'm not taking you to see an awful thing like that."

"I don't know. It sounds like a pretty interesting movie to me," Clint said lazily, winking at Kat.

At once Kat ran over to Clint and grabbed his arm. "Would you take me, Clint? Would you please?"

"Well, your dad would have to agree to it."

"Clint will take me, Dad," Kat announced triumphantly.

Lewis stared at his youngest daughter, wondering, not for the first time, what in the world she would be like when she grew up. He saw no signs of femininity about her, except that of late her angular boy's figure had begun developing a little. "Well, if Clint wants to take you to see such a horrible thing and pollute the innocent mind of a child, I suppose I can't do anything about it."

"I'll put my hands over her eyes so she can't see the bad parts," Clint promised, grinning. He turned and said to Hannah, "And you can put your hands over mine."

Hannah laughed. "All right, we'll go. But we'll probably all have nightmares."

Shortly after that, the family went to bed. Josh stayed in the parlor, for he knew it was his father's habit to read for a time in his easy chair. He sat down across from Lewis and said, "I'll be leaving next week, Dad."

Putting the paper down, Lewis said with surprise, "Leaving? For where?"

"There's a mill opening up in Tennessee. They're going to need a lot of men, the paper said."

"Where'd you hear about this?"

"Austin Whelock came by and told me."

"It's too soon for you to go."

"No, it's not. I'm getting nervous. I need to find some work and help with the expenses around here."

Lewis looked down at his hands, a troubled expression sweeping across his face. He was silent for so long that Josh asked, "What's wrong, Dad?"

"I wish I could afford to send you back to college. I feel terrible that I've wasted everything."

"It's not your fault," Josh said quickly. "A lot of good men got caught in this crash. I had my chance to finish college—I could have graduated a long time ago. It was my fault, not yours."

"Well, at least you'll be here for the wedding. I'm awfully glad to hear that."

"Wouldn't miss it for a thing!"

Lewis Winslow looked at his son and felt a warm surge of pride. "You've changed, son. I'm afraid I'm going to have to tell you how proud I am of you."

Josh flushed. "I haven't done anything to be proud of yet, Dad."

"You will, though. Jenny says you'll be an archeologist."

"If I do, I'll be the oldest one alive. I'd have to go back to college first, and then find someone willing to take me on. That would be hard."

"She says you can do anything you want to."

"She's overestimating my capabilities. But anyway, Dad, I'm glad you're getting married. I love Missouri Ann."

"I'm glad to hear that," Lewis said, smiling. Then a strange expression crossed his face. "One thing worries me, though."

"What's that?"

"Missouri says that we're going to have children, and I'm too old for that."

"No, you're not. And if she says so, I guess it'll happen. I never saw a woman like her." Josh felt a warm affection for his father. "I hope you have half a dozen kids."

"Please, Josh, don't say things like that!"

"Seriously, Dad, I'm glad you have somebody. Missouri Ann's a fine woman." He smiled and came over and put his hand on his father's shoulder. "Mom would have loved her."

"She would, wouldn't she?"

"Yes. I really think so. Good night, Dad. I'll see you in the morning."

CHAPTER EIGHT

TWO BECOME AS ONE

★ ★ ★ ★

Bethel Church was packed, for although the Winslows had not been inhabitants of Summerdale, Georgia, for a lengthy time, they had made many friends. The matter of Josh Winslow's conviction for bootlegging and his surprisingly short sentence had made the entire community aware of the family. Bootlegging had become, more or less, a cottage industry in the county. The most likely suspects, although never yet apprehended, were the Cundiffs and the Skinners. Brazenly, Dora Skinner sat in the back row of the church, even though everyone there knew she had pulled Josh Winslow into the crime that had led to his conviction and imprisonment.

Ivy Witherspoon, the master gossip of the community, was present, as she was at every wedding and every funeral—or any other activity that did not charge admission. Mrs. Witherspoon was a sixty-five-year-old widow, a thin woman with a dark complexion and a pair of gimlet eyes set much too close together over a thin beak of a nose. Her lips also were thin—in fact, everything about the woman was thin, as though she had not been dealt a full measure. Her voice, however, in striking contrast to her slight features, was thick, strong, and potent. When she spoke, her words could be clearly heard over the soft organ prelude.

"I'm surprised Dora Skinner has the nerve to come inside the house of God!"

Mrs. Witherspoon's companion, Laurel Henderson, nodded primly. "I think you're right." She was a woman as round and mountainous as Mrs. Witherspoon was thin. Her numerous double chins quivered with indignation as she turned to stare at Dora Skinner. "She has no shame, of course, but this is really too much."

"Everyone knows what she is. I'm surprised the deacons didn't stop her at the door."

"You're *exactly* right, sister!" Mrs. Henderson agreed.

The two women sat there eyeing Dora, who was more amused than offended by their overloud comments. She was a strongly built young woman of nineteen, who exuded sensuality as some women exude virtue. She was wearing a blue dress intended for a woman without her abundant curves so that she appeared to be bursting out of it. Her eyes were an odd color, more hazel than anything else, and there was something feline in her facial expression. Indeed, her face was shaped much like that of a Siamese cat, and her eyes turned slightly upward, adding to the impression. She stared boldly at the two women and smiled and nodded at them, forming a profane word with her lips that could be plainly read. The two women turned several shades of red, swiveled around, and refused to look at her again.

Dora had come to the wedding of Lewis Winslow and Missouri Ann Ramey on a whim. She had been waiting for Josh to come visit her and had been peeved when he had not. She loved to draw men to her, and some said that she chewed them up and spat them out when she grew tired of them. Josh had been different. He was educated, cultured, and fine looking. He had also been a drunk, of course, but then most of the men she knew were. Dora did not look upon drunkenness as wrong. Every article of clothing she owned and every bite of food she put into her mouth was purchased by the sale of moonshine. She herself was active in the manufacture and distribution of the vitriolic liquor that had been known to cause blindness and even death.

Dora sat quietly, running her eyes over the congregation. She knew them all, even though she never attended church, and more than once she would meet the eyes of some man who found it impossible to hold her gaze. *I could tell these nice church people a thing or two about some of these men,* she thought. *They're so holy!—but they come scraping at my door after dark.*

A door opened at the front of the church, and three men emerged: the Reverend Devoe Crutchfield, Lewis Winslow, and Josh Winslow. Dora did not move, but her eyes fastened on Josh. When his eyes swept the church and met hers, she saw him suddenly draw his head back, and his lips tightened into a thin line. She smiled at him and lifted her hand in a familiar greeting. She was amused when he reddened and turned away, fixing his eyes on the door from which the bride would emerge. Dora loved the chase. For her the only game in life was that of man and woman. Anything else was not worth her time. She leaned back and smiled slightly, for she loved a challenge. She had cast off many men, but none had ever walked away from her whole and healthy. *You just wait, my darling Josh,* she thought with a thrill of anticipatory pleasure. *You and I will have a little talk after we get this wedding out of the way. . . .*

★ ★ ★ ★

Missouri Ann stood as stiff as a ramrod but considerably more attractive than she usually appeared in her old work clothes. She was a tall woman with a surprisingly slender waist, which was well set off by the wedding gown. She was big boned and strong, and her cheeks and lips were rosy with a little rouge applied by Jenny. Her fists were clenched so tightly that her knuckles were white.

"Relax, Ma," Jenny said. She had been kneeling to adjust the skirt of the white gown and rose with a smile. "It'll all be over before you know it."

"I wish we had run off somewhere and just got married in a preacher's house." Missouri Ann's lips were pressed tightly together, and she was breathing rapidly as if overexerted.

"Now, slow down," Jenny soothed.

Hannah came to stand beside her, nodding with a smile.

"That's right," she said gently. "Take a slow, deep breath—that's it. It's the happiest day of your life."

"I feel like I'm about to step into a barrel of snakes. I never felt this skeered in my life!"

"Didn't you get scared at your first marriage?"

"No—we just went to the preacher's and got married in his living room, and it was done in five minutes. With all this fussing around and wedding dresses and such like, and all those people—I don't know what to do!"

Hannah exchanged a quick glance with Jenny. Her eyes were compassionate. "You're going to do fine. There's nothing to it."

The two young women had spent a great deal of time over Missouri Ann. She was rural to the bone and had never been to a formal wedding, much less taken part in one. Now as she stood there, Jenny felt a sharp stab of pity. *It must be terrible for her. She knows absolutely nothing about things like this.* Reaching up, she arranged a lock of Missouri's hair and said, "You look absolutely beautiful. Dad is going to be shocked when he sees you."

"Do . . . do you really think so?"

"Of course I do."

"Well, what do I do now?"

"Don't you remember the rehearsal?" Hannah asked gently. "We went through it all."

Missouri Ann swallowed convulsively. "I don't remember a thing."

"Kat will walk up the aisle and throw flowers. Then Hannah and I will go down one at a time," Jenny said. "And then you step out and go down the aisle. When you get there, Dad will greet you, and you'll turn around and face Brother Crutchfield. Just say what he tells you to say, and you'll be fine."

Suddenly Missouri Ann laughed shortly. "I haven't been so skeered since I got surprised by that grizzly lookin' for her cubs. I had only one shot in my rifle. If I hadn't hit her right in the brain, she would have et me."

"Well, Dad's not a grizzly. He's happier than I've seen him in years."

"All right. If you say so."

The three women stood there, and then Kat came bursting in.

She was wearing a new pink dress with a bow in her hair and a basket of flower petals in her hand. "They're ready to start! Do I go now?"

"Yes, go now. You look very pretty."

Kat hitched her skirt up and shook her head. "I don't like dresses. Overalls are more fittin'."

She left the room, and Jenny said, "The longer we live down here, the worse her grammar gets. She does look pretty, though."

Hannah had the door cracked, and she watched for a moment, then said, "Here I go." She stepped out, and Jenny took her place.

In a few moments, Jenny said, "My turn. Now, you walk very slowly, just like we practiced. All right, Ma?"

The words seemed to encourage Missouri Ann. She nodded but could not utter a word.

Standing there listening to the music with the women who were about to become her legal daughters, Missouri Ann Ramey could hardly believe what was happening. When her first husband died a couple of years ago, she had resigned herself to a solitary life in a small house in the deepest part of the woods. She had learned to fend for herself, and the thought of remarriage had never once entered her mind. But as time went on she began to yearn for a husband and started to think about having more children. When she found Lewis Winslow almost unconscious with a broken leg, God spoke to her and said in effect, "You will marry this man, and you will bear his children." Thinking back, she remembered how she blurted out this revelation to Lewis and how he had turned pale and would have run away if he'd had two sound legs. A reluctant smile tugged at her broad lips, and she shook her head. "It's a wonder he didn't run off—broken leg or not," she muttered.

And then the sound of the wedding march came, and Missouri Ann suddenly bowed her head. "Lord, I'd appreciate it if you'd help me get through this."

Opening the door, she began to walk down the aisle, and somehow a great calm settled on her. She looked over the congregation and noticed Mayor Potter Flemming with his wife, Ellen, turning to smile at her. H. G. Huntington and his much younger wife, Edith, were smiling also. There was Jude Tanner, the big blacksmith who played the mandolin, and Dr. Harrison Peturis, a big shambling bear of a man with salt-and-pepper hair and a full beard. Jesse Cannon, who had served under General Longstreet in the Civil War, sat with his wife, Dolly.

She passed them all, and a feeling of pride swelled within her as she realized that, despite her apprehensions, these people were her friends, and they wished her well.

Finally she looked up and saw Lewis waiting for her at the altar, so handsome that she felt inhibited in his presence. She faltered and he smiled broadly. The smile did everything. It made her feel like a woman. He always made her feel like this—like a beautiful, delicate woman, despite her size and lack of culture. She came to stand beside him, and then she turned, and Devoe Crutchfield began speaking.

"We are gathered together in the sight of God and in this company to unite in holy wedlock this man, Lewis Winslow, and this woman, Missouri Ann Ramey. . . ."

Missouri Ann listened to the words. They had a beauty and power that swept through her so that tears came to her eyes. There was something so solemn and so rich in those words—words that had been spoken millions of times, she supposed, yet somehow she knew she and Lewis would love each other as long as they both lived. Finally, when Lewis had slipped the ring on her finger, Devoe Crutchfield said, "I now pronounce you husband and wife."

Missouri Ann turned, and Lewis put his hand on her cheeks, leaned forward, and kissed her firmly on the lips. Then he whispered, "I love you, Missouri Ann."

The world seemed to explode with color and music for her, and she smiled broadly and said, "I'll be the best wife I know how, Lewis."

The couple turned and walked out to the triumphant swell of the small pedal organ, and the congregation broke into spontaneous applause as the two disappeared out the front door.

★ ★ ★ ★

The Bethel Church was a converted barn, made into a church

when Devoe Crutchfield had been dismissed from the First Baptist Church in town after a disagreement among the elders over an alleged scandal. The rift had caused a painful split in the church, with much of the congregation supporting Reverend Crutchfield and following him to the new church. Many others in the community had joined as well, some who had never set foot in a church before, coming to hear his powerful preaching and getting baptized into the faith. The congregation showed their support by working endlessly to transform the old barn into a comfortable and roomy church, donating their time and whatever materials they could find. The men had divided the large space in two—one half for the sanctuary, and the other half for a meeting hall, where the reception for Lewis and Missouri Ann now was being held.

The large room was quite bare, with wooden walls and floor, so the voices and laughter caused quite a commotion as the guests enjoyed their punch and wedding cake. Despite the jovial atmosphere and happy occasion, Josh Winslow had an urgent desire to whirl and leave through the nearest door. He knew that Dora Skinner was standing across the room from him. His eyes had met hers once, and though he had turned away, he was swept by feelings for her he did not want to admit he still had. Every day he fought against powerful memories of Dora and of their intimate moments together, thoughts that sometimes assaulted him unexpectedly at night when he was almost asleep. His desire for her had tormented him in his prison cell, though he had hoped that after his conversion such impulses would wane, as had his desire for whiskey.

But it was as though Dora sent out some strange and mysterious signal that exploded in his brain, especially now that she was in the same room with him. Even in the midst of the laughter and rejoicing about him, he struggled to shove the unwanted images and memories out of his mind.

"Aren't you going to say hello, Josh?"

Swallowing hard, Josh turned and kept his face as still as possible. "Hello, Dora. It's good to see you again." This was a lie, but it was the polite thing to say.

"Why don't you fix me some refreshments. I like a man to wait on me."

The words dripped with meaning. There was a brilliant light in her wide eyes, and her lips, red and soft, seemed to draw Josh's gaze.

"Of course," he said quickly. He turned and busied himself getting a slice of cake and a glass of punch. When he came back he handed them to Dora, who said, "Let's stand over there. I want to hear what you've been doing since you got out."

There was no avoiding this, so Josh followed her. He caught a glimpse of Jenny, who was watching him unsmilingly. He took his eyes away from his sister and tried to act nonchalant. "How have you been, Dora?"

"I've been fine. . . ." She drew out the last word in a sultry voice. "Ever so lonesome, of course, while you were gone."

He remembered the slight huskiness in her voice from other, more intimate, circumstances. He could not drive the images from his mind, and he was well aware that Dora knew exactly what her presence was doing to him. It seemed to bring her a mixture of satisfaction and possibly greed. She did not physically touch him, but in all other ways he was intensely aware of her presence, of her lips, eyes, and hands, and of the lush figure that strained against the material of her dress.

"I'm surprised you haven't been by to see me."

Josh then did look into her eyes. "I've been a little busy."

"Too busy to see me?"

Josh had never known such an inner struggle. He wondered briefly, *God, why are you letting this woman get to me like she is? Why don't you just rip it out of me? I wish you would, and I ask you to do it now.* He waited for God to answer his prayer, but for some reason he felt the urges within him increase rather than diminish. He felt he had to get out of there, and he suddenly knew he had to break this off. "I've got something to tell you, Dora."

"What is it?" Her eyes were teasing and her lips provocative.

"While I was in prison I found the Lord." He saw a sudden change in Dora's eyes and felt strengthened, knowing that some-how this had struck a chord in her. He then spoke earnestly, telling her how God had taken away from him all desire for drink and ending with, "So I won't be going back to my old ways."

"You don't want to drink anymore?"

"No, it's a miracle."

"And you don't want *me* anymore, Josh?"

Josh hesitated only for a fraction of a moment, but Dora saw it. He said, "I'm not going to let myself think about that. What we had was wrong, Dora. Maybe you don't think so, but I do. It cost me my reputation and a month of my life, and I'll be carrying some memories around I'd just as soon not."

Dora stared at him intensely. "You think that now, but that's not the way it will be."

Josh said plainly, "Let me go, Dora. You have to. We have nothing for each other."

Dora Skinner had never been dismissed. Anger flickered in her eyes and something else—a grim determination—but she smiled and said, "I'll be seeing you, Josh. You'll be back." She turned and walked away, leaving the room. The eyes of practically everyone in the reception hall followed her, then they swung back to look at Josh. Josh went over to Jenny at once and said, "That's all. It's finished."

Jenny put her hand on his arm. She wanted to hug him, but she contented herself by saying, "I'm very proud of you, Josh." Then hesitantly she added, "But Dora isn't going to give up."

"You're right about that. It's a good thing I'm leaving soon."

★　★　★　★

The morning sun was bright and warmed the cold earth as Lewis and Josh stood in front of the bus station. The loamy odors of the field and the rising temperature heralded the approach of spring to both men. Josh had said good-bye to all the others, but Lewis had insisted on driving him to the bus station. He had also insisted on buying Josh his ticket, and now as they stood there waiting for Josh to board with the other passengers, Lewis reached into his pocket and pulled out some bills. He pushed them toward Josh, but Josh at once shook his head. "Dad, please don't do that. Take it and use it for fixing up the place. You've done enough buying the bus ticket."

"You may need it, son. I know you're broke."

"I won't starve. Hopefully I'll get one of those jobs."

"How will you live until then?"

"I've got a little money." Indeed, Josh did have the money that the warden had pressed into his hand. It wasn't much, but he knew that at least he would not starve. "I'll be sending back money as soon as I get a paycheck. I want to help fix the place up. I want it to be the showplace of the county, Dad. You and Ma will be dressed up just like rich planters one of these days, and I'll be proud to say that's my dad and my mom, the best mom and dad anybody ever had."

Lewis blinked and then chewed his lower lip to disguise his emotion. At one time he had almost given up on this boy, but now God had intervened, and it made Lewis feel as if he were swelling up inside with the pride that now came to him. He looked at Josh, studying the clear gray eyes of the tall, strong figure, and then he reached down and pulled his watch from his vest. He loosened the chain and extended it toward Josh. "You can't refuse this," he said.

"Dad, I can't take your watch! It was Sky Winslow's."

"Yes, it was. It's got a good heritage. We've got a good family, son."

Josh took the watch and stared at it. He had admired it all of his life, and now his hands trembled slightly as he held it. Sky Winslow had been his hero. He had cherished the stories of the man who had been almost a legend in his own time. He held it, knowing that he could not refuse it. "I'll keep it the rest of my life, Dad. I'll give it to your grandson one day."

"Good, son!"

"Get on if you're goin'!" the bus driver yelled at them.

Josh reached forward, embraced his father, and received his hug. The two men stood there a moment, and then Josh stepped back. "Good-bye, Dad. I'll write. Take care of the family."

"You take care of yourself. God bless you, son."

Lewis Winslow watched Josh get on the bus. He stood waving as Josh pressed his face to the window. Finally the bus pulled out, and Lewis waited until it had disappeared, then turned and walked slowly back to the truck, feeling a sense of pride in Josh that stirred him more than he thought possible.

CHAPTER NINE

A MATTER OF PRIDE

★ ★ ★ ★

By the time the pale sun had positioned itself high in the sky, Josh was already filled with a despondency that was shared by many other men who stood in front of the ugly brick building. The sign hanging on the front read Ingalls Manufacturing Company. The sign was new, even though the building was old. Some architect had, no doubt, been told that beauty was not a necessary ingredient for a building dedicated to the manufacture of wheelbarrows and other construction equipment, and he had obviously been obedient to the suggestion. The building was nothing more than a matchbox enlarged ten thousand times, with opaque-glass windows widely spaced along all three floors. They seemed to stare out at the men gathered beneath the facade with malevolent intent. The brick itself had been stained by time and weather and had degenerated from what had probably been a dull red into a smoky, leprous gray. The factory sat in the middle of a field shorn of every blade of grass and every tree, anything that had life, so that the hard gray surface lay bare to the pale rays of the March sun. The sun itself seemed to be a dull orange wafer pasted in the sky, giving off neither heat nor warmth but simply hanging there, a dreary ornament for an unattractive world.

Josh felt his shoulder nudged and turned to see a thin man whose clothes hung on him, accentuating the sharp angles of his shoulder blades. The coat was so small that his bony wrists stuck out, and his fingers were scarred, the knuckles nearly twice the normal size. He cracked his hands together and twisted his catfish mouth into a sneer. With a vile curse he said loudly in Josh's ear, "There ain't no jobs! There never was any jobs."

Josh turned quickly and stared into the man's muddy brown eyes. They seemed to be opaque with nothing behind them, no sign of life or joy or humor, simply instruments that enabled him to make his way through the world without running into things. "Why, there have to be jobs. Why would they advertise?"

"Advertise? They ain't advertised! You didn't see it in no paper, did you?"

"A friend of mine said he did."

"Well, your friend is a liar. It's always this way. Somebody says, 'We'd better hire five new men,' and by the time the gossips get through with it and it gets to punks like you and me, they're sayin' they need five hundred."

Josh stared at the gangling form, taking in the gaunt face that looked as hopeless as the many others milling around the pair. All wore tattered clothing, mostly old suit coats, and almost all of them had soft felt hats pulled down over their heads as far as possible. "I don't believe it," Josh said defiantly.

"You probably believe in the Easter bunny, too, and the tooth fairy. I'm gettin' out of here. It's a waste of time." With a final curse and lifting his raw-knuckled hand with a shake at the Ingalls Manufacturing Company, the man turned and shoved his way out of the crowd, using his shoulders to clear a way. There were murmurs of discontent, but the men were too cold and weary and hungry to fight among themselves.

Josh's feet hurt, and he was hungry. He had had only a doughnut and two cups of coffee for breakfast, and now gloom settled over him like a palpable curtain. He had been so hopeful when he'd left home, but as soon as he had arrived at Ingalls and seen the huge crowd of men milling around, he had begun to doubt the truth of what he'd heard. He slapped his arms to get his circulation going and saw that the crowd was thinning out.

They simply turned and walked away, hopelessness written on their features. A stubbornness rose in Josh Winslow, and the thought pounded at his mind, *Well, I'm not leaving. I've come this far, and I'm going to stay until they tell me to my face that there are no jobs.*

The virulence of his thoughts surprised him, for he had taken the easy way for most of his life. Born into a rich family, spoiled and given every luxury, he had not been trained to throw himself against an obstacle. He remembered how shocked he had been when the market had crashed and he had found himself destitute, along with the rest of his family. Shame brushed against his mind as the memory came of how he had drunk himself into insensibility and finally had wound up selling moonshine liquor so that he could buy more whiskey. He quickly put that out of his mind, for he had learned that those thoughts would bring him down quicker than anything else. He remembered his friend from prison, Thad Gilbert, who had led him to the Lord, saying, *"The minute you begin thinking, Josh, that you can't do it, that all is going to go wrong, that God's just a figment of your imagination, that He's forgotten you—you can believe you didn't think of those things yourself. The devil can put doubts in your mind. The thing to do, brother, is simply look right up and tell the old devil, 'You didn't die for me on a cross. Jesus did, and He's told me that everything He begins He finishes. So you go right ahead and take your best shot, for I'm on the side of Jesus, and He never loses!'"*

Josh smiled as he thought of his friend Thad and wished that he were there with him. He had read in the Bible's book of Acts about a man named Barnabas, who was called "the son of consolation," and more than once he had thought of Thad Gilbert in that role. The man had simply been able to take anyone who was down and lift him up and encourage him.

The morning wore on slowly, as time always does when one is cold and hungry and fighting against doubt. It was nearly noon, and some of the men brought out sandwiches from their coat pockets. Others had brought lunch pails with Thermos jugs full of steaming coffee. A man beside Josh had brought two such jugs. One contained hot soup, and just one whiff of it made Josh grow almost ravenous. The man, a short, chubby fellow with bright blue eyes and full red lips, caught Josh's eye. "Here," he said. "I can't eat all this soup."

"I can't take your meal," Josh protested.

"Why, Lord bless you. Jesus gave me this soup, and I'm giving it to you in His name."

Josh immediately smiled. "You're a Christian, then."

"Why, bless God I am. I'm saved, sanctified, filled with the Holy Ghost, ready for the rapture, and in love with Jesus. Here, brother."

Josh took the cap of the Thermos, which the bubbly young man had filled to the top. There was no spoon, but he sipped the soup carefully, delighting in the rich seasoning. "This is the best soup I've ever had. My name's Josh, by the way."

"I'm Aloysius. Just call me Al. The Lord told me when I got up this morning to fix a double portion. That I'd be meeting one of His family members, and I was supposed to see that he got a good meal. So your Father in heaven is looking out for you, Josh."

Josh ate the soup slowly, savoring each sip, and then accepted a half cup of steaming black coffee. The first sip made him blink, and Al laughed. "That coffee would raise the dead, brother. I don't believe in weak men, weak women, or weak coffee. How long have you been a soldier in the army of the Lord?"

"Not very long," Josh replied. "I was saved in a prison cell."

"I was saved in a flophouse. I'd been so drunk I could hardly lift my head, but God reached down, shook me out, tied me in knots, and then set me free."

The young man had apparently memorized the entire Bible and was a tremendous encouragement to Josh. Every other word Al spoke was a verse of Scripture, and Josh looked around and noticed that those within range of his voice were listening covertly. Aloysius simply bubbled over with joy and invited everyone near him to take Jesus Christ as their Lord and Savior.

"I wish I had your boldness, Al. I'm pretty shy about sharing my faith."

"Why, you just need what the apostles needed. You remember when Jesus was taken and crucified? Why, them apostles ran like scared rabbits. They hid out in a room, and Jesus had to go find them after His resurrection. Walked right through the door. Won't that be somethin' when we won't be stopped by no doors? But after Pentecost, why, there wasn't no fear in them. They were all filled with the Holy Ghost. Jesus said, 'You wait and tarry until you be endued with power from on high.' That's what you need, brother. Power from on high!"

A tall man with a stocking cap and a face scarred with small-pox grunted, "I don't believe none of that stuff."

Al jammed his hand down in his pocket. He brought out a New Testament and said, "Here you are, brother. Let me point out a few things. I've got a little soup left. You eat the soup and drink the coffee, and I'll read to you from the Word of God."

The tall man stared at Aloysius and then laughed harshly. "I'll take the soup and the coffee, and I guess I'll have to take the preachin' that goes with it. Turn your wolf loose!"

Josh listened, fascinated, as Aloysius spoke to the man about the glory of God and the death of Jesus on the cross. He was shocked when the man ate the soup and drank the coffee, then simply stood there. Many others were listening carefully, and finally Josh saw tears run down the man's face. Suddenly Aloysius turned and said, "Come on, Brother Josh, you and me's going to pray our friend Slim through to glory."

Josh had never done such a thing, but he had seen Thad and others in the prison do so. He put his hand on the man's shoulder and began to pray. He was awkward, not knowing exactly what to say, but he could feel the man's shoulders quivering, and after he had prayed, Al led the man in a prayer of his own. Finally the man looked up, and something in his expression was totally changed. Al exclaimed, "You done see the glory, brother! You're a child of the King right now. You take this Bible, and you read it. God's going to do great and mighty things in your life. I feel it in my spirit."

Josh felt good after this. He saw others who were not as happy, and some of the men were mumbling about not needing any preachers. Several jeered at Al and at Josh, saying, "Where's your God with people starving to death? Why doesn't He give me work? I've got a hungry wife and kids starving."

Josh had no answer for this. He was no theologian. All he

could say was, "I don't know all the answers, but I know Jesus is real, and I know He's the only hope any of us have."

Aloysius took up the refrain, and he spoke enthusiastically until one of the doors of the factory opened, and a man wearing a herringbone suit, a white shirt, and a maroon tie stepped outside. He was obviously one of the owners, and immediately cries began to come out. "Where are the jobs? Give us work! We need work, mister!"

The man held up his hand and said, "My name is Ingalls." He waited until a quiet fell over the group and then looked around. He was a stern-looking man, but there was no cruelty or meanness in him that Josh could see. He looked grieved, and for a moment he simply stared at his feet. Then he lifted his head and said in a clear voice, "I'm very sorry that this has happened. We needed a few hands, but rumors took over. And although we tried to make it clear we were not hiring anymore, obviously you men did not get the word."

"Ain't there no jobs at all?" a voice cried out angrily.

"I'm afraid not. I'm so sorry. I wish I had jobs for every one of you men. If I were you, I would leave and go home." He turned and stepped inside the door. Angry cries followed him, but Josh shook his head, filled with disappointment. "Well, Aloysius," he said, "there are no jobs here. I might as well go back home to Georgia."

Aloysius had sobered, but he nodded firmly four times saying, "Amen—amen—amen—amen! If I die starving to death, Brother Josh, I'm going to starve to death trusting God. You remember the patriarch Job. He said, 'Though he slay me, yet will I trust in him.'" He slapped Josh on the shoulder and took his hand and said, "God's going to do a great work in your life, brother. Never give up on Jesus!"

"I'll do that."

"You got a home to go to, brother?"

"Yes, but I hate to go back and tell them about this."

"Every man's got to eat his peck of dirt." Al sighed, then smiled and said, "Christians never say good-bye, you know! So if I don't see you again in this world, brother, we'll be gathered around the throne."

Josh felt the hard grip of Aloysius, who then turned and left him. Josh joined the men walking away from the factory. Most of them started down the road, lining both sides of it, and Josh knew there would be no hope of catching a ride. No one would stop in the midst of a crowd like this for fear of being swamped.

★   ★   ★   ★

By four o'clock Josh had already worked off the cup of soup and the doughnut he'd had for breakfast. He felt as hungry as a starved wolf but deliberately chose to ignore that as much as possible. The crowd of men had thinned out. Many had turned off on side roads, but Josh had kept plodding on until now he was alone. He recalled Al's cheerful spirit and wished that he had some of the man's courage. "I wonder if I'll ever be as strong in the faith as he is. I'm pretty weak right now, I think."

He trudged along wearily, keeping his eyes down on the road before him, feeling the loneliness of the land. Fields stretched out on either side of him, and stalks of the past harvest were gray and lifeless. The sky was also gray so that it seemed on the far horizon that the earth and the sky met without a visible line, one simply melding into the other. Passing by a cornfield with a few ragged stalks left, he heard the raucous cries of crows and looked up to see three of them perched in the naked branches of an oak tree. A few withered leaves still held their grasp, but the crows seemed to be harbingers of doom. Although Josh liked most birds, he had never liked crows and had gotten into furious arguments with Hannah, who loved all birds. Josh remembered saying once, "They're evil birds. I hate them."

Hannah had rebuked him. "They are *not* evil. God made them what they are."

"Well, He should have made them different," Josh had retorted but then immediately regretted it.

He turned away from the dark trio and continued to walk. A house rose up in front of him over on the right. He could see yellow lights in the windows and knew that the inhabitants were warm inside and probably cooking supper. As he came even with the house, he had the impulse to go up to the door, knock, and ask for work in exchange for food. Hunger drove him, but his pride was stronger than his hunger, and after standing irresolutely for a time, he whirled and walked on stiffly down the road. *You're a fool, Josh Winslow! Too proud to ask for something to eat!*

He left the house behind, and then suddenly his thoughts began to go back over his life. He thought of how he had wasted such great opportunities. He thought of the college he had attended and all of the help and encouragement he had gotten there, but he had wasted even that. He thought of friendships he had wrecked because of his selfishness and refusal to bear responsibilities. Memories of his family that he had utterly failed came to him, filling him with a deep shame, and, as always at times like this, his years as a drunk rose to torment him.

"What do I have to be proud of?" He spoke the words aloud, and they seemed to disturb the world about him. They hung on the raw breeze coming out of the north, a breeze that chilled him and cut to the very bone. He walked on and muttered again, "What do I have to be proud of?"

★　★　★　★

The sky was opaque now. The sun had hidden its face, and there was no moon that Josh could see. In the entire sky overhead not a single star burned, and darkness seemed to cloak the road ahead of him. He knew he had to find some shelter from the plummeting cold. Suddenly something touched his hand, and he flinched. Then several tiny sensations on his other hand came, and he realized the worst. "Just what I needed," he muttered disgustedly. "It's starting to rain." He moved on, turned up his coat collar, rounded off his hat brim, and began to look for anything that would give him shelter for the night. He had not gone a hundred yards before he saw a vague outline of a ruined house close to the road on his left. He moved quickly and saw that it was nothing but two chimneys left from a burned-out house. They had evidently been at either end of it, but now nothing was left except the blackened ashes.

Well, one thing was left—a small barn, which had apparently escaped the conflagration. He stepped forward, then stopped abruptly, for he saw that two men had already staked out their claim on the barn. "Hello," he called, and they turned quickly. Josh stopped when the two came toward him in a most alarming way. They separated instead of staying together, and in the fading darkness his heart sank as he realized they were not the most friendly of men. Both were large and bulky and were as soaked as he was from the cold drizzle that was steadily falling. "You mind if I share your barn?" Josh asked, trying to sound friendly.

One of the men stepped up no farther than two feet away and peered at Josh. He had a doughy face with huge lips and small eyes. His sodden wool cap was pulled down over his head, and there was a brutal light in his eyes. "You got anything to eat?"

"No, not a thing," Josh said, then added quickly, "Maybe I'd better go on. I can make another mile or two."

The hobo suddenly reached out and grabbed Josh's arm. The strength in his hand was frightening, almost simian. The fingers seemed to close down to the very bone, and Josh almost cried out. He jerked away and said, "Take your hands off me!"

The other hobo had approached from a different angle, and now Josh saw that he had a club or a stick of some kind in his hand. Josh backed away, saying, "You fellas won't get anything out of me. I haven't got a dime, and I've got nothing at all to eat."

The taller of the two men, the one with the club, grinned. His teeth were broken, yellow, animalistic. "You got a nice coat, boy. I needs one of those in this rain." He yanked at Josh's coat, popping off the buttons as he tore it from him. Josh's feet slipped in the muddy ground as he struggled to get away from the man. He was only too glad to let him take his coat, but he wasn't about to let him get his money, which he had secreted in his pants pocket.

"Hey, would you look at that fancy pocket watch! Whoo-wee! Where'd a bum like you get a thing like that?"

Josh's heart sank as he looked down and saw his grandfather's watch swinging from its chain, where it had fallen out of his vest pocket. He lunged to get away, but two sets of massive hands held him in place and pinned him to the ground.

"Just hand it over, and you can go on your way," one of the men sneered as he snatched at the watch.

At that instant Josh knew he had reached a point in his life when he would not give another inch. He had always given up before when met with a challenge, taken refuge in his family's money or in his father's protection. He had simply walked away, but now in a flash he remembered the smile in his father's eyes as he had given him the watch and how he had said, "*I'll keep it the rest of my life, Dad. I'll give it to your grandson one day.*"

Josh knew then that he would die before he would give over Sky Winslow's watch to these thugs. The two men were heavy, but he was lean and wiry. If he could break from their grasp he could make a run for it. With a sudden strength he didn't know he had, he raised his legs and kicked each man squarely in the face. They both staggered back, holding their faces and howling in pain. Josh jumped up from the mud and began to run as fast as his well-muscled legs would take him. *I can probably outrun them,* he thought, but the tall man recovered quicker than he expected, and he felt the club crash against his back. The pain was agonizing, and he fell to his knees. He caught himself on his hands and knew that another blow was coming. He threw up his arm and partially deflected it, but the other tramp was there, the larger one. Josh caught a glimpse of the kick as it came. It caught him in the ribs, and pain such as he had never felt before shot through him. He fell over gasping, and looking up, he saw the taller tramp raise the club. He tried to protect himself, but he was too weak and too late. It smashed against the ribs that had just been kicked, and the world exploded with a burst of orange light and unbelievable pain. He had time for only one thought. He knew they were going to beat him to death, and he thought, *A good thing I found Jesus when I did!*

CHAPTER TEN

"ETERNAL ONE, YOU GOT ME INTO THIS!"

★ ★ ★ ★

Shifting her blanket roll from one shoulder to the other, Kefira looked up and noted that rain was in the offing. The sky was dull, and although it was only eleven o'clock in the morning, the sun seemed to be hiding. Only a vague, pale circle marked its existence, and Kefira shivered and pulled her coat more tightly around her as she trudged along the roadside. Once she looked up and saw a flight of birds high in the sky. They were in a V-shaped formation, and Kefira followed their flight, fascinated by the order they kept. As always when she saw something unusual, she immediately began to worry it and pick at it, exactly as a dog would pick at a mysterious object.

I wonder how they decide which bird gets to go to the front of the V. Is he the smartest one? Do the others mind not getting to lead? These thoughts flowed through her mind smoothly, and she kept her eye on the birds until they disappeared. They were headed north, and for a fleeting moment she envied the speed of their passage, especially now that a cold drizzle had begun to fall. She'd dreamt last night of a beach and waves marching almost like soldiers to break upon the white sand. Even though she had been sleeping in a cold barn wrapped in her two blankets, she had seemed to sense the warmth of the sun-heated sand and waves, as warm as bath water. Wryly she smiled at her own imagination. "You think too much. That's what's wrong with you, girl," she murmured. Her words broke the stillness of the air, and she suddenly heard the sound of an automobile. Quickly she stepped to the side of the road and then turned to examine the approaching vehicle. She had been offered rides many times by men, some alone, some with a companion, but during her days on the road, she had become as wary as a wild animal. After her close call with the hobo on the train, she'd had another scare when the authorities had spotted her and tried to apprehend her. She had barely escaped and decided that riding the rails was too risky. So she continued to make her way south by road, mostly walking, but sometimes hitching a ride if the driver looked safe enough. She kept the loaded pistol she'd found in the hobo's bedroll in her side pocket and had made up her mind exactly what she would do with it if she had to protect herself. Several times she had gotten rides with couples, or with a woman alone, and now she was pleased to see a woman seated beside the driver in the approaching black truck. She did not lift her hand, nor in any way indicate a plea for a ride, but simply stood there. She never thumbed for rides as many did. She somehow felt this was an imposition. Once she had reasoned it out with herself. *People buy those cars. They work for the money to pay for them. They keep gas in them and keep them repaired. And I'm asking them to give me what they've worked for.* She knew something was not quite right about this, for she had no compunction about asking for food, but that she always took in exchange for work, refusing to accept it unless she could do something. Many a house she had stopped at had accepted her offer to wash dishes or clean rooms or work in the yard for food.

Fleetingly, as she saw the truck beginning to slow down, she thought how different it was in the South. Northern people were somehow less approachable. Since she had been in Tennessee, she had been fascinated by the slow drawls of the people. They had smiled more quickly, and this surprised her for some reason. She had heard somewhere, or read, of southern hospitality and had marked it off as simply the remark of one who was proud of his origin and wanted to promote his home country. But there was something to it, she decided, and she waited until the truck stopped and then walked up to the side where the woman stuck her head out. "Are you going far?"

"Yes, ma'am, I am."

"Why, it's rainin' already and fixin' to pour something fierce. Get in, dearie." The woman was in her sixties, Kefira surmised, and by stooping she could see the man was approximately the same age. The truck was old and battered, and the radiator seemed to hiss like a teakettle, but the engine chugged along evenly enough, though somewhat noisily. The woman opened the door, and Kefira tossed her blanket roll in the back and sat down.

"My name is Kefira," she said.

"Kefira! What a beautiful name! My name is Anna McKinney, and this is my husband, George."

"I'm pleased to know you, missy," Mr. McKinney said, nodding. He wore a felt hat pushed back on his head, and his eyes were warm and friendly. "It's startin' to come down now. You was fixin' to get wet."

"I guess I was. I sure appreciate the ride."

McKinney urged the truck forward, and it responded with a series of jerks and then maintained a steady pace. Kefira knew that these two were curious about her. She waited for them to ask the inevitable question, *What's a young girl like you doing hitchhiking on the road?* And finally it came.

"Are you a long way from your home, Kefira?" Mrs. McKinney asked.

"I don't really have a home anymore, ma'am. I come from the North. It's so bitter cold up there that I wanted to head south. I'm going all the way to the Gulf of Mexico. I want to see the beaches there and the warm water."

"Why, I been down that way myself. Down to Pensacola, Florida." George McKinney nodded. "You'll get warm there. Not right now, of course, but in spring and summer you'll heat up. I got sunburned until I looked like a boiled lobster."

Suddenly Kefira began to cough. She yanked a limp handkerchief out of her side pocket and buried her face. The coughing struck her hard for a moment, but finally she caught her breath and cleared her throat.

"Why, dearie, you got a bad cold there!"

"I guess I do have a little cold."

"You don't need to be out in weather like this."

"Oh, I'll be all right. I'm very strong. It's only a cold."

The rain began beating down, making a pinging noise on the radiator and the hood and the top of the truck. Anna McKinney cast covert glances at the young woman, and something seemed to pass between her and her husband. She asked no more questions, but when the car turned down a side road, Kefira said, "Oh, you can let me out here."

"You can't get out in this. It's raining buckets," the older woman said. "You can stay at our house until the rain quits."

"Maybe you'd let me work. I'm very strong, and I can do anything."

"Why, of course, there's always plenty to do at our place," Mrs. McKinney said cheerfully.

Kefira breathed a deep sigh of relief, for she was tired. Life on the road was harder than she had dreamed, and she had slept little since leaving the train. The nagging cough had kept her awake, and now as the car pulled in front of a rambling house painted a rather startling shade of green, she was relieved to know that at least for a while she had to make no decisions at all.

"You come on inside, dearie."

Glad enough to heed Mrs. McKinney's instruction, she followed the woman in. The house was warm, and Kefira looked around as she pulled off her cap and ran her hand through her damp hair. The house was cheerful looking, with gleaming oak and walnut furniture, and yellow-and-white wallpaper that added a homey touch. She had yanked her bedroll out of the truck and now stood there holding it.

"Why don't you use one of our spare rooms," Mrs. McKinney said. "You might want to lie down and rest a bit while I fix something to eat."

"Oh no, ma'am, I want to work!"

"Well, come along. You'll want to put on some dry clothes anyway. You're soaked through and through."

Kefira was glad enough to do this. She followed the woman to a room off of the hallway, and Mrs. McKinney waved her hand, saying, "This was our daughter Sara's room. She's married now. You can change clothes, then come out, and we'll see what we can find to eat."

"Thank you very much, Mrs. McKinney."

As soon as the door was closed, Kefira unrolled her bedroll. She had learned to keep her clothes dry by wrapping them in oilcloth, and she quickly shucked off her shoes and skimmed out of her coat, shirt, and men's trousers. She then dried herself off as well as she could. The clean clothes felt good against her skin, and when she was dressed, she went out into the kitchen. "What can I do to help?"

"I'm just going to heat up leftovers. We had company last night, and I always cook too much, and the fire's still hot in the stove. You sit right there."

"I'd really rather work, ma'am."

"We'll find something for you to do later. Do you like hot tea?"

"Why, yes I do."

"Let me fix you some. It's my own special blend." Mrs. McKinney stared at her. "As a matter of fact, with that cough you've got, I'd better fix you up some of my special hot toddy."

Five minutes later Kefira was sipping Mrs. McKinney's "special hot toddy." She did not know the contents of it, but it bit at her throat. She could taste lemon and spices and something stronger. She gasped but grinned and said, "I've never tasted anything like this."

George McKinney had come clomping in with a load of firewood. He laughed and said, "That special toddy will set you free, missy. I think it'd raise Lazarus."

"Don't you be sacrilegious, George!"

"Why, I'm not!" George came over and said, "Let me have one of those toddies." There was a certain mischievousness in the man that Kefira spotted at once.

"You're not getting any toddy because you're not sick! Here, you help me set the table."

"I'll do that." Kefira got up, and despite Mrs. McKinney's protests, she helped set the table.

"We've just got a few leftovers here," Mrs. McKinney said, "but we'll make out."

Anna McKinney's idea of a "few leftovers" was pork chops, thick chunks of round steak, black-eyed peas, mashed potatoes, and a strange item called pickled okra that Kefira had never heard of before. The food was heated until it was steaming hot, and when Kefira sat down without preamble, the other two bowed their heads, and Mr. McKinney said firmly, "Lord, everything we have comes from you. This food comes from you, and we thank you for it. We ask you especially, Lord, to bless this our guest, Miss Kefira. Watch over her, Lord, and keep her safe. In Jesus' name. Amen."

Kefira tried to eat daintily, but she was famished. She sampled the pickled okra and blinked with shock.

"It's got a little of my special peppers in there," Mrs. McKinney said, "but in weather like this it tastes good. Nothin' like spicy pickled okra to set a body up when the weather's turnin' dicey."

Kefira ate until she was ashamed of herself, and then Mrs. McKinney brought out a plate covered with a cloth. She whipped off the cloth and said, "I didn't do too good with this apple pie, but maybe you'd like to try it."

Kefira ate a generous slice of the pie and then took a cup of the scalding hot coffee. "I've never had as good a meal in my whole life as this, Mrs. McKinney," she said. "I'm ashamed for eating so much. You must let me work to pay for it before I leave."

George McKinney stared out the window. Rain was coming down in sheets now, and he shook his head. "It looks like when the flood came and the ark got lifted up." He turned back and nodded firmly. "You ain't goin' nowhere in that downpour, Miss Kefira. You'd look like a drowned rat."

"You look tired, dear. Why don't you go take a hot bath and then lie down in Sara's room, cover up, and just rest."

"Thank you," Kefira whispered, "I'd like that." She suppressed a cough, but the older couple caught it.

"You come along, now. I'll show you where the towels are. We'll heat some water, and George can carry it up. One of these days we're going to get us a fancy hot-water tank, but right now we'll heat it on the stove."

Kefira was as tired as she had ever been in her life. The huge meal had stultified her, and she went without argument to the bathroom, where she was handed a big fluffy towel and a washcloth, and Mrs. McKinney said, "I made this soap myself. It's better than any store-bought, I say."

Kefira took the jar and touched the creamy soap. "Mmm, it smells so good!"

"I always put somethin' sweet smellin' in it. Lilac water, I think this is. George will pour your hot water pretty soon. Then you lie down and sleep as long as you want. You look so peaked. You probably ought to sleep all afternoon and all night."

"Oh, I won't do that!"

Kefira went back to the bedroom and looked at the sodden clothes. They were dirty and grimy, and she thought, *I bet they wouldn't mind if I washed my clothes, but I'll do that after I take a nap.*

Ten minutes later she was soaking in the hot tub and had never felt such luxury in all of her life. George had made several trips up the stairs to fill the tub to the brim for her. The homemade soap was like nothing she had ever touched before, and she lathered freely, reveling in the feeling of cleanness. She actually fell asleep in the tub, awoke with a start, then laughed at herself. She got out, dried herself off, and slipped into the soft pajamas and terrycloth robe Mrs. McKinney had loaned her, and then went down to the room. Mrs. McKinney had turned back the covers, and laying the robe aside, Kefira got in between the sheets. They also had a fresh lilac smell, and when she lay back, she gasped at the softness of the bed. She had never felt a mattress like this. She sank down deep into it until she felt as though it had swallowed her. The pillow was also soft and yielding and molded itself around her head. She had time to see that the quilt over her was sewn into a fantastic pattern of colors—reds, yellows, blues—but she knew no more, for she sank into a deep, untroubled, dreamless sleep.

★　★　★　★

When she awoke, Kefira was startled to see morning sunlight streaming into the window. She had slept all night! The storm had passed and the day promised to be a beautiful one. She was even more startled to see piled on top of the dresser all of her clothes—laundered and neatly ironed. Mrs. McKinney must have been up half the night scrubbing and drying her grimy, mud-splattered clothes.

Coming out of the room fully dressed in her clean clothes, Kefira caught the smell of meat cooking and of biscuits baking. She entered the kitchen, and when Mrs. McKinney turned to her and greeted her warmly, Kefira shook her head in wonder. "I can't believe I slept all afternoon and all night! When I woke up I didn't know where I was."

"Well, you needed the sleep, dear." Mrs. McKinney was standing before the stove with a pan of fresh biscuits she had just taken out of the oven. "Just in time for breakfast. George," she called out, "come and eat!"

Mr. McKinney came into the kitchen and nodded. "Good mornin', lady. You got your beauty sleep, I take it."

"I really am embarrassed. I ate like a hog and slept the clock around."

"Reckon you needed it," McKinney said kindly. "Have a seat there."

Kefira wanted to help, but Anna McKinney waved her aside. "It's all ready. Just sit."

Once again George bowed his head, thanked God for the food, then, in a way that warmed Kefira's heart, called her name and asked a blessing on her. Kefira protested at the plate that was put before her containing three eggs and biscuits almost as big around as a saucer. "I can't eat all this!"

"Do the best you can. That's all a mule can do," McKinney grinned. "And try some of these grits."

"Grits? What are grits?"

"Oh, don't ask. Just eat 'em. Put some butter and a little salt on 'em. You'll like 'em."

Kefira did indeed like the grits, as she liked everything else. She had a queer feeling of safety as she sat there with the McKinneys. The two talked about the little things that made up their lives, and she found herself wondering if there were many people like this in the South. She suspected there were.

"Do you know anybody down on the coast, dearie?" Mrs. McKinney asked.

"No, but I'll be able to get work there, I hope, and I'll make friends."

"You come from New York?" George asked curiously.

"Yes, sir. I've lived there all my life."

"What's it like there? I've seen pictures and seen it in the movies, and I think it'd scare me to death to live in a big place like that."

Kefira began to tell them about New York City. The two sat there listening intently and asking questions. Anna asked, "What kind of a church do you go to there in New York? Is it big or little? We go to a little church ourselves."

Kefira hesitated. "Well, actually, Mrs. McKinney, I don't go to a church. I go to a synagogue, or a temple as it's called sometimes."

"Oh, are you a Jew, then?" George asked, leaning forward, his eyes bright with interest.

"Yes, I am." Kefira braced herself. She had unpleasant memories connected with her Jewishness. She did not know what to expect, but all she saw in the simple faces of the two before her was interest. "I don't believe I've ever met a real Jewish person before," George said simply.

"You should come to New York. You would meet plenty of Jewish people there."

"What's it like in a temple? I mean, I don't want to be nosy, but we don't know anything about the way you people worship."

Kefira told the couple about the services in the synagogue. They listened avidly, and then Kefira realized with a start that they had been talking for almost an hour, and she laughed awkwardly. "Please, ma'am, let me do some work for you. You've done so much for me."

"Well, all right, if you insist. You can help me make bread."

"I've never done that before, but just show me what to do."

"You've never made bread?"

"In New York, there's a bakery on just about every corner. I never needed to make it myself."

Mrs. McKinney mixed up the ingredients, then showed Kefira how to knead the large lump of dough. Then she set the bowl of dough in the warm oven to rise.

"We'll make two loaves and should have plenty left for some nice rolls for dinner."

Kefira quickly learned how to handle the sticky dough and to shape the rolls. The task was simple and pleasant, and the two women listened to the radio while they worked. Finally, after the loaves and rolls were in their pans, Kefira washed the bowl and utensils and wiped down the table while Mrs. McKinney covered the pans with clean dish towels. Kefira asked, "What will you do with them now?"

"We'll just let them rise once more and then I'll bake them. Thanks for your help, dearie."

Kefira looked out the window and saw George splitting wood with an ax and said, "You've been so kind to me. I can't tell you how much I appreciate it." She began to cough again, and this time the violence of it shook her.

"You'd better have some more of my special toddy. Are you troubled a lot with your lungs?"

"No. I did get wet a few days ago, though, and didn't get dried out quick enough. I expect it's just going into a chest cold."

Anna shook her head. "I think we'd better doctor you up a bit."

"No, I'll have to be going soon. The rain has stopped now. I'd like to work some more to make up for what I've eaten, though."

"Oh, don't be foolish, child! That was nothing."

Suddenly the older woman turned and put her eyes on Kefira. "You mind if I ask you a real personal question?"

"Why . . . of course not."

"Have you ever read any in the Bible?"

"Your Bible? The Christian Bible? No, I haven't."

"But you've heard of Jesus."

Instantly Kefira grew cautious. "I've heard of Him, yes, especially around Christmastime and Easter."

"What do you think of Him? I just can't understand what

people think of Jesus who don't know much about Him. My daddy was a Methodist preacher, and all I ever knew was about Jesus. I was converted when I was seven years old, and I've served the Lord ever since."

Actually Kefira did not want to discuss Jesus, and her discomfort must have shown on her face.

"Oh, don't pay any attention to me. I don't mean any harm," Anna said quickly. She changed the subject and Kefira was glad.

When George came in, Kefira asked, "Is there anything I can do outside, any yard work, Mr. McKinney?"

"Why, bless you, girl, not a thing. But it looks like it's cloudin' up again and is goin' to rain a bit more. Hadn't you better wait it out here? We'd be glad to have you."

"Thank you, but I need to be heading south."

Both tried to persuade Kefira to stay, but she was determined. The McKinneys also insisted on loading her down with what food she could carry. Kefira did not offer them what little money she had, for she knew that would not be right. Finally she was ready to go. "Good-bye," she said simply. She wanted to do more, and finally she came over and gave her hand first to Anna and then to George. "You've been so good to me. I'll never forget you."

"We'll be praying for you, Kefira," Anna said simply. She handed the girl a small book and added, "I'd like for you to have this New Testament. I've about wore it out. You might like to look into it."

Kefira took the small book, smiled, and put it into her blanket roll. "Thanks for everything."

George nodded. "The Lord will watch over you."

"Thank you," she said, and turning, she left the house. They followed her out to the porch, and she walked away, turning once to wave at them. They stood framed there, George's arm around his wife, and both of them waved again. Kefira somehow knew that this was one of those images she would keep for many years in her memory. She had been so affected by the obvious concern of these two people, their kindness, their generosity, their warmth.

All day long she trudged, and three times vehicles stopped to offer her a ride, but each time the drivers were male, and she simply ignored them and trudged along.

She stopped once to eat a beef sandwich that Mrs. McKinney had fixed and three of the pickled okra that bit at her tongue. That cheered her up, and she continued walking. A drizzle came late in the afternoon. She took shelter under a large tree, but still it soaked her clothing, and she thought regretfully of how nice it had been to be dry and warm for a time.

She rested awhile and then walked farther. Early in the evening she thought about finding a farmhouse where she might ask to sleep in their barn. She had done that before, but the road was lonely and there were few houses. As she walked along, she thought of the prayers that George McKinney had prayed for her by name, and a warmth washed over her.

Suddenly she remembered prayers that her own father had prayed. He had held her on his lap and prayed for her every night. She remembered it so well. Once she remembered him praying for God to help him find a watch he had lost, and she had asked him, *"Papa, does God hear about little things like that?"*

His answer still was with her, and she seemed to see his warm brown eyes and his strong hands. *"Yes, liebchen, He cares for everything."*

Perhaps it was this memory that suddenly created a strange desire in her. She used to pray as a little girl, and even as a young woman, but after her father's death and as her life had gotten harder, she had fallen out of the habit. She had even wondered many times if there even was a God who heard prayers. Now suddenly she found herself praying. "Eternal One," she prayed, "look down on me in mercy. I have not been faithful to you, but have pity on me. Help me this day to please you—" Suddenly she remembered the way her father closed every prayer. "And let me be a help to someone else this day." She smiled wryly, thinking of that phrase her father had always used, and then she shrugged, feeling somewhat foolish. *The Creator of the universe is not interested in what one young woman among all the millions will do today.*

She walked along, staring at the ground, and the darkness was falling so quickly it troubled her. She heard a sound and stopped abruptly. There ahead of her, over to the side of the road, directly in front of a skeleton of a burned house, was a small barn. She saw three men, and shock ran through her as she saw one of the men knock another down with what appeared to be a club. She heard the man cry out, and then the large man suddenly drew back his foot and kicked him. She was close enough to hear the thud of the blow and winced. Then the man delivered another kick, and the other began striking the fallen man with the club.

Afterward Kefira could never remember what went on in her mind at that instant. She later thought it had something to do with the prayer she had prayed just a short time before. *And let me be a help to someone else this day.* She saw that the fallen man was already badly hurt, and she ran forward, pulling the pistol from her pocket.

"Leave him alone!" she shouted, her voice startling her as well as the two men. Both men suddenly stood up, and one of them, the larger one, started for her.

She could see his eyes glittering like a wild animal and knew there was no mercy in him. Without a second thought, she raised the pistol and pulled the trigger.

The shot rang out and instantly the man grabbed the side of his head. Kefira had simply wanted to fire a warning shot, but the bullet had clipped the man's ear, and he stood there staring at her in shock. She took two steps forward and raised the pistol and shouted, "Leave that man alone. Get out of here!"

The other man cursed and started toward her, and Kefira loosed a shot so near to the man's head that he flinched and cursed. "I'll shoot you both if you don't get out of here right now!" Kefira yelled, and she leveled the pistol firmly, not knowing if she really could carry out her threat or not.

The two immediately turned, the man dropping his club, the other holding to his ear. They fled, stopping just long enough to pick up their bedrolls, and Kefira watched them until they disappeared in the gathering night.

Suddenly she felt weak as the strength flowed out of her. *If I had shot an inch to the right, I'd have killed that man.* The thought ran through her like an electric shock. She stared at the gun, then felt something like pride. She looked up at the heavens and wondered, *God, is this the one I'm supposed to help?* She stuffed the gun in the side pocket of her coat and ran to the fallen man. He was lying on his back, and she dropped down on one knee beside him. His head was bleeding, and his eyes were closed. He was not dead, for she could see his chest rising and falling, and his head moved slightly from one side to the other.

"Mister, can you hear me?" She touched his face, but he did not move or speak.

"Please wake up." She leaned over and studied his face and for a moment was completely confused. She did not know how badly he was hurt, but the rain was starting to fall again. She stood up and peered into the darkness. She knew there was no house back the way she had come, and she saw no lights farther down the road in the direction where the man's two assailants had disappeared.

She looked down at the man and then ran quickly to the barn. It was unlocked, and one of the doors sagged where a hinge had fallen off. She stepped inside but could not see anything in the darkness.

"I've got to get him out of the rain. Then maybe I can get help." Running back to the fallen man, she grabbed his clothes and heaved at him. He groaned with pain but did not awaken. It was a titanic struggle to drag him the ten feet to the barn, and by the time she got him inside, the night had almost fully fallen. She fumbled in her bag and pulled out a candle and matches. Her hands were trembling as she lit the candle, but the pale amber flame flickered to life. She looked around, not knowing what to do next. She knelt beside the unconscious man, studying his face. She had learned to read people rather well, and she saw nothing vicious in his face—only a helpless wounded man who needed her help. Kefira laid her hand on his chest and thought for a moment, then took a deep breath. "Well, Eternal One," she said aloud, "you got me into this, so please help me do what has to be done!"

CHAPTER ELEVEN

"I GUESS I BELONG TO YOU"

★ ★ ★ ★

Kefira's voice sounded small in the emptiness of the barn, and she felt somewhat foolish speaking to God in such a fashion. In all truth she was afraid, for she did not know the extent of the man's injuries. He might die, and how would she explain that to anyone? Looking around, she saw that the barn, abandoned though it was, had evidently been used as a storage area. Several empty wooden boxes were thrown over to the corner, and she quickly turned one upright, dripped several drops of the hot wax from the candle, then set it firmly on the box. It threw off little enough light, but at least she was not alone in the intense darkness.

"I've got to keep him warm," she whispered. Quickly she found that some of the boxes were falling apart, and although she had nothing to chop with, she managed to break off several boards, some of them almost rotted. They were dry, though, and she cleared a space on the bare ground and began to make a small pyramid of the smaller pieces. She found what evidently were fruit boxes, very fragile wood that looked as if it would burn easily. Breaking these, she added them, then brought the candle over and held it under the wood. Soon the fire began to nibble at her kindling, and she replaced the candle. As the fire caught and she cautiously added pieces to it, it threw a light over the interior. Someone had stacked some firewood at one end. It was old and covered with mold but dry, and soon she had a fire that gave off not only a cheerful yellow light but warmth as well. She went over to the wounded man and pulled at him until he lay parallel to the fire. He groaned with pain and grabbed at his side, but he did not awaken. She studied his face, and holding the candle close, she cautiously examined the wound on his head. "I've got to do something with that. It's still bleeding."

She opened her bedroll, pulled out a saucepan, and balanced it on the fire. She had a frying pan also, and she went outside and caught some of the rainwater from the eaves. The rain was falling more steadily now, but the roof evidently was sound. She managed to heat a little water, then set the saucepan down, and going back to her bedroll, she searched for something she could use to dress the wound.

She had no bandages as such, but she took part of her underwear, a vest made out of cotton, and decided that would do. Opening her pocketknife, she cut the vest into several long strips, then carried them over to the man. She knelt down and, dipping one of the strips into the warm water, began to bathe the cut. She had no practical experience in treating wounds, but she was relieved to see that the cut was shallow, although it was still bleeding freely. When she had washed it as well as she could, she took several of the strips and managed to tie a bandage around his head. During this time he made no move at all, and his breath puffed his lips out. She held his head for a moment after she had finished and studied his face. He was a good-looking man, somewhere in his late twenties, she supposed, and she felt an odd sense of pleasure and possession.

Finally she laid his head down gently, put one of the blankets over him, and added two more small pieces of wood to the fire. She sat down then, rinsed out the saucepan carefully, opened a can of beans, and poured it into the pan. She added some rainwater and began to heat the stew.

Once she thought she heard something outside and jerked in fear. Her hand went at once to the pistol, and she stood there in the flickering light of the fire absolutely motionless. Nothing happened. No one came, and she went to the door looking vainly, hoping that a vehicle would come by and she could flag it down. But the road seemed deserted, as it had all afternoon. Evidently there were few inhabitants and the road was little used.

She started to go back to the stew when suddenly the man spoke, or at least uttered some sound. It was a wordless cry, but at once she went to him and knelt down and stared into his face. His eyes were open, and he stared at her without comprehension for a moment.

"How do you feel?"

The question seemed to mean nothing to the man, but then he blinked and twisted his head. "Where—?"

"Don't try to talk. You've been hurt."

The man looked around wildly, threw his arm out, and tried to turn over. He cried out, gasping in pain.

"Where do you hurt?"

"It's . . . my side."

"Lie still," Kefira said. She carefully unbuttoned his vest and shirt. She saw no open wound, but his left side was already discolored, and she could tell there was an unnatural puffiness about it.

"I think you have some broken ribs," she said. "You need to see a doctor."

She watched his eyes, but he closed them for a moment. The pain must have been intense. She said nothing, and finally he opened them and said, "What happened? Wait . . . I remember."

"There were two men."

"I know. They were trying . . . to rob me," he gasped. Suddenly he reached around, feeling for something.

"What is it you want?"

"My watch. Did they get my watch?"

"No, it's still here." She touched the watch, still hanging from its chain in his vest pocket. She saw him relax then and lie back. "I thought they were going to kill me."

Kefira nodded. She was relieved that he was talking and was not going to die immediately at least. "One of them was beating you with a club, and the other was kicking you. Why didn't you give them the watch if that's what they wanted?"

"No, it was a family watch. My father gave it to me."

Kefira shook her head. *What good's an old watch when you're dead?* She said nothing about the watch, however, asking instead, "Are you warm enough?"

"I guess so." He stared at her for a moment, then said, "I guess you saved my life. I don't know how you did it."

Kefira did not know how to answer. "I shot at them and scared them away."

The man's eyes opened wide. "You shot at them!" he whispered. "You carry a gun?"

"Yes."

"I guess that's a good thing for me, huh? By the way, my name's Josh Winslow."

"I'm Kefira Reis."

"You actually shot at them," Josh whispered. "I can't believe it."

"I meant to scare them, but—" She broke off and said in some confusion, "I'm not a very good shot. I hit one of them in the ear. That was probably a good thing. I think they were going to kill you."

"Could I have a drink of water?"

"Yes, I'll get it." Kefira got the water bottle and poured some into her tin cup. She lifted his head and saw that it hurt him, but he drank thirstily. "More?" she asked.

"No, that's enough for now." He looked at her strangely and then asked, "What are you doing out here, Miss Reis?"

"I'm on the road. I guess you are too."

"Dangerous for a young woman to be out like this. Don't you have any family?"

"No."

At her single-word reply, the man looked at her more closely. She was conscious of his gaze and said, "I'm heating up some food. But you'll have to sit up, I think."

She busied herself stirring the beans, and when they were hot she helped him move to a sitting position against the wall. From his grim expression, she knew the pain was intense, but he was evidently half starved. He devoured the beans and the home-baked bread Mrs. McKinney had wrapped up and given her, and finally he shook his head. "No more. That's fine."

Kefira had eaten also, and now she washed out the dishes with the rainwater falling steadily from the eaves. She came back and added another piece of wood to the fire. She was aware that he was watching her, and finally she turned to face him. "Why are you looking at me like that?"

"I was just thinking. I read about a tribe of Indians some-where in South America. They had a custom there that when a person saves someone's life, that person sort of belongs to them."

"You mean like a slave?"

"I don't know. I don't remember. But, anyway, I guess I belong to you, Kefira."

Kefira was half amused by this and intrigued. She started to speak, but then she saw Winslow's eyes drooping. "Here," she said, "lie down. You need to stay warm. In the morning I'll go for help."

He did not answer, and she saw that he was suffering badly from the beating. She eased him over gently until his blanket was under him, then covered him up with it. She put the other blan-ket over him, then sat down beside the fire to watch him. When fatigue overwhelmed her, she pulled the second blanket back and lay down beside him. He was unconscious and did not move, although he moaned more than once. She pulled the blan-ket over them both but knew she would have to stay awake to keep the fire going. When sleep threatened to come, she got up and sat before the fire.

In the morning, the rain stopped, and Kefira was coughing almost steadily. She bent over and said to the man, "I've got to go get help."

He must have been awake, for he answered immediately in a hoarse whisper. "Call Reverend Devoe Crutchfield at Summer-dale, Georgia. I don't know his number, but he'll get someone to help me."

"Devoe Crutchfield at Summerdale, Georgia. I'll do that." Kefira rose and left at once. It was dawn now but only barely so; the sun was just peeping over the eastern horizon. She had dried her clothes out thoroughly, but her cough was no better.

She had walked no more than five minutes when she heard the sound of an approaching vehicle. As the car drew close she waved frantically. It pulled up, and she walked around to the driver's side, where she saw a man inside. "I need help," she said. "There's a man that's been badly hurt back there in that barn."

"Get in, miss."

Kefira did not open the door. Instead, she studied the driver's face. He was obviously a farmer, perhaps in his midforties.

He said, "It's all right, miss. I'll help you with him."

Kefira decided he was a truthful sort, and she climbed into the car and pointed. "It's down there."

"What happened to him?"

"He was badly beaten by two men just about dark last night. I got him into the barn out of the rain, but he needs to see a doctor."

"My name's Jethro Higgins," the man offered.

Kefira gave him her name but volunteered no information. When the car pulled up in front of the barn, he said, "This is the old Henderson place. It burned down a year ago." Kefira got out at once, and Higgins followed her inside. While Kefira made sure that the fire was completely out, Higgins, a tall, rawboned man, walked directly over to Josh and stooped down. "How you doin'?" he said quietly.

"Not . . . so good."

"We'll take care of that. I need to get you into the car."

Josh Winslow nodded and Higgins helped him up. The young woman got on the other side, and the two of them steered him out. Kefira opened the door, and Higgins carefully lowered him onto the backseat. "Take it easy," he said reassuringly. "We'll get you to a doctor in no time."

Kefira carefully shut the back door and then got in the front seat with Higgins. She looked back over the seat and saw that the injured man's face was pale, and he was biting his lower lips as though to keep from crying aloud.

Higgins turned the car around and said, "My place is just three miles down this road. We'd better go right into town to the doctor's office. This fellow's pretty badly hurt."

Kefira started to thank him and then a spasm of coughing overtook her. Higgins looked alarmed. "You don't sound too good yourself, miss. Are you all right?"

"Just a bad cold."

"Sounds worse than that to me. Better have Dr. Jamison look you over too."

As for Josh Winslow, the ride was torment, and getting there was worse. It had taken all his concentration to keep from crying out when the tall man and the young woman had helped him to the car. Now he heard voices, and he felt hands on him, and it felt as though he were being torn apart. He remembered only a soft voice encouraging him. "You'll be all right," and a gruff voice saying, "Bring him on into the office." Then they lifted him, and mercifully he knew no more.

CHAPTER TWELVE

WHEN A MAN SEES BEAUTY

★ ★ ★ ★

The lion crouched with his head held high, and Kefira felt terror rushing through her body. She tried to shut off the sight. The large animals had always frightened her, and this was the most monstrous beast she had ever seen. She had walked through the sand, and overhead the skies had been dark and foreboding. She could not remember how she got to this place that seemed to stretch out forever—flat without variation. Once she had broken into a run, hoping to find someone to help or a structure where she could take refuge, but suddenly before her had appeared the form of a savage beast.

Stopping dead still, Kefira felt her heart beating until it seemed almost that it would tear itself out of her breast. She put her hand on her chest and pressed against it. Desperately she wanted to shut her eyes, or better still, to turn and flee, but the strength had drained from her, and she did not have the power even to stand. She slumped down on her knees, transfixed by the sight that seemed to enter through her eyes and into her head and swell there until it filled her entire body.

A shaft of sunlight shot down from the heavens and fell directly on the head and shoulders of the beast. She saw his paws were stretched out in front of him—and then she saw that this was no lion. She had seen lions in the zoo and once at a circus, but this beast, though he had the body of a lion . . . had the face of a man.

She could not turn away, and she saw that the face was scarred and battered, the nose almost gone, and there was some sort of headdress that spread out from where his ears would be. The fear of it came like a flood then, and she began to cry. Then she heard a voice. It was not the strange beast that spoke, but the voice came from somewhere deep within her. It was a comforting voice, soft and soothing, and it did not come with words, at least not words that she could understand. It was more of a sense of someone entering who calmed her fears, and she suddenly knew that everything would be all right.

Kefira stiffened and opened her eyes. She looked around wildly, then sat up and stared about the room. The dream had been so real. She could almost feel the individual grains of sand under her feet and the hot wind of the desert on her cheek. "But what is it?" she whispered. "What does it mean?"

Recognition came flooding back then, and she threw back the covers and sat on the side of the bed. She knew this room. At least she remembered being brought here by a woman who had spoken kindly to her and told her to sleep—that she was not well.

The room was cold, and Kefira shivered and at once began getting into her clothes. Her bedroll was not there, and she could not remember what she had done with it. As she hurriedly dressed, she remembered the doctor standing beside the man called Winslow, along with the couple taking them in. *What were their names?—Higgins, that was it.* The memories came quickly now, and when she was fully dressed, she pulled her thoughts away from the dream and to the injured man. He had been conscious most of the time, and Kefira had waited until after the doctor came out of the room. His name was Jamison. He was a tall, spindly man made up of spare parts, it seemed, but he had a kindly face and a soft accent in his voice. *"He's going to be all right,"* Dr. Jamison had said. *"He's got some ribs that are either broken or so badly cracked they might as well be. He's going to have a lot of pain. I wrapped him up—not that that does much good. Every time he breathes he's going to hurt those ribs, but I'm leaving some pain-killer. Keep him dosed up, and don't let him do too much. I'll stop in tomorrow.*"

Kefira stepped outside the door, struggled against the temptation to cough but could not help it. She coughed so hard she leaned against the door. After the coughing spell passed, she touched her face. It felt hot, and she knew she had a fever. Shaking her head, she muttered, "I can't be sick. I just can't." She was light-headed, but her limbs felt heavy, and despite her resolution, she knew with a sense of growing desperation that she was as sick as she had ever been in her life.

★ ★ ★ ★

She was standing over him when he opened his eyes, and memory came flooding back. "Hello," he said and licked his lips. "I feel like I've been drugged."

"The doctor gave you medicine to make you sleep. How do you feel?"

Josh arched his body slightly and then twisted his lips up with a grimace of pain. "I feel like I've been torn in two." He thought for a minute and then said, "I'm sorry I've forgotten your name. I guess I was out of it."

"Kefira Reis."

"Did I tell you mine?"

"Yes, Winslow—Joshua Winslow."

Josh turned experimentally from side to side. The pain was consistently bad. Every time he moved, it was as if someone was stabbing his side with a red-hot sword. A thought occurred to him, and he looked up at her. "If I sneeze," he said, alarmed at the thought, "I think it *would* tear me in two."

"Then don't sneeze."

Josh managed a grin. "I don't know how you do that." She coughed suddenly, and he looked at her more closely. "You don't look so good yourself."

"Just a cold."

"You've been sleeping out in this weather?"

"I usually find shelter."

At that moment Mrs. Higgins came into the room. "Oh, you're up, Miss Reis!" She was a tall, strongly built woman with a homely face and a pair of honest blue eyes. "How do you feel?"

"I'm all right."

Mrs. Higgins stared at her, took a step closer, and after an examination of Kefira's features, shook her head. "You've got a fever, haven't you?"

"A little bit, but I'll get over it."

"I've got some breakfast made. I came in to see if you could eat anything, young man."

"Nothing wrong with my appetite," Josh said. "It's just all the rest of me that hurts."

"I'll bring it in to him," Kefira said.

"Fine, and you need to eat something yourself."

The two women left, and Josh lay on the bed thinking about what had happened. The attack now was like a very bad dream. He could remember the faces of the men only slightly, but the memory of the kicks and blows was graphic indeed. He lay there careful not to move, occupying himself again with an effort to neither cough nor sneeze. He thought about the cough of the young woman who had saved his life. *I wonder if she had the doctor look at her.* The thought of the doctor came rushing back into his memory. He remembered asking him how long he would hurt like this, but he could not recall what the doctor said. Only that it was not something he was pleased to hear.

Looking out the window, he saw that the skies were clearing and the sun had risen. He had no idea of the time, and looking over to a golden oak dresser against the wall, he saw his watch and chain there and felt a sudden pride. "They didn't get you," he spoke aloud to the watch. "They may have broken every rib I own, but I hung on to you, didn't I?"

His grim determination to keep the watch, even at the cost of his life, was something new for Josh. He had always drifted with the current and had never fought for anything in his life. Now as he lay there taking shallow breaths to keep the pain away, he knew he had passed a test. He had a friend in college, Tom Jenkins, who had once said while the two were out drinking together, "College is nothing but a series of obstacles. They put a hurdle in front of you, something you have to do, and you jump it. Then as soon as you get over, they put another one there. Whether it's tests or courses it doesn't matter, and I don't think they care, just as long as you go over the hurdles." Jenkins had taken another drink and grinned rashly. "That's what life is, Josh, my boy, nothing but a series of hurdles. You'll knock one down every once in a while. Just keep running. Don't ever stop."

Joshua wondered where Jenkins was. He had not heard from him in years. *Probably successful,* he thought. *He was going to be a lawyer, and I guess he made it. He was a pretty determined fellow.*

In the midst of his thoughts, Josh looked up to see Kefira coming in with a tray.

"Mmm . . . I can smell it from here. What delectable did you bring me?"

Kefira just set the tray down and said, "You're going to have to sit up. You might strangle and choke, and that wouldn't be good."

"It would be a shame after all the trouble you've gone to on my behalf." Josh gave her a boyish grin. "Here, let me work myself up." He began a series of small movements, pushing and lifting himself carefully, and after what seemed like an inordinate amount of time, he finally sighed with relief. "Whew," he said. "Anyone would think I was ninety years old."

Kefira lifted the plate and handed it to him. He put it in his lap, took the fork, and stared at the food. "Scrambled eggs, ham, and homemade biscuits. Nothing like country cooking, is there?"

"People eat well here in the South," Kefira said, smiling sweetly. She went over and picked up the cup of coffee and drew up a chair and sat down beside him. "I'll hold this for you." She coughed suddenly, turning her head away, then clearing her throat. "You probably need to eat all you can."

"Aren't you going to have any?" he asked as he took a mouthful.

"I don't much feel like it," Kefira admitted. "Not with his cough and fever."

From time to time he looked over at the young woman who sat with her eyes on him. She was still wearing men's clothes, including a gray shirt that was unbuttoned at the throat. She had smooth skin, a beautiful complexion, and her hair was the blackest thing he had ever seen. He took another bite of eggs, chewed thoughtfully, then sneaked another glance. He had thought her eyes were black, but now he could see they were dark blue. He suddenly realized she was aware of his scrutiny and might be embarrassed, so he turned his eyes back to his plate and ate the remains of the biscuit loaded with peach preserves, then handed her the plate and took the coffee. He washed the last remnant down with strong drafts, then handed her the cup. "I feel better now."

"The doctor said some of your ribs may be broken. He wasn't quite sure."

"They feel like it, but I'll be all right."

"Your family is coming to get you. Did Mrs. Higgins tell you that?"

"No, did you call?"

"No, Mr. Higgins called. I'm not too good with telephones, but he talked to the minister you spoke of, and he promised to have someone here as soon as possible."

A feeling close to despair washed over Josh. It must have shown in his expression, for Kefira asked, "What's the matter?"

"I left home to go get a job so that I wouldn't be a burden to my family. Times are tough, and now here I've made things even worse. I'll be a cripple they'll have to take care of."

"I'm sure they won't feel that way," Kefira said quickly. "You couldn't help what happened."

Josh turned to face her. He breathed deeply until he felt his muscles contract and the pain start. "I guess not," he said. "I tried to run away, but I wasn't quick enough." He looked at her closely. "Do I remember you telling me you shot one of those fellows?"

Kefira answered defensively, "I was going to shoot in the air, but I'm not very good, so I nicked him in the ear."

Josh felt laughter coming on, but he knew that would hurt. He held his side as he chuckled lightly. "I was out cold by that time. I don't even remember hearing the shot, but it's probably a good thing. They would have killed me if you hadn't come by."

He sat there relaxing, and a calico cat jumped up on his lap and settled down there, purring. "Well, hello there. You're a friendly one."

The cat began kneading him, lifting his front feet rhythmically and sinking his claws into Josh's flesh. "Ow, that hurts!"

"Here, you can't do that," Kefira said to the animal. She reached out and picked up the cat. He allowed himself to be lifted, dangling limply, and when she put him on the floor, he stared at her with offended dignity, then stalked out of the room.

"Quite the comedian," Josh remarked.

Kefira said, "Could you drink some more coffee?"

"No, not right now. Sit down and talk to me a minute if you're not busy." He studied her face again and saw that she was flushed. "I'm worried about that cold of yours. What did the doctor say?"

"He was too busy with you. Besides, I'll be all right. I've had colds before."

Josh said, "Please sit down. I can't do a thing but lie here."

"Maybe I can find you something to read."

"I'd rather talk."

Kefira seemed to hesitate, then put the dishes on the tray and returned to sit down beside him. There was a placid quality in her that Josh liked immediately, but there was also strength in every line of her features. He could not tell about her figure under the shapeless clothes she wore, but she appeared to be trim and in good physical condition—except for the cold.

"How big a family do you have?" Kefira asked. She listened carefully as Josh spoke of his family, and then when he asked her about her own, she said, "I only have one brother."

"Oh, your parents aren't living, then?"

"No."

"Where does your brother live?"

Kefira hesitated, then said, "In New York."

"Why did you go on the road instead of staying with him?"

Kefira saw no reason to lie. "He's in prison."

"Oh, I'm sorry to hear that," Josh said quickly. He wanted to ask what the man had done but felt he could not. "How much longer does he have to serve?"

"Only about a year and a half. When he gets out, I want the two of us to live together."

"What's his name?"

"Chaim." When Kefira saw Winslow's brow contract in a puzzled frown, she said, "That's spelled C-h-a-i-m, but it's pronounced 'High-im.'"

"Chaim? What kind of a name is that?"

"It's Hebrew."

As she expected, Josh was surprised. "You're Jewish, then?"

"Yes."

"I'm sorry about your brother. I guess a year and a half seems like a long time. You have no other relatives at all?"

"No, not really."

Josh saw that she was watching him and shrugged his shoulders, bringing a twinge of pain. "I've been in jail myself," he said. "So I know what it's like."

"What were you in jail for?" Ordinarily Kefira would not have asked the question, but this interested her. He did not look like a criminal type, and she watched his face as he suddenly smiled.

"Selling bootleg liquor. I was a drunk too."

"You don't look like a drunk—or a criminal."

Josh smiled and shook his head. "'One may smile, and smile, and be a villain.'"

"What does that mean?"

"It's just a line from a play. It means we're not always on the inside what we seem to be on the outside."

Kefira recognized the truth of this well enough. She leaned forward and asked, "Was it very hard being in jail?"

"No, actually it wasn't. I wasn't in for long, and I got plenty to eat and I had a place to sleep, of course. Actually these last couple days have been harder than the time I was in jail."

"But you'll be going home now."

"Yes, and they ought to throw me out."

"Throw you out! Why would they do that?"

"Because I'm the black sheep of the family—the bad one."

"I don't think you're so bad," Kefira said. She pulled out a handkerchief and began to cough, and the effort was obviously painful for her. When she recovered, she asked, "How's your head?"

"Fine, I guess. The doctor changed the bandage."

"Yes, he didn't have to take any stitches."

They sat in silence for a minute, then Kefira stood to her feet, "I think I'll go see if I can help Mrs. Higgins with the work."

"All right. Thank you, Miss Reis."

"You can call me Kefira."

"That's a pretty name. What does it mean?" He saw a smile touch her lips and said, "What's so funny?"

"It's my name. I don't often tell a goy what it means."

"What's a goy?"

"Somebody that's not a Jew." She smiled and said, "It means 'little cub.' I guess I was named after a lion or something. Maybe I had a bad nature when I was a baby."

"I don't believe that, but you have the courage of a lion to stand up to those two thugs. I'll never forget it, Kefira. Never."

His words obviously embarrassed her, and she ducked her head, saying, "I'll bring you some more coffee after a while. I expect you'd better rest."

She left the room and went into the kitchen. Jethro and Edith Higgins were there eating breakfast, and Mr. Higgins rose and motioned to a chair. "Sit down, miss. Plenty of food."

"I'm not very hungry."

Mrs. Higgins shook her head. "You should have told the doctor you were sick. I meant to, but I got so occupied with your man that I forgot."

"He's . . . . he's not my man."

"What happened?" Jethro Higgins asked. He listened as she recounted the story, then grinned broadly. "So, you carry a gun, huh?"

"I do. Does that shock you?"

"It was a lucky thing for Joshua Winslow you had it. From what you tell me, those two thugs meant business."

"I hate guns," Kefira said. "I hope I never have to pull the trigger again."

Mrs. Higgins sipped from the white mug she held between

both hands and asked her husband, "What did the minister say? The one you called."

"He said somebody would come right away to pick him up." Mr. Higgins turned and asked Kefira, "Will you go with him?"

"No, he's a stranger to me. I'm going to the coast. Down to Florida. Maybe to the very end of it." Her face was flushed with fever, but excitement danced in her eyes. "I've looked at the map so often. I'd like to go out to the very tip of Florida where it sticks out into the ocean."

The two studied her, and when she got up and left, Higgins said, "She's a strange one, isn't she, Edith?"

"Poor child. She's evidently got nobody. I wish she'd stay around here. We could find her something to do."

"Sounds like she's pretty set on heading for Florida."

"Nothing there for her. She needs friends and a family. She'd be a pretty girl if she'd put on a dress."

"She's pretty as she is."

"Suppose it was some of our kin, Jethro. Think how bad we'd feel. There are evil men out there. She's had proof enough of that."

"She seems pretty set. I think she's the kind of person that finishes what she starts."

"Lucky for Mr. Winslow she does."

★　★　★　★

"You're the best checkers player I ever saw, Josh. I usually can hold my own down at the general store. There's some experts down there." Jethro Higgins grinned and looked down at the checkerboard. "That's all they do is play checkers. Not worth a dime."

"I've always been good at checkers and chess," Josh stated matter-of-factly.

"Chess—I don't know how to play that. Looks complicated."

"I suppose it is. I always liked it, though. Guess I like a challenge."

Jethro was sitting in a chair pulled up close to the bedside table in Josh's room. It was late afternoon. The two had played three games of checkers, none of which lasted long, for Josh was indeed very good at the game. The two men had nibbled at the sugar cookies Mrs. Higgins had brought in and washed them down with strong drafts of black, unsweetened coffee. Josh had refused sugar and cream, and Higgins had nodded his approval. "Real men don't need that," he grunted. "Just hot and black."

"I do like coffee."

"So do I." Higgins grinned. "The worst cup of coffee I ever had in my life—was real good!"

Josh laughed at the statement and then caught himself. "Ow, that hurts."

"You're gonna be laid up for a while. Have to take it easy."

"I know. I hate it."

"Your family will take care of you."

"That's just it. They don't need a helpless man to wait on and eat their food."

"Things pretty bad with your folks?"

"They're better off than some. We do own the place we're on, and we've got a good man to help out—my brother-in-law. He knows everything about farming and gardening." Josh went on for some time speaking of Clint Longstreet's capabilities and said thoughtfully, "I don't know what we would have done if it hadn't been for Clint. My sister Kat—she's just thirteen—says that she thought he was an angel when he helped us get out of New York. We didn't have much but the clothes on our backs and Clint's old truck, but we made it."

"Pretty country down in that part of Georgia. I went through there once. Looks a lot like this country."

"It is pretty down there."

"One time I was down—" Suddenly Higgins broke off. He rose and went over to the window. "It's a truck. Don't believe I know the fellow. He's getting out. I expect it might be the fellow come for you."

Indeed, it proved to be. Josh sat still, and Higgins left the room. Josh heard voices, then footsteps as Clint Longstreet stepped inside. He was wearing a red mackinaw coat and a cap with flaps tied up over the top. He smiled and strode over to

Josh, saying, "My, my—some folks will do anything to get waited on."

"How are you, Clint?"

"I'm fine, but what about you? You don't look too bad."

"Well, that's good news 'cause I feel bad enough."

"He's got some busted ribs," Higgins said. "His head's not too bad, though—seems to be able to think pretty straight. You fixin' to take him on home?"

"Don't guess I ought to start tonight."

"I don't know about his ridin' a long ways. He hurts pretty bad, and the roads ain't too good."

"You're right about that." Clint nodded. "Full of chuck-holes."

Josh waved his hand dismissively. "Just fix me a bed in the back of the truck. I'll be fine."

"Well, you can't leave until tomorrow anyway. We'll put you up tonight. As a matter of fact, you might ought to stay two or three days."

"It's your say, Josh," Clint said. "If you want to stay and mend up, I'll hang around."

"No, let's go tomorrow early."

"Well, it's about suppertime," Jethro said. "You two can talk. I'll come back and get you when it's on the table. You think you might be able to sit up at the table, Josh?"

"Sure, I'll give it a try."

As soon as Higgins left, Josh made a helpless gesture. "Well, here's the bad penny turned up again. I sure didn't last long without crying for help."

"What happened? I didn't get the full story. Just that you got beat up." Clint sat down in the chair that Higgins had vacated.

"Well, if it hadn't been for a young woman named Kefira Reis, I guess you'd be comin' to get my body." He launched into the story, leaving nothing out, and when he had finished he said, "If it hadn't been for Kefira, it would've been all over for me, Clint."

"Sounds like my kind of woman. Pretty homely, is she?"

"Homely! No, what makes you say that?"

"Well, you don't expect good-lookin' women to roam around alone like that."

"She's very pretty!"

"But packs a gun, 'eh? I wonder what kind."

"I don't know. You'll have to ask her."

At that point Mrs. Higgins came in and said, "If you can get to the table, Mr. Winslow, supper's all ready."

"Just call me Josh, please, and I'll be pleased to join you."

Josh started to get up, but the sudden movement sent a pain ripping through him. He lay back and gasped. "On second thought, I don't think I'd better try to stand up."

"I'll bring you some food in here," Mrs. Higgins said quickly, then turned to Clint. "You come and eat at the table with my husband and the young woman, mister."

"Everybody calls me Clint," he said as he left the injured man's room and went to the table.

When he entered the dining room, Clint was startled at the beauty of the young woman who sat there. Even in her rough clothes and her black hair tied back, he agreed with Josh's assessment of her. He introduced himself at once. "I'm Clint Longstreet, Josh's brother-in-law."

"He told me about you," Kefira said. "How is he?"

"He's hurtin' a lot."

Higgins nodded. "Broken ribs are some of the worst things a fellow can have. I broke a couple of mine once fallin' out of the hayloft. Life was sure miserable for a while. Couldn't hardly breathe. Sit yourself down there, Clint."

The meal was plain, but there was plenty of food: fried pork chops, canned corn, purple-hulled peas, and fresh corn bread. Clint looked at the young woman and said, "Josh told me how you saved his bacon."

Kefira looked rather pale except for the color in her cheeks from the fever. She shook her head and whispered, "It wasn't much."

"Not the way I hear it."

Clint wanted to know more about this young woman, but he could see that she was not well. After supper he went back to Josh's room and said, "You didn't lie about that girl. She's a beauty. What's her name—Kefira? Funny name. Never heard it before."

"She's Jewish."

"That right? Well, she's a looker, but she seems right poorly."

"She needs to go to bed and stay there, but she's real stubborn. She says she's got to get to Florida, somewhere on the coast."

Clint scratched his cheek. "I'm not sure I ought to haul you back. Some of the roads are really rough, Josh. It'll shake you to pieces."

"I can't stay here and be a burden on the Higginses." He smiled grimly, "I'd rather go home and be a burden on you and the folks."

"It's your say."

"Just fix me a bed and drive as slow as you can. I'll make it all right."

★   ★   ★   ★

Later that evening Clint sat in front of the wood stove talking to Higgins, deciding he liked the man a great deal. "Good of you to take in my brother-in-law."

Higgins looked up, surprised. "Well, what would a man do? Kick him out?"

"Some would."

"Not much of a man who'd do that." Higgins was systematically peeling an apple. He had peeled the whole thing, leaving only one long peel, and now he opened the door of the wood stove and threw it in. The fire crackled and snapped, and the heat radiated throughout the room. Shutting the door, he took a bite of the apple, munched on it thoughtfully, and went on. "He really don't need to make no long, hard trip."

"That's what I told him, but he's stubborn as a blue-nosed mule."

"I figured that. Well, how will you do it?"

"Don't know, but I'll go as slow as I can, of course, but he could be thrown around a lot in the back of that big old truck."

Clint spent the rest of the evening losing at checkers to Josh, and then he went out and found Kefira sitting alone in front of the stove. Mr. and Mrs. Higgins had gone to bed early. "He's hurtin' pretty bad, miss," Clint said. He took a seat in the rocker and was quiet for a moment. "I hear you're in a hurry to get down to the big water."

"Yes, I would like to get there," she said with an effort.

"Look, how about this," Clint said. He leaned forward and spread his hands in an expressive gesture. "I ain't no doctor, but I know you ain't feelin' good. If you're like I am when I get one of these colds, it could last a long time."

"I'll just have to weather it, Clint."

"I got me a problem, Kefira. I can drive as slow as I can, but Josh is going to be thrown around some. He needs somebody with him in the back of that truck. It's going to be tough enough as it is, so here's what I was thinking. You come along with me. You stay in the back, and you hold him as still as you can. We'll fix a nice bed, and we'll bolster him up. I brought plenty of extra covers with me. But there's going to be lots of bumps, and he needs somebody with him." He watched her face and saw a negative expression and then said quickly, "Help me get him home, and then you'll have lots of folks to take care of you until you're over this cold. We owe you something for saving Josh. His dad would want you to do it."

"But I don't even know them."

"You'll love 'em. They're fine people. Besides, I don't see any other way to do this." Then he played his highest card. "Look, you make the trip back with me and stay at our place until you get well. Then, if you want, I'll drive you all the way to the coast."

Kefira straightened up. The red spots in her cheeks were growing, but his offer suddenly seemed too good to be true. "All the way to the coast?"

"It's not too far, actually. I wouldn't mind seeing that country again myself. How about it? Is it a deal?"

Kefira nodded quickly. "Yes, it sounds good to me."

Kefira felt bad enough that she wanted to go to bed immediately. She said good-night to Clint, went to the kitchen cabinet, and found the bottle Mrs. Higgins had left there for her. She took two big tablespoons of the rank-tasting medicine and then capped the bottle with a shudder. She went to bed and discovered that whatever the medicine had in it worked. She coughed a great deal at first but finally fell into a drugged sleep.

★　★　★　★

"I'm right worried about you, young lady," Edith Higgins said. "I don't see why you don't just stay with us. We'll take care of you until you get well."

"That's very kind of you, but I really need to be with Josh. It's going to be a hard ride on him."

"Yes, it will." The two women were standing out beside the truck, and they turned as Josh emerged. Clint held him on one side and Higgins on the other. He walked stiffly, and pain etched its marks on his face. He kept his eyes down, and when they lifted him up to put him in the truck, he cried out involuntarily.

"Sorry, Josh. No way to do this easy." He crawled up into the enclosed back of the truck and arranged Josh on the bed he had made, sticking a pillow under his head. He jumped out then and said, "If you're ready, Kefira, I guess we'll hit the road."

Kefira turned and shook hands with both of the Higginses. "Thank you so much," she whispered. "You've been so kind."

"God bless you, dear. You take care of that cold."

"Good-bye," Higgins said. "You take care of that young fellow, now."

Kefira nodded and climbed up into the back of the big old truck.

"I'll shut this door," Clint said. "There's a hammer up there. If you want to stop, just bang on the back of the cab. I'll pull over."

"All right."

Light came in through the cracks of the wooden cap over the truck bed, so Kefira moved over to where Josh was lying down. "Is it very bad?" she asked.

He did not answer, and when she leaned forward, she saw

that his eyes were glazed. "Mrs. Higgins . . . dosed me up. I don't . . ." His eyes fluttered, then closed, and Kefira saw that he was unconscious. She sat down beside him, leaning against the side of the truck. The engine started with a roar, then it moved slowly forward. Josh's body rocked slightly, and she reached out and held his shoulders. As the truck picked up speed, she felt about as bad as she ever had in her life. Finally she could not sit up any longer but moved to lie down beside him. She put her arm over him and was glad that Clint had braced him on the other side with quilts and blankets. He could not actually move or roll over, and as the truck rumbled on, she herself went to sleep.

★   ★   ★   ★

Clint pulled up in front of the Winslow house, shut off the engine, and leaped out. He was stiff from the long trip, but he moved quickly. When he reached the back of the truck, he saw Hannah coming out, followed by Jenny and Kat. It was Hannah who said, "How is he, Clint?"

"All right, sweetheart." He reached over and took her kiss. "Well, actually he's in a lot of pain." He hesitated, then said, "The only way I could get him here was to have some help holdin' him still. The young woman agreed to do it."

"A young woman!" Kat exclaimed, her eyes bright. "Who is she?"

"I'll tell you the whole story later, but she saved his life. She's sick too—with a real bad cold and fever. Maybe even pneumonia."

"Well, let's get her out of there at once," Jenny said.

At that moment Lewis came running out of the house and stared at Clint. "Is he all right?"

"It's going to be a chore getting him into a bed. His ribs are busted, and he really feels poorly."

"Chester Taylor is inside. He can help us carry him in."

"Okay. Where will we put him?"

Hannah said, "In the last room on the east side."

Clint nodded, opening the back door of the truck. He kneeled in and said, "Well, this looks bad! Kefira, you all right?" He got no answer, turned, and said, "I think the young woman's sicker than I thought. We'll take her in first." He moved forward and saw that Kefira was indeed out of it. She was lying perfectly still, her arm thrown across Josh's chest. Clint picked her up awkwardly and then scooted to the back of the truck, and when he stepped out, her head fell back.

"Why, she's unconscious," Hannah said. "Come along, Clint. We'll put her in the upstairs bedroom."

"We'd better go get Doc Peturis," Lewis said.

Clint followed Hannah into the house, put the young woman on the bed, then said, "I'll go get Josh."

It was a struggle getting the injured man out. He had taken enough of the painkiller so that he was only partially conscious, but still he cried out with pain. They lifted Josh up and carried him into the house.

Finally both of the patients were in bed.

As for Kefira, she was aware of voices and movement, but she could not seem to come out of it. For a time she thought she had died and wondered vaguely if she would see her parents.

She felt her clothes being pulled off and tried to protest, and then she was being washed with warm water, and finally she felt smooth, fresh clothes. She tried to open her eyes and did slightly, and she saw the faces of two women hovering over her. She tried to speak but could not, and instead dropped off into a warm blackness.

PART THREE

The Dream

★ ★ ★

CHAPTER THIRTEEN

JUST A DREAM

★ ★ ★ ★

Kefira opened her eyes and for just a moment was filled with stark terror. She was frightened as badly as she had ever been in her life, for she had no idea where she was, and in that single moment she could not even remember the recent events of her life.

Closing her eyes, she took a deep breath and kept perfectly still. Her mind seemed to swirl, bringing memories of dreams, some of which were very frightening. Slowly the maelstrom that was her mind grew calm, and memories began coming back slowly, fragments at a time. She remembered burning up, it seemed, and somehow gentle hands had cooled her body. A face came to her then . . . a woman's face, kind and yet strange to her. She could not remember who it was, and she desperately wanted to.

From somewhere a rhythmic sound came to her, and she recognized the ticking of a clock. The regularity of it and the ordinariness of it brought a sudden sense of relief. *A clock. I'm in a bed in a room and there's a clock ticking.*

She heard another sound then, the sibilant whispering of the wind, and this also eased the fear that had almost paralyzed her mind. Opening her eyes, she saw a window and outside a tree.

A bird was sitting on a branch, and as Kefira studied the bird it tilted up its head and began to chirp melodiously. She watched the bird until she heard footsteps approaching. Turning her head she saw a woman wearing a light blue dress and over it a white apron. It was the face, she realized, that she had seen in the dream, and when the woman spoke her voice was pleasant.

"Well, you're waking up." She stooped down, put her hand on Kefira's forehead, and held it there for a moment. "Your fever's gone. I'd guess you're thirsty, aren't you?"

"Yes!"

The woman turned to the bedside table, and Kefira followed her with her eyes as she poured water from a pink glass pitcher into a large glass. When the woman held it to her lips and helped her to sit up, Kefira gulped it eagerly, spilling some of the fluid down her chin. She drained the glass and whispered, "Thank you."

"My name's Hannah Longstreet, and I already know you're Kefira Reis."

"What . . . what is this place?"

"This is my home. My husband brought you here after you helped with Joshua."

Memories then came flooding back to Kefira. She licked her lips and sat up straighter in the bed. She felt weak and drained but was relieved that her mind was now clearing. "How is Josh?"

"He's very well," Hannah said. "The doctor said he's going to be fine. He was actually more worried about you than he was about him." Hannah's eyes focused on the young woman, and she said, "Are you hungry?"

Suddenly Kefira realized she was ravenous. "Yes, I am."

"You lie right there and drink water in little sips. I'll pour you another glass. I'll be back soon with something to eat."

Kefira watched Hannah pour the glass of water, took it in her own hand, then watched as the woman left the room. Things were still confused. She felt as if she were working a jigsaw puzzle with some of the pieces missing. Slowly she sipped the water and then lay back against the pillows. She turned to watch the bird outside the window and recognized it as a mockingbird. The wind had ruffled its feathers, but it tilted its head back and sang a song so happy and energetic that Kefira longed to be as free in heart as that small bird.

★ ★ ★ ★

When Hannah entered, Josh looked up from the book he was reading. "How is she this morning?"

"Fine," Hannah said. "She's awake. Why don't you go in and talk to her while I fix breakfast."

"She feels like talking?"

"Well, she feels like listening." Hannah smiled slightly. "Go on, now, and keep her company."

Josh put a marker in the book, closed it, and put his hands on the table. Very slowly he rose, moving like an old, old man. He had discovered that any sudden move or any twisting of his body was sure to bring the stabbing pain that took his breath away. He had sneezed once and had thought the act would tear his body in two. Since then he had learned to control sneezes by pinching his nose.

Moving slowly, he left the parlor, walked down the hall, then knocked gently on the door. Without waiting, he stepped inside and saw that Kefira was sitting up in the bed holding a glass in her hand. "Well, I'm glad to see you in the world of the living again." He walked slowly across the room and, turning a cane-bottomed chair around, sat down very carefully. He expelled a sigh of relief and then nodded. "I never appreciated what a great thing it was just to walk without hurting." He saw that her face was pale and her eyes were filled with an expression he could not read. "How are you feeling?"

"I'm . . . much better."

"You gave us all quite a scare." Josh nodded. "You were the star patient around here for a while."

"How long have I been here?"

"Three days. Don't you remember any of it?"

"Not really."

"You were pretty sick. You had us all worried, Kefira."

He saw that she had drunk most of the water, and he reached

out and took the glass. The move made him wince, but he grinned and said, "I'm better too. The first couple of days I couldn't even turn over." He poured the glass three-fourths full, handed it back to her, and watched as she sipped it. "You know, Kefira," he remarked, "I guess I owe you another debt. It seems like you've made a habit of taking care of me."

A slight color tinged her cheeks as if she were not used to compliments.

Kefira glanced at his face and was once again impressed with what a fine-looking man he was. He was lean and his cheeks were somewhat sunken from his recent troubles, but he had the clearest gray eyes she had ever seen, and there was a sense of fineness about him that she was unaccustomed to. His features were clear and clean and crisp, and there was somehow an aristocratic look about the long nose, the high cheekbones. He was freshly shaved, and his skin glowed in a healthy fashion. "Your ribs are broken?"

"No, just cracked, Doc Peturis thinks." He shook his head ruefully. "If cracked ribs hurt this much, I'd hate to have them broken!"

Kefira listened as Josh talked easily. He had a wide, mobile mouth, and his chin was a trifle pronounced, which gave him a rather stubborn look. But there was, at the same time, a lack of roughness about him that she had come to expect from men, and she found him fascinating.

Hannah interrupted their conversation, coming in with a tray bearing a glass of milk and a bowl of something that sent up a breath of pale steam.

"You scoot on, Josh. After Kefira eats I'm going to help her wash and put on a fresh nightgown."

Josh got up, smiled at Kefira, and said, "Well, thanks again for saving my life."

Kefira did not know how to answer that, but she did manage a smile. The smell of the food reached her, and she turned and watched eagerly as Hannah came over and set the tray down on the bedside table. "Here," she said. "Don't worry about spilling some of it. I'm going to wash that gown anyhow. It's hot. Don't burn yourself."

Kefira ate gingerly. The broth was hot and had bits of chicken and vegetables in it. It was delicious and she ate it all and drank the milk too.

"Now then. You can have some more later," Hannah said. "I think it's better to eat smaller meals more often, especially if you've been sick. Now, with your permission, I'm going to clean you up a little bit and change your sheets and your nightgown."

Hannah got her out of bed, helped her remove her gown, washed her with warm soapy water, rinsed her off, then put her in a fresh nightgown. After stripping off the covers and putting on fresh sheets, she helped Kefira back into bed and said, "Now, does that feel better?"

"Oh yes, much better!"

The door opened suddenly, and Kat Winslow entered. Her eyes alive with curiosity, she walked at once to Kefira's bedside. "Hello," she announced loudly. "My name's Kat, and yours is Kefira. Josh told me."

"That's right. Is your real name Kat?"

"No, it's Katherine, but everybody calls me Kat. I even sign it Kat. Katherine sounds too formal, I think. You've got a pretty name—Kefira. What does it mean?"

"Now, Kat, you leave Kefira alone," Hannah said, gathering up the sheets. She laughed, adding, "Run her out if she bothers you, Kefira. She'll pester you to death with questions."

"I will not!" Kat said indignantly. But as soon as Hannah left, she pulled the chair up close and said, "I want to hear all about it. Josh told me you shot a man who was trying to hurt him. Is that right?"

"Yes, it is."

Kat's eyes grew even larger, and she breathed, "I want to hear *all* about it."

Kefira found the girl nearly as fascinating as her brother. She was somewhere around twelve or thirteen, as far as she could guess, and had the same gray eyes and tawny hair as Josh. She was wearing a pair of overalls, none too clean, and dirt was underneath her fingernails. As Hannah had warned, she fired off one question after another.

"Are you married?"

"No, I'm not."

"Why not?"

Kefira laughed. She was drowsy from the food and the comfort of a bath and the fresh sheets, but she found herself liking Kat very much. "I suppose I never found a man I liked well enough to marry."

Kat said, "Ma prayed for a man and God sent my father to her."

Kefira remembered Josh mentioning something like this and knew Kat referred to her stepmother. "Josh told me," she said.

"Maybe you'd better try that." Kat nodded innocently.

Josh entered at that moment and said, "Try what?"

"Kefira hasn't got a husband, so maybe she ought to pray that God would send her one like Ma prayed and got Daddy."

Josh's eyes sparkled and danced with humor. He reached over and pulled Kat's hair. "You leave Kefira alone."

Kat started to protest, but Josh said, "You go along, now, and let Kefira rest."

"I'll go, but I'll come back. When you get up, I'll read to you, Kefira. I'm a good reader, and then I'll show you my egg collection."

As soon as Kat left like a miniature whirlwind, Kefira said, "I guess I've forgotten what you told me about your stepmother."

"Well, you'll have to know Missouri Ann to understand it," he said. He took a seat, smelling the fragrance of the soap that lingered and noticing that her face was shiny. "It's a strange story. You see, Missouri Ann is very close to God. Her first husband died about three years ago and she was pretty happy living alone. But then she found Dad with a busted leg and rescued him. She says God told her she was to marry him and have his children, so she took him in and announced that God had sent him." Josh laughed.

"I remember you telling me about that now. Things aren't too clear just yet."

"Well, Missouri Ann's a strange woman. She thinks there's

only one right person to marry. If you marry the wrong one, you're in trouble."

"She thinks that?"

"She told me a story one time," Josh said, nodding. "She thinks it's an old Indian legend. That God made one whole creature, and the creature was very happy. But something bad happened, and the creature got separated into two halves. The halves went all throughout the world, trying to find each other among all the other separated creatures. They couldn't rest until they found the exact half they were originally created with." Josh smiled, "I always thought of it like a paper doll torn in two. The only one that would match would be the one torn off from it."

"Is that what you believe?" Kefira asked.

"Oh, I don't know. You'll have to ask Missouri Ann. It's her theory."

As if on cue, the door opened and Missouri Ann came in and asked, "Well, how's the patient?"

Kefira studied her carefully. She was a tall woman with a square face, black hair with a streak of silver, and blue-gray eyes. She came over at once and looked at Kefira. "Well, you're better. The good Lord has healed you, I see."

"I'm much better, thank you."

Josh rose and said, "I'm going to move around a bit. You take good care of this patient, Ma."

As Josh left, Missouri Ann smiled. "It makes me feel good to hear Josh call me 'Ma.'"

"He was telling me how you met your husband. That you believe God sent him."

"They make it sound easy. What they don't tell you is that I was getting lonely after my first husband died. I prayed for a companion for a year before Mr. Winslow came along." She stood over Kefira, felt her forehead, and then said, "Most people give up on praying too quick. You've got to keep at it."

Kefira liked the woman instantly. She mentioned tentatively, "I need to get up and do something."

"Like what?"

"Well, help with the work."

"No, God sent you here to rest up. He brought you for that

purpose, and that's all there is to it."

Kefira was growing very drowsy, but this statement attracted her attention. "You really think God cares about things like that? I mean, I'm just one person out of millions."

"The good Lord knows the fall of a single sparrow. Why wouldn't He care about one of His own?"

"I don't feel like I'm one of His own."

"Well, you're wrong, then." Missouri Ann smiled gently, and her voice was warm. "You're one of His own, and God's going to do great things. Now, you go to sleep. There'll be plenty of time to talk later."

Actually Kefira was terribly sleepy. She felt the woman's hand on her hair stroking it, and it gave her a sense of warm security. She closed her eyes and tried to say something but dropped off to sleep—a soft, gentle, easy sleep with no dreams.

★　★　★　★

A strong wind was tossing the trees outside, and Kefira lifted her eyes from the food she was preparing to look out the window. She had always liked the spring, and here in the South it evidently came early. A short-tailed striped cat walked by, his eye on a bird perched on a fence out in the field, and he took off in a blur, but of course, the bird flew away, escaping with no trouble.

"What's that? What are you cooking, Kefira?"

Kefira had learned that Kat had more questions than anyone could possibly have answers. For the past week since Kefira had made a rapid recovery, Kat had stayed almost under her. Now she crowded in, looking at the dough Kefira was kneading. "You ask so many questions, bubee."

"Bubee? What's that?"

"That's what Jews call people they like very much."

"How do you spell it? B-o-o-b-y?"

"No, b-u-b-e-e."

"I wish I could speak another language. Maybe you could teach me yours."

"You wouldn't have anyone to talk to after I leave, I would think. There aren't many Jews in this part of the world."

"But what is it you're cooking there?"

"It's called *vareniki*. It's really just little bits of dough filled with jelly or fruit or meat. Just about anything. Here, you stuff some of them, and afterward we'll fry them in fat."

Kefira had improved so rapidly that she had gotten out of the bed, determined to do something to help. She had persuaded Missouri to let her cook a Jewish supper, and Missouri had been fascinated.

Kefira knew mostly Jewish recipes and was not sure how the family would like them. As they worked, Kat spoke excitedly about the meal, about her school, about finding a new bird's egg. *She's so full of life,* Kefira thought, *and so filled with joy. It's good to watch her.*

"Kefira, can I ask you something?"

Kefira laughed. "You've asked me a thousand questions in the past week. I suppose one more won't hurt."

"Well . . . there's this boy at school, and I think he likes me."

"Oh, is that right?"

"I think so. He always comes to sit by me when we eat lunch, and he watches me."

"What's his name?"

"Johnny Marr."

"And what about you? Do you like him?"

"I don't know. I'm not sure I'm supposed to."

"What does that mean?"

"He makes me feel kind of funny."

"And why is that?"

"Oh, I don't care about stuff like that—boy-girl stuff, I mean."

"I think that's very wise, Kat. There'll be plenty of time for boys when you grow up into a young woman."

"Did boys like you when you were thirteen?"

Kefira suddenly had memories of how Howie Schwartz had followed her constantly when she had been exactly thirteen. She had been pleased but confused. "It's a hard time—thirteen. You're not a little girl and yet not a woman either. Sort of in between."

"You mean like a mule?"

Kefira laughed. "I don't know about mules, but I know thirteen's a hard age for girls—and I expect for boys too."

The conversation was interrupted when Missouri Ann came in. "Can I be of any help?"

"I don't know how this meal's going to go over. Jewish cooking is different."

"It'll be a change from squirrel and dumplings," Missouri exclaimed.

Missouri Ann began to work around the kitchen, listening as Kat spoke incessantly with Kefira. For a time she turned to watch the young woman and, as always, was concerned about her spiritual condition. Kefira was actually the first Jew she had ever met, and she longed to see her find the true Messiah.

★ ★ ★ ★

The meal was a tremendous success. The family ate everything, demanding to know the name of each dish.

"This is great. Doesn't taste like the fish I cook," Jenny said. "What do you call it, Kefira?"

"We call it *gefilte fish*."

"Well, it sure is different," Clint said. "How do you fix it?"

"Oh, you just chop the fish up, add onions and seasoning, and then cook it in salt water."

"And this stuffed cabbage. What do you call that?" Lewis demanded.

"We call it *holishkes*."

"Well, it's really great. And this pudding is wonderful—never tasted anything better. What do you call it?"

"It's just a bread-suet pudding. We call it *kugel*. It's always better cooked with raisins, I think."

"How do you say 'this is real good' in Jewish, Kefira?" Kat piped up.

"Me ken lecken di finger."

"That sounds like licking your finger!" Kat said, her eyes enormous.

"Actually, that's what it means. It's so good one can lick his fingers."

"Kefira's going to teach me to speak Hebrew."

"Well, actually it's not Hebrew but Yiddish. Very much like Hebrew, though."

Josh ate slowly with enjoyment. He had never eaten Jewish food before that he could remember and found it delicious. He was also pleased that Kefira had made this effort, and he saw that there was a glow in her as every member of the family admired her cooking.

After the meal Missouri Ann said, "Now, you go out for a walk or something, Kefira."

"No, I'd like to help with the dishes."

"Plenty of hands here to do that. You go along, now."

Kefira smiled shyly as Hannah came over and gave her a hug, commenting on her great success as a cook. "Thank you," Kefira said. "It wasn't much, really."

Kefira left the house, and as she walked along the path that led down to the river, she could feel the touches of spring already in the air. When she got to the water's edge, she stood for a long time listening to the gurgling sounds the water made as it poured over the rocks. Once a fish broke the surface, startling her, and she remembered that she had promised Kat she'd go fishing with her.

She moved downstream, slowly thinking of how strange it was to find herself on a farm in Georgia, so far from New York. The week had been the most pleasant she could remember. She had never seen a family any closer than the Winslows, and their Christianity puzzled her. She had been afraid of Christians for years, but she had seen nothing but kindness and goodness in these people. *I wonder if all Christians are like that. No, they're not all that way, because I've seen some that are cruel.* The thought troubled her, and she struggled with it for a time.

She had almost decided to go back when she heard a dog barking and turned to look back toward the house. She was struck by the scene before her: the freshly painted white two-story house, fields stretching toward distant mountains on one side and toward a forest on the other. Even the large dog in the yard, barking at something high in a tree, seemed familiar—and she suddenly realized how alike this place was to the dream she had had all those months ago in New York. She heard someone call her name and dismissed her fancy.

She looked around and spotted Josh coming along the path that bordered the river. He was carrying a small rifle under his arm and greeted her cheerfully. "Thought I'd come out and maybe get a rabbit or a squirrel but no luck. Mind if I join you?"

"No, it's a beautiful evening."

"Spring's almost here," Josh said. He noted that a little wind was running its cool breath over the water. "Always liked this river," he said. "It seems to sing a little song as it makes its way down toward the ocean."

"This will really go to the ocean?"

"Eventually." Josh nodded. "Let's sit down awhile. I'm still feeling some strain." The two sat down on a large tree that had fallen over years ago, and Josh leaned the rifle carefully against it. "This river will go down to a bigger river, maybe the Chattahoochee, and the Chattahoochee will go to the ocean." He found her watching him in a strange way and noted how beautiful her eyes were. "Then it'll rise out of the ocean," he continued. "The sun will shine and draw the water up, and it'll make a cloud. Then it'll come back over land, turn to rain, and start its journey all over again."

"I never thought about that."

"Things don't change much. As wise old Solomon said in the Old Testament, 'There's nothing new under the sun.'"

The two sat there, with Josh speaking lightly about the world and the way it worked, and finally Kefira turned to him. "Josh, what do you really want?"

Startled, Josh faced her, his eyes widening. "Why, I guess I'm not quite sure."

"You must want something. Didn't you dream about something when you were a boy?"

Josh did not answer for a moment. A troubled expression touched his gray eyes, and then he laughed ruefully. "Well, as a matter of fact, I always wanted to be an archeologist."

"That's someone who digs up bones, isn't it?"

"Bones and other things."

"Why didn't you become one?"

"Because I was a fool. We had too much money. I got to drinking. But there was a time when I had a chance." His eyes grew animated as he said, "One of my college professors was an archeologist named Phineas Welles. I read all of his books and went with him on a dig."

"What's a dig?"

"That means you dig up bones and things, like you said. That time we were digging up Indian mounds in Louisiana."

"You like that?" she asked curiously. "It sounds boring."

"Oh, it isn't!" Josh exclaimed. "It's the most exciting thing in the world, at least to me. Why, you never know what you're going to find next."

Kefira listened as Josh spoke with enthusiasm. Once he threw his arm out to illustrate a point and grunted with pain, but he continued speaking of his dream. Kefira thought suddenly of the dreams she had had, especially the ones in a strange land with the enormous stone lion with a man's face. She had dreamed of that several times.

Finally Josh grew silent, and Kefira asked, "What's wrong?"

"I'm just sad, Kefira. There was an article in the paper just this week about Dr. Welles. He's gotten so famous now that he even makes the national news. He's planning a dig in Egypt."

"And you'd like to go with him."

"More than anything in the world, but of course, it's impossible."

"Why is it impossible?"

Josh turned to her and saw that she was watching him carefully. Her eyes were wide spaced and so dark blue that they seemed to have no bottom. She had a woman's clean-edged lips, and a summer darkness tinged her skin where her dress opened at the neck, showing the smooth ivory of her throat. She was wearing a dress that had belonged to his sister Jenny, and he could not help but be aware of her gentle curves in the soft cotton frock. The light was kind to her, revealing the womanliness in face and figure, her face a mirror that changed as her feelings changed. Somewhat confused by his sudden awareness of this young woman who had come to mean so much in his life, he dropped his eyes. "I couldn't do it," he said. "I'd have to go back to college and learn ancient languages."

Kefira reached out suddenly and took his hand. She did this unthinkingly, for it was something she would not normally have done—in fact, had never done—but the dejection in Josh's sad face and stooping shoulders touched her. "You can do it if you want to, Josh," she whispered.

Josh was startled by her touch. He turned to her and saw the concern in her face. He suddenly lifted her hand, kissed it, and saw a rich flush come to her cheeks. "There's a kind heart speaking there." He stopped for a moment, then did something that shocked them both. Maybe the urges of a lone man always move toward a compassionate woman, but suddenly he wanted to touch her, for her nearness brought forth longings he had not felt for some time. It was not just her physical beauty that drew him, but that which lay beneath. There was a sweetness in her that trouble had not destroyed, and though he didn't understand why, she had the power to stir him and to touch his loneliness. He reached forward, kissed her on the lips, and for one brief moment she returned his kiss.

Her lips were soft and yielding under his, the lips of a giving woman—and then she suddenly pushed him back and anger flared in her eyes. She struck him in the chest with her fist and said, "Don't you ever do that again, Josh!"

Josh blinked and said quietly, "I'm sorry. I meant nothing by it, Kefira, but you're a comfort to a lonely man."

"Never touch me again!" Kefira rose, turned, and walked away, her back stiff and straight.

As Josh watched her go, he thought of what a hard time she must have had with men in her life, and knew he had been wrong. "What were you thinking about?" he accused himself bitterly. "You should have known better." The evening seemed spoiled now, and he sat there heavily, unable to recapture the excitement that had come to him. But he knew he would remember her kiss for a long time.

CHAPTER FOURTEEN

A HOUSE FILLED WITH LOVE

★ ★ ★ ★

Kefira found a special pleasure in helping Hannah, Missouri Ann, and Jenny. She had risen early on Saturday morning and all day long felt strong enough to work around the house. Actually there was plenty of work to do, for as she had discovered, the nearly hundred-year-old house had been allowed to run down considerably before the Winslows moved in and started fixing it up. She learned that it had been the girlhood home of Lewis's first wife, and almost every day someone managed to speak of how grateful they were to have had such a refuge when the Wall Street crash took away all their resources.

Kefira was both intrigued and troubled by the casual yet fervent way Missouri Ann and the other family members spoke of Jesus. She had been raised among people who despised Jesus Christ, so much that some of them simply refused to say the name. The best friend of her father had turned crimson when he spoke of the Christian faith and insisted on calling Jesus "that man." Such feelings had been common enough in New York among the Jewish community, and Kefira had absorbed it along with other cultural biases. Now, however, she saw that the Winslow house was filled with love, and for some reason this troubled her. Before she had come here, it had been easy to dislike Christians, but how could she dislike these people who laughed and obviously enjoyed life and had taken her in almost as a family member?

Perhaps her relationship with Kat had something to do with Kefira's warm feeling for the family. She had never met a youngster more natural or uninhibited. Kat simply said whatever came into her mind so that she was a creature without guile. It was April now and spring had come to the land, bringing the verdant odors of the earth, the loamy smell of the fields, and the warmth that would quicken the seeds Lewis and Clint planted. Kat had lured Kefira out on her expeditions into the woods, and Kefira was amazed at how the girl loved the out-of-doors. Kat seemed to know every footpath through the woods bordering the farm and had taken Kefira to the spots in the river where fish could be pulled out almost at will. There was a naturalness about Kat Winslow that made Kefira wish she herself had some of that same quality. At times she worried about the girl, who seemed to have no idea that there were monsters in the world—dangers and problems that lurked, waiting to destroy the naïve and the innocent. Kat simply moved through the world with wide-open eyes and somehow managed to keep the sweetest spirit Kefira had ever seen.

Kefira was mopping the hall that separated the bedrooms on the second floor when Kat thundered up the stairs. "Kefira, you've got to come and see our program at church!"

Kefira was wearing her hair tied up with a bandana to keep it clean, and she straightened up and smiled. "What kind of a program?"

"It's a play, and I've got a wonderful part!"

"What kind of a play is it?"

"I'm not going to tell, but you have to come. You will, won't you?"

Kefira had been waiting for Missouri Ann or Lewis or perhaps Josh to invite her to church, but so far they had not. Now the invitation came so naturally that she felt some assurance. "I suppose I could go. I'd like to see you in the play."

Kat danced over, reached up, and pulled Kefira down and kissed her noisily. "It'll be great! There'll be good singing too, and afterward there's going to be food to eat!"

"That's what food's good for," Kefira said, laughing. She watched as Kat went sailing down the stairs, taking them three at a time, and then looked up to see Missouri Ann come out of the bedroom on the end.

"Kat makes enough noise to wake the dead," Missouri Ann said, chuckling.

"She asked me to go to a program at church. Do you know anything about it?"

"Oh yes. She's been practicing for a couple of weeks now. I hope you'll come."

Kefira hesitated, and a troubled light came into her clear, dark blue eyes. "I've never been inside of a Christian church before."

"Well, I've never been in a synagogue either, but I'll tell you what. You go to church with me, and I'll go to synagogue with you."

Kefira smiled. "Is there one close?"

"Not that I know of. But maybe you can tell me what happens in one of your services. I'd be happy to learn all about it. And if we can find out if there's a synagogue near here, I'll go visit it with you."

Kefira knew that Missouri Ann Winslow would do exactly that. She had learned to respect this woman, so strong of body and so close to the earth. In a way she was Kat grown-up, with a naturalness and an inner beauty that intrigued Kefira. "All right," she said. "I'll take you up on that."

★ ★ ★ ★

Josh was sitting very still staring into the fire as Kefira came into the parlor late that same evening. She saw the newspaper on his lap and noted that he quickly folded it and put it away as he looked up to greet her. "It's been a long day. You're working too hard, Kefira."

"I don't think so." Kefira moved over and picked up the poker. She loved to stir the fire and watch the golden sparks rise up through the chimney. "We don't really need a fire tonight. It's so warm, but I like fires. We never had an open fireplace where I grew up. I don't think anyone did."

"We did at our house in New York. Of course, I was too dumb to appreciate them. I've gotten to where I like everything about fires. I even like going out cutting the trees and sawing them and then splitting them."

Kefira sat down and glanced at the paper and waited for him to mention it, but he did not. "Kat asked me to go to church for her program."

"I hope you'll go. She's real excited about it."

"I promised her I would, but I'm a little bit afraid. I've never been in a church before."

Josh smiled easily. "Nobody will jump on you, I'm sure. It's not a regular service anyway. A program for the children mostly. I'm glad you're going."

The two sat there watching the fire, and occasionally the logs gave off popping sounds, then sighed and settled down. The clock ticked loudly, and Josh mentioned that this clock had been in their family for a long time. "Our mother told me about it before she died. She loved it better than any other piece of furniture in the house. I'm glad it's still here."

"You miss her a lot, don't you, Josh?"

"Yes, I guess I always will." He turned and chewed his lower lip thoughtfully. "Missouri Ann is a wonderful woman. I'm glad Dad found her. Or she found him. However it was."

"What are you reading in the paper?" Kefira finally asked.

A disturbed look crossed Josh's countenance. "I was reading again about the dig my old professor, Dr. Welles, is going to make in Egypt."

Kefira remembered the last time they spoke about this, when he had kissed her. Neither had ever mentioned the moment again, and her guard had been up. But since that afternoon Josh had made no more advances, and she had grown comfortable again in his company. "I'd like to see you go on that dig, Josh," she said suddenly.

"I don't see how I could."

"Do you know how lucky you are, Josh?"

"Lucky!" He shook his head. "I'm a jailbird without a dime."

"But you know what you want to do."

"Knowing what someone wants to do isn't doing it. I missed my chance."

Kefira somehow felt strongly about this. She was surprised at what an intense interest she felt in Josh Winslow's life and well-being. Knowing that she had saved him from a terrible beating, perhaps saved his life, gave her a possessive feeling she could not explain. Leaning forward now, she said in an intense tone, "I think you ought to do what you want to do. There are so many people who can't, but you could, Josh."

"It would take money and I'm broke. Besides, I'm too old to start."

"You're strong and young, and money is not the biggest problem in the world. Suppose you were blind or crippled? Then you'd have no chance."

Josh gave her an astonished look. "Well, that's right, of course," he said. "But it's just like a mountain, Kefira."

"I heard your stepmother reading from your Bible the other day. It came from your New Testament. It was something about if a mountain's in your way, just speak to it."

"That's right," Josh smiled. "But I don't have Missouri Ann's faith."

Kefira said no more. She grew quiet, and finally she rose and said, "Good night, Josh. I wish you'd try to be what you want to be."

As soon as she left, Josh picked up the paper and read the story again. He had practically memorized the article, but now something began moving deep down inside. He was suddenly aware that Kefira's words had touched him deeply. *I've had life so easy, and now this thing that I want so much is right in front of me. I don't even know if Professor Welles would remember me, and there are probably fifty men begging him to be included in the expedition. There's no reason why he should choose me. Doesn't make any sense.* These thoughts rushed through his mind, but then again he remembered Kefira's intense expression and the warmth of her words as she had spoken. *"I wish you'd try to be what you want to be."* He got up too quickly, took a deep breath at the stab of pain, then went over to stand over the fire. He stared down into it, thinking intently and wondering if he had enough gumption to even try what Kefira suggested.

★　★　★　★

Kefira had expected to be as tense as a coiled spring at the church service but had been surprised to find out that after the initial fear, she relaxed and enjoyed the play very much. She knew several of the people who had gathered for the program, and several of them had come up to speak to her. She had felt inhibited at first and had said little as she sat between Josh and Jenny during the performance.

The action took place on a makeshift stage with curtains, which, Jenny informed her, she had worked on along with the other ladies. The play was composed of Bible stories from the New Testament acted out by the children. Kefira, of course, was not familiar with these, but she could follow the action quite easily. She was particularly delighted by Kat, who threw herself into the role with great vigor and spoke her lines loudly enough to be heard outside the church.

"She overacts a bit, but isn't she great?" Jenny whispered.

"She's wonderful," Kefira whispered back.

After the play ended, a tall, gangly, rather homely man stood up, and Jenny said, "That's Reverend Devoe Crutchfield. He's the pastor."

"Is he the one who was in love with you?" Kefira asked.

Jenny looked flustered. "Nothing like that! We're good friends."

Kefira was not sure about this, but she had no time to think, for Reverend Crutchfield had begun to speak. He had a good strong baritone voice and spoke warmly of the efforts of the children and those who had helped with the play. Finally he said, "I know you wouldn't expect to get by without a sermon. You can't keep a preacher quiet. However, I don't have one for you today." His eyes went over the congregation, and he said, "I was reading in the book of Deuteronomy in the first chapter this morning, and I was struck by one phrase. Moses had led the people out of Egypt, out of slavery and into the wilderness, but as you may remember, was not permitted to go to the Promised Land. He displeased God, as far as I can tell, once in his whole life, and God said because of that, Moses would not be permitted to go into the land for which he longed. I guess sometimes God seems hard, but I've often thought that instead of going to an earthly Promised Land, Moses went to be with God in the real Promised Land."

Kefira listened closely, for her father's favorite book had been the book of Deuteronomy. He had read it aloud so often that she had almost memorized it, and she recognized the instance of which the pastor spoke and listened as he read from the Scripture:

"'Joshua the son of Nun, which standeth before thee, he shall go in thither: encourage him: for he shall cause Israel to inherit it.'"

Reverend Crutchfield looked over the congregation and by accident, perhaps, his eyes met those of Kefira Reis. He smiled slightly and then raised his voice, speaking to the congregation. "God uses His people to encourage one another. He did not say to an angel, 'Gabriel, my servant Joshua is about to lead my people in Canaan. Go encourage him.' Gabriel would not have been half as fitted to do the encouraging as Moses and the people of Israel were. A brother's empathy is more precious than an angel's sympathy. An angel had never experienced the hardness of the road, nor seen the fiery serpents, nor led the stiff-necked multitude in the wilderness as Moses had. God usually works for a man by a man. He uses all of us to form a bond of brotherhood and sisterhood, and we're dependent on each other. So I ask you this evening to take this text as God's message to you. Encourage those whom you encounter. Speak cheerily to the young and the anxious who don't know what to do with their lives. Lovingly try to move stumbling blocks out of their way."

Kefira, who had come prepared to pay no attention to doctrine whatsoever in such a place as a Christian church, found herself warming to this advice. Perhaps because what she was hearing came from her father's favorite book, she leaned forward to listen more carefully, not conscious of the glances she got from Josh beside her.

"Comfort the sorrowful and do what you can for the desponding," the reverend continued. "Speak a word in season to him that's weary, and encourage those who are fearful to go on their way. God encourages you by His promises, and Jesus encourages you as He points to the heaven He's won for you. I encourage you this evening to take this word from God personally. Someone needs your voice of assurance. Give it to him or her by the Spirit of God."

Suddenly Kefira leaned back, and she reached over and took Josh's arm and turned her head toward him, whispering, "You see. The reverend says to encourage people, and that's what I've tried to do with you, Josh."

Josh sat absolutely still, aware of Kefira's hand on his arm. Then he turned to face her and whispered, "You're quite an encourager, Kefira."

The two, for that one single moment, felt as if they were alone. Reverend Crutchfield was still speaking, but each of them felt a special communion, something that had passed from one spirit to another, and this made Kefira feel very good inside.

Reverend Crutchfield ended his short comments with, "I'm going to take a few moments to allow God to speak to your hearts. If God has given any of you a special blessing, or if you have a special need, just let it be known."

Kefira did not know what this meant, but suddenly a tall, lean man sitting in the front row arose and said with a joyful voice, "I want to thank God for healing my daughter, Carrie. We'd just about given up, but the prayers of God's people went up, and now Carrie is right here with me, completely healed by the miracle of God." He reached down and held up a small girl, and the room was filled with voices saying, "Amen" and "Bless you, brother."

For some time people stood up, some of them weeping as they shared sorrows, others telling triumphant stories of what God had done for them. Kefira had never encountered anything like this. She had seen friendship and good strong ties between members of the synagogue, but this was a real family. It was obvious from their dress that most of these people were poor. But as they spoke of their faith in Jesus Christ, she could not help but be moved.

The service ended, and Kat came out at once, her eyes glowing. "Did you see me, Kefira?"

"I did, and I heard you too. You did wonderfully well. I was *very* proud of you."

Kefira sat next to Missouri Ann in the front seat of the truck for the ride home, and the others were loaded into the back. Missouri Ann asked her, "Did you enjoy the play?"

"It was very good, and the people standing up and talking. What did the preacher call it?"

"A testimony service."

"They all believe so much in God."

"Well, of course they do!" Missouri Ann said. "That's what a church is. Do you have anything like that in your synagogue?"

"Not really," Kefira said slowly. "I've never seen anything like that. Do you do it often?"

"Fairly often at our church. Sometimes people have so much to say that Brother Crutchfield doesn't get to preach, but that doesn't bother him. We all love to hear the stories of victory in God's people."

Kefira said no more, but all the way home and later in bed that night she went over the scene again and wondered, *How can these Christians be so different? There's something in them I don't understand.* It troubled her, and she went to sleep thinking about Josh and about the preacher's advice to encourage him. She had taken it personally, and now she felt that she had done the right thing.

★ ★ ★ ★

Two days after the play, Kefira was helping Missouri Ann peel potatoes when Clint came in with an envelope in his hand. "A letter for you, Kefira."

"For me? It must be from my brother." Taking the envelope, she saw that her name and the address were in a handwriting she didn't recognize. The postmark was from New York. Nervously she opened the envelope and read the few lines. It was on the letterhead of the state prison system of New York and said briefly:

> *My dear Miss Reis,*
>   *I am the chaplain at the prison here, and I am grieved to inform you that your brother is very ill. If it is at all possible, I think you should come and visit him. I've gotten your address from the letters you mailed to him and think it might be wise if you would come as quickly as possible.*
>
>   *Sincerely yours,*
>   *Chaplain Daniel Stokes*

Kefira's face gave her away, and Missouri Ann asked, "What is it, dear, bad news?"

"It's my brother. He's in prison, and he's very ill." She folded the envelope with unsteady hands and said, "I have to go to him."

"Of course you do, but you can't go tonight. You'll have to wait until morning."

Kefira hardly heard Missouri's words. She was thinking, *How can I possibly get back to New York? I don't have any money. I'll have to ride the rails, and I think Chaim must be very ill indeed for the chaplain to write the way he has.*

Kefira said little that night at the supper table. She was relatively sure that Missouri Ann had shared her bad news with the others, for she caught the sidelong looks they gave her. After supper she went to her room and went to bed early, tossing for a long time, trying to think of a way to get to New York more quickly.

A light tap at her door gave her a start, and she climbed out of bed and opened the door. She found Missouri Ann wearing a robe and slippers and holding a lantern in her hand. "I need to talk to you, Kefira."

"Why . . . come in."

Missouri Ann entered, set the lamp down, and turned to face Kefira. "I've been praying for hours, and the Lord has spoken to me. I want to pray for your brother."

Kefira stared at the older woman. "Well, of course, if you'd like." She bowed her head, but Missouri Ann pulled her over to the bed and the two knelt down together. For a long time there was only silence, so much so that Kefira wondered if this was all there was to the prayer. But then Missouri Ann began to call upon God. There was an earnestness in her voice almost like pain, and Kefira had never heard anyone ever pray like this. It was as if one of her own children were dreadfully ill, and Kefira found herself transfixed by the agony of the woman.

The prayer lasted for a long time, but finally Missouri Ann grew silent. She turned then and tears, Kefira saw, were running down her cheeks. "Your brother is healed."

Kefira did not know what to make of this. "Why, that's . . . that's good, Mrs. Winslow."

"You don't believe me, but it's so. Look at the clock. It's two in the morning. Wherever your brother is God has touched him, for the Lord God himself has told me so." Missouri Ann got to her feet, and Kefira followed suit. Missouri Ann put her arms around the young woman, hugged her, and then picked up the lantern and left without another word.

Kefira was mystified. She went back to bed and thought about the strange encounter for a long time before finally dropping off into a troubled sleep.

★　★　★　★

"Kefira, I stayed up most of the night, and God gave me another word for you."

Kefira had come down the stairs and was met at the foot of them by Missouri Ann.

"What is it?" She hardly knew how to take these declarations. She was not accustomed to people saying that God had spoken to them personally, and it frightened her.

"You must go to your brother at once."

"Yes, I know that, Mrs. Winslow."

"God told me that Josh should go with you, and He told me to give you the money so that you can take the train." She handed Kefira an envelope, and Kefira stared at it. "I can't take your money."

"God told me to give it to you. Don't worry, daughter. You can't outgive God. God will probably restore this to me thirty or even a hundredfold."

Kefira stood there looking into the plain strong face of Missouri Ann Winslow. She did not know what to say, but a lump formed in her throat. No one had ever done anything like this for her before.

Missouri Ann added, "I had a word for Josh too. I've already given it to him. He knows he's got to go with you. God gave me a specific word for him."

"A word? What was it?"

"It came right clear. God told me to tell Josh, 'Go with Kefira to New York, and you'll find your dream.'"

Kefira could only stand there helplessly, but tears rose in her eyes. She had never seen kindness such as filled this house, and now she threw herself into Missouri Ann's arms and clung to her, weeping as she had not done for a long time. Finally she drew back and said, "If your God can do this, He can do anything."

"He's a big God, daughter. Trust Him!"

CHAPTER FIFTEEN

A NOTABLE MIRACLE

★   ★   ★   ★

Looking out the window of the train, Kefira noted the familiar signs. They would be arriving at Sing Sing in a few moments, and she straightened up and fought off the fear and depression that had filled her. All the way from Georgia she had been torn between hope and despair. She remembered the prayers of Missouri Ann and the confidence in the woman's voice and in her eyes—but life had treated her harshly enough that she had come to expect the worst.

Turning away from the window, she said, "We're almost there, Josh."

Josh glanced out the window and then met Kefira's eyes. He noted that lines of strain marked her face and that her eyes were cloudy with doubt. He reached over and squeezed her forearm, saying quietly, "It'll be all right, Kefira. You'll see."

Kefira shook her head and murmured, "I don't think so. I'm afraid, Josh."

"There's a verse in the Bible that says 'With God all things are possible.' I believe that. Not as much as Missouri Ann maybe, but I know it's true."

A warmth came to Kefira then, and she was very conscious of his hand on her arm. Suddenly she thought of how she had struck him when he had kissed her. The scene had troubled her, for as she thought back on it, she knew his embrace had been innocent. He had not been like other men, and she was wise enough to realize that. For some time she had been trying to find a way to tell him this, and now as the train began to slow down, she said quickly, "Josh, you'll never know how much it helps to have somebody with me. I've been alone so much, and I am so grateful that you came with me."

"I'm glad I'm here."

"And, Josh . . ." Kefira hesitated for a moment, then met his eyes. Her lips were soft and tremulous as she formed the words, "I'm sorry for the way I acted down at the river."

Instantly Josh knew what this apology had cost Kefira. He squeezed her arm again and then removed his hand. "It was nothing, Kefira. But I want you to know this. I'll always be a brother to you."

Something about this disturbed Kefira. She shook her head and said at once, "You're *not* my brother, Josh."

Josh was surprised, but at that moment the conductor came through calling out, "Ossining! All out for Ossining!" The train came to a grinding halt, and Josh got up and stepped aside to let Kefira precede him down the aisle. When they had stepped out onto the platform, Kefira said, "We get on that bus to go to the prison." She led him to the bus and the two got on. When the visitors were all inside and seated, the driver shut the door and moved out slowly. Josh sat quietly beside Kefira during the short trip to Sing Sing Prison, studying the faces of those who were on their way to visit the inmates. Most of them, it seemed, were from a lower station of life, but he saw one woman dressed in expensive clothes wearing a brilliant diamond on her left hand. She was an attractive woman in her fifties, he supposed, and there was something in her carriage that caught his eye. "I wonder who she's going to see," he whispered to Kefira.

Kefira came out of her thoughts and studied the woman. "She's rich, isn't she?"

"I expect so, judging from that rock on her finger."

"Maybe she's visiting her son, or it could be her brother or husband."

"Things like this level people," Josh murmured. "I mean, she's no better off than that woman sitting in front of her. She's obviously poor, but both of them have the same problem."

"I suppose most of us have the same problems really."

"That's what the Bible says. It doesn't always appear that way, but Job says, 'Man is born unto trouble, as the sparks fly upward.'"

"My father used to quote that Scripture a lot. It's from the book of Job."

"I believe it is. Your father read to you a lot from the Scriptures, didn't he?"

"Every night. I still seem to hear his voice sometimes."

After passing through the prison gates, the bus pulled up in front of the gray building. "That's it there," Kefira said as they stepped off. The visitors all headed toward the reception area, and when they were inside, Kefira said to the guard checking identification, "I would like to see Chaplain Stokes."

The guard lifted his eyes and considered her for a moment. He was a thin man with a thin mouth and a careless look on his face. "Go wait in that room right over there. I'll send word for him to come."

Josh presented his driver's license, and the guard looked at the list. "You're not on the list. You'll have to wait here while the lady visits her brother."

"That's fine. Is it all right if I wait for the chaplain with her?"

"Yes."

Kefira and Josh went into the room that the guard had indicated, which contained a few straight-back chairs and a small table—nothing else. They sat down, and the tension built up in Kefira. She was unable to speak, and her mind was so totally concentrated on her brother, she was startled when the door opened and a short, heavyset man strode in.

"I'm Chaplain Stokes," he said. He had rosy cheeks and bright blue eyes and a wealth of blond hair, carefully combed.

"I'm Chaim Reis's sister," she said as she rose from her chair. "My name is Kefira."

"Yes, I know about you. Chaim has told me."

"This is my friend Joshua Winslow."

"Glad to know you, Mr. Winslow."

"How is my brother?" The words rushed breathlessly from Kefira's lips, and she felt strangely weak. For some reason she had been haunted by the idea that Chaim had died and the chaplain was here to break the bad news.

Chaplain Stokes saw the young woman's agitation. "I've got good news," he said. "He's much, much better."

"Thank God!" Kefira breathed. She felt weak for a moment and put her hand to her forehead, swaying slightly. Instantly Josh was beside her, his arm around her, supporting her. She leaned against him, grateful for his thoughtfulness.

"Here, you'd better sit down," the chaplain said. He waited until Josh helped Kefira to a chair, then said, "He was very ill, Miss Reis. The doctors were not at all optimistic, and I think Chaim himself had about given up on living."

"What was it, Chaplain?" Josh asked.

"The doctors never really decided. He got a terrible rash that went into a fever and that went into pneumonia. It went around. Several of the prisoners caught it, and two of them died. We get a lot of people from different places here, and the doctors think one of them brought something in. It could have even been a disease from overseas. Maybe from South America or somewhere."

"Could I see him, Chaplain?" Kefira asked.

"Of course."

"The guard said I wouldn't be able to go," Josh said.

"Oh, it'll be all right. I'll take you on my authority. Come along both of you."

The two followed Chaplain Stokes out of the small room and down the corridor. It was not the same route that Kefira had taken before to the visitors' room, and the chaplain explained, "He's not in his cell now. He's in the infirmary. He'll be there until he's fully recovered."

Chaplain Stokes led the way until they reached a door labeled INFIRMARY in plain block letters, and a guard greeted the chaplain pleasantly as they entered. "He's in this ward over here," Stokes said.

He led them into another room where there were six beds.

Only two of them were occupied, one by a man who lay flat on his back staring up at the ceiling, but Kefira cried out with joy when she saw Chaim sitting up in the other bed with a book.

"Chaim!" she said and went to his side at once.

"Kefira, it's you!"

Josh stood back, watching as the two embraced. He got a favorable impression of Chaim Reis, who was in better condition than he had expected. He saw the resemblance between the two, for Chaim had the same dark blue eyes and black hair and high cheekbones as his sister. The chaplain stepped outside, murmuring something Josh did not hear, and then Kefira straightened up and said, "This is my friend Joshua Winslow. Josh, this is my brother, Chaim."

As the two men shook hands, Josh was aware of Chaim watching him carefully. "I'm glad to meet you, Chaim. Kefira's told me so much about you."

"She's told me a little bit about you too, in her letters."

"If it hadn't been for Josh's mother, I couldn't have gotten here so quick. And she insisted that Josh come along to look after me."

Chaim smiled then, and the resemblance to his sister was even clearer. They had the same way of smiling and the same way of holding their heads to one side when they spoke.

"I appreciate what you've done for my sister."

"I guess she didn't tell you all of it. It's what she's done for me that's important."

"Oh, don't go into all that, Josh!" Kefira said quickly.

"I'll go into it this much," Josh said. "Your sister saved my life."

Chaim turned instantly to look at Kefira, who flushed and said, "He's making more of it than there really was."

But nothing would do except for her to tell the story. Chaim listened with deep interest, and finally when she had finished, he smiled and said, "And so my sister really saved your life!"

"Oh, it wasn't that dramatic. Tell me about yourself, Chaim. How do you feel? Oh," she said, "we brought you some fruit."

Josh had been carrying the basket of fruit and supplies that they had brought with them. Chaim picked up an apple and stared at it. "A real apple," he said. "I haven't had one since I've been here. Do you mind if I eat it now?"

"Of course not. Go right ahead," Kefira said.

The two watched as Chaim bit into the apple and chewed it slowly, savoring the taste. "One of the things I miss in here is good fresh fruit."

Chaim insisted that Kefira tell him what she had been doing, and as he ate the apple with great enjoyment, his dark eyes went often to Josh Winslow. He said nothing until she had finished, then he said to Josh, "I'm thankful to you and your family for taking care of my sister."

"Well, it was probably my fault she got sick, so it was nothing we need to be thanked for. My family has pretty well adopted her."

Kefira said, "They are a wonderful family, Chaim. I hope you get to meet them when you get out." She reached out and pushed a lock of black hair from his forehead and said, "I'm so glad you're better. I was frightened nearly to death."

"It was pretty serious. I thought I was going to die."

"I guess the doctors must have done a good job on you," Josh commented. "I understand it was a serious illness that went through the prison."

"I don't think the doctors had much to do with it."

"What do you mean, Chaim?" Kefira asked, surprised by his words.

"I was dying, sis. It was like being sucked into a big black hole, and late one night I knew that death was coming for me. I'd heard of people who knew death was coming, but this was real. I felt myself slipping away, and then—" Chaim suddenly ran his hands through his hair, and a strange look crossed his face. He reached out and took Kefira's hand and said, "Something happened. I suddenly knew that I wasn't going to die. It was as if God himself came into the room and put his hand on me."

Suddenly Kefira asked, "When was this, Chaim?"

"It was last Thursday, about two o'clock in the morning."

Kefira felt electricity run through her, and she turned to Josh, who was watching her carefully. "That was when Missouri Ann came into my room to pray for Chaim. I remember looking at the clock, and it was exactly two o'clock."

"Who is this?" Chaim asked, puzzled.

"It's Josh's stepmother. Her name is Missouri Ann. She came to my room and said she had to pray for you. We knelt down beside the bed, and I didn't understand it all. But you should have heard her, Chaim. She prayed like her heart was going to be torn out of her. I was actually afraid for her she prayed so hard. And finally she turned to me, and she said, 'Your brother's healed.'"

Chaim stared at her open eyed. "I've never heard of such a thing!" he exclaimed.

"Neither have I, but it was exactly two o'clock in the morning on Thursday."

Chaim dropped his head and stared at his hands that he had clasped together. He squeezed them together, and finally he looked up and said, "I knew God was in it, but I've never heard of anything like this before. You know what, sis? I've doubted God ever since I've been here. Everything's so terrible. But now I don't think I can do that anymore."

Kefira moved forward and put her arms around her brother and held him. "Neither can I, Chaim," she whispered huskily.

★　★　★　★

"I've decided to take your advice, Kefira."

Kefira looked up at Josh. The two were on the bus headed back for the train that would take them back to New York City.

"What do you mean, Josh?"

"I'm going to see Professor Welles."

"The man who's taking the trip to Egypt?"

"Yes, I'm going to ask him to take me with him." He turned to her and laughed ruefully. "He probably doesn't remember me. He may even have me thrown out."

"No he won't! I think that's wonderful, Josh! I'll tell you what. Why don't we get a place to stay tonight, and then I can see some of my old friends."

"All right. Missouri Ann gave us enough money to stay a few days at a hotel, but it'll have to be a cheap one, I'm afraid."

"Anything will do."

The two found rooms in a run-down hotel on the Lower East Side. They were on the same floor but not adjoining. When they had deposited their meager belongings in their rooms, Josh said, "It probably won't take me long to get thrown out of Professor Welles's offices. I'll meet you here at six o'clock."

"All right, Josh, but remember. If God can heal my brother, He can give you this position."

Josh suddenly reached out and took both of Kefira's hands in his. He smiled down at her and shook his head. "You'd better be careful or you're going to have as much faith as Missouri Ann." He squeezed her hands, turned, and left.

Kefira watched him go, and then she left the hotel herself. Her old neighborhood was not too far, and she decided to walk. As she moved down the streets of New York looking at the familiar buildings and watching the faces of the people, it seemed she had been gone for years.

Curiosity overcame her, and she deliberately walked by the shop where Adolph Kurtz had sent her off on her travels by his unwanted attention. When she reached it she was surprised to see that the building was empty and had a FOR RENT sign on it. She wondered what happened to Kurtz and knew if she could find Millie Johnson, she would get the entire story.

She went at once to Millie's house. She knocked on the door and was met by a tall, gaunt woman. Millie's mother, she supposed.

The woman asked, "Can I help you?"

"I'm looking for Millie."

"Oh, she doesn't live with us anymore. She got married."

Kefira was disappointed, for she had hoped to see her old friend. "May I ask where she lives now?"

"She and her new husband moved down to Pittsburgh after the wedding."

Kefira thanked the woman and turned to leave. Then she quickly turned back. "I noticed that the shop where she worked is closed."

The tall woman laughed abruptly and forcefully. "I'll say it's closed! Adolph Kurtz put his hands on one woman too many."'

Blinking with surprise, Kefira asked, "What do you mean?"

"He was trying to force himself on one of the women there, and her husband came in and caught him." A broad smile creased the woman's lips, and she shook her head in satisfaction. "He fixed Kurtz for good. Put him in the hospital for two months. He lost his lease and went broke."

Kefira thanked the woman again. When the door closed and Kefira turned away, she was seized by a savage satisfaction. "He got what he deserved," she murmured. As she walked away down the street, she found herself reveling in the downfall of Adolph Kurtz. But then she began to have second thoughts. *He was an evil man, but I don't think I should rejoice in anyone's misfortune.* She was surprised at this streak of generosity in her and could not imagine where it had come from.

★　★　★　★

"I'd like to see Dr. Welles please."

"He's back in his office. What's your name? I'll see if he's got time for you." The speaker was a small woman, rather sprightly, in her midsixties.

"My name's Joshua Winslow."

The woman stared at Josh suspiciously, her dark eyes almost glinting. "You sit right over there. I'll see if the doctor's available."

Josh felt chastened by the woman's attitude, and he did not sit. *I may not be here long enough to make it worth my while sitting down*, he thought. Anxiety gripped him and his hands were sweating. He had not realized until this moment how much he wanted to go on the expedition with Dr. Welles. It had all begun with Kefira's urging, and now he steeled himself to failure. *It's been so long ago, and we weren't really all that close.* He hesitated, then said, "God, I ask you to help me get this job."

Even as he said the prayer, he heard footsteps and turned to see Phineas Welles bustling down the hall. He was shocked, for the professor looked exactly as he had the last time he had seen him all those years ago. Welles approached with a smile and out-stretched hand, saying, "Well, well, well, it's you, Joshua!" Welles was a small man no more than five-six with graying blond hair, light blue eyes, and fair skin. He had a high forehead and a mild appearance, except that his eyes gleamed when he was excited. They gleamed now.

"Joshua, my boy, how wonderful to see you again!"

Josh took the professor's hand, and relief washed through him. "I wasn't sure you'd remember me, Professor."

"Remember you! Why, I may be getting older, but I'm not senile yet. Come back into my office. I want to hear all about what you're doing. How in the world did you ever find me?"

Josh felt his arm seized, and he was practically dragged down the hall to the professor's office. The professor motioned to a chair, but Josh remained standing as he answered questions that the professor threw at him, trying to be absolutely honest with him. Finally the professor asked, "What are you doing here, my boy?"

"I came to ask you for a job." There, the words were out. He saw surprise wash across the professor's mild features and has-tened to say, "I know you must have turned away hundreds of men for this dig, but I'll work for nothing. Just for food, and I'll find a place to sleep." The words began to tumble over Josh's lips, and he had no idea what an appealing figure he made as he stood there—tall and fine looking and yet somewhat pathetic in his eagerness.

"I'll have to tell you this, Professor. I haven't led a good life. My family spoiled me rotten, and when we lost everything in the crash, I got into illegal activities. Delivering moonshine in Geor-gia. I went to jail for it."

Welles listened quietly. He was sitting across from Josh, and now he said briskly, "Well, I'm glad you told me all this, Joshua. I'm sorry that you've had such troubles."

"All my own fault, Professor. All of my making."

"And so you want to go to Egypt. Well, I remember what a hard worker you were. I'll tell you what," he said. "My brother Conrad is funding this expedition. He's the one with the money in the family." A sour look came to him for a moment, and he shook his head. "He wants me to find riches over in Egypt. Golden masks and things like that. He's read about Howard Carter and Lord Carnarvon—the men who discovered Tutankhamen's tomb, you know—and he thinks all we have to do is go over there and turn over a shovelful of sand and find another unrobbed tomb. Why, my boy, I doubt there's another tomb in Egypt that hasn't been plundered."

"You'd never be interested in that. What are you going for, Professor?"

"My boy, I have a deep feeling that somewhere in Egypt there's a record of the Hebrews. Maybe even of Moses himself. Maybe even of Abraham. He was in Egypt, you know."

"Yes, I know."

"Well, I'm going to find it. My brother's furnishing the money, and I've got a chance. I'd like for you to go with me."

Josh felt like shouting. He got to his feet and stepped quickly to take the professor's hand. "I can never thank you enough, Professor!" he exclaimed. "I'll do anything."

"Well, don't make so much of it, my boy. It's going to be a lot of hard work. You remember how it was in the digs—you worked for six months for one moment's triumph. Listen, you'll have to go to my brother's office first." He reached into his pocket, pulled out a card, and handed it to him. "He will have to approve you. Go see him at once, then come back. If he says he'll take you, then we'll both be happy."

Josh left the office and almost broke into a run. He found himself wanting to shout, but then caution came to him. "I've got to please Conrad Welles, and from what I hear about him, he's a hard man to please."

★   ★   ★   ★

"I'm not going to put up with this, Diana!" Conrad Welles stood before his daughter, a grim look in his hazel eyes. He was a strongly built man, tanned, with iron gray hair and a square face. He was obviously accustomed to having his own way, and now as he stared at Diana, he said roughly, "You're not going to drive a car anymore! The very idea of getting arrested for driving while intoxicated! I'm ashamed of you!"

Diana Welles took after her mother. She was tall and willowy with blond hair, green eyes, and rather spectacular coloring. She was not at all upset by her father's warnings, and now she simply reached up and patted him on the cheek.

"You can't keep me from driving, Dad. Unfortunately—from your point of view—I have money that mother left me."

This was, indeed, a sore point for Conrad Welles. After his wife had died in an automobile accident, he discovered that in her will she had left her sizable fortune directly to Diana, so from that point onward, Diana had done exactly as she pleased.

"I'm spoiled, and it's all your fault," Diana said. She pulled her father's head down and kissed him on the cheek. "Don't worry about me, Dad. I'm all right."

"Your mother could have raised you better than I have." This was a stupendous admission for Conrad Welles, who never liked to admit that anyone could do anything better than he. There was affection in his words as well as regret. He missed his wife, and he did feel that Diana would have been a different woman had her mother lived. At the age of twenty-seven Diana had married a Hollywood movie star, who had proved to be completely worthless, had divorced him, and since then had led a dissolute life. Still, Conrad Welles loved this daughter of his. She was, he understood, much like him—self-willed, strong-minded, and determined to win at whatever she did.

The buzzer on Welles's desk sounded, and he turned away from Diana, pushing the button. "What is it, Irene?"

"A gentleman to see you, sir. He has a note from your brother."

"Send him in."

Diana walked over to the window and said, "I'll be going now. I'll see you at dinner tonight."

"All right, but please don't drink and drive."

"You worry too much, Dad."

Diana turned to go, and the door opened. She took one look at the man who entered and stopped dead still. For one moment she did not speak, and then she said, "Josh, it's you!"

Conrad Welles stared at the man who had come in. He was not expensively dressed but was a rather handsome fellow—lean and tall with tawny hair and gray eyes. He saw shock come into the man's eyes and then heard him say, "Why—Diana!"

Diana went at once and put her hand out, and Conrad saw the man take it. He seemed speechless, and Diana said, "Why, you're more handsome than you were back in college!" She turned and said, "Dad, this is Josh Winslow. We went to college together."

Conrad moved around and took Winslow's hand. "Glad to know you, Winslow." His eyes went to Diana, who was smiling brightly. "So, you were in college with my daughter."

"Yes, sir, but I didn't make it all the way through, as I'm sure she did."

Diana laughed. She had a good laugh, wholesome and healthy. "No, you're wrong. I didn't make it either. We're two dropouts, Josh. I'm surprised, though. You were the smartest one in the whole class. Uncle Phineas loved you."

"What's this all about? You knew Phineas in those days, Winslow?"

"He was one of my professors, Mr. Welles."

"Josh was his favorite student," Diana said. "I think he was mine too." Her eyes danced with pleasure, and she laughed. "I still remember those times we had in Louisiana on the dig with Uncle Phineas."

"I remember them too," Josh said. Then he turned to Welles, saying, "I've asked your brother to take me on the expedition, but he says you will have to approve my employment."

"Well, I'm sorry, but I've already hired all the men Phineas will need. He'll be working with a primarily Egyptian crew on this dig." As Welles spoke these words, he watched the reaction of the young man. He had turned many men down and expected some sort of strong reaction, but he did not get it. Winslow simply nodded and said, "I was afraid it would be that way. Thank you for your time, Mr. Welles."

He turned and said, "It's good to see you again, Diana."

He left the office and passed through the reception room.

When he was out in the hall, however, he heard his name and turned around to see Diana. She came up to him and said, "Don't be discouraged, Josh. I'll talk to Dad. Where can I call you?"

"I don't have a phone."

"Well, here. This is my number. You call me tomorrow." She came and stood beside him, pressed herself against him, and said in a silky voice, "Do you really remember the old days, Josh, the times we had?"

"I could never forget, Diana."

She smiled and touched his cheek. "Be sure and call me tomorrow. I'll work on Dad. It'll be all right. You'll see."

CHAPTER SIXTEEN

TWO FOR THE PRICE OF ONE

★ ★ ★ ★

"I know a place we can eat, Josh," Kefira said. "It's not too far from here, and it's very good—and it's cheap too."

Josh smiled at Kefira. The two of them had met as agreed at six in front of the hotel, and now he said, "That's good. I'm starved."

"It's only a few blocks. We can walk."

The two of them made their way along the busy street, and Josh commented once, "I've gotten so used to being in the country that this all seems strange to me."

"You know, I feel the same way, even though I haven't been gone long. I'm glad to be away from New York, though. It doesn't have very many good memories for me."

For a moment Josh considered asking her what she was planning to do now, but he had slept poorly the previous night thinking about this very question. She was so alone in the world, and now that there seemed to be some possibility of his going to Egypt, the thought of her future troubled him. He said nothing about this, however, until she led him to a small restaurant and stopped him before going in. "It's Jewish food. You might not like it."

"I liked it when you cooked it," Josh said. "I don't see why I wouldn't."

The two went inside, and Josh saw that, indeed, it was a small place. There were no more than seven or eight tables, and most of them were full. He heard someone call Kefira's name, and he turned to see a short, very heavyset woman with black hair and eyes to match come forward.

"Why, Kefira, it's you!"

"Hello, Sarah. It's good to see you again."

Sarah was obviously the proprietor. She wore a black dress with a white apron over it. "You come and sit down. I want to hear what all you've been doing." She turned and said, "Ah, is this your husband?"

Kefira flushed. "No, this is a very good friend of mine. Mr. Joshua Winslow, this is Sarah Goldman."

Sarah stared at the young man, clinically examining him, then smiled. "You come, and I will feed you. You need to fatten up."

"Well, that's speaking right out," Josh said, grinning. He went to the table against the back wall and pulled the chair out for Kefira.

She looked at him, surprised and yet pleased at his fine manners. She was not used to such things and, flashing a glance at Sarah, saw that she noted it too. She waited until Josh sat down and then she said, "We want the very best you have, Sarah."

"Ah, that's what your papa always said." She turned to Joshua, saying, "Her father. What a *mench* he was!"

"What's a *mench*?" Josh asked.

"A good man," Sarah nodded knowingly. "And her mama. Such a fine woman. And how is your brother?"

"He's doing fine, Sarah. He'll be out in about a year."

"That is good. I miss your family. Now, you sit right there, and you must eat everything I bring out to you."

The meal that she brought out seemed enormous to Josh. First there were *holishkes,* or stuffed cabbage, for each of them, and then there was a fish called lox, which was really smoked salmon, followed by *lokshen,* noodles which were highly spiced and very delicious. Josh was eating enthusiastically when a memory came to him. He looked up at Sarah as she laid another dish on the table and said, "Me ken lecken di finger."

Sarah's eyes widened with surprise. "Oh, so you speak Yiddish!"

"Not really. It's just something that Kefira taught us when she was cooking for us."

Finally Sarah brought out a dish of small pastries, and Josh said, "I know what these are. They're vareniki."

Sarah laughed. "You are a smart young man. Do you like your supper?"

"Very much, Miss Sarah."

The two sat there drinking the strong tea that Sarah served them in small cups, and finally Josh said to Kefira, "I have some news."

"Did you get the job?" Kefira leaned forward, her eyes intent.

"Not yet." Josh explained his visit with Professor Welles and then his subsequent interview with Conrad Welles. "He told me no, but his daughter was there—Diana. She caught me as I was leaving and said not to give up. She asked me to call her tomorrow. She thought maybe she could talk her father into hiring me."

"Why would she do that? You don't know her, do you?"

"Well, as a matter of fact . . ." For some reason Josh found it hard to explain Diana to Kefira. He took a quick sip of the tea and then found the words to say it. "As a matter of fact, Diana and I are old friends. That is, we were in college together. I was on a dig with her uncle, and she went along. It was the mound digging that I told you about."

"But do you think she can tell her father what to do?"

"She always has," Josh said wryly. "She's very spoiled, I'm afraid."

"What is she like?"

Josh looked up with surprise. "Well, her father's a very wealthy man. She's always had everything she wanted. She married a movie star. I saw it in the papers, but later she divorced him. I don't know why."

"But what does she look like?"

"She looks good enough."

"Josh, tell me what she looks like. Why won't you talk about her?"

"I *will* talk about her," Josh said, irritated for a moment. "She's tall and has blond hair and green eyes."

"Is she beautiful?"

Josh twisted his head nervously. "Yes, I suppose you might say that."

Kefira continued to pursue the question of Diana Wells in a most uncomfortable way as far as Josh was concerned. She wanted to know everything about the woman, and finally she stared at Josh and said, "I don't see why she should try to get you a job—unless you two were very close."

Josh did not answer immediately, and suddenly Kefira knew that there was more to his relationship with this woman than he was telling. She stared at him fixedly for a moment and then shook her head. "Well, I hope you get the job."

"I probably won't," he said. "But now tell me about what you did all day. . . ."

★ ★ ★ ★

Josh slept poorly that night, and in the morning waited impatiently until ten o'clock. He did not think it would be proper to call Diana any earlier, but finally he left his hotel room, went downstairs, and used the phone in the lobby. He dialed the number Diana had given him, and at once her voice spoke out. "Hello?"

"Hello, Diana, this is Josh."

"Oh, Josh, I'm so glad you called. Look, everything's going to be fine. I talked to Dad, and he's agreed that you can go on the dig."

"Diana, that's wonderful! How did you do it?"

Diana laughed throatily. "Women have their ways. I'll tell you what. My father's pretty busy today, but let's you and I go out tonight and have dinner. Afterward you come home with me, and we'll corner him."

Josh hesitated only for an instant. Somehow this seemed a

roundabout way to get a position, but still there was no other door open. "All right, Diana, but it can't be anything fancy. I don't have the clothes for it."

"I'll pick you up in front of your hotel. Where is it?" Josh gave her the name of the hotel, and she said, "I'll pick you up at six. Be ready. We'll have fun, just like old times."

"All right, Diana." Josh hung up slowly and for a moment he was perturbed. He was still bruised emotionally over his affair with Dora Skinner and had no desire to get involved in the same way again. Still, Diana was the door to the dream of his life, and he really had no other choice. He went back upstairs and knocked on Kefira's door. She opened it at once, and he saw that she was fully dressed. "Let's go have breakfast," he said. "I've got some good news."

"What is it, Josh?"

"I just called Diana, and she said she's got her father talked into the notion of hiring me. He's busy today, but she wants me to meet him tonight."

"That's wonderful, Josh! Maybe you and I can go out and have supper together."

"Well, actually she wants to meet me for supper, but you and I can have breakfast and lunch."

Kefira stared at Josh, then said briefly, "That's fine." She stepped outside, closed the door, and the two went down to breakfast. Josh spoke very rapidly, for he had seen something come into Kefira's eyes when he had mentioned having dinner with Diana. For some reason this made him feel guilty, although he could not imagine why.

They ate breakfast at a restaurant across the street. The breakfast special was ham and eggs, but Kefira said, "I can't have the ham, but I'll have the eggs."

Josh said, "Maybe you could have something else. Eggs won't last you long."

"They're fine."

There was a constraint between the two, and Josh tried to break it by speaking of the possibilities in Egypt. But he finally came to what had been on his mind ever since the possibility of his leaving the country had become real. "What do you want to do, Kefira? Where do you want to go?"

"I'm going to the coast. That was where I was going when we met. I just got interrupted a bit."

"Yes, by saving my life," Josh said. He stirred his coffee idly, staring down into the cup, then took a sip from it. "Look," he said, "why don't you go stay with my folks. They would love to have you."

"I couldn't do that."

"Why not?"

Kefira could not answer truthfully. As a matter of fact, she herself had an inclination to go back to the Winslow house. It had been a place of refuge for her, but somehow she knew with Josh gone it would not be the same. "I'll stay here for another week, perhaps, and go see Chaim as often as I can. Maybe it's selfish of me to go south. Maybe I need to get a job where I can visit him."

"New York's a hard place for a young woman alone."

"I know that well enough."

Josh found himself unable to speak what was on his mind. He wanted to see Kefira safe and secure, and the idea of going off to Egypt and leaving her all alone troubled him, but he had no answer for it. Finally, when they had eaten breakfast, he said, "Why don't we just enjoy New York today."

"All right. You can show me where the rich people live, and I'll show you where the poor people live."

Josh laughed. "I'm poor people now, but at least maybe we can go to some museums."

Kefira said, "That would be nice."

The two of them left the restaurant and began walking down the street. Each of them was troubled, but neither could speak of what was on their hearts.

★　★　★　★

"This is some car, Diana, but you always did like fast cars."

"Yes, and so did you, if I remember."

"Well, that life's gone."

"You never did tell me exactly what happened, Josh. Oh, I know your family lost all of its money in the crash, but what have you been doing?"

"It's not a happy story, Diana. I went downhill pretty badly. Took to drinking too much, got in trouble, and did some time in jail."

Diana was fascinated by this but not troubled so far as Josh could see. He told her the whole story that night at dinner. She had great intuition, this Diana Welles, and put her finger on the trouble at once.

"So this woman, Dora Skinner, you fell in love with her, and she got you into trouble."

Josh stared at Diana. She was wearing a softly printed dress with yellow, blue, and pink flowers scattered randomly over a light green background. It was sleeveless with a low neckline and a long, softly pleated skirt.

"I can't blame it on Dora, and I wasn't in love with her."

"But you did have an affair with her?"

Josh looked down at his hands and did not speak for a moment. "I can't deny that. It was the wrong thing to do, and I've been sorry about it."

"Have you seen her since you got out?"

"Yes."

"She's still got her hooks in you, hasn't she, Josh?" Diana was staring at him intently.

"It was just a . . . just a thing of the flesh. That's all it was. Altogether wrong."

"You weren't always concerned about right and wrong. I remember that from our time together." Diana grinned, and her eyes danced with laughter.

"I wasn't all that good if you'll remember."

"I do remember. Do you regret it, Josh?"

In that instant Joshua Winslow, thinking of his brief affair with Diana Welles, could not answer honestly. He had been young, and the times had been wild. It was the height of the Roaring Twenties, and he had lived the life of pleasure. He had been serious enough about his studies, but after the books were closed and the classes were over, he and Diana had engaged in all of the activities of flaming youth. There had been plenty of money for liquor and good times, and he remembered vividly some of the hours he had spent with Diana. "It was all a long time ago, Diana. We were very young."

"And now you're an old man with a long white beard," she jeered. "No wine, women, and song for Josh Winslow, the old patriarch."

Josh laughed at her. She had always been amusing, and he had always enjoyed the way she poked fun at him. "That's pretty much the case. I need a job, and I've always had a dream of being an archeologist. I'm getting a late start, so I really am an old man with a white beard as far as that's concerned."

"Don't be foolish, Josh. You can do it. You were always head and shoulders above the rest of us. Uncle Phineas said you would have been the greatest archeologist around if you had stuck with it."

"Did he really say that?"

"More than once. He's very fond of you." She leaned forward, and the lights overhead caught the diamonds around her neck. They glittered and flashed with cold blue fire. Her eyes glittered as well as they fixed on him. "I'd like to see you do well." She put her hands out, and Josh reached out and took them involuntarily. She squeezed his hands and smiled. "I still remember those things we did together." For an instant she saddened, and then she pulled her hands back. "I've made a lot of mistakes since then. You probably read about some of them in the papers." Josh did not answer, and she shrugged. "Well, we can't wipe out the past." She made herself smile again and then said, "Come on, let's go talk to Dad. You just go right in with all flags flying. I've got him talked into the notion of hiring you."

★ ★ ★ ★

Diana drove Josh to the Welles home, which was indeed a mansion, and led him to her father's study, where she announced she was leaving the two of them alone to talk. She winked at Josh and left with a smile.

Conrad Welles was a man of direct ways. He met everything the same way—head-on. Someone had described him as a man with his head bowed as if he were going to ram it through an oak door. Now he said almost roughly, "All right, Winslow. Diana has talked me into hiring you. She'd drive me crazy if I didn't. She has a way of doing that."

"Well, I'm sorry if she's been importunate, but I do want to go on this expedition more than anything I've ever wanted. As I told your brother, money's not important to me."

"Don't be a fool! Money's important to everyone," Welles growled.

Josh shrugged. "I expect you're right there, Mr. Welles. Maybe I was sounding a bit noble, but I just want you to understand that I'm serious about this. I've wasted a lot of years, and I want to become an archeologist. It's too late, really, for me to go back to college, but your brother is the finest archeologist in the world. I just want to be with him and follow him around. Why, I'll shine his shoes or do anything he wants done."

"That's good because that's your assignment. He's not as healthy as he should be, and I want you to take the hard work off of him. Don't let him work himself to death."

"I'll do my best, Mr. Welles."

Welles then spoke crisply of the duties he expected Josh to fulfill. He named a salary that was higher than Josh had expected and said, "It's all set, then. You're ready to leave?"

"Yes, sir, at any time."

"Good. We won't be leaving until May the eleventh, but I want you at my brother's office tomorrow morning to help him start packing up."

Suddenly an idea flashed into Josh's mind. Perhaps it had been there in some fashion before, but now it seemed to explode, fully developed, in his brain. He said eagerly, "Mr. Welles, I have a friend. Would you like to have two helpers for the price of one?"

Conrad Welles stared at Josh. "What are you talking about, man?"

"I have a friend who needs a place to work."

"Is he an archeologist?"

"No, I'm not talking about a skilled laborer. I'm talking about ... well, a cook, for example. She's a wonderful cook, and—"

"A woman! Have you lost your mind? I'm not hiring any girlfriend of yours."

"She's not that, Mr. Welles. Just listen to me if you will for five minutes."

Welles stared at Josh with displeasure. "All right, five minutes, but it'd better be good."

Josh gave his history with Kefira Reis as briefly but as clearly as he could. When he had finished he said, "So she has no place to go. The salary mentioned is far more than I expected. Just give half of it to her, and you'll have two people there."

"It's too dangerous for a woman."

"Look, she carries a gun. She shot a man who was going to kill me. I think she can take care of herself probably better than I can. And think about this, Mr. Welles. You say your brother's not in the best of health. Kefira's a wonderful cook. She could make life very easy for him. Doing his washing. Taking care of him. Seeing that he eats right ..." Josh poured out the advantages of having a woman along, and finally he was surprised when Welles laughed.

"All right—all right, I'm convinced! All I want to know is one thing. Are you two having an affair?"

"No, of course not!"

"Don't be so righteous and holy! It has been known to happen, you know."

"I've told you the absolute truth, Mr. Welles. I feel like a brother toward her. She has nobody, and she saved my life. If I could do this for her, I'd feel that I had made up for that."

Welles stood silently staring at the young man. "All right, you take her to see my brother. Tell him I have agreed to hire her, but he has to approve her."

"Thank you very much, Mr. Welles. You won't regret it. She'll be a great help to your brother."

★ ★ ★ ★

The New Testament fascinated Kefira. She had heard of Jesus. She knew what Christmas meant to a Christian, but suddenly as she read, the man Jesus seemed to reach out to her. She was startled by a knock on her door. She knew it had to be Joshua, so she shoved the New Testament into her purse and went to the door. When she opened it, she saw his eyes were blazing with excitement.

"I've got great news, Kefira."

"What is it, Josh?"

"I've got the job."

"That is wonderful!"

"Yes, but it's even better than you think. While I was talking to Mr. Welles, it suddenly occurred to me that there might be a job for you too."

Kefira stared at Josh. "I don't know anything about archeology."

"No, but you can cook, and you can wash, and you can dig. It's a lot of hard work. That's what these expeditions are. Professor Welles is a bit frail. He needs somebody to look after him, and so I convinced his brother that you'd be good for the job. And the salary's good too." He named the figure and saw surprise wash across Kefira's face. "And the good thing is we won't be spending any of it. There's nothing to spend it on out in the desert, so when the job's done we'll come home with some money. You can help Chaim when he gets out." He knew this would be pleasing to her, and he saw that the idea took hold of her at once.

"I don't know. I never thought of such a thing."

"Neither did I. It just came to me while I was talking to Mr. Welles. Look, this is so much better than just going down to the coast or wandering around. It's something we can do together, and you can be a great help to the professor."

It took very little persuasion because Kefira was quite apprehensive about the future. When Josh painted the advantages of the job in such glowing colors, she finally said, "All right. I'll do it if you think it's best, Josh."

"It'll be wonderful! Come on. We've got to go talk to the professor. He has to approve your employment."

★　★　★　★

"And so, Professor Welles, your brother says he thinks it would be a good idea for Miss Reis to accompany us. She's a fine cook, I can testify to that."

"Wait a minute, Josh," Kefira protested. "I cook mostly Jewish food."

"I love Jewish food," Professor Welles beamed. "I ate it all the time when I was on the dig in the Holy Land."

"And she can help with the washing, and she can do some of the digging too, under instruction, of course."

"All right." The professor was delighted. He said, "Well, of course, it's always good to have extra help. And a good cook is hard to find. The last one we had nearly poisoned me. It's fine with me. I'd be glad to have you, my dear."

"Thank you, Professor," Kefira said. A sense of security suddenly came to her, and she felt warm gratitude toward Josh.

As they left the professor's office, he said, "Come along. Conrad Welles wanted to meet you if his brother approved."

The two made their way to Conrad's office, which was not far from the professor's, and when they were announced and entered the room, Josh was surprised to see Diana there.

"Hello, Diana," he said. "This is Miss Kefira Reis."

Diana nodded, saying noncommittally, "I'm glad to know you, Miss Reis."

"Good to meet you, Miss Welles."

Conrad Welles had been sitting behind his desk, but he got up now and came over to stand before Kefira. He stared at her for a moment and said, "It's a rough life on a dig. Do you think you can put up with primitive conditions? No bathroom and all that?"

"Yes, sir, I think I can."

Conrad's eyes suddenly twinkled. "Do you still carry a pistol?"

"I have it right here in my purse."

"A pistol!" Diana exclaimed. "You carry a pistol?"

"She carries it for protection," Josh said hurriedly. "As a matter of fact, if she hadn't had it, I might not be here."

"That sounds like an interesting story."

Kefira was studying the tall blond woman. "I'd be happy to tell you all about it sometime, Miss Welles."

Diana stood perfectly still, her eyes locked with Kefira's, then she suddenly smiled. "We'll have plenty of time," she said. "I haven't had a chance to tell you, Dad"—she turned to face her father—"but I've decided to go to Egypt for the dig."

Conrad Welles stared at his daughter. "It's the first I've heard of it."

Diana turned and smiled at Josh. "I made up my mind rather suddenly. It'll be like old times, won't it, Josh?"

Kefira watched Josh and saw something pass across his features. She knew suddenly why this woman had decided to go on the dig, and although she was young and inexperienced, she understood as well that Josh Winslow was going to find more in Egypt than old bones.

CHAPTER SEVENTEEN

LAST NIGHT IN NEW YORK

★　★　★　★

With a flourish Josh drove the nail into the packing case, hit it with a resounding blow, then lifted the hammer in triumph. "That's the last of it," he exclaimed, "and I'm glad of it!"

Kefira had been moving boxes across the crowded room, but now she stopped and turned to smile at Josh. "It's been a real job, hasn't it? I didn't know it was going to be this much work just to get ready to go to Egypt."

Josh put the hammer down carefully, flexed his finger, and shook his head. "I think you have to do quite a bit of planning. You can't step back over to New York and buy something that you forgot to take. It's pretty primitive out where we're going." He arched his back and tested his side and felt only a slight twinge. The work getting ready to go had been hard, but the cracked ribs seemed to have knitted themselves together. "Let's have a cup of coffee," he said. "I'm dry as a bone."

The two moved over and cleared a place on the table, and Kefira filled two white mugs with coffee from the battered pot. "The professor insists on taking this old pot," she said as she put the cups down. "It looks like it came over on the *Mayflower*, but he says it's the only pot in the world that makes coffee right."

"He's a funny guy. Kind of set in his ways."

"But he's a wonderful man. I like him very much."

Josh tasted the coffee cautiously, then sighed. "That's good. Maybe he's right about the coffeepot." He looked up and smiled at Kefira, noting the weariness around her eyes. "You're tired out," he said. "I guess we all are, but in the morning we get on the ship. Then we can just take a rest. There won't be any work to do until we get to Egypt."

"I've never been on a big ship. I expect I'll get seasick."

"Let's hope for better things. They tell me that seasickness is bad. I had a cousin who went to Europe on the *Lusitania* once, and he said once was enough. He said when you first get seasick you're afraid you're going to die—then after a while you're afraid you *won't* die. Pretty bad stuff."

The two sat there in the midst of the cluttered room talking and enjoying the coffee. Both of them were exhausted after the extensive preparations. Josh had run all over the city finding the items the professor wanted to take. In addition to this, he had taken up the study of reading hieroglyphics. He had begun this study years before while a student in college and had done well at it. But it was a complicated subject and called for all of his mental energy. The professor had been tutoring him and promised to continue doing so during the ship voyage as well.

They had almost finished their coffee when the door swung open and Diana burst in. As always, she could not enter a room at a sedate pace but always seemed to be rushing to some extremely important appointment. She came over at once and put her hand on Josh's shoulder in a familiar fashion. "Come on, Josh. We're going to celebrate tonight."

"Celebrate what?" Josh said. He was rather uncomfortable with the familiarity Diana showed him and was very much aware of Kefira's steady gaze on the act.

"Why, we celebrate getting packed and getting away from New York."

Diana was wearing a calf-length dress made of a soft, light fuchsia material that clung to her rather seductively. Over it, she wore a short jacket with padded shoulders, unfastened between waist and hip. A small close-fitting matching hat perched on her head at a jaunty angle. She looked expensive, as always, and

Kefira felt like a dowdy bird indeed next to this gloriously arrayed young woman.

Josh looked down at his work clothes and said, "I'm not dressed to go to a fancy place."

"Well, I am, so one of us will be enough. Come on, there's a restaurant I want to take you to."

"We've got to leave pretty early in the morning, Diana," Josh protested.

"You're talking like an old man. Come along." Suddenly Diana looked over toward Kefira. "You're welcome to come along too, of course."

"No thank you, Diana," Kefira answered quickly. "I believe I'll just go to bed early."

Josh rose and accompanied Diana out of the office, but when he looked back he saw Kefira still sitting, and she looked very much alone. "I hate to leave Kefira alone," he said as they left the building and were getting into the flashy Deusenberg.

"Why, she didn't want to come. I asked her," Diana said. "Come on. Shake off your troubles. We're going to have a great time tonight."

Back inside the room, Kefira rose and began to wash the cups. She stood wondering whether or not to pack them and finally decided there would be cups, at least, for sale in Egypt. She was depressed, and she knew it had something to do with Josh and Diana Welles. Ever since Diana had announced that she was going on the trip, she had monopolized Josh's time. Somehow she had managed to put Kefira into a subordinate position, and while she was polite enough, there were times that she seemed to treat Kefira as one of the lowest order of servants.

Kefira began tidying up, checking boxes to be sure they were secure and well labeled. She heard the door close and looked up to see Professor Welles enter. He smiled at her but said in a worried tone, "Why, my dear, you shouldn't be working this late! You should be in bed. I'm afraid we've been asking too much of you."

"Oh, that's not so, Professor Welles," Kefira said at once with a smile. She liked the professor very much indeed. She knew he was an intellectual giant. His pictures were in the paper, and everyone spoke of him almost in awe. He was the foremost authority in the world, so Josh had told her, in Egyptology. But in many ways he was almost childlike. He was forgetful to a fault, and it took a great deal of Kefira's time keeping up with the things that he simply let slip his mind. It pleased her that she had been able to help him with personal things. He loved her cooking, and she had checked his wardrobe and been shocked to find that he was packing dirty clothes. She had firmly taken charge of his entire wardrobe and seen that everything was cleaned and pressed and had thrown away some socks that were more holes than fabric.

"I think everything's ready to go, Professor," Kefira said.

"That's fine—fine!" Professor Welles beamed at her. "Now I feel much better with you to take care of me. I'm not very good at looking after myself," he confessed.

"I'm glad I can help. I don't know anything about archeology. I wish I knew more."

"Well, you'll know more when we get back. A great deal of the field is learned simply by doing it. You can only learn so much out of a textbook, but actually putting a shovel in the ground is another thing."

The two chatted amiably, and then Phineas said, "Where's Joshua? I expected he'd be here with you."

"Diana came by and wanted him to go out and celebrate."

Something in Kefira's tone tugged at the professor's attention. He examined her carefully and saw that the young woman was somewhat depressed. He was not as good at reading people as he was at reading hieroglyphics, but still he had become very fond of this young woman and was sensitive to her moods. He had wondered from the beginning about her relationship with Joshua, and now he thought he had part of the answer. "You'll have to forgive Diana. She's very impulsive."

"It's all right. She wanted to celebrate."

"Diana's a dear girl, and I love her, but she's been terribly spoiled." Phineas sighed and shook his head sadly. "And I'm afraid I'm partly responsible for that. I could never say no to her. Neither could her father. If her mother had lived, I think she might have been a different young woman. Stella had a great deal of native intelligence, and she knew Diana had a willful spirit."

"She's very beautiful."

"Oh yes, she's always been that. Even as a child. I wish she weren't."

"You wish she weren't beautiful?" Kefira looked up quickly. "Why would you say that?"

"Physical beauty isn't always an asset." He smiled, looking more like a cherub than ever. "Since I've never had any, I've analyzed it quite carefully. You know the Bible says, 'Favour is deceitful, and beauty is vain: but a woman that feareth the Lord, she shall be praised.'"

Immediately Kefira asked, "Where's that in the Bible? In the New Testament?"

"Oh no, it's in the Old Testament. The book of Proverbs, last chapter, thirtieth verse. In the Hebrew it sounds much more impressive." He spoke again, this time in apparently fluent Hebrew.

"You speak Hebrew, Professor?"

"Oh yes, it's a relatively simple language to learn," he said carelessly.

"Why did you learn to speak Hebrew?"

"I wanted to read the Bible in the original language, so that, of course, meant Hebrew as well as Aramaic and Greek."

"You learned those languages so you could read the Bible in them?"

"Oh yes, it was quite fun, actually. And it's come in handy. Where we're going, Aramaic is still spoken at times."

"How many other languages do you speak?" Kefira asked.

"Oh, I don't know. Let me see. German, of course. French. A little Spanish. Portuguese, Mandarin, Russian—oh, I don't know. Two or three more."

"That is miraculous!"

Phineas looked at her. "Oh no, not miraculous. God gives us different gifts. He gave me the gift of languages, and I learned them very easily. But you have gifts just as valuable in God's sight."

"Me! Why, I can't do anything."

Phineas smiled gently. "Yes you can. You have the gift of love in you. I've seen it from the first."

Kefira was astonished at Phineas's words. "What do you mean, Professor?"

"I don't know how it is, but some people have loving hearts and some people just don't. It's the greatest gift of all, I think. I would trade all my knowledge of languages just to be able to love people like I know you do."

"You can't have seen that in me! You haven't been around me that much."

"You'll find it to be true, though."

Kefira was shocked at the professor's words, and she grew very quiet. Finally she shook her head. "I've had a pretty hard life, Professor, since my parents died, and I'm afraid I've had bad thoughts about people. I get angry and I want to get revenge."

She looked up, and suddenly there was a vulnerability in her countenance. She had a beautifully fashioned face, all of its features generous and capable of robust emotion. But there was a hint of her will and pride in the corners of her eyes and lips. "I have to tell you that I don't love God."

"You don't? You amaze me, my dear."

"When my father died it all began. Then my brother went to prison, and since then I've had a hard time with . . . well, with men who've been abusive. And then my mother died. So it keeps coming back to me. Why does God do all these things? You know, I'm ashamed to admit it, but I even think of God as my enemy."

"I think, child, He is your beloved enemy."

"What does that mean, Professor? Beloved enemy? I've never heard anybody say that."

"Well, sometimes I wish you'd get a copy of the New Testament."

"Oh, I have one!"

"Then read in the book of Acts the story of a man called Paul. His original name was Saul of Tarsus, and he was very much opposed to Jesus Christ. As a matter of fact, he had authority and imprisoned people who were Christians. He was on his way to put more people in prison when he was suddenly struck down by a blinding light from heaven. Oh, it's an exciting story! And Paul, of course, was amazed and shocked and stunned when a voice spoke to him. And the voice said, 'Saul, why persecutest thou me?' And Saul said, 'Who art thou, Lord?' And the voice said, 'I am Jesus whom thou persecutest.'"

"I never heard of anything like that."

"Well, Paul came to know Jesus during that experience, but before that, he had thought of Jesus as his enemy. But all the time Jesus loved him and was determined that He would save him from his sins. So, my dear Kefira, you may think God is your enemy, but He loves you. So think of Him as a *beloved enemy*—at least until that time when you can think of Him simply as your beloved."

Kefira felt something begin within her, deep inside. It was like a warmth, but it was not that exactly. As soon as the professor had mentioned the name of Jesus, she realized that she could not ignore Jesus any longer. But she did not want to admit this, so she said, "I'll read the story tonight."

Phineas reached over, patted her hand, and held it. "You have a sweet disposition. You'll need it when we get to Egypt. The one certainty about these trips is that things *always* go wrong." He released her hand and said, "You'd better go to bed now. I can see you're tired." He stepped toward the door and then turned back and remarked, "Diana has too much money and too much beauty. She's always gotten what she wanted, but remember that verse in the Bible. 'Beauty is vain, but a woman that feareth the Lord, she shall be praised.' That's my prayer for you, Kefira."

Kefira stood there as the professor left. She was tremendously moved by the verse that he spoke, and suddenly she had a desire to read the story of Paul. Quickly she locked up the office and went to her room. She found the New Testament at once, sat down, and began looking for the book of Acts. She had some difficulty finding it, but when she did she immediately began with chapter one and read eagerly.

★　★　★　★

"Come on, Josh, I'm starved."

Josh stood aside and watched as the uniformed valet stepped out from under the restaurant awning and slid behind the wheel of Diana's car.

"I'll park the car for you, Miss Welles," he said with a smile.

Josh and Diana approached the entrance, and a uniformed doorman opened it, greeted Diana by name, and said with a broad smile, "Good to see you again, Miss Welles."

"Thank you, Harry. Good to be here."

As they stepped inside, Josh at once felt out of place. He had put on a coat, but still, one look around revealed that these were indeed society people. The women were dressed in expensive gowns and wore glittering jewelry. Many of the men were wearing evening dress, and Josh shook his head. "You know I feel as out of place as a bullfrog on a freeway with his hopper busted."

Diana laughed and took his arm. "That's all right. Some real strange types come in here."

"What's the name of this place?"

"It's called the Colony. It started out when prohibition began with a restaurant in the front, and in the back the gamblers and the prostitutes plied their professions quite successfully. A man named Cavalero owns it. I'll introduce you to him."

The Colony was packed. Tables were as close together as possible, but there was an empty space, evidently, for a floor show. A band was playing, and the room was filled with smoke and laughter and the voices of the diners. Waiters moved around carrying silver trays high over their heads. Some of them pushed food around on wheeled carts.

A tall olive-skinned man with Mediterranean features approached and bowed from the hips. "Ah, Miss Welles, I have your table ready. Believe me, I had to fight to save it."

"Thank you, Mario. That was sweet of you."

The two followed Mario to a table far back in the corner, and Mario pulled the chair out for Diana and said, "I'll have a very special wine sent out to you, if you would trust me, Miss Welles."

"I always trust your choice in wine, Mario."

The maitre d' left, and Diana smiled and reached over and put her hand over Josh's. "I hope you're hungry. The food here is wonderful. Here, see if there's anything you like."

The menu proved to be impressive. It included dishes like eel ragout, pompano en papillote, pheasant Souvaroff, and dozens of others.

"I don't know what most of this is."

"Let me order," Diana said. "We'll have crepes suzettes and chicken curry. That's very good."

Diana gave their order crisply to the waiter who came, and Josh occupied himself by looking around. When the waiter left, Josh said, "There's John Barrymore."

"He comes here pretty often. He drinks so much that they have to water down his liquor."

"That's too bad. I hear he's a great actor."

"Very fine indeed! I saw him play Hamlet once. I wish we had time to catch his new film. You should have come to New York earlier."

Josh turned to face her. "Well, Diana, I really couldn't. I was either in jail or recovering from broken ribs."

"How are your ribs?"

"They're all right now. I'll be able to dig with the best of them, but it's a good thing Kefira was there. If she hadn't been there with her thirty-eight, I think I'd've been in a grave somewhere."

Diana's eyes narrowed. "So you've said. I can't believe she really shot the man who was beating you."

"She sure did. Just in the ear, of course."

"She's a pretty tough cookie. Not many women could pull a gun on a man."

"I think she's not as tough as she likes to make out. Actually, she's a very sensitive young woman. She's been hurt pretty badly."

Diana nodded absently, and then the two were interrupted as a man in a tuxedo stepped up to a microphone. "And now, ladies and gentlemen, for your entertainment we have with us tonight the great Al Jolson. Come on, Jolie, let's hear it!"

Al Jolson stepped up to the microphone, and for the next thirty minutes his voice filled the room. He sang the songs that had made him famous—"My Mammy," "California, Here I

Come," and a number of others. He was an exuberant man with flashing eyes, and he held the audience in the palm of his hand.

By the time he was through singing and had waved cheerfully and disappeared, waiters began bringing food to nearby tables. Josh was stunned by the flamboyant tradition of the restaurant. They brought out food skewered on flaming swords. Josh noticed and pointed out to Diana that one party even had hot dogs served to them on flaming swords, and another had twelve ripe olives brought in on long brochettes by twelve individual waiters.

"They like to show off a little," Diana said, laughing as one waiter walked by with meat impaled and flaming. "Any minute now they'll be bringing in the manager on a flaming sword."

Josh grinned at Diana and shook his head. "It all seems sort of frivolous."

"That's what it is—frivolous. What the world needs is more frivolous things, Josh." She had had several drinks and had been rather surprised when Josh refused to join her. His refusal, however, did not affect her own drinking. Her eyes danced with pleasure as she began teasing him about the old days and the fun they'd had in college.

Josh listened and smiled, but finally their food came, and they applied themselves to it. They both had healthy appetites, and once Diana said, "You'd better enjoy this. I imagine we'll be eating mostly out of cans on the dig."

"Not really. Kefira's a wonderful cook. She's introduced me to Jewish food. It's spicy, and she really knows how to cook a good meal."

Diana nodded, then at once began making plans for the rest of the evening. Evidently, Josh realized, she was planning to make a long night of it, but he determined that after the meal, he would go back to the room and try to get what rest he could.

They stayed at the restaurant for two hours, for there were several other acts. During this time Diana drank a considerable number of glasses of wine, and when they left she was somewhat unsteady. He held her arm, and when the car was brought up, he said, "I'd better drive, don't you think?"

"Nonsense, I'll drive."

With some trepidation, Josh got into the car and watched as Diana put the car in gear. She shot out from the parking space with a screaming of tires, and he said, "Diana, take it easy!"

"Taking it easy is for other people, Josh, not for you and me."

The ride to his hotel was perilous. Diana drove carelessly and narrowly missed having several head-on collisions. She stopped the car in front of the hotel where Josh was staying and turned to him. "Why don't I come up for a while? We can talk about old times."

"That's not a good idea, Diana. We've got an early call in the morning, and you've had too much to drink."

Diana suddenly reached over and put her arms around him and pulled him forward. She kissed him hard, then laughed. "You're nothing but an old puritan, that's what you are! The old Josh wouldn't have turned down an offer like that."

Josh smiled faintly. "I guess he wouldn't have, but things have changed a lot."

Diana shook her head. She still had her arms around his neck and was holding him tightly. "You've got some bad ideas in your head, Josh, but we'll have plenty of time in Egypt. I hear there's a beautiful moon there. Out on the desert sand you'll change your mind."

Josh got out of the car and leaned over to say, "Be careful."

"Careful is for old ladies. I'll see you in the morning, Josh."

The Deusenberg shot off, and Josh watched as it weaved its way down the street. "I hope she gets home all right," he murmured, then turned and entered the hotel.

CHAPTER EIGHTEEN

MEETING ON DECK

★　★　★　★

The morning of May the eleventh went quickly for Kefira. She was up by dawn, and after a quick breakfast she and Josh went to the docks. Josh watched carefully as the crates and baggage were loaded, and then the two of them went up on deck. The ship was a beehive of activity, and it was exciting to Kefira to watch as the late passengers came running to get on board.

"Look, there's Diana," Josh said. A taxi had pulled up, and Diana had gotten out. She moved rather slowly, and Kefira said, "What's wrong with her?"

Secretly Josh thought she probably had a hangover, but he said, "I guess it's a little early for her." They watched as she came up the gangplank and then disappeared.

For over an hour the two stood there, and Kefira's eyes were wide with excitement. "I've never done anything like this, Josh!"

"I never have either. I'm glad we're doing it together."

Kefira felt pleased by his words, and the two waited until the ship cast off. They watched as the tugs pulled the *Empress* away from the dock and then carefully shepherded her out into the open sea.

They made their way to the stern of the ship and stood there until the New York skyline grew indistinct and finally disappeared.

"Well, we're on our way, Kefira," Josh said. The two of them were leaning on the rail and staring at the sea that separated them from America. "Are you afraid?"

"A little bit," she confessed. "What if the ship sinks?"

"It won't do that." Josh smiled.

"I'm not afraid, then. But it may be a long time before we get back."

"That's right. The professor said the dig may take several years, but we'll come back before then, I'm sure. You'll want to be back when Chaim gets out of Sing Sing."

"What about you, Josh?"

"This is a great break for me, Kefira. I can learn from the professor. Why, it's like having a university walking around in one man's shoes. He knows everything!"

Kefira turned to face him, and he studied her countenance. Her hair rose back from her temples, flowed over her head, and was caught into a ball behind. Her face was expressive, as much as he had ever seen it, and he saw pleasure graphically registered in the light and shadow of her feelings. She usually had a composed expression, but now a little-girl eagerness displayed itself. Josh watched the slight changes of her face, the quickening and the loosening of the small expressions that came and went in a fugitive fashion. She wasn't exactly smiling, but the hint of a smile hovered around her mouth.

Kefira studied Josh and noticed that he held his long lips together on the edge of a smile. Josh seemed to have a way of looking at things, or people, as if absorbing them without judging some as more important than others. He was, Kefira had discovered, a man who could be gallant to women, but she did not understand whether it was because he had some deep feeling about any one particular woman.

"I'm glad we're in this thing together, Kefira," Josh said, his warm, clear eyes looking directly into her own.

"So am I," she replied, and at that moment she felt complete and whole and confident.

★ ★ ★ ★

Kefira had brought no fancy clothes, so when Phineas knocked on her cabin door to announce, "We're going to eat at the captain's table tonight," she had been disturbed. She went through her scanty wardrobe and finally sighed and chose the only dress that even came close to being ornate. It was a very simple dress of light blue with a high rounded neckline, three-quarter-length sleeves, a sash around the waist, and a midcalf-length skirt.

She donned the dress, put on the simple pearl earrings that had belonged to her mother, one of the few things of hers she had left, and walked toward the dining area. She found the party already gathered, and at once noted that Diana was wearing a light orchid dress with a low décolletage inset with chiffon. Diamonds glittered at her throat and earlobes, and Kefira felt out of place.

Phineas took her arm at once, saying, "Come along, Kefira. I want you to meet the captain."

The captain was a tall, cheerful-looking man with a full white beard. His name was Ralph Toliver, and he was in his midfifties as far as she could determine. He greeted Kefira courteously with a smile and then seated them at his table. The meal was ornate and very rich. Wine was served, which neither Kefira nor Josh tasted.

Kefira kept very quiet listening to Captain Toliver as he spoke of his adventures on the seas. He was a fascinating speaker and managed to draw in the others. Finally he turned his eyes on Kefira and smiled humorously. "You two ladies had better be careful. These sailors are like all sailors everywhere. They'll try to romance you."

Diana glanced at Kefira and shook her head, and a mischievous light danced in her eyes. "They'd better not try to romance Miss Reis. She carries a gun and has been known to shoot men with it."

Everyone's eyes turned on Kefira, the officers staring at her with disbelief but interest.

"I'm sure you're speaking metaphorically," Captain Toliver replied, studying Kefira carefully. "She doesn't look like a gun-packing lady."

"Oh, it's true enough. Tell them about it, Kefira."

Kefira could not say a word. She wanted to leave at once she was so embarrassed, but Josh came to her rescue. "Miss Reis was once compelled to carry a gun because she was in very dangerous territory. As a matter of fact, if she hadn't been, I think I would probably be six feet under right now."

The first officer, a short, rotund man with merry blue eyes, said, "That sounds like some story, but I'm willing to risk it. Would you dance with me, Miss Reis?"

Glad to leave the table, Kefira got up. She found the first officer, whose name was Don Cunningham, a very nice young man. As they were waltzing about the floor, he said, "I don't suppose you'd care to tell me about your adventure with the gun?"

"Oh, there wasn't really much to it, Mr. Cunningham."

"Well, I think I'm safe—I'm harmless enough."

Kefira smiled, for she liked the officer. "That's the first mark of a man making his move. He announces he's harmless."

"Oh, but I mean it!" Cunningham protested. "I've got a wife and two children at home."

Kefira smiled and began asking the names of the children. When they returned to the table, Josh whispered to her, "Don't let it get to you, Kefira. Diana didn't mean anything."

"I'm sure she didn't."

The meal was interesting, and Diana made no more remarks about Kefira.

After the meal was over, the professor said, "Kefira, if you'd like, I'll show you some of the plans I've made."

"I'd like that very much."

Kefira accompanied Phineas to his cabin, and he began to show her maps and diagrams, most of which she did not understand.

"How do you know where to dig? Do you just start anywhere?" Kefira asked.

"Oh no, there are signs. You want to dig where people once lived, and people leave their mark whenever they inhabit a place for a long time." He rummaged through some large sheets of paper, then said, "Look, here's where we'll be going. It's very close to the Valley of the Kings. Have you heard of that?"

"No, I'm afraid not."

"Well, it's a burial place used by many of the pharaohs. I expect every grain of sand there has been turned over and many discoveries have been made."

"So, you're going to dig there?"

"I don't think there's anything much left there to find, but when I was in Egypt several years ago, I made a side trip from the Valley of the Kings, and I found this little tell."

"Tell? What's a tell?"

"It's a low mound, usually with a flat top. Here, I have a diagram of it."

Kefira looked at the drawing and studied it carefully. "It looks just like a small hill that's been cut off flat on the top."

"Yes, that's exactly what it looks like, and they're called *tells*. You see, back in ancient days, a settlement would grow up on the plain, but time and storms and wars would come along and flatten the village. But it was still a good site, usually close to water, so other people would come along and build on that old site. They'd repeat the cycle, and so what you have is layer upon layer of different civilizations."

Kefira listened eagerly as the professor explained his plan. His eyes sparkled as he said, "This is just a little tell. I expect it's been overlooked, but when I was there before, I found one piece of pottery that shouldn't have been there. I was just digging around without much aim, and I came across it. The pottery went all the way back maybe to 2000 B.C. It shouldn't have been on top, but it could have survived from a previous civilization."

"And so we're going to dig there?"

Phineas nodded, and excitement made him restless. He slapped his hands together and then waved his arms around as he spoke. "What I want to find, Kefira, is evidence of the Hebrews in Egypt."

"You mean like Moses?"

"Even further back than that. We know from the Old Testament that Abraham went from Canaan to stay in Egypt during a time of famine. I'd like to find some evidence that he was actually there."

Kefira was very interested in this. She knew the book of Genesis very well and listened as the professor explained his desire to find some trace of the patriarchs.

"My brother's not very interested in this sort of thing," he said. "He wants me to find a tomb with gold and jewelry and valuable things. I'm afraid he's more interested in that than in anything of historical significance."

Kefira stayed for over an hour listening to the professor, and then she left and went to her own cabin. It was a very small cabin, but it had a bunk and a porthole through which she could look out at the sea and a small chest in which she kept her clothes and personal things.

She opened the chest, took out the Yiddish Bible that had belonged to her father, and began reading again the story of Genesis. She found the part about Abraham, and when she went over it, she thought, *What a wonderful thing it would be if the professor could find evidence of Abraham's sojourn in Egypt.*

★   ★   ★   ★

"It's going to be a great dig, Diana," Phineas said. The two of them were in his cabin. She had come by to borrow a book, and the two had fallen into a long discussion about the possibilities. Diana, despite her frivolous life, had actually become somewhat of an expert on pottery, and Phineas said, "I'm glad you're along, Diana. You know, you could become a leading authority on pottery if you'd give yourself to it."

Diana said, "I'm afraid that would call for more character than I have."

"I think you have more character than you think, dear." Phineas was genuinely fond of Diana. He had helped raise her after the death of his sister-in-law and had been grieved to see the direction the young woman's life had taken. They talked for a while and then Phineas remarked, "I'm very glad Kefira is with us, but I think you'll have to be more careful, Diana."

"Careful? How? What do you mean?"

"That remark you made at the captain's table. It embarrassed her."

"She's too easily embarrassed, then," Diana laughed. "She'd better hope I never say anything worse."

"I wish you would be more careful."

"I'll try. Well, good night, Uncle. I'm going to take a turn around the deck." She kissed him on the cheek and left.

The wind was warm, and the ship was forging through the dark waters. Overhead the skies were bright with stars, and Diana enjoyed her walk. She had made almost a complete round when she found Josh leaning on the rails, staring out at the ocean. "Hello, shipmate," she said. Walking over, she stood beside him for a moment, then said, "Are you excited, Josh?"

"Never been more excited in my life. It's a miracle of God that I'm here. I wish I'd prepared myself more for it, though."

"No point grieving over what you haven't done."

"I suppose that's right."

"Anyway, there have been some great archeologists who had very little formal training. You always had a gift for the digs. Remember how we all wanted to start on that big mound down in Louisiana, but you got stubborn? You just bulldozed us into digging in a smaller one. Even Uncle Phineas was swept away with it."

"I remember. I don't know why I felt that way."

"Well, anyway that had all the prize finds in it. Phineas says that kind of instinct is worth more than a college degree."

The two stood there reveling in the warm breeze and in the glorious display of stars overhead. The moon was dazzling too, and its reflection glowed in a silvery path that led to the horizon. "I guess I mentioned it before," Diana said slowly, "but that was the best time I ever had in my younger days."

"It was a good time for me too."

Diana leaned against him, her shoulder touching his. "We'll do big things together, Josh. I feel it."

Josh was intensely aware of the pressure of her arm against his. He knew that at one time he had felt a passion for this woman stronger than anything that had ever touched him, and as he stood there beside her, he also knew that he could be drawn to her again. There was something in her that attracted men, and he felt it. He was still, however, not over Dora. He had been scarred deeply by his relationship with her, and now, though Diana was no Dora Skinner, he still felt uneasy about the strength of his feelings for her. He made his excuses as soon as he could, then went at once to his room. He slept poorly that night, whether from excitement over what lay ahead or apprehension about his feelings for Diana he could not say.

★　★　★　★

"Well, we land in Egypt tomorrow, Kefira," Josh said. The two had gone up on deck after supper. The night was mild, and the ship was forging steadily through the dark waters.

"I'm glad I didn't get seasick," Kefira said. She leaned against the rail and stared down at the white frothy waves as the ship plowed through the darkness. The moon was so bright she could see clearly in all directions. "Isn't this a beautiful night?" she said.

"Sure is." Josh had noticed that Kefira had been very quiet at supper. She had left early, and now he sensed that she was unhappy. "Is there something wrong, Kefira?"

"Oh no, not really."

"Don't fool me, now. We know each other pretty well."

Kefira did feel somewhat depressed, and she could not account for it. She had been excited ever since she had known she was going to Egypt. She had gone back to visit Chaim and found that he was improving. She had mailed a letter for him the day they had left, but still she worried about him. She felt uncertain, and her future seemed rather dim. The others knew what they were doing, but all she could do was cook and do menial jobs. And she felt uncomfortable around Diana Welles.

And beneath all this there was another trouble. She had been reading the New Testament and found herself caught up with the story of the Gospels. She had completed the book of John, and the stories of Jesus had so moved her that she had found herself almost weeping. At first she had tried simply to put the New Testament away, feeling that such emotions were wrong. She remembered what the professor had said, that Christ was her "beloved enemy," and over and over again she read in the Scripture where Christ did love those who were in trouble, and those who weren't, for that matter. He had so much love that it touched—and troubled—Kefira greatly.

Now, as she stood beside Josh in the warm light of the moon overhead, she felt lonely and said finally, "I guess I miss my parents, and I'm worried about Chaim." She looked up at him and said, "Sometimes I feel like I've lost my way, Josh, and that everywhere I turn is the wrong way."

The moonlight, Josh noticed, was kind to Kefira, illuminating the full, soft lines of her body, the strong and pleasant contours of her face. He had always felt she was attractive, and now staring down at her, the soft fragrance that came to him slid through the armor of his self-sufficiency. She was sad now, but he knew there was a fire in this young woman that made her lovely, and he felt the things a man feels when he looks upon beauty and knows it will never be for him. It concerned him that she was sad, and he suddenly reached out and touched her cheek, marveling at the smoothness of it. It was an innocent gesture, but she was startled, he saw, and at once removed his hand. "Don't shoot me, Kefira." He smiled. "I'm harmless."

Kefira laughed then and said, "I won't do that, Josh. You're my best friend."

"That's good. I'm glad you feel that way. I'll tell you what. Let's stay up all night and just watch for land."

"We'll be too tired to work if we do that."

"Don't worry about it. I just want to remember this time. It's been so good."

They stood side by side and were silent as the ship sliced through the water. For a long time neither of them spoke, and finally he turned to her and said, "I'm glad I'm your best friend, Kefira."

Studying him for a moment, Kefira had a thought. "We can never be more than friends, Josh, you know that."

"Why would you say that?"

"We're too different."

"I don't think we're all that different."

"Yes, we are. I'm a Jew and you're a Christian." She hesitated then and added, "And besides, you're used to women like Diana."

Josh did not answer for a moment, for her words had affected him in a powerful way. He had been struggling with his feelings for Diana. On the one hand, he knew it was a purely physical attraction, and yet there seemed to be more to it than that. Now he said quietly, "I've given up on trying to read the future, but I know this. You're a wonderful young woman, Kefira, and the man who gets you will get a prize."

Kefira's cheeks grew warm, and as she looked into his gray eyes, she felt as pleased as she had ever felt in the presence of a man. She was shocked when he added, "You know, I was reading in the Old Testament this morning. I'm reading it through. I'm just finishing up the book of Proverbs. I was reading the last chapter. It describes a virtuous woman and almost the last verse says, 'Favour is deceitful, and beauty is vain: but a woman that feareth the Lord, she shall be praised.' That's you, Kefira."

Kefira was shocked, for Josh quoted the exact verse that the professor had applied to her!

Josh was struck by her silence, and he leaned forward and saw tears glistening in her dark eyes. "Don't cry."

"I can't help it!"

Josh felt the strong magnetic pull of this young woman. He took her hand and squeezed it, and then said, "Well, we'll always be the best of friends, won't we?"

Kefira's throat was full and she could not tell why. She whispered huskily, "Good night, Josh," then turned and pulled her hand away. She went at once to her cabin, and when she closed the door, she leaned back against it. She could not speak, so full was the emotion that raced through her. Finally she whispered the words that she had tried to contain. "I'm in love with Josh Winslow!"

The words shocked her, and she dashed the tears from her eyes. "Nothing can ever come of it," she said fiercely. A great sadness filled her, and as the ship rushed through the night, she knew that nothing she could say or do would ever change what she felt for the young man who had come into her life so abruptly.

PART FOUR

The Prize

★ ★ ★

CHAPTER NINETEEN

AT THE DIG

★ ★ ★ ★

As the *Empress* pulled into the port of Alexandria, Josh felt a thrill of anticipation. His eyes took in the flat country, and although it was impossible to see inland very far, he knew that soon he would be standing on the same ground on which the pharaohs had trod. The docks, he saw, were crowded, swarming with native workers trundling loads to various ships.

As the *Empress* pulled alongside the long stone quay, he heard Phineas say, "Well, we're here, Josh. It always gives me a thrill to come back to this land."

Josh grinned and turned to face the professor. "I've got a strong feeling we're going to find what we're looking for."

Phineas's round, cherubic face broke into a smile. "All archeologists think that, but the truth is there are more disappointments than victories in our profession, my boy. You work six months and get absolutely nothing—but then one day your shovel turns over something that you've been waiting for all your life and it makes it all worthwhile."

The two men stood there until the gangplank went down, and then Phineas said, "Well, we'll have to find our man. I've never met him, but he comes well recommended." His eyes swept the dock, and he nodded. "That could be him coming up the gangplank now. He looks like somebody important."

The two men made their way to the upper reaches of the gangplank, and a tall man with dark olive skin stepped on board. He was a handsome fellow with dark brown eyes and wore a turban and a white robe belted with a crimson sash. "Dr. Welles?"

"Yes, I'm Welles." The professor stepped forward and took the man's hand. "You must be Amir Ben Kalil."

"Yes, indeed. I'm very happy to meet you, Professor. I was so excited when you chose me to join your expedition."

"Mutual, I'm sure. This is Joshua Winslow, my assistant."

Josh stepped forward and took the man's hand. His grip was crushing, and Josh had to exert his strength to keep his bones from collapsing. "I'm glad to meet you, sir."

Amir smiled, his teeth white against his olive skin, and said, "I assume that you're anxious to get started, so I have hired a boat to take us up the Nile to our dig site."

"Fine—fine! We can't get started too soon. Come along, and I'll introduce you to the other members of our group."

"I'll go be sure that everything gets loaded, Professor," Josh said.

Amir turned and pointed. "You see that short, heavyset man with the blue turban? He's in charge of the boat. He will load the goods for you if you will point them out to him."

Amir had spoken carelessly as if to an underling, and Josh, for an instant, was affronted. But then he shrugged, realizing that in reality he *was* an underling.

Phineas and Amir started along the deck but stopped when the two women appeared. "Ah, here they are! May I present my niece, Diana Welles, and this is another of my assistants, Kefira Reis. Ladies, this is our new associate, Amir Ben Kalil."

Amir's eyes took in the two women, and he bowed deeply. Stepping forward, he took Diana's extended hand, kissed it, and then did the same for Kefira.

"I am honored to know you, Miss Welles. You're the professor's niece?"

"Yes," Diana said, smiling. "And you're the man who's going to help us find the golden mask of one of the pharaohs."

Amir laughed. "I would hope so, but it may take a little time."

He turned then to Kefira, saying, "And you are an archeologist, Miss Reis?" He was studying her carefully, and something in his eyes changed.

"Oh no," Kefira said quickly. "I'm just a helper. I try to take care of the professor's needs and do the cooking."

Amir said, "Sometimes the cook is the most valuable member of an expedition. I will look forward to our meals."

"Amir has gotten a boat," Phineas said. "We will have to get everything loaded on it, and then we'll sail up the Nile to the site. We'd better hurry, I think."

★   ★   ★   ★

The craft that glided smoothly up the broad brown river had but a single triangular sail. It had no motor, but the wind drove it along at a rapid clip. The supplies had all been stored below, and the native crew of four adjusted the sail from time to time. At other times they gathered around the single mast, speaking in their own language.

Amir had come to stand beside Kefira, who was holding on to the low rail. "This is the heart of Egypt, Miss Reis. The Nile Valley."

"It's very unusual. I've never seen anything like it."

They had been sailing now for some two hours, and Kefira commented, "This is such fertile land. Look at how green everything is."

"Yes, it is especially so at this season. At this point the Nile Valley is five miles wide. Look, you see those steep cliffs there and again on the other side there? They shelter the valley from the desert wind. Everywhere in the valley there's fertile black silt, but when you reach those cliffs, nothing grows. It's nothing but sand and rock, no vegetation, and sparse animal life. For the ancient people this desert was a region of great danger. They visited it only for the beautiful hard stones that could be quarried there and sometimes crossed over it on an adventurous trip to a foreign land."

"Are you Egyptian?"

"No, I am Arab." Amir hesitated, then stared at her. "I take it you are of Hebrew ancestry."

"How did you know that?"

"By your name, of course, and also by your appearance. You have the look of a daughter of Abraham."

"I'm proud you should think so."

For some reason Kefira felt somewhat uneasy under the piercing gaze of the Arab. He was an exceptionally handsome man, with smooth, almost classic features. His skin was lighter than she had expected, and he was tall and lean but obviously a powerful man. His hands, she noticed, were strong looking, but he had the long fingers that one expected of a concert pianist or an artist. She was fascinated by him and yet at the same time was somewhat nervous in his presence. "Will we be going far up the river?"

"Not really. We will disembark at a small village called Amarna. If we went farther, we would go to the ancient city of Thebes. And someday you will want to take a trip to the Valley of the Kings, which is where many of the ancient pharaohs were buried. But we should arrive by midafternoon."

He smiled, bowed slightly, and said, "I must go speak with Professor Welles. Let me know if there's anything I can do for you."

"Thank you very much." Kefira watched the tall man leave, then turned again to view the fertile fields of the Nile Valley flowing by on either side.

★ ★ ★ ★

"This is Lisimba, Miss Reis. He will be your assistant." Amir frowned and said, "If he gives you any trouble, simply beat him. Or if you would prefer, I will do it for you."

Kefira turned to see if Amir was serious, and he seemed to be. "I don't think we'll have to resort to that," she said quickly.

"These natives are no good. You have to beat them to get the best out of them." Amir whirled and walked away, and Kefira turned to the man who stood before her.

Lisimba was very small, several inches smaller than Kefira herself. He wore a simple tunic, belted by a strap of frayed leather. His feet were bare, his arms thin and stringy. His face was ugly. There was no other way to describe it. It was almost like a monkey face but was redeemed by the bright, cheerful brown eyes and the smile that twisted his lips upward. He was dark, baked by the sun, and Kefira was uncertain of how to treat him. "I don't think we'll have any beatings here, Lisimba."

"No, missy. Lisimba will work hard. God bless you very much."

"Well, I'll have to tell you that I'm new at cooking on an expedition like this, Lisimba. You'll have to help me."

"Oh yes, missy. You come with me. There is a market. You will buy fresh food for supper tonight."

The sailing craft had docked and was being unloaded into a truck that was backed up to the wooden dock. Amir had indicated they would have to wait until morning to leave for the digs, so Kefira had determined to cook her first meal, and she was nervous about it. She had gotten some Egyptian money from the professor, but it was a mystery to her how to convert dollars into Egyptian coinage.

Lisimba bobbed along beside Kefira in a strange, hobbling gait, a cross between a hop and a skip. He grinned incessantly and punctuated many of his sentences with expressions like "Bless the Lord" or "Praise God."

The market he led her to was simple, made up of stalls on both sides of the narrow street. Lisimba was at her side as she selected the fresh vegetables, many of which she did not recognize. He bargained vociferously with the venders. Kefira quickly learned you did not pay the first price they asked and was shocked when Lisimba called one man a "thief with a camel's nose" for trying to overcharge a lady. Such insults, apparently, did not mean anything, for the man had simply lowered his price grudgingly until an agreement was reached.

When they reached the meat section, Kefira was appalled.

Animal carcasses hung in the open air, covered with flies. The stench was unbearable, and she turned to Lisimba. "This is awful!"

"You do not like the meat?"

"No, there are flies all over it."

"If you like, we can buy a live animal and we can keep the flies off."

Kefira hesitated, then shook her head. "I don't know anything about butchering animals."

"I know everything about such things, praise the Lord," Lisimba said eagerly. "Come. Over there we can buy a nice juicy tender lamb. You know how to cook lamb?"

"Not really."

"Then perhaps you will allow me to help you."

"I'm afraid you'll have to, Lisimba. I'm glad you're here. As you can see, I don't know what I'm doing."

"You will learn very quickly. I will show you," Lisimba said eagerly.

The two purchased a half-grown lamb, which Lisimba said would make the best meal, and then they started back, with Lisimba leading the lamb.

When they reached the docks, Kefira found that Josh had set up her tent, as well as one for Diana. He looked at the lamb and said, "Is that supper tonight?"

"Yes, you should have seen that meat market. Meat hanging in the open. Flies all over it."

Josh suddenly laughed. "I want to watch as you butcher that cute little fellow."

Kefira frowned. "You're awful, Josh! You know I couldn't do that."

"You're just like my sister Jenny. She hates to eat deer because she says they're so beautiful. She eats them, though, I've noticed. Try to do a good job," he winked at her. "You want to impress us all on your first meal on the expedition."

★ ★ ★ ★

Anxiously Kefira looked over the meal she had prepared. The men had gone to wash up, and as they returned, she said nervously, "I hope you're not expecting too much."

"It will be delicious, my dear. Your cooking always is," Phineas said cheerfully.

The men sat down, and Kefira began setting out the meal.

"This smells wonderful. What is it?" Josh asked.

"It's stewed lamb, and I made some black bean soup."

As she put the dishes on the table, Professor Welles said, "I think we'll ask God to bless the food. Josh, would you pronounce the blessing?"

Josh asked a quick blessing, and then the men dug in. Amir tasted the stewed lamb and said with surprise, "Why, it's perfectly seasoned! You are a chef indeed, Miss Reis."

"Well, I have to give credit to my assistant." Kefira turned and nodded to Lisimba, who was standing close by. "He showed me how to do it."

"What is this?" Amir asked, holding up a small piece of pastry.

"It's called *teiglach*. It's my specialty."

Josh bit into one of the bits of pastry and exclaimed, "Why, this is good! What's in it?"

"Cheese and bits of lamb."

Diana served herself a second helping of stewed lamb. "I'll have to say, Kefira, you are an excellent cook."

"Thank you, Diana."

When the meal was almost finished, Kefira brought out her masterpiece—a sweet carrot compote. As the members of the party sampled it, they all pronounced it delicious.

"I've been on some digs," Phineas said, "where we had to threaten to shoot the cook, but I can see we won't have any problems this time. My compliments, my dear."

As the others spoke up their commendation, Kefira felt a great release. She had been worried as to whether she could handle the kind of cooking that would suit the others, and now she felt confident.

After the meal, the others left to see to the storing of the supplies on the truck, and Kefira helped Lisimba clean up.

"I don't know what I would have done without you, Lisimba," Kefira said, smiling.

"You will be a great cook," Lisimba said. He flashed a smile at her, his little monkey face twisted, and said, "You will make a good wife for some man. This is good practice for wives-to-be."

Kefira did not answer but instead said, "Are you Muslim, Lisimba?"

"No, missy, not Muslim—not anymore. I am a Jesus man now."

This surprised Kefira. She had assumed that the small man was a Muslim, understanding that most of the natives were. She waited for him to say more, but he chatted on about the supplies and the food, punctuating his remarks with expressions of thanksgiving.

As soon as the meal was cleaned up and preparations for breakfast complete, Kefira went to the tent. She undressed, put on a cotton gown, and after washing her face and hands, got under the covers on the cot. She fell asleep almost immediately, but she slept fitfully. Several times that night she dreamed of a sharp black stone and of a house beside it with a goat on top. She had dreamed this for weeks now, and she could make no sense out of it. Finally she drifted off into a deep, solid sleep.

★ ★ ★ ★

They arrived at the dig site early in the day. The work went well, and by sunset the camp was fairly well established. The large wall tents were up in a line, one for each of the members of the expedition, and one that would serve as an office and a depository for the relics they found. There were two smaller tents for sanitary purposes, for which Kefira was grateful. Another tent was the cook tent, where the stove and oven were kept, along with a table and chairs for the meals. The groceries were stored here in crates to keep out any wandering visitors, and Kefira had worked quickly to provide a simple meal at noon as they set up the tents. Everyone had worked hard, and once Amir had come into the tent to get water. He was a suave man and seemed to be studying her carefully. Finally he thanked her for the water, then said, "Be very careful about leaving camp, Miss Reis."

"Why don't you call me Kefira? Everyone else does."

"Why, thank you. I will. But as I say, I would not advise you to go alone outside of the area."

"Why not?"

"Some of the people in this area," Amir said carefully, "are not on good terms with the Jews."

Kefira turned to face him. "That was true in New York, where I lived."

"It is different here," Amir said patiently. "These people are very primitive. There are ancient feuds and superstitions about the Jewish race."

"What about you, Amir? Do you dislike the Jews?"

Amir laughed. His eyes were bold, and he studied her for a moment. "I hope to show you that I can be very close to Jews."

There was a tone in his speech that Kefira disliked, but the words themselves were inoffensive enough. She nodded, then went back to her work, and after Amir left, she said, "Lisimba, we have to have another good supper."

"Tonight we will have roasted lamb, and perhaps you will fix some more of your Jewish food."

As the two worked, Kefira finally asked what had been on her heart. "How is it that you are a Christian, Lisimba? Not many of your people are, I think."

"You are right, missy," Lisimba said sadly. He turned to her with a mournful look on his ugly face. "But I will tell you why I am a follower of Jesus. You see, I was a slave."

"You mean a real slave in chains?"

"In chains and beaten and all that goes with slavery." He paused and asked, "Are there slaves in your country, missy?"

"Not anymore. We had a war there, and they were all freed."

"Ah, that is good! But in many of the Muslim countries there is slavery. Young girls are sold into slavery by their parents when they are mere children. Others go into slavery for debt. That was my fate. I went in debt to the wrong man, and when I could not pay, he took me for a slave."

"How terrible!"

"It was not pleasant. He kept me chained to a post every night, and he beat me severely."

Kefira listened with horror as Lisimba spoke of the nature of being a slave. She had never given this a thought, since slavery was not a part of American life, but now she felt the horror of it, the absolute hopelessness as Lisimba spoke on about what it was like. "I was no more than an animal to my owner. He would work me until I could work no more. Had I died, he would have thrown my body into a ditch."

"But how did you get free?"

Lisimba's face brightened up, and his face was quite bearable when he smiled. "I found a portion of the Word of God. It was only a small part of the Bible and very worn. It was printed in Egyptian, and I think the good God must have put it in my way. I found it, and I kept it secret. It was part of the Gospel that told of Jesus and His mercy. I read it every night until I had it memorized." Tears sprang to his eyes, and he said, "And then I prayed to this Jesus God. I asked Him to set me free, and He did, missy. He did!"

Kefira was fascinated. "How did that happen?"

"I do not know. I know when I called on Jesus, He did something in my heart. I was miserable and unhappy and angry, but when I called on Him it was as if . . . as if I were put in a place where my heart was light and easy."

"But you were still a slave."

"Yes, I was. And every day I prayed for Jesus to set me free."

"How long did you pray?" Kefira asked cautiously. She was fascinated by the story, and there was no question in her mind as to the sincerity of the little man.

"I prayed for three years, and one day a man came to my master. I had never seen him, but he was a relative of mine. He had succeeded in business and had become a Christian. He told my master he wanted to buy me, and he paid the full price. And when we were alone, he said that Jesus God appeared to him and told him to come and buy my freedom." Tears were running down Lisimba's dark cheeks, and he said, "So Jesus set my soul free, and then He instructed my cousin to buy my physical freedom. That is why I sing the praises of the Lord Jesus every day."

Kefira was tremendously moved by the story. She sensed the sweet spirit in Lisimba, and for all of his ugliness, he was one of the happiest men she had ever seen.

That night she went to bed and thought for a long time about what had happened to Lisimba. She could not doubt his words. The truth shone from him, and when she went to sleep that night, she dreamed again of the sharp black stone rising high into the air and the house with the goat grazing on top.

★　★　★　★

By dawn Kefira had breakfast cooked, which in this case was bacon and eggs and bagels. She could not eat the bacon, but the others ate voraciously. When they had finished, Phineas announced, "Well, it's time to go to work. I've printed a schedule that we will stick to very carefully."

Kefira joined the others in looking over the schedule:

5:00 A.M. Reveille
5:30 A.M. Breakfast
6:00 A.M. to 2:00 P.M. Work
2:00 P.M. Lunch
3:00 P.M. to 4:00 P.M. Siesta
4:00 P.M. to 7:00 P.M. Work
7:30 P.M. Dinner
8:30 P.M. to 10:00 P.M. Plan work for next day. Examine results
　　of day's work.

Diana said indignantly, "Why, we can't work like this! There's no time to do anything but work."

"That's what we're here for, my dear. I'm sure we'll find time to make exceptions. Now we're all going to the tell. We'll start today."

He led them out to the tell, which was only a hundred yards away, and they all stood looking at the slight mound. "The important thing right now—I might say, the all-important thing—is where do we start?"

"That is very important, Professor," Amir said quickly. "I think we should start on the east side."

They all walked over the tell, which was no more than an acre in size, and for some time Phineas was deep in thought. He shook his head finally and said, "If we start at the wrong place, we can waste a tremendous amount of time. It's very important that we find some artifacts immediately. My brother Conrad will be wanting evidence that we're doing well."

Kefira, of course, kept silent during all of this. She listened as the professor and Amir discussed where to begin, and finally Phineas turned and said, "What do you think, Joshua? Would you be happy with Amir's decision?"

Josh looked somewhat disconcerted. "Well, I have so little experience, and I'm sure Amir has a great deal. But from what I've read of the excavation of other tells, the best would be the northwest area."

Amir looked incredulous. "Why northwest, if I may ask?"

"Because it appears that out of a hundred communities, more than ninety of them placed their major buildings in the northwest area."

"Why would they do that?" Amir demanded.

"I don't think anybody knows." Joshua shrugged. "Perhaps because of the sunset."

Amir argued vehemently against it, but finally Phineas said, "Amir, I am a scientist, but there is such a thing as luck. There's also such a thing as a hunch, as we say in America. I respect your opinion, but I believe we will start in the northwest."

Amir was obviously affronted. "These things should never be left to amateurs!" he huffed.

"You'll just have to live with this decision," Phineas said mildly. "Don't worry. We'll get to the eastern area soon enough."

"Very well," Amir said stiffly. "Let's get to work."

★   ★   ★   ★

The stars were as sharp and clear as diamond points overhead, and looking up Josh said, "Just think, God knows the names of every one of those stars."

Diana, who had asked Josh to walk with her around the camp before bedtime, smiled at him. "I'm sure He does." She had worked hard all day at the dig, and now she said, "This is going to be a lot of hard work, Josh, isn't it? It always is."

"That's what we came for." He stopped and turned to face her. "I just thank the Lord I'm here. It's a miracle, and I know I have you to thank for it, Diana. If you hadn't talked your father into hiring me, I'd be back on the farm in Georgia."

"I'm glad you're here too." Diana came close to him and put her hand on his chest. "We're going to have a good time on this. There'll be hard work, but there'll be time to relax as well."

She reached up then and touched his cheek. "What kind of woman is it you want, Josh?"

Josh was taken off guard by her question. He made no immediate answer, but Diana knew the question had touched him. She somehow guessed he harbored a picture of the ideal woman in his mind and in his dreams. She stood there, wanting him and wanting to be seen by him, not as the world judged her but as a woman to be desired. Her own desires were burning within her, and she was not ashamed of them. She had known Josh as a young man and they had found passion together, and now she expected it to come again. She watched him carefully and knew that he was filled with restless, vague wishes and that he did not yet know what those wishes were. But she knew he had to have love, and since she herself needed this more than anything else, she waited for his answer.

As for Josh, he struggled with the natural impulses that rose in him. Diana was a powerful enough force to be felt, and suddenly he could not squelch the heavy insistent appetite. He pulled his mind away from her by force of will and then said almost hoarsely, "Diana, you ought to be more . . . careful of yourself . . . with men, I mean."

"I can't be like that, Josh. I can't lock myself away. If we care for each other, why shouldn't we have each other?"

Josh suddenly straightened up and shook his head. "That may have been the way I thought when we first met back in our college days, Diana, but I'm a Christian now. I know that might sound pompous to you, but it's the only answer I can give you."

Diana knew better than to argue against his belief. She looked up at him and said, "We belong together, Josh. I know you still care for me, and I care for you." Her voice grew soft, and her eyes seemed to envelop him. "We have to seize what little joy we can, Josh. That's all there is in this world."

"No, I don't agree, Diana. Please, you don't know what it does to me when you—" He could not finish his sentence and said almost harshly, "Time to turn in. We've got a hard day tomorrow."

Diana was satisfied. *I touched him. He's fighting, but this religion of his will fade away. He wants me, and I can make him want me more.*

CHAPTER TWENTY

"JESUS HELD ME TOGETHER"

★ ★ ★ ★

The date was May 29, and Kefira knew that the weather back in New York would be mild—spring was usually quite comfortable. But here in the flat plains of Egypt, the bright sun already beat down with summertime strength.

Kefira stood on the tell and surveyed the surrounding area. As far as she could see, there were no trees. The tents made a line that broke the flatness of the terrain. Far off to her right an outcropping of rock arose, the two lines of rocks forming a wadi or a small valley. To the north a flock of sheep was barely visible, the dark red robes of the herdsmen making a small splash of color on the bland landscape.

The excavation that day had surprised her. She had imagined workers throwing dirt high in the air, working with feverish activity. Instead, shovelful by shovelful was examined carefully by the professor or Diana, with Josh watching on the sidelines. It was all rather boring, and Kefira had waited all morning for them to find something. Instead the native workers had hauled away wheelbarrow after wheelbarrow to a small wadi, dumping their loads there.

Now she saw the professor go down on his hands and knees and wave the barrows back. He had a brush in his hand and was studiously sweeping away the dust from something. She carefully stepped closer as he picked up an object and said with satisfaction, "The first find of our expedition."

They all crowded around as Phineas held up a small disc. "What is it?" Diana asked, peering at it.

"I think it's a button. It has an eagle on it. It must be from one of Napoleon's soldiers." The professor took a small white card out of his pocket and began to write on it. When he had finished, he handed it to Kefira and said, "We label everything we find like this." Taking the card, Kefira saw he had drawn a picture of the button, and at the bottom of the card he had written, *Button from one of Napoleon's soldiers.* Beside the button, he had noted, *Scale 1-1.* And at the top left, he had carefully printed, *Level one about seventeen fifty.*

She looked up and said, "How would a French button get in Egypt?"

"Napoleon thought to expand this as part of his empire. He had to stop, though, when Lord Nelson defeated his navy at the Battle of the Nile and he was cut off. Still, this button may have come directly from one of his soldiers, or a native may have found a coat and brought it here. No way of telling."

Kefira handed the card back and smiled. "You keep careful records, Professor."

Phineas nodded. "That's what archeology is. Records."

★ ★ ★ ★

The careful digging of the trench went on for several days, and a number of artifacts were turned up. There was a gold coin with a picture of Caesar on it, a Roman sword missing its handle, likely hewn of wood now rotted away, and a considerable amount of pottery, which Diana identified.

Kefira was pleased with the way she kept the group well fed, and also with the way she took care of the professor. He had a way of losing things, and she, with Joshua's help, organized his writings and the findings in a careful, methodical way.

Kefira had asked to do some of the work of digging, and

under the supervision of one of the crew, she put in her time under the blazing sun. Josh, whose skin was fair, burned if he did not cover himself and wear a broad-brimmed hat, but Kefira simply turned a rich golden color, and she took no harm from it.

It was on a Thursday afternoon, while Kefira was very carefully removing sand, when she made the most significant discovery of all. She had become quite proficient at gently scooping away sand with a cup. It was dull work, but she had learned how important it was to let nothing go by. Emptying the cup, she began to brush away at the sand when suddenly her fingers encountered something hard. Carefully she took a brush and swept the sand away and then she stopped suddenly. She began to tremble and said in a strange voice, "Josh, I think I found something."

Josh, who was working ten feet away, came at once. Peering over, he caught his breath. "You have. I'd better get Professor Welles." He left and was soon back with the professor, along with Amir and Diana. The professor was staring at the object, and he looked up and smiled.

"Kefira, you found a grave."

"Someone's buried here?"

"Yes, and it's very well preserved." He began to clean the sand away, and soon a hand was clear and part of a forearm. Everyone was excited, and for the next day and a half they took turns clearing the sand away from the body Kefira had discovered. As they did, the professor explained to Kefira, "The body, as you can see, is in a sleeping position, with the elbows and knees drawn together. Many bodies are found in this position. The body was placed in a pit with provisions for the afterlife— we'll probably find a few artifacts here, such as food containers."

"But how can a body still be here after all these years?"

"Probably no place in the world would a body be better mummified, with the possible exception of someone being frozen in a glacier. Here, you see, the sand absorbs all the water from the body. It dries it out and preserves it. It's not at all unusual to find burial places like this. Many times we find them under houses."

"People buried their dead under their house?"

"Oh yes. That was very common."

The digging went on until the body was finally clear.

"It's a woman," Professor Welles said softly. "Look, her hair is even preserved. It's a reddish color. And there's another body here, a small child."

Kefira said nothing, but she felt a great sadness. She kept back while the others worked, and finally Josh called out, "Look, I don't believe it!"

Everyone moved in closer to see what Josh had uncovered. "It's a cross," he said.

Kefira leaned forward and saw that in the woman's hand, which was partly beneath her body, was an object that did indeed look like a cross.

"It's made of silver, I think," Josh said. He looked up at the professor. "That pretty well dates it, doesn't it? It would have to be from some time in the first century A.D."

"Yes, it's a find indeed."

Amir had leaned forward, his eyes gleaming. "This will be worthy of some attention. A Christian burial here in this part of the world and at a very early date. Congratulations, Professor."

"The body won't last long now that it's been uncovered, unless we take special care," Professor Welles said. "You're the expert in that, Amir."

"Yes, I will take care of it at once."

Later that afternoon Kefira was seated on the sand watching as Amir carefully transferred the body to a case that could be sealed airtight. It would be taken to the museum in Cairo, where it would be preserved.

Josh came over and sat down beside Kefira. "You're very quiet today."

"I've been thinking about that woman and her child."

Josh looked at her and saw that her eyes were sad. "Why does it trouble you?"

"I've been thinking about her, wondering what she was like. She must have been happy when her baby was born. I could just imagine her riding the child on her knees, kissing the baby's cheek, just as I'd do if I had a child." She looked at him, and her eyes were enormous. "I've always been interested in people,

Josh. I see them laughing or crying, and I wonder why. I hardly ever pass a man or a woman without wondering about their story. Has their life been good or bad?" She looked up and said, "Have you ever stopped to think how close heaven is for all of us, and yet how far it is when we lift our hands to touch it?"

Josh felt a surge of compassion. "Don't be sad," he said. "Just imagine that she had a good life."

"But she died so young, and her baby along with her."

"Don't be afraid. Don't ever be afraid, Kefira. God is good, and He cares for us."

"You really believe that, don't you, Josh?"

"Yes, I do."

"I'm glad you think like that. I hope you always will."

A gust of wind lifted a lock of her black hair, then dropped it over her forehead. She brushed it back and looked down at her hands for a moment. When she looked up, he saw there were tears in her eyes. "I cry too easily, I guess. Her troubles are over at least. Most of ours still lie ahead of us."

Impulsively Josh reached over and took her hand. It was warm and strong, and he held it, squeezing it to give her a little comfort. She turned to face him, and he saw her need for love and assurance and faith. "You'll find your way like I did."

Kefira felt the strong grasp of his hand; then he released her, and she got to her feet. "I'm sorry to be so moody. That's the way women are, I guess."

"It's the way men are too," Josh said, getting up to stand beside her. "I'm glad you feel deeply about things, Kefira."

She smiled briefly, then turned away. She went at once to the tent and began working on the meal with Lisimba at her side. She could not keep from thinking about the woman buried in the sand with her baby, and Lisimba noticed her quietness. "Why you not talk much, missy?"

"I've been thinking about the two bodies we found, the woman and the little baby. It makes me sad to think of it."

"No, she is with Jesus. Do not be sad."

"How do you know that?"

"She had a cross in her hand. Mr. Josh told me. She was a Jesus woman."

Kefira turned and looked at the man. He was ageless. He could have been anywhere from thirty to seventy. The desert seemed to have embalmed him almost as much as the woman they had found. She smiled at him, for she had grown fond of the man. "I wish I had your assurance, Lisimba."

"You will have after you are saved."

The words caught at Kefira. "After I'm saved? What do you mean by *saved*?"

"Why, all of us need to be saved. We are all bad creatures. Me, I was the worst of sinners, but the Bible says that all people sin."

"Of course, that's true. But there's nothing we can do about it."

"Oh no, that is not right, missy!" Lisimba protested. "Let me read you. There is a book in the Bible called Acts."

"Yes, I've read some of it, about the man called Paul who was struck down on the road to Damascus."

"Yes, Paul was saved like that. Tonight before you sleep, read in the sixteenth chapter of this beautiful book. It tells the story of two men, Paul and Silas, who were preaching about Jesus. They were thrown in jail and had their feet in chains, and they were whipped for preaching. I know the rest by heart. You would think that men in jail with their feet bound, with their backs bleeding, would be very sad, would you not?"

"I would think so."

"But the Bible, it says, 'And at midnight Paul and Silas prayed, and sang praises unto God: and the prisoners heard them. And suddenly there was a great earthquake, so that the foundations of the prison were shaken: and immediately all the doors were opened, and every one's bands were loosed. And the keeper of the prison awaking out of his sleep, and seeing the prison doors open, he drew out his sword, and would have killed himself, supposing that the prisoners had fled. But Paul cried with a loud voice, saying, Do thyself no harm: for we are all here. Then he called for a light, and sprang in, and came trembling, and fell down before Paul and Silas, and brought them out, and said, Sirs, what must I do to be saved?'"

Lisimba fairly quivered with excitement. "You see? This man

he knows he is bad, but he wants to know how to be bad no more. That is what being saved means."

Intrigued, Kefira said, "And what did the prisoners tell him?"

"Ah, in verse thirty-one, they gave him the answer, 'And they said, believe on the Lord Jesus Christ, and thou shalt be saved, and thy house.' And that is what happened, missy. The jailer he believed and was saved and was forgiven for his sins, and his whole house gave their hearts to Jesus. Oh, what a happy story! How great is our God to save us from all of our sins. Hallelujah! Praise the name of Jesus!"

Kefira was moved by Lisimba's story. She worked the rest of the day, and the first thing she did that night, after going to her own tent, was to turn to the book of Acts and read the entire story. She read it slowly, thinking carefully about it, and wondered, *How could a man love those who had beaten him with a whip? I couldn't do that!* She read the story again, and the question came to her, *Can it be true? Can a person be saved and have his sins forgiven?* All she knew of faith was from her Jewish background—there was nothing like this in her imagination.

Going to bed, she lay awake for a long time thinking of Lisimba's excitement and joy, and going over the story of Paul and Silas and the conversion of the jailer. Finally she dropped off to sleep and dreamed again of the black rock rising like a needle in the air.

★　★　★　★

The work progressed steadily, and all of the team members fell into a regularity of life. It seemed they all followed the schedule Phineas had laid out, and Kefira found herself enjoying the life. The work was hard and demanding, but during the nights she would sit around the campfire listening to the others, saying little herself. She continued to read the New Testament, shocked at how hungry for it she was finding herself to be. She was fascinated by the character of Jesus of Nazareth. He was nothing like she had imagined. She knew now that she had allowed her thoughts of Him to be colored by those she had seen who called themselves Christians. She found in the New Testament that even the close followers of Jesus had faults, and somehow that comforted her. She loved the stories of Jesus when He met those who were ill and simply touched them and they were healed. She read over and over again about the prostitute He had forgiven, and how Jesus loved people no matter how bad they were.

Her relationships were good with everyone except Amir. He had taken occasion more than once to lay his hand on her shoulder and squeeze it. Whenever he came near her, she immediately put up her defenses. One evening when she was cleaning up by herself, he came in and spoke to her pleasantly. "You did well on the dig today, and the meal tonight was good. You're working hard."

"I don't mind, Amir."

He came over then and stood beside her. "You and I ought to drive into the village sometime. There are some things I could show you there."

"Oh, I don't think I could do that. There's too much work to do."

Kefira was taken completely by surprise when he suddenly seized her, pulled her close, and kissed her. She was so shocked by his brazen action that she did not resist for a moment, but then she put her hands against his chest and shoved herself forcefully back. "Don't you touch me again!" she said quietly but with a direct intensity.

"Don't tell me you've never been kissed before."

"You heard what I said."

"Yes, I've heard that you carry a gun and that you shoot men who take liberties. But I think all women want to be loved. They just need a strong man."

"Amir, stay away from me," she warned.

Amir laughed and shook his head. "You Jewish women are a funny sort, but I'll win you over."

Kefira told no one of what had happened, but she was careful to never allow herself to be alone with Amir again.

★ ★ ★ ★

Josh got a severe case of sunburn the next day, and Phineas ordered him out of the sun. He came into the cook tent to watch Kefira as she prepared the meal and to drink the water she gave him from time to time. Lisimba was scurrying about peeling and dicing vegetables, and at the same time, as usual, he was talking about the Bible. He loved the stories of the Bible, the Old Testament and the New, and was continually speaking of them.

Josh listened as Lisimba told Kefira the story of Jesus walking on the water. He spoke with great gusto and dramatized everything with wild hand gestures. Sometimes he became so excited he literally danced.

" . . . and so Jesus tells Peter to come to Him on the water, and Simon Peter—he jumps out and he starts for Jesus, walking on the water his own self. But he don't go far when he suddenly looks around and sees the storm, and then he makes a bad mistake, missy. He doubt Jesus, and he suddenly sinks down in the water. He begins to scream 'Help me!' and Jesus, He go picks him out of the water and throws him in the boat. That Peter," Lisimba said, shaking his head sadly, "he should have gone all the way to Jesus."

"You really believe that story, Lisimba?" Kefira asked.

"Oh yes, missy. Jesus can walk on water. He is a big God. He made the water. Why can He not walk on it?"

Josh grinned and listened as Lisimba rebuked Kefira, and when the small man left the tent, he said, "You've got a good preacher there, Kefira."

Kefira came over and sat down beside him. "Drink some more water," she said, "and put that compress back on your head."

"It's just a little burn, not sunstroke."

"You do what I tell you."

"You're pretty bossy," he complained, but he took the damp cloth and put it on his forehead. "You two have gotten pretty close, haven't you?"

"Lisimba? Yes, he's a lovely man."

"Lovely! He's ugly as an ape!"

"I don't mean outside. He has more joy than anybody I've ever seen."

Josh had been very careful to put no pressure on Kefira, but now after sitting silently for a moment, he said, "I don't want to offend you, Kefira, but one of my prayers is that one day you'll know Jesus."

Kefira looked at him quickly. She did not answer for a time, and then finally she asked, "Why would you want me to be a Christian?"

"Because I think everyone needs Jesus. You know there's a verse in the book of Colossians that says Jesus holds everything together, all the stars in place. He keeps the earth from flying off in some crazy direction, and He keeps life together." Josh had grown very serious, and now he said, "He kept me. Jesus is all that held me together, Kefira. If it hadn't been for Him, I don't know where I'd be."

Kefira put her gaze on him, studying him intently. Finally she said, "Do you love Jesus, Josh?"

"Yes, I do," he said quietly. "Not as much as I should, but that's part of the Christian life. You know how the longer you are around some people, the more you love them. I haven't been a Christian very long, but the more I think of Jesus, the more I seek Him, the more I love Him. I think that's what heaven will be," he said quietly. "Just learning to love Jesus and each other more and more throughout all eternity."

"That's very good." Kefira's voice was soft, and she was quiet for a long time. "I've been reading about Jesus. There's nobody else like Him in all of history, but have I been wrong all my life? My whole family is Jewish. None of them believe in Jesus."

"I can't answer all your questions, but I'm glad you're learning about Jesus. One day you'll cry out to Him, and He'll just come in and take over your heart."

Disbelief clouded Kefira's features. She shook her head and got up and said no more.

★　★　★　★

The weeks wore on, and very few finds were made in the tell. Amir had been growing steadily more discontented. He began trying to persuade Phineas to change locations, but Phineas was steadfast. "No," he said firmly, "we'll stay here. I'm sure there's something here, and we'll just have to be patient."

Diana had heard this conversation, and privately she agreed with Amir. She found Josh and said, "I'm going into town to get some supplies. Come with me."

"I've got a lot to do, Diana."

"Don't be such an old stick. I need the company. Come on."

The two of them climbed into the truck and drove into the village. They bought the supplies and loaded them in the truck. As they were climbing back in, Diana looked around with a scowl on her face. "There's not a thing to do in a dump like this. Don't you ever wish you were back in civilization again?"

Josh had not yet started the motor. He sat in the driver's seat, sweat running from his forehead. He mopped it and shook his head. "No, not really. This is what I want to do."

"I think I agree with Amir," Diana said abruptly. "I don't think there's anything at the tell where we are now. I think we ought to move."

"Your uncle doesn't agree with you."

"He's a very stubborn man. Oh, I know he seems meek, but he's like a snapping turtle hanging on when he gets an idea." She reached out and put her hand on the back of his neck, and he turned to face her with surprise. "I've been thinking, Josh. This is no way for you to live."

"Why, I don't mind it. The hardships, you mean?"

"No, just being off the beaten track." Diana had been thinking about this for some time. She was a woman of moods and had become more and more disenchanted with life on the barren desert. "I've been thinking a lot, and I want you to listen to me, Josh."

"All right. What is it?"

"You'll get tired of this pretty soon. I want us to go back to the States, and I want you to get to know my father. You'd like him. He's gruff, but he's got a good heart. He has his hand in a lot of things, business things. You two would get along. He'll give you a job. Something that's exciting with some money in it. We could do it together. We could travel, see the world and have fun."

Josh was very aware of her touch. At the moment, hot, dirty, sweaty, and tired, her words seemed to make sense, but he had already made his choice. He knew it was time that she understood how he felt. Turning to her, he said, "Diana, what we had for each other is over. At the time it was the greatest thing in my life, but I'm a different man now. I'm not the man for you. We'd make each other miserable, and I think deep down you know it."

As Josh spoke, Diana let her hand remain on his neck for a moment, then abruptly pulled it away. "Let's go back," she said.

"I didn't want to offend you, but we could never have anything for each other long-term. We're too different."

And then Diana Welles, for once in her life, gave up. She hated to be defeated, but she saw that Josh was steady, rocklike, and she realized he was speaking the truth. "All right, Josh, I gave it a whirl. You can't blame a girl for trying, can you?" She turned to him and smiled slightly, then said, "Go on back to camp. We're a finished item."

Josh started the truck and felt a weight fall away from him. He knew he had done the right thing. He was sorry that Diana was hurt, but he knew her well. He knew she would find somebody else—and that she would never be happy with what she found.

CHAPTER TWENTY-ONE

THE FIND

★ ★ ★ ★

As June came to an end, Kefira found that she had settled in to the work and life in the desert better than she had expected. She had grown somewhat accustomed to the heat, never really liking it but learning to ignore the searing sun at midday. At night the winds sometimes felt almost cool in comparison with the day, and it was during those times that she would sit after finishing her work and read the New Testament, which had become a part of her life.

Late one Wednesday she had finished washing Phineas's shirts and shorts and hung them to dry, and afterward had gone to his tent, giving him clean sheets. She had become very fond indeed of Phineas, and he of her. He often made such remarks as, "If it weren't for Kefira's cooking, we'd all be at each other's throats. I've seen it that way on digs in the past." Kefira's face would flush with pleasure at his remarks, but she noticed Diana did not particularly enjoy them.

Now, drawing the canvas chair to the front of her tent, she opened the New Testament. As she held it in her hands she wondered, *What would Papa think of my reading the New Testament?* The question troubled her deeply. Her uncle had been a rabbi in the old country, and her father had longed to be one, but circumstances had not permitted it. Her Jewish heritage ran deep and the thought of forsaking it, which had occurred to her of late, gave her a pain in her heart. For a long time she sat there simply holding the worn black book, thinking of her parents and of Chaim. She had written him several times since she'd left, but there had been no answer, and she assumed it was difficult to get mail from the States to Egypt. She found herself praying then, as she often did, for his safety and health, and that when his time in prison was over he would find a good life. Abruptly she halted her prayer, realizing that she had no right to pray. From far off came the plaintive cry of a wild dog, and Kefira waited until it faded, then murmured, "What right have I to pray to God? I've thought of Him as my enemy for taking my parents. Why should He hear a sinner like me?"

She opened the book at random and began reading in the middle of a chapter:

> *And one of the Pharisees desired him that he would eat with him. And he went into the Pharisee's house, and sat down to meat. And, behold, a woman in the city, which was a sinner, when she knew that Jesus sat at meat in the Pharisee's house, brought an alabaster box of ointment, and stood at his feet behind him weeping, and began to wash his feet with tears and did wipe them with the hairs of her head, and kissed his feet, and anointed them with the ointment.*

The words struck Kefira powerfully. She well knew that the attitudes of the ancient Jews—and even some of the modern ones—toward women were harsh. Her father had told her that some Jews, when they said their prayers, always added the phrase, "And thank you, God, for not making me a woman." He had shaken his head and told her this was wrong, but Kefira had never forgotten it. She had read in the Old Testament of the inferior position of women, how they had been treated almost as chattel, and it had angered her.

She read the verses again, and for some reason the plight of the woman touched her heart. She had been aware of destitute women on the streets of New York and had never been able to understand how a woman could fall to such a position. As she read of the woman finding Jesus and weeping, her tears falling on His feet and wiping them away with her long hair, she felt compassion. *Poor woman! What a terrible life she must have led!*

And then Kefira thought, *The righteous, self-respecting Jews would have nothing to do with a fallen woman. What will Jesus do to this woman, obviously a prostitute, who comes and takes such liberties with Him? Why, He'll probably tell her to go at once and leave Him alone!*

She looked down to the next verse:

Now when the Pharisee which had bidden him saw it, he spake within himself, saying, This man, if he were a prophet, would have known who and what manner of woman this is that toucheth him: for she is a sinner.

That's exactly what I would expect a good Jewish man to say, Kefira thought. *He expects Jesus to command the woman to leave Him alone, just as I do.*

She began reading at the next verse:

And Jesus answering said unto him, Simon, I have somewhat to say unto thee. And he saith, Master, say on. There was a certain creditor which had two debtors: the one owed five hundred pence, and the other fifty. And when they had nothing to pay, he frankly forgave them both. Tell me therefore, which of them will love him most?

Again Kefira paused and thought of what she had read. "What a strange thing to say," she murmured. "I love the parables Jesus gave, and this is obviously one of them. But anyone would know the answer to that. The one who is forgiven the most will love the most."

She looked down and began reading again:

Simon answered and said, I suppose that he, to whom he forgave most. And he said unto him, Thou hast rightly judged. And he turned to the woman, and said unto Simon, Seest thou this woman? I entered into thine house, thou gavest me no water for my feet: but she hath washed my feet with tears, and wiped them with the hairs of her head. Thou gavest me no kiss: but this woman since the time I came in hath not ceased to kiss my feet. My head with oil thou didst not anoint: but this woman hath anointed my feet with ointment.

"Good for you, Jesus!" Kefira whispered fervently. "Just exactly what he deserved, the self-righteous pig! Good for you, Jesus!"

She read on:

Wherefore I say unto thee, Her sins, which are many, are forgiven; for she loved much: but to whom little is forgiven, the same loveth little. And he said unto her, Thy sins are forgiven.

Joy flooded Kefira at that moment. She could almost see the scene in her fertile imagination. The self-righteous Pharisee, the prophet Jesus, and the woman crouching at His feet with tears flowing down her face. She could hear the sternness of Jesus' accusation as He spoke to His host, and then, when she read the words, *Thy sins are forgiven,* tears came into her eyes. She could not continue reading for a time and had to pull out a handker-chief to wipe the tears away.

"What kind of a man is this who would forgive so freely?" she whispered. She looked down and read the last two verses:

And they that sat at meat with him began to say within themselves, Who is this that forgiveth sins also? And he said to the woman, Thy faith hath saved thee; go in peace.

Closing the New Testament, Kefira clasped it in both hands. She leaned forward in her canvas chair and put the small book to her forehead and closed her eyes. The peace of the desert brought a great quietness, but she was far away in her imagina-tion. She was sitting in that room and thinking of Jesus and the poor sinful woman. *How she must have felt,* Kefira thought with a burst of emotion, *when He said, "Thy sins are forgiven." And when He said, "Thy faith hath saved thee." And then He told her, "Go in peace." How I would have liked to be there to see that.*

For a long, long time Kefira sat there with the New Testament pressed against her forehead, her eyes tightly closed. She found herself wanting to weep, and she did not know why. She felt also a great void within her own heart, for she had hardness there against men and even against God for allowing her life to be so difficult. Now, however, as she read of Jesus and His loving spirit and His generosity and kindness toward a sinful woman, she whispered, "How can I hate a man who does such things as this?"

The silence ran on and still she sat there, until finally she whispered, "Oh, Jesus, if this is the kind of a man you are, I cannot hate you any longer." She did not know how to pray, for she had prayed mostly in formal patterns, but now out of her heart came the prayer. "Show me the way, O almighty and eternal God. If this Jesus is your son, make me to know it. That I too may fall before Him and weep as another sinful woman once did."

★ ★ ★ ★

The confrontation exploded almost like a mine going off and caught Phineas by surprise. He had been working over his diagrams in the tent, which he had made into his office and was now cluttered up with artifacts and findings. Amir had come in and without preamble had stated, "We must change locations, Professor Welles. We are wasting our time here."

Phineas put down his pencil on the small desk, leaned back in his chair, and shook his head. "I'm sorry to disagree with you, Amir, but I feel that would be a sad mistake."

Amir's face darkened, and he said loudly, "You do not know this land as I do. I know you have a reputation, but I have lived here all of my life, and I tell you we're wasting money and time. There is nothing here to find of any importance."

"Amir, please be patient," Phineas said, sighing. "I expect that we've all felt as you do. When I was on the dig at Crete, I felt exactly the same way, and many times I was ready to leave. But I had an able assistant who kept encouraging me. I grew angry with him at times, but I'd listen to him. And you've heard of the great finds that we made there."

"This is not Crete! This is Egypt!" Amir said vehemently. "When I agreed to cooperate with you on this dig, I assumed that you would listen to me, but you have not. We have dug nothing out but a few unimportant items, and there is nothing here except more of the same! I insist that we leave!"

The argument grew more heated. Even the professor lost his temper, which was a rare thing.

"You are here as a colleague, Amir, but I am the senior member of this expedition. And I am telling you now that I do not want to hear any more about leaving."

Amir stared at the smaller man. Hot words came to his lips, and he let them fall, but then he said, "If I leave, you will have great difficulty in continuing."

"It would be unfortunate," Phineas said sharply, "but we would do the best we could without you."

"But you do not have influence with the government as I do. You could be stopped in a moment if I dropped a word in the right place."

"I think after that threat there's nothing more to be said. There'll be no more talk about it."

Amir glared at Welles, turned and left, and shortly afterward Josh came in. "I couldn't help overhearing. Amir was pretty loud," he said. He studied the professor and said, "Do you think he'll cause trouble?"

"I hope not, Joshua. He is right about one thing. He's an influential man with the government in Cairo. The laws and regulations are very strict about excavating here. It all must be cleared through the department there." Phineas sighed and ran his hand through his scanty hair. "I don't know why things like this have to happen. It's hard enough doing the work without fighting dissension like this."

Josh could not help thinking it would have been better if Amir had not been involved in the expedition at all, but he knew it was useless to take that line now. "I'm sure we'll find more significant artifacts, Professor. We'll just have to work harder."

"You're a comfort, Josh. I'm glad you're here with me. I've watched you work, and I know you have a great future in the field. How are you coming with your hieroglyphics?"

"It's a lot harder than French or German, but you've been such a help to me. I'm sure I'll master it. I always admired the way you could read hieroglyphics as easily as I read a news-paper."

"You have a gift for language, and you'll learn."

Josh left the professor and went to the cook tent, where he found Lisimba peeling potatoes. "Need any help, Lisimba?" he said with a grin.

"No, you dig, I cook with missy." He smiled and nodded over to Kefira, who was chopping a fish into small pieces.

"What are you cooking now?" Josh asked her.

"Gefilte fish. Lisimba found some fresh fish from heaven knows where, and I missed gefilte fish."

"I remember you fixed that for us back in Georgia."

"That's right, I did." She smiled at him, then added, "Some-time I'll make you gefilte *kishke*."

"What in the world is that?"

"It's stuffed intestines."

Josh laughed. "It sounds like something they would eat down south. Only there they call it 'chitterlings.'"

"There's also gefilte *helzel,* stuffed chicken neck skin. We'll try that sometime."

"Well, if you make it, I'm sure I'll like it." Josh sat there chatting idly with her and finally remarked on the scene between Amir and Phineas. "He was really sore. He talked about walking out."

"I never have liked that man. He's arrogant," Kefira said. "I wish he would go away."

"I guess we need him. He has influence with the government. He could cause us trouble."

"That is true," Lisimba said, nodding. "He is a very important man in Cairo. He has very influential friends, but the Lord Jesus will not let him hurt the good professor."

"That's good news. We'll both pray about that." Josh grinned and took a sip of his coffee. He remained for a time and then left to go back to the dig.

Lisimba had been watching Kefira very carefully. He finished peeling the potatoes and then began slicing them up into slivers. "You like Mr. Joshua, do you not, missy?"

Kefira was startled. "Why . . . we're very good friends."

"Yes, I can see that."

Kefira stared at Lisimba and saw he was laughing at her. "What do you mean by saying such a thing? That's all we are, just friends."

"Miss Diana she likes him too."

Kefira felt a blush heat her cheeks. "I suppose she does. They are very old friends."

"But he like you best."

Kefira burst into laughter. "You're quite a psychologist, aren't you, Lisimba!"

"What is that?"

"Someone who claims to know how people feel and why they act the way they do."

"Oh yes, Lisimba very good at things like that. It is very easy, for one look in your eyes and I see you have a heart for Mr. Joshua. And I see he looks at you in a way he does not at Miss Diana."

Kefira stared at the small dark face of Lisimba and then smiled. "You just cut up those potatoes and don't take so much interest in me and Joshua."

"But you are so very *interesting*, missy!" Lisimba grinned. "I cannot help myself."

Kefira shushed him and then turned back to her work, but she thought of Lisimba's words and wondered if they were true. Diana had monopolized Josh's every free moment, making several trips into the village, and she had, without admitting it even to herself, resented it. Now she reflected on Lisimba's words, and she wondered if there was anything to them.

★　★　★　★

The desert sun of July was just as hot as that of June. Josh and Kefira took their turn out under the blistering sun digging away, and the trench had grown long now. There had been many finds, for obviously this had been an old, old city, or perhaps town would be a better word. They had discovered combs and mirrors and Egyptian gods but nothing of any earthshaking significance.

At midday on the third of July, Josh was at the end of the tunnel digging away. They had reached a point where there was much rubble, and he had to use a shovel to break some of it loose. His mind was far back at his home in Georgia, but he came to himself with a start when his shovel struck a solid stone.

"What can this be? Must be a wall of some kind," he muttered. He began more carefully to clear away the rubble, and finally he knew that the professor would be interested. He called out, "Professor, I found something here!"

The professor ambled over, got into the trench, and said, "What is it, my boy?"

"It's rock of some kind. Look, it's not native."

"No, it's not an outgrowth. It's a building stone." Excitement crept into the professor's voice, and he said, "We may have found something here. This looks like it could be some sort of door."

Word spread throughout the camp, and soon everybody was there, staring. Josh and the professor cleared away the rock, and the crew carried it off in wheelbarrows. Finally Josh said, "Look, there's some kind of an inscription down here. Let me clear away the rest of the rubble."

Amir was standing close behind Joshua. "Let me see! Let me do it!"

Josh stepped back, for he was, after all, only a minor member of the crew. He watched as Amir quickly and efficiently cleared it away, and then he heard the man exclaim in Arabic something he could not understand.

"Look at this," the professor said. "It's the governor's seal."

Amir was cleaning frantically to clear the seal, and finally when he turned around and spoke to the professor, there was awe in his voice. "It is the seal of Mensah."

"I believe you're right," the professor said, and for once he was excited. "Mensah. Everyone has looked for his grave."

"Who is Mensah?" Joshua asked.

Diana was standing beside him, touching his arm. "He was the right-hand man of Pharaoh Mentuhotep II of the eleventh dynasty. Many thought Mensah was more powerful than the pharaoh. There are plenty of records about his achievements, and many thought he would be the next pharaoh. But he disappeared, and his tomb has never been found, although plenty of people have looked for it."

"That is right, and if this is correct, we have the find of the century here!" Amir exclaimed.

Great excitement prevailed then, and the professor declared a celebration. For the rest of the day they took turns working at the wall, until the door to the tomb was finally clear.

Josh found himself standing beside Kefira and reached out and hugged her. "We'll be telling our grandchildren about this someday, Kefira. It's a great find."

Kefira was aware of his arm around her, but he seemed unconscious of it. She smiled up at him and said, "I'm so glad for you, Josh."

"We may be here for a long time. It'll be a great opportunity for us."

Kefira looked around and said, "Did you notice that Amir left?"

"No, I didn't." Josh glanced around and saw everyone except Amir there at the trench working excitedly. "Where could he have gone?"

"I don't know. I thought it was strange that he would leave in the midst of all this excitement."

Josh suddenly realized he had his arm around Kefira. "Hey, I didn't mean to squeeze you to death. I'm just so excited."

"That's all right." Kefira turned, saying, "I've got to go fix supper."

★　★　★　★

The supper had been a victory celebration, but everyone noted Amir's absence. Diana said, "I can't imagine where Amir has gone. You'd think he would want to be here."

"Important finds like this have to be recorded, my dear," Phineas said. "I'm sure he's just gone to Cairo to make sure that our find has been recorded. Well, we had a lovely victory dinner," Phineas went on. "It was delicious, Kefira."

"Thank you, Professor."

"Yes, it was very good," Diana said. She had never complimented Kefira before, and now she raised her glass of wine and said, "Here's to you, Kefira Reis."

Joshua and the professor raised their glasses and toasted Kefira, whose cheeks reddened. "It was only a dinner," she said.

Diana stared at her critically and then said something that Kefira did not soon forget. "You have won, Kefira."

"Won what?" the professor asked with surprise, looking at his niece.

"It's a woman thing. You wouldn't understand." Diana patted his arm and then changed the subject.

After the meal the professor and Diana went to their tents. Kefira started to clean up, but Lisimba said, "No, missy, this is Lisimba's job."

"Why, thank you, Lisimba."

"Let's go out and look at that door one more time, Kefira," Josh said.

"All right. I'd like to."

The two left the dining tent and walked across the desert. "It seems almost cool tonight," Josh said. "But that's just in contrast with the heat of the day."

"I love the desert at night," Kefira said. "It's so quiet and peaceful."

They reached the ditch and stood looking down, and the silver moonlight illuminated the door. "I wonder what lies behind there. I want to tear it down and start looking. It could be anything."

"What sort of thing could it be?"

"Well, the pharaohs buried themselves pretty ornately. Death was very important to them, and as you know, preserving their bodies was too. But they made one mistake about their burials."

"What was that?"

"They were buried with precious things, gold and silver and jewelry, so sooner or later grave robbers were likely to come along. Most of the tombs were robbed and the mummies treated pretty roughly. As a matter of fact, there's only been one pharaoh's tomb found pretty much intact."

"Which one was that?"

"You've heard me talk about it. Howard Carter and Lord Carnarvon found the tomb of Tutankhamen. Its contents were almost untouched. They found weapons, clothes, furniture, and jewelry, as well as the famous coffin and the mask."

"Oh yes, I've seen a picture of that!"

"It made Carter famous as an archeologist."

"So, you're hoping there will be an unrobbed tomb here."

"That's what we're all hoping for. It would be the find of the century. Well, not as important as the pharaoh's, but almost."

The two stood there talking, and from time to time Kefira would turn to look up at Josh, and he would watch the slight changes of her face, the quickening and loosening of small expressions. Her black hair rose back from her temples in its thick masses, and he thought how beautiful it was. Once he said something that amused her, and he saw some private joke dancing in her eyes.

She seemed happy, and he knew this was unusual, for he had never ceased to marvel at the range of her spirit. He had seen hurt stain her eyes. And he had seen bitterness from time to time. But now a shade of loveliness seemed to come to her, and he listened to the cadence of her voice.

Finally she noticed his silence. "Why are you so quiet, Josh?"

He turned to face her and put his hands on her shoulders. She was wearing a khaki shirt and pants, and he could not ignore the clean-running physical lines, the lovely turning of her throat, and the strong, rounded shoulders. Her waist was small, her curves feminine. She was watching him with an innocence he had noticed in her from the very beginning. He knew she didn't realize how beautiful she was, and since he was a man like other men with all the same impulses, he was drawn to her as a lonely man is always drawn to a woman. But he knew that no other woman had ever touched him as deeply as this one. All of his past history with women suddenly seemed cheap and tawdry, for Kefira had not only an outward beauty and grace, but she was rich in a way a woman should be. She was like music that stirred his soul.

"What's wrong, Josh?"

Josh reached out and drew her close. He waited for her to protest, but she did not. She lifted her head and looked at him, and he knew then that he cared for her as he never had for another. He saw emotion leave a fugitive impression upon her face, and he thought, *I know her better than I've ever known any woman.* And then he lowered his lips and kissed her.

Kefira knew he was going to kiss her, but she did not feel the fear that usually came. She waited, saying nothing, but when he put his arms around her, and she felt his lips on hers, she knew that this man was like no other man, at least for her. She put her hands behind his neck and held him, and as his lips pressed against hers she found herself thinking, *So this is what love feels like.* . . . She had already admitted to herself that she loved Josh. But she had never allowed herself to hope that Josh might love her too. But now as he held her gently and yet with a force that took her breath away, a flame of hope leaped up to take its place.

When Josh lifted his head, Kefira let out a small sigh.

"I have to tell you, Kefira," he said quietly, "that I feel something for you that I've never felt for any other woman. You have a sweetness in you and a goodness, and everything you do is true and right."

"No, I'm not that way," Kefira whispered. She kept her hands on his neck and wondered at herself. "I've been so afraid of men, Joshua, but I'm not afraid of you." She stepped back then, and he released her. They stood there quietly, neither of them knowing exactly what to say. Finally she whispered, "Good night," then turned and walked away.

He stood there watching her go, and as she walked across the moonlit sand, he thought, *This is like nothing ever was. I've never felt anything like this for a woman before.*

★　★　★　★

The next day Kefira felt uneasy around Josh. At breakfast she did not even look at him and knew that he noticed. There was a painful shyness in her, for she had lain awake for a long time thinking of his caress and knowing that she would remember it for months, maybe even longer. His kiss had been gentle, and his words had been like balm over her spirit. She had long known that he had been with other women, including Diana, but he had said that she was like no other woman. And the sweetness of this filled her.

Finally, after breakfast was over, he came to stand beside her and said, "Good morning."

Rich color touched her cheeks, and she smiled. "I didn't mean to ignore you. I'm a little embarrassed."

"There's no need to be." He wanted to reach out and touch her, and she read the impulse in his eyes. Flustered, she said, "I'd better help Lisimba."

Josh suddenly smiled, and then he said, "After supper tonight, let's go out and look at the door of the tomb again."

Kefira knew he was teasing her, but she liked it. Her lips curled upward in a smile, and joy danced in her eyes. "I'll have to think about that. I'm not sure it's safe for a girl to be alone with you."

"You're safe enough. I'm just a poor fellow with lots of inhibitions."

"I'm not sure I believe that," Kefira said. "But we'll see."

The sun was high in the sky, and Josh and the professor were carefully clearing away more of the wall that spanned each side of the door. It was Josh who looked up and said, "Someone's coming."

"Probably Amir coming back with permission to do the opening," the professor said.

The two men climbed out of the trench, and Diana joined them, and then Kefira stepped outside of the tent.

A vehicle pulled up with a symbol on the side that said Department of Antiquities. Three men got out, one of them Amir and the other two strangers.

The professor greeted them. "Good morning, Amir."

The professor got no further, for one of the men, a short, fat, greasy man with small, piggish eyes said, "I am Amun Ibn Jabari. I am the Commissioner of Antiquities."

"I'm glad to know you, sir."

"I have come to inform you that you are not permitted to continue this work, Dr. Welles."

Phineas stared at the man and then at Amir. "What can that possibly mean, Commissioner?"

"It means that the dig will be under the name of Amir Ben Kalil."

"We have been working together, of course."

"Your name is not on the papers that give permission. You are an intruder here, sir, and I inform you that you will vacate these premises at once."

"What are you talking about!" Josh exclaimed. "This is the professor's dig."

"I do not know you, nor do I want to. As commissioner, I am giving you twenty-four hours to vacate this site."

Phineas Welles looked into Amir's eyes and said, "You shouldn't do this thing, Amir. It isn't right."

Amir sneered. "You've heard the commissioner. You have twenty-four hours. I will expect you to be gone so that I may continue my work." He wheeled and walked back to the car, and the commissioner said with a warning, "I trust I will not have to use force. You are a respected man, sir, but your papers are not in order. I would suggest you vacate immediately."

Diana turned to her uncle. "He can't do that, Uncle Phineas!" Anger blazed in her eyes, and her voice was high with incredulity.

Phineas looked at the paper the commissioner had given him. "I'm afraid we must leave," he said, resigned.

"But, Professor, this is your dig! There has to be some recourse!" Josh exclaimed.

Professor Welles looked at the officials who were leaving, his eyes dwelling on the tall form of Amir. He turned to them and, with great sadness in his voice, said, "I have never learned not to trust people, and now I must pay for it."

CHAPTER TWENTY-TWO

MIRACLE IN THE DESERT

★ ★ ★ ★

"You can't let this get to you, Kefira," Josh said. He took her by the arm and turned her around and noted that her face was flushed. Her eyes flashed with anger, and Josh shook his head, adding, "You can only hurt yourself this way."

"But he had no right! He's a thief!" Kefira's face was contorted with rage. She had become very close to Phineas, and she knew how much this dig meant to Josh. For two days she had been furious, slamming pans around, speaking in short sentences, and had made herself so unapproachable that even Lisimba had grumbled at her ways.

Josh shook his head sympathetically. "I know it's easy to let yourself go, but there's nothing we can do about it."

"I'd like to shoot him!"

"No you wouldn't. That's just your anger talking."

Kefira brushed a lock of raven hair off of her forehead and squared her shoulders. Cold little points of light seemed to dance in her eyes, and a rocky expression had drawn her features into disagreeable lines. Temper flushed her face, and she said, "How can you be so—so easy about all this, Josh? It means your whole life, in a way. You've dreamed about this for years, and now it's within your grasp. And that hoodlum has stolen it!"

"I know it's hard, and we're all disappointed, but you only make matters worse by letting bitterness get to you."

"I can't help it," Kefira said. "It's just the way I am."

"No, it's not the way you are," Josh said. He laid his hand on her shoulder and squeezed it. "You've got more sweetness and goodness and gentleness in you than any woman I've ever seen, and I don't like to see you like this. It's not what you are."

Josh's words fell on Kefira like soothing oil. She bit her lip and looked down at the ground, conscious of the warm pressure of his hand on her shoulder. Finally she looked up, took a deep breath, and said, "All right, Josh, but I don't forgive easily."

She turned and walked away, and Josh stared after her. He had not seen her like this, although he had known there was a hard streak intermingled with her gentle spirit. "She's going to get into trouble if she doesn't conquer her anger." He turned and walked over to the professor's tent. Phineas was sitting down staring off into space, and Josh said, "Am I interrupting anything?"

"Oh no. Come in, Josh. Have a seat." Phineas waved to an empty chair and then put his eyes on Josh. "I'm afraid we're going to have to take a new run at this thing. I've let most of the workers go until I figure out what to do next. I've wired my brother what's happened, and he's ready to come over and strangle Amir. He has a great deal of anger in him, and he's used to getting his own way."

"I'm afraid Kefira's out of hand too. She's running around like she wants to bite somebody, mostly Amir, I guess."

"I hate to see it."

"So do I. I was hoping she'd be over it, but it seems to be getting worse."

Phineas bounced a pencil point on the tip of his index finger, then laid the pencil down on the desk. "We're going to have to move to another site, but so help me, I don't have another idea in my mind. I've had this tell in my heart so long that I haven't had time to think of anything else."

"Well, we'll find something, I'm sure. You haven't given up hope, have you?"

"No, but I'm just a little disconcerted. To be interrupted like that right at the moment of triumph—that makes it worse." He grinned suddenly, and his eyes twinkled. "I've had to struggle a bit with my anger. Last night, after I was in bed, I thought of ways to punish Amir. Then I realized that that wouldn't do."

"We all have a little bitterness and anger. We don't like people taking things that belong to us."

"I suppose that's human nature."

"It really is. You know, there's a verse in the Bible that says, 'Only by pride cometh contention.' Can't remember where it is," Josh muttered. "Somewhere in the book of Ecclesiastes, I think, or Proverbs. But in any case, it's true enough. We're selfish to the bone, and when somebody interferes with us, we strike back."

"You know, I read a study on that two years ago. This social scientist of some sort—a psychologist, I believe—would call people in for an interview, and there would be things on the table—coffee cups, ashtrays, boxes of paper clips. All sorts of things. This psychologist would begin interviewing the person, and then he would slowly move one of the items a little closer to the fellow. He kept moving things closer, and the more items he moved, the more nervous the subjects got." Phineas laughed aloud. "Finally they became unable to concentrate, and the psychologist said they were angry because that was *their* space and somebody was taking it."

"I guess it's the Adam in us, but I'm working on it."

"So am I . . . so am I," the professor said. "We'll find something. Don't worry, my boy."

★ ★ ★ ★

A few hours after this conversation, Josh looked up to see a car approaching. They had moved away from the site and had set up their tents near one of the few wells in the country. "Who's that, I wonder?" Kefira asked. She had come up to stand beside Josh, and her eyes glinted. "Probably somebody to run us off of this place."

But the intent of this visitor was quite different. The car stopped, and a man got out. He was dressed in a white suit of

English cut and wore a sun helmet. The professor came out and said, "Why, that's Charles Oaken. I was on a dig with him three years ago." He greeted the visitor with a hearty, "Hello, Charles!"

"Hello, Phineas." Oaken was a tall, limber individual of some forty years. He had light skin that was badly sunburned, and his blue eyes sparkled. "I hear you got thrown out of your dig."

"My fault, I'm afraid, Charles. I didn't see to the proper paper work."

"No," Oaken said and laughed. "I heard he diddled you out of the lost tomb of Mensah."

"Well, you don't have to be so blasted happy about it, Charles," Phineas grumbled.

"Stepped on your sore toe." Charles turned and said, "I don't believe I've met these young people." He took the introductions, nodded, and then said, "I suppose all of you are thinking of ways to strip Amir to the bone after what he did."

"Well, I am!" Kefira huffed. She did not like the visitor being so cheerful in the face of their plight, and her demeanor was stern.

"Don't shoot, Miss Reis," Oaken said. "I have some news that may make you feel a little better."

"What kind of news, Charles?" Phineas asked quickly.

"It's about your dig and the lost tomb of Mensah. Amir had the photographers all there ready to become a celebrity the world over. He opened the door, and guess what was there on the other side?"

"I suppose a perfectly preserved mummy and lots of gold and jewels," Josh said.

"Not at all, young man! The fact is the door was fastened onto a solid face of rock."

A moment's silence fell over the three, and then Phineas began to laugh. "That old trick! Well, I'm glad now that I didn't have to face the music."

"What does this mean, Professor?" Kefira interrupted the two men, who were now laughing.

"Oh, it was an old trick of some of the pharaohs, Kefira," Phineas explained. "It was hard work keeping their tombs concealed, and some of them would make up false tombs. They would simply put a wall and a door over a sheet of solid rock, and the grave robbers, after going to all the trouble of getting through, would find nothing but rock."

Kefira stared at him and then smiled. "So Amir didn't get anything!"

"He got plenty of laughs from the newspapermen who had come from a long way. Some of them are pretty sore. I don't think he'll want to be showing his face again soon."

The visitor stayed for a while, then took his leave, and Josh could not resist saying to Kefira, "Well, you see how much good all your anger did? Amir didn't get a thing out of it."

Kefira reddened. "I suppose you're right, but he didn't mean for it to happen that way." She shook her hair, and it cascaded down her back, a black waterfall glistening in the sun. "I suppose you think I'm a terrible person with a horrible temper."

"No, Kefira, I think you're a sweet, generous, wonderful woman who let her temper get away with her."

Kefira laughed. "Good, and you're to minimize all my faults and find all the nice things you can to say about me."

★　★　★　★

At supper that night Diana had been strangely quiet. Finally she looked at Phineas and said, "There's nothing going on here, is there, Uncle?"

"Not really, Diana. We'll try to find another spot, but it'll take a while."

"I think I'll go back to New York."

Kefira looked up swiftly and saw that Diana's face was fixed, but then suddenly the woman turned to her and smiled. "I think you can take care of these men without me, can't you, Kefira?"

"I'll do my best."

"But are you sure you want to do this, Diana?" Phineas asked, a worried look on his face. "I'd been counting on you."

"If you develop anything big, maybe I'll come back. But the way these things are, you could go for a year or two without anything that would require me. No, I think I'll go on back."

After the meal, Diana made it a point to find Josh and have a word with him. "You're not too surprised, are you, Josh?"

"About your going back? Well, I am a little."

"You know me pretty well, I think. I can never stick to anything." She reached up and put her hand on his cheek. "I thought we could go back and find what we had before, but someone said you can't step in the same river twice." She removed her hand and said, "You won't miss me too much, I don't think."

"Of course I will."

"I'm sure you'll find some feminine company." She tossed her head back and laughed. "I'm not very subtle, but you're following Kefira around like a moon-faced calf. Why don't you make love to her?"

Josh stared at her. "Well, I just don't—"

He could not finish, and Diana shook her head. "You're hopeless, Josh." She sighed, then turned and strode away.

★ ★ ★ ★

Kefira could not sleep. She woke up two hours before dawn and dressed. It was too early to start cooking, so she read the New Testament for a time but soon grew restless. She stuck the book in her shirt pocket and went out to watch the sun rise. She was not quite oriented to their new location as she had been at the tell. The country was flat, but there were some low hills rising over in the east. They looked very close, and she began walking toward them in the moonlight. The moon was full and shed its silver beams down, and the country was quiet. It was the coolest time of the day, and she knew it would soon be blistering hot.

As she walked, she thought about her life. Her thoughts went back to the prison cell at Sing Sing where her brother was locked up. It always grieved her to think about this, and she forced it out of her mind, trying instead to think of what Chaim would do when he got out. She was disturbed about what had happened at the tell, but she knew somehow she had to make enough money to help her brother make a new start.

The walking was pleasant, and the sand was firm underfoot, not shifting, as it had been in some spots. She saw what looked like a tent off in the distance, and she grew interested. As she walked toward it, however, she began thinking of the Winslows and the time she had spent in their house. She remembered it all as if it were a dream. There had been such love and happiness there. There had been joy too, and she remembered Kat's innocent laughter as the two of them had pursued a wayward possum in the woods.

What would it be like, she thought, *to live all the time with people loving each other and having relatives all around? I'd give anything to live like that. . . .*

Her thoughts took her then to Josh, and from there to Diana. She could not help feeling a surge of joy that Diana was leaving. She admitted to herself that she had felt jealous of Diana's possessiveness and had felt, while she was around, that Josh could never turn loose his thoughts of her. Josh had told her plainly enough that he had felt himself in love with her once, that they had had an affair, but he had also told her clearly that Diana was not for him.

Kefira had a way of getting lost in her thoughts, of going over things in the past, exploring events, bringing up faces with a startling clarity. She did this until finally she saw that what she had taken for a tent was simply an outcropping of rock. Looking east, she spotted a wadi on one side and followed it for a while out of curiosity, but she did not see much to interest her, except a delightful desert mouse with large ears and a very long tail.

Finally the sun began to shed milky gray light in the east, signaling the approach of sunrise. *I'd better get back,* Kefira thought. *I'll be late for breakfast.* She turned and started back, still thinking mostly of what she would do with her life if she had to leave and go back to the States, and the thought depressed her. She gave in to it for a time, then finally shook her head. "I can't be thinking of things like that. I'll be all right." She followed her footprints back along the wadi to where she had entered the dry creek bed, then headed west toward the camp.

Without warning, a strong wind kicked up, spraying sand and dust in her face. She pulled her neck scarf up over her head and over her eyes and kept walking. As the wind became stronger, she could hardly walk against it, and soon she was forced to stop. She tried to look around through the thin cotton neckerchief. The sun had been obscured by the flying sand and now the entire sky was milky. She was no longer certain if she was walking away from or toward the sun.

In confusion, she did the only thing she could think to do. With nothing to shelter her from the stinging sand, she sat on the ground and prayed aloud. "Please, God, make this wind die down so I can get back to the camp."

Within seconds, the wind calmed as quickly as it had begun. Breathing a sigh of relief, Kefira stood and located the sun in the east and began to walk in the opposite direction. She searched for her footprints, but everything had been obliterated in the wind. Quite certain that she was walking in the right general direction, though, she picked up her pace, but fifteen minutes later she stopped and looked around in confusion. The camp was nowhere in sight, and she felt a shiver of fear. "I must be going in the wrong direction. Perhaps it's over this way." Turning to her left, she walked steadily, looking ahead at the horizon. The longer she walked, the more frightened she became. She had heard stories of people lost in the desert who had become dehydrated and died for lack of water. Her fear grew as nothing appeared on the horizon, and she stopped and looked around again uncertainly. The land all around was flat. Nothing broke the horizon except the low hills behind her in the east. She breathed another prayer and began walking in a westerly direction.

The sun rose slowly and an hour later Kefira knew she was utterly lost. The earth was beginning to heat up from the warm rays of the sun, and she was already thirsty. "They'll come and find me," she whispered. "All I have to do is keep my head."

But somehow keeping her head seemed difficult. She had no watch, but she knew that time was passing by the way the sun had risen high in the sky. She was completely disoriented now and had not the vaguest idea of which way to go. She could have missed the camp completely, and she realized that it might now be in any direction at all. Being in the city had taught her nothing about being lost in a featureless desert, and as the sun beat down on her, Kefira Reis felt terror as she had never known it. She stopped, not knowing what to do. *I may be walking away from the camp,* she thought. *The best thing I can do is stay still and wait for them to come find me.*

She spotted a small sand dune not far away and began to walk toward it. A small wadi behind the dune offered a tiny bit of shade. There was no water, although there had been at one time. Crouching down to shade herself as much as she could from the blistering sun, Kefira knew for the first time in her life what the fear of death really was.

★ ★ ★ ★

"What do you mean she's not in her tent!" Josh exclaimed. "She *has* to be!"

Diana had gone to seek Kefira at Josh's request. He had gone to the cooking tent, where Lisimba had already started working on breakfast. But he had said, "Missy is not here. Probably still asleep."

Diana had wandered in, and Josh had said, "Go see if you can wake Kefira. I think she's overslept."

Diana had returned quickly, saying, "She's not there. She's not in the sanitary tent either. I looked there too."

An alarm went off in Josh's head. Warning flowed through him, ringing like a clear bell. "She might be with the professor."

He went at once to Dr. Welles's tent, followed by Diana. But when the professor stepped outside and they asked after Kefira, he looked surprised. "Why, I haven't seen her since last evening!"

"She's not here. We've searched everywhere," Josh said, his voice strained.

"Do you think she could have been kidnapped?" Diana asked suddenly.

"That's not likely," Josh replied.

The three stood there uncertainly, and finally Josh said, "She likes to take walks. Let's spread out and see if we can find her. Just call out her name."

Lisimba's aid was quickly enlisted, and the four of them took off in different directions. Josh moved out two hundred yards calling her name, but only the sound of his own voice echoed back. He looked with despair at the flatness of the land and shook his head. "This is too slow," he muttered. "We'll have to use the truck."

He hurried back to the camp and found that the others had had no success. "I'll take the truck and make circles. Diana, you go with me. You can help look."

Josh got to the truck, turned the key—and nothing happened.

"What's wrong with this thing?" Josh said angrily, pounding his hands on the steering wheel. He tried again and still no response. He got out and threw back the hood. He found nothing wrong and then muttered, "The battery's dead."

"Do we have a spare?" the professor asked worriedly.

"No, we should have, though, out here by ourselves like this. We'll have to send someone to the village, but I doubt if they have one."

"I'll go to the village," the professor offered, "and the rest of you can continue looking. If I can find a battery, I'll bring it back."

Josh knew it was at least an hour's walk to the village, and they couldn't just sit and wait for the professor to return. "We've got to find her soon," he said. "She could dehydrate in this sun, and besides, it's not safe for a woman out there."

Josh went at once and filled two bottles with water, tied them together, and slung them over his shoulder.

Diana said, "Josh, don't you get lost." Worry was in her voice, and she said, "As soon as my uncle gets back with a battery, we'll come out and find you."

"That's good, Diana."

"She'll be all right. Don't worry."

Josh tried to smile but said, "I pray God she will," and he started walking.

Diana watched him until he became nothing but a dot. She saw him turn left and knew he was making a circle, and as she looked around at the land, she saw what an immensity of ground there was to cover. She said to Lisimba, "Well, Lisimba, you're a praying man. I expect you'd better start."

Lisimba nodded, bobbing his head up and down. "I have already started, Miss Diana."

* * * *

The heat was like the blow of a fist, and Kefira kept her eyes shut against the glare of the sun's beams. She had resisted the impulse to get up and start running and crying out for help. The temptation had come to her, but she knew there was no hope in that. She opened her eyes into slits and saw that the sun was past the meridian, and she knew it was at least one or two o'clock, the hottest part of the day. Her mouth was dry, and her lips felt parched. Every tissue in her body cried out for moisture. She had followed the professor's admonition to drink water constantly in small sips, so she had not felt the effects of the sun while on the dig. Besides that, she had taken care to rest in the shade part of each day, but now she had been under the blazing heat of the Egyptian sun for more than eight hours, and she felt light-headed.

The thought of death came to her more than once, and the fear that was stronger than anything she had ever known was still there. She hated the thought of dying, for there was so much she wanted to do. She thought of leaving Chaim and how he would need her, and she thought of Josh and knew she would never have with him what her heart cried out for.

The seconds and minutes seemed to move slowly, and Kefira looked up and saw two vultures circling overhead. They were so high they were mere dots, and she wondered if they had found her. This increased her fear, and she shut her eyes more tightly.

As the time passed, she felt the lostness of her spirit, and then she thought of death itself—and what came on the other side of death. The Jewish religion had little to say about it, but she knew that Christians were very positive about heaven, believing that the moment they ended this life they would step into the presence of a holy God and a living savior.

For a long time she thought about this, and finally she began to pray. At first it was merely a cry, "Oh, God, help me! Don't let me die out here!" But then a strange awareness came to her. She felt that she was, somehow, in the presence of God and did not know what to say or what to think.

"Help me, God, because I cannot help myself."

Suddenly she thought of the story of Jesus and the prostitute. How she had come to Him weeping, and how He had simply said to her, *"Thy sins be forgiven."* And then He had said, *"Thy faith has saved thee."* This story had never left her mind, and now she cried aloud, "Oh, Jesus, I am no better than that woman! I'm *worse* than she is! I'm just a sinner. But I'm afraid, and I need you. I need you to help me. I believe that you forgave that woman's sins, and I bring my sins to you, and I ask you to forgive me. That's all I know how to do, Jesus."

Suddenly deep within Kefira, something began to happen. She started to weep and did not know why. The tears flowed, and she covered her face with her hands. She knew she was still in terrible danger, but now there was a difference. The fear began to leave, and she knew she was in the presence of God himself. "I don't know how to become a Christian," she sobbed, "but I will do anything, Lord Jesus. Forgive my sins and take me to yourself."

She said no more but sat there, and the peace that came to her was beyond belief. She kept her eyes closed, but she felt almost as if an arm had been placed about her and someone was whispering peace into her ear.

"Is that you, Lord Jesus?" she whispered, and then in the silence she heard no voice. But in her heart there was a peaceful certainty she had never experienced before, and she knew that she had found her Messiah.

★　★　★　★

Josh was flushed with the heat of the sun. He had drunk half of one of the bottles of water and could spare no more. He had made three circles and seen absolutely nothing. With almost every step, he was praying that God would guide him.

He pulled out his watch and saw that it was after three o'clock. *She must be terrified, lost like this. God, help me to find her!*

He pushed forward with his breath coming short as he punished himself with the pace. There was no thought of giving up, and he kept hoping to hear the sound of the truck, but there was nothing but silence. From time to time he would call out, but his voice seemed thready and futile in the vastness of the desert.

He followed a track broken across the desert and passed by a small wadi. There was no water in it, and he knew by this time Kefira must be terribly thirsty.

He pushed on, and ten minutes later he raised his voice and called, "Kefira—Kefira!"

He kept walking, and then suddenly a tiny movement caught his eye. He looked up, shading his eyes. He ran forward staggering, the bottles bumping against his side, and then he saw the flash of blue, and he knew that he had found her. "Kefira—!" he cried. He ran until he saw her climb out of the wadi and stumble toward him. She would have fallen, but he caught her before she fell. Joy raced through him, and he whispered, "You're alive—you're alive, Kefira! Thank God you're alive."

Kefira felt his arms around her holding her up, and she heard his voice thanking God for her safety. She had no strength and began to slump. He helped her to sit down and uncapped one of the bottles. "Take a little," he said.

The water was heavenly, and she drank several swallows before he pulled it away. He said, "You can have more later. Not too much right now." He sat down beside her and held her in his arms, and she put her face against his chest. "I was going crazy, Kefira."

She held on to him for a time and felt him rocking her back and forth as a man would rock a child. Then she lifted her eyes and through chapped lips, she said, "I've found the Messiah!"

Josh stared at her for a moment, and tears came to his eyes. "You accepted Jesus?"

"Yes, He came to me, and He gave me peace. And He brought you to me, my dear."

The two stood there, a mere speck in the vast desert. The sun was beating down, but Kefira Reis knew she had found what she had sought for all of her life. The God she thought was her enemy was now her beloved enemy—not even that. Simply *her beloved*!

CHAPTER TWENTY-THREE

THE NEEDLE

★ ★ ★ ★

Kefira bent over the table, her brow contracted, and chewed her lower lip. She studied the sheet of paper she had been writing on, and then shook her head. *I don't know how Chaim is going to take this,* she thought. *He may hate me, but I have to tell him.*

> *And so, my dear brother, I have become a believer in Jesus the Messiah. I tremble when I write this to you, for you are all the family I have. I know this decision would have hurt our parents terribly, and I fear it may hurt you, but I have to be absolutely honest with you. I've told you how I thought I might die, and I have told you how I have been reading the Christian Bible for some time, and how the figure of Jesus has become more and more appealing to me. Oh, Chaim, I wish you would read the New Testament! We both had the wrong idea about Jesus. He is love itself. He showed nothing but compassion toward everyone He met who was in trouble or sick. He was stern only with the self-righteous, but to those who confessed themselves sinners He showed nothing but a love such as I cannot describe.*
>
> *Since that moment in the desert when I cried out to Him to save me, I have been filled with an absolute peace. Even at that moment when I thought death was near, there came into my spirit and into my heart a great quietness that was like nothing I had ever known*

before. Everything, I knew, was going to be all right. Even if I died,
that would be all right too, for I would be with Jesus.

Kefira put down her pen and rubbed her eyes and then prayed silently. *Lord, help me to say the words that will help Chaim understand what has happened to me. And I pray, Lord, that you will save him and bring him into a knowledge of you, the savior. I can't do this alone, but, O Jesus, you can do anything. So I pray you will open his heart to receive you.*

Picking up the pen, she began to write again. The letter got longer, for she felt the need to let him know fully what was in her heart.

The work here has gone very badly. Professor Welles seems to have lost heart. He was always so cheerful and so filled with excitement. It was a joy each morning to fix his breakfast, for he would come in rubbing his hands, his eyes sparkling and talking with such great excitement. But that is all gone now. I think he had placed every hope he had in the tell where we were digging. I have come to admire him so much, and it hurts me to see him so affected by the way things have gone.

And Josh is saddened too. He saw this as a chance to begin a new career. He has had a bad life, Chaim, but he has turned from it. I know you would admire him if you could be with him. He is, in many ways, the best man I have ever met.

Kefira suddenly stopped and stared at what she had written. "That's not honest," she whispered. "I must tell Chaim the truth." She began to write again with a hand not quite steady.

You are my brother, and I must tell you that I am in love with Joshua Winslow. This is not a sudden thing, I realize now. We have not known each other all that long, but from the very beginning I felt something for him. Perhaps it had something to do with caring for him when he was injured and helpless. I do not know how love comes, but I must tell you, my dear brother, I care for him greatly. I think he cares for me too, and since Diana Welles left, he has been happier, more free, it seems. I think she had some sort of hold on him, and now that is broken. He has not been a perfect man all his life, but now he is a devoted Christian and determined to serve the Lord with all of his heart. And I admire this in him. I do not know

where this will lead, but he cares for me. I think he is afraid of his
past. He has made mistakes with women, and, of course, he knows
that I have had unfortunate experiences with men. So we are a little
bit guarded around each other.

I cannot send packages from here, but I am sending money to
the chaplain with instructions to provide what you need. There is
nothing to do with money out here, so I am so happy to be able to
meet some of your needs.

May God richly bless you and keep you. The day will come
when you will be free from prison, and I must say that my prayer
for you is that you will be free in your spirit as I am now free.

Your loving sister,
Kefira

Sighing deeply, she put the pen down, flexed her fingers, and then read quickly over the letter. It did not satisfy her, but then nothing would, except to have been able to go to Chaim and tell the story of her new life in person. The words seemed so weak, but it was the best she could do. She folded the letter, put it into an envelope, and addressed it. Finally, standing up, she stretched and bent over, blew out the lamp, and got into bed. It was very late, but she was not tired. For a long time she lay there thinking about her brother, and then finally said simply, "Lord, I cannot help him, but you can. Please touch his heart."

Kefira had discovered that prayer could be like this. She had always prayed formal prayers before, but now she was discovering that sometimes a single sentence, just a word or a phrase uttered to God, would bring her peace. This intrigued her, for she had always been prone to worry about things, keeping them until they became a burden. She remembered the Scripture she had read before she began the letter. *Cast thy burden upon the Lord,* and it gave her joy to know that she could do this.

Slowly she began to grow sleepy, and her last thoughts before she drifted off were rather hazy. She was thinking about the professor and about Josh and even about herself, how they all longed to find success in their mission. "Things have gone so badly, Lord Jesus," she said. "Please help us to get on the right track." She prayed this prayer until she drifted off to sleep.

* ★ ★ ★

Josh did not notice anything particularly different about Kefira the next morning, except perhaps she was a little quieter. As usual, she and Lisimba fixed a very good breakfast, and then she sat down and ate with him and Phineas. Josh did most of the talking, for he saw that the professor seemed rather overwhelmed. He made himself keep the conversation going, and finally when the meal was over he said, "Well, we've got to keep going. We'll find something, I'm sure."

"I'm not sure, Joshua." Phineas drew his hand across his face and shook his head. "I have no earthly idea of where to go next. This has never happened to me before. Always, on every expedition, the problem was not so much where to dig as how to get to it and how to keep the work going. Now I seem to be a ship without a rudder."

Josh spoke rapidly, trying to convince the professor, but finally he ran out of things to say and fell silent.

"I have something to tell both of you," Kefira said.

Joshua noticed that her face was strained, and he had a sudden fear that she might be falling ill.

After a moment's silence in which Kefira seemed to struggle, she said, "I've not known whether to tell you about this or not, but now since everything's gone so badly, I think I must. You will probably think it's crazy."

"What is it, child?" Phineas asked, his eyes becoming more alert. "Is there some sort of trouble?"

"Not trouble, but I don't know what you think about dreams. I've had the same dream over and over again."

"What sort of a dream, Kefira?" Josh asked gently. He saw she was having difficulty and said, "In the Scripture God spoke to people through dreams many times, and you know my stepmother. She believes greatly in dreams—that God sometimes uses them."

"I've always dreamed very vividly. As a matter of fact, I dreamed about Egypt before I even knew I'd be coming here. I didn't know what it meant, of course. I dreamed about the sphinx and the pyramids and the desert." She turned to Josh and said, "And, Josh, I dreamed about your house before I ever saw it."

"Our house in Georgia?"

"Yes, when I was in New York before we ever met. I had the most vivid dream. I didn't understand it. I dreamed I was walking down a road, and there in front of me was the house, two stories, four columns, freshly painted white . . . just exactly as it is. Why, I even saw a woman hanging out clothes—and Stonewall, that bluish dog. I saw him." Her eyes grew excited, and she said, "I saw it all."

"You really saw all this?" Josh asked, incredulous.

"Yes, but those aren't the dreams I'm talking about."

"What did you dream, my dear?" Phineas urged her.

"It was the dream of a place. There were no people in it," Kefira said thoughtfully. "All I saw really was some kind of large black rock that was very sharp and pointed. It seemed to point to the sky almost like a finger. It was out by itself in the desert— just like out there," she waved with her hand, indicating the desert that lay outside the camp. "Nothing but emptiness, and this one black stone pointing up. And beside it was a house made out of stone, and there was grass on top of the house, and a goat was eating the grass."

"Well, I've seen that kind of house many times," the professor said quickly. "You've probably seen them too. The people sometimes build flat roofs, and the grass seed takes root. I haven't seen a goat on one, though."

"Was the dream the same every time?" Josh inquired.

"Every time. I dreamed it again last night," she said, "and just before I went to sleep, I prayed that God would show you where to dig, Professor."

"Why, how kind of you, my dear."

"Do you think that this dream could mean something?" Kefira asked. She was embarrassed now that she had told it and then shook her head. "It probably doesn't mean anything. There probably isn't any stone like that except in my dream."

"Oh yes, missy, there is such a stone!"

All three of them turned at once to see Lisimba, who had

been standing back waiting to pour their coffee. Now he bobbed his head up and down and grinned mightily. "Yes, indeed, there is such a stone. I have seen it myself."

"You have!" Professor Welles exclaimed. "Where?"

"It is not too far from Thebes, but it is out in the desert. Far out."

"What did it look like?" Kefira asked eagerly.

"It looked like you said. A black finger pointing at the sky. It is well known to the natives. They call it the needle."

"And you've seen it yourself, Lisimba?" Josh demanded.

"Oh yes. I was working for a man, and we went that way, and I saw it. One of the men who worked with me lived close by. He told me that place was haunted. It is not good."

"But was there a house beside it?" Kefira asked, her eyes bright.

"Yes, just as you said. A stone house is not far from it. We passed by very quickly, but I remembered it, for I had never seen a rock so sharp. There was no goat on the house when I was there," he said apologetically.

Kefira turned to the professor and said, "I don't know anything about archeology, but I've had this dream five or six times, and it's always the same. Could it possibly be that God is telling us that that is the place to go dig?"

Professor Welles stared at her for a moment, then slapped his thighs. "Well, by George, I don't have any other ideas! I think it's worth taking a look at anyway." He laughed. "Please, don't either of you tell any reporters about this. I like to appear a little more scientific than going out on an expedition based on a woman's dream."

"I think we ought to try it, Professor," Josh said quickly. "We don't have any other options really, so I say let's go take a look at it."

"All right, we'll do it!" Phineas said firmly. He rose and said, "Let's pull the tents down and get out of here as quickly as we can."

The work then began with the professor and Josh shouting orders to the pared-down crew, and Kefira and Lisimba began packing away her cooking gear. Once Josh came in for a drink of water, and she said, "Josh, it may all mean nothing."

"Who can tell? God works in mysterious ways sometimes, Kefira." He reached out and took her hand and held it for a moment. "Don't worry about it. We can't be any worse off, and I'd like to see that black needle myself!"

★　★　★　★

Kefira was sitting in the front seat between Joshua and Lisimba. The winds were driving the sands in swirling tiny whirlwinds, and she strained her eyes ahead. Ever since they had left on their quest, she had been terrified, thinking that it was all merely a dream. She had said almost nothing, but Josh and Lisimba had carried the brunt of the conversation.

Suddenly Lisimba said, "There, you see him?"

Both Josh and Kefira eagerly strained their eyes, looking forward. "I see something over there," Kefira said. "Is that it?"

"Yes, go that way, Mr. Josh."

Josh turned slightly and saw in his rearview mirror that the professor was following close behind. "Mighty barren out here," he said, "but then most of Egypt is."

Kefira did not answer. She had all her attention focused on the sight before her. As they drew nearer, her heart seemed to leap into her throat. "Look, Josh, do you see it?"

"I sure do. Never saw anything like it."

As they drew near, Kefira exclaimed, "Look, there's the house over there—and look, Josh, there's grass on it and there's a goat!"

Josh gasped with surprise. "You're right—there *is* a goat!" He turned to Kefira and, taking one hand off the wheel, put his arm around her shoulders and squeezed her. "Just like in your dream."

"Yes, the Lord God, He gives us good dreams sometimes," Lisimba chortled.

Josh brought the truck to a stop twenty feet from the house and from the large rock that was set firmly in the earth. He got out of the truck, helped Kefira out, and the two of them waited until the professor climbed out of the other truck and came to stand beside them. "Well, Professor, what do you think?"

Phineas's face was totally expressive. His eyes were dancing, and he said, "I'll tell you one thing. That's not a native rock. That was brought in from somewhere. Let's take a look at it."

They advanced and went around the rock, which rose some twenty feet in the air. It had probably been roughly square at one time, but was worn now by the abrasive actions of the wind and sand.

The professor dropped on his knees and began digging. "Get a shovel," he said. "We've got to see what's on the base of this."

Josh ran and got a shovel, and he applied his muscle power. Soon he had a trench dug completely around it, a foot and a half deep. "Look," he said, "it's square at the bottom." His face was alight, and he said, "What does that mean, Professor? That it was a monument?"

"Yes, and I think all the words that were carved into it have worn away, but we'll dig down and see." He looked up and said, "What about the house?"

"I haven't seen anybody," Kefira said. "It seems to be deserted."

The four of them went to the house, and Lisimba cautioned them, mentioning, "Some say it is haunted with bad spirits."

"I don't think we need worry about that," Phineas said cheerfully. He led the way inside, and indeed, the house was empty. There were a few pieces of broken furniture, but the house seemed to have been more recently occupied by wild animals and birds than anything else.

"This is strange," Phineas murmured, frowning. "A house out here and not inhabited."

"Well, I don't think anyone could farm this land," Josh observed.

"It was probably greener a thousand years ago. Much of this land was."

Going outside, the three of them stood considering the black rock and the house. The goat on the top looked down at them, chewing placidly.

"I wonder where that goat finds food and water. Can't live on just what's growing on the house, especially without water."

"There's probably a small spring somewhere close around. There would have to be to support him. Did you notice there were other animal tracks too?" Josh asked.

"Let's set up the tents," the professor said. "We've got to think about this."

Setting up the tents occupied some of their time, and Kefira fixed a quick meal, but none of them were particularly hungry. The professor had gone to gaze at the stone, looking up at it and then getting down and digging like a terrier at the base.

"This is the strangest thing I've ever heard of," Kefira said. "Do you think it means something?"

"I believe the professor thinks so. He wouldn't be so busy otherwise."

Five minutes later the professor came back, and a smile wreathed his face. "Well, I found something. An inscription at the base. It's only the name of the quarry and the quarry master, but I can date it from that. This stone," he said, "goes all the way past the time of the early days of the pharaohs." He smiled with satisfaction. "And if there's a stone like that, it was put here for a purpose, and we're going to find it."

"Professor, do you mean it?" Kefira cried with delight.

"You'll see whether I mean it. The first thing I'm going to do is get in that truck and go make sure that we're in good standing with the authorities at Cairo." He frowned and then shook his head. "No one is going to take this away from us."

Ten minutes later the professor was on his way, driving the truck across the desert at full speed. Kefira and Josh stood watching him. "I believe God is in this, Josh."

"I think you're right."

The two of them watched until the truck disappeared, and then Josh said, "Well, there's nothing much to do until the professor gets back. Maybe I can spend some time with you."

Kefira suddenly laughed. "Well, I'm not going anywhere alone this time, that's for certain. Now, let's see if we can find that spring. . . ."

★　★　★　★

As it happened, Kefira and Josh had plenty of time to spend together. The professor was gone for two days, and Kefira enjoyed every moment. They did find the tiny spring, enough to supply their needs, and they had plenty of food. The few workers they'd retained enjoyed loafing, and Kefira and Josh spent every waking moment together. It was a wonderful time for Kefira, and each day she found out more about this man whom she had grown to love. He said nothing to her about his feelings, but often he would take her hand and smile at her in a way that warmed her deep inside.

★　★　★　★

The professor came roaring back with a full crew. He got out of the truck waving a paper, and when he reached them, his eyes were electric. "No one can say we haven't followed the official line on this. We have full authority to dig anywhere in this area."

"That's wonderful, Professor!" Josh exclaimed. "But where are we going to start?" He looked around at the vacant spaces and shook his head. "We can't just stick a shovel in that sand."

"No, we're going to start in the logical place," Phineas said.

"The logical place. Where's that?" Kefira asked.

"Under the house itself." He saw their surprise and said, "In ancient Egypt many people buried their dead beneath their houses. I don't know what was here before, but I'm banking on the fact that since it's happened before, it can happen again. So come along. Let's start dismantling that floor."

They went inside at once, both Josh and Kefira filled with excitement. The floor was covered with a layer of stones four inches thick. "This stone had to be brought in from somewhere," the professor said. He had wiggled a crowbar into a crack and pried up one of the rocks. He studied it, saying, "I'm thinking it came from Aswan, but we shall see."

The professor and Josh quickly removed a section of the floor and then began to remove the material beneath it. "This isn't sand," Josh said. "This house was built on something else."

"Probably on top of another structure that had been flattened by wars or storms," Phineas agreed.

The search went on all day, and the workers were kept busy hauling out their wheelbarrows full of dirt. That night they had uncovered half the floor but had found nothing save one or two interesting artifacts. One was a comb made out of ivory.

"That ivory didn't come from here," Josh said.

"No, from India probably. But the pharaohs knew ivory. And this," Phineas said, "is most interesting."

Kefira came closer and saw a fragment of pottery no more than three inches square. "What's interesting about that?" she said.

"The writing on it," the professor explained.

Kefira stared at it and shook her head. "What kind of writing is it?"

"It's hieroglyphics, and it's of the time of very early Egypt. So we're at the right spot. I'm sure of it."

★ ★ ★ ★

The next day, however, the professor was not so sure, nor the day after. They had removed the entire floor and had made sample digs but had found only a few minor pieces.

"How deep are we going to go, Professor?" Josh asked.

"You've got to remember, Joshua, that the desert shifts. You remember how deep we had to go in some of those simple little burial grounds in Louisiana? Have you ever been to Israel?"

"No, never."

"I think the biggest surprise for me there was when I saw Jacob's well."

"Why, I read in the Bible where Jesus met a woman at Jacob's well."

"Yes, it was in Samaria. Well, I knew the well was there, so I was anxious to see it. It's always been a favorite story of mine. So I went there, and I saw a house there, and I thought that must be the well. I went over to it and found out that it had become a tourist attraction. They charged to see it. Not much but a little. So I paid and went into the small house, expecting to find it."

"Was it there?" Josh inquired.

"No, there was a set of stairs that went down some thirty feet. There was a place hollowed out, and there was the well."

"The well was thirty feet underground?"

"Yes, that well was up on top of the surface when Jesus sat there and talked with that woman. But over hundreds of years, even thousands, the earth had filled in. That's the way it is with the earth."

★ ★ ★ ★

The dig went on for a week. They were not removing shovelfuls at a time, but teaspoons. They kept finding evidence of ancient Egypt. The professor found a gold scarab and murmured, "This is a treasure. This was not owned by a poor person."

He handed it to Kefira, who examined it. "Why, it looks like a beetle."

"That's what a scarab is. Egyptians worshiped beetles as they worshiped nearly everything else."

Handing the item back, she said, "We go so slowly."

"The old-school archeologists destroyed a lot of things. We might find one tiny piece of evidence here if we're careful, but if we use shovels, we could miss it. Be patient, my dear."

Kefira was patient. She did the cooking, and she also helped with the painstaking business of taking out the rubble and sand a spoonful at a time. Whenever she saw something in the ground, she would often proceed with only a brush, carefully brushing away the sand until the object was revealed and then she would call the professor to make a judgment on it.

One day she had been digging very carefully. She was kneeling down, and her knees were beginning to ache. Suddenly the spoon she was using to move the fine silt struck something hard. She blinked and scraped again. Carefully she tested the earth and knew that whatever it was, was very large. "Professor," she said, "I found something."

As always when one of them made a find, the other two

would rush over. "What is it, my dear?"

"I don't know. Here, you'd better see. It seems like a big flat stone."

The professor gave her a startled look and then stooped down and began working with it. Josh and Kefira bent over, Josh holding a flashlight. The professor scraped carefully and looked up with his eyes dancing. "I think we found something here."

"What do you think it is?"

"It's stone, all right, but like that needle out there. It's been hauled in. Here, help me, Josh. We need to clear away."

All of them worked diligently but carefully. An hour later they had cleared an area five feet square. The professor was totally silent. He had found something that startled him. The others leaned in and saw that he had found some writing. They did not speak for fear of disturbing his concentration.

Finally Phineas Welles looked up, and his lips were trembling. He could not speak for a moment, and finally Josh cried, "What is it, Professor?"

"It's . . . a tomb, if I'm not mistaken." He waved a hand that was not quite steady toward the seal. "You see that seal? It says it is the seal of Mensah."

Josh and Kefira both stared at him, for he had mentioned often that this would be the greatest find in modern archeological history.

"Is that what it says, Professor?" Kefira asked.

"I believe it is. I think we have found a tomb, and pray to God that it might not be a false one."

"It could be like the one back at the tell that Amir claimed, couldn't it?"

"It could be, or it could be that tomb robbers have been here, but I doubt it. Somewhere there's an opening. If this is the opening to the tomb, it doesn't look broken into to me. Just think of it. If we could find a tomb with the body of a man like Mensah and all of the treasures buried with him, it would be the dream of my lifetime."

★ ★ ★ ★

They worked into the evening until they were exhausted, clearing more away until finally the opening to whatever was below was cleared. The professor said, "If it's like other tombs, this will give access to a stairway, and then there will be a tunnel leading to the burial chamber. But we must go very slowly. Get some rest."

The professor went to bed, but both Josh and Kefira were too excited. She fixed coffee, and they drank it together, talking late into the night. Finally Josh said, "Let's walk around. I can't sleep."

"All right, Josh."

The two walked outside and made their way toward the needle. They stood staring up, and Josh put his arm around her waist. "You're quite a dreamer, Kefira Reis."

Kefira turned to face him, and he kept his arm in place. She put her hands on his chest and looked up at him. She did not mean to say so, but somehow she could not keep it back any longer. "Joshua, do you know that I care for you?" she whispered softly.

Josh was absolutely still for a moment, and then he lowered his head and kissed her. She returned his kiss with a firm pressure, and he drew her closer. He had a dread of making a mistake with this girl, but her words had touched something in his heart.

"I'm glad you do, Kefira, for I love you with all my heart." He stroked her hair and then kissed her again. He feared that his ardor would be too great for her, yet her arms drew him close, and he knew then that this was right. When he lifted his head, he said, "Will you marry me and live with me and be my wife?"

"Yes!" Kefira reached up and put both hands on his cheeks. She held his face like that for a moment, then put her arms around him and laid her cheek against his chest. "I was so afraid you wouldn't love me."

"That's the one thing in this world you'll never have to worry about."

The two stood holding each other, while overhead, a silver disc of moon shed its light upon them. There in the silence, Josh and Kefira knew they had found something in the land of Egypt more precious than any archeological find.

CHAPTER TWENTY-FOUR

THE PRIZE

★ ★ ★ ★

The work progressed very slowly, so slowly that Kefira grew impatient. Every day she helped Josh, Professor Welles, and the crew uncover what lay beneath the ancient house.

It took over a week of careful, painstaking labor to unearth the stairway beneath the house. Some of the stones were heavy, and Josh had to do most of that work, but finally the flooring was removed, and they stared down into the darkness. The professor threw a beam from his flashlight and said in a hushed whisper, "It's possible no one has been in this place for thousands of years. I haven't seen any sign of grave robbers. It's a miracle!"

The professor went first, followed closely by Josh and Kefira. At the foot of the stairs they found a landing, but it was filled in with rubble.

"Where did all this come from?" Josh asked in bewilderment.

"I think it's possible that whoever built this tomb—Mensah perhaps—ordered it filled in to keep robbers out. They were very conscious of grave robbers in those days."

"Well, there's bound to be a door here."

"I'm sure there is, and let's hope it's sealed and the seal is unbroken. But first," the professor said, "we've got to examine this rubble carefully."

Piece by piece, and in small buckets, the rubble was removed. Finally on the first day of August the rubble was cleared, and the professor stood with Josh and Kefira, staring at the door before them. It was sealed in, and he went over it carefully with his fingers. He turned and said in a voice not quite steady, "It hasn't been broken into. I think we may have found something really great." He passed his hand over his forehead and said, "This has happened before so many times, when people got this far and then found that robbers had gone in and spoiled everything."

He turned to the seal and ran his fingers over it. It was the seal of the royal cemetery. He turned to them and nodded. "This is clear proof that a person of very high standing was buried here. I think whoever designed this was very wise. I believe he had seen the damage done to other tombs and decided to hide his own very well." He smiled slightly and said, "Khufu, who built the largest pyramid, the great pyramid, made a mistake. He wanted his body to be hidden, and then he built a building half a mile high and almost a quarter of a mile wide so nobody could miss the location."

"That wasn't very smart, was it?" Kefira said seriously.

"No, and in the Valley of the Kings, the pharaohs, very conveniently for grave robbers, put themselves in one small area. But this man evidently came out in the middle of an empty desert. He had the tomb built, then disguised the entrance with this ordinary-looking house. It took a long time, I would think, depending upon how long the tunnel is and how big the chambers are. But I would suspect he had all the dirt hauled off and that he worked for a long time. I wouldn't even be surprised if he didn't have some of the workers killed to keep the location secret."

"What a gruesome thought," Kefira said, frowning.

"There are more gruesome things in this world than you can think of, Kefira." Phineas smiled. "Well, we'll open this door and see what we have. We'll take one stone out first and then see what's on the other side."

For two hours the men labored, taking turns chiseling away

the mortar that held the stone together, and finally Josh said, "I believe I can pull it out now, Professor."

"Do so then, Joshua, and let's take a look at what we've found."

Josh got his fingers in the crevice and began to work the stone outward. Finally it came free, and he staggered back before putting it down.

The professor stepped forward with his flashlight and looked through the opening. He was silent for a long time, but neither Josh nor Kefira wanted to disturb him.

Turning to face them, the professor's face was alight with eagerness. "It's a tunnel," he said. "There seems to be a great deal of rubble in it. But the tunnel must lead to the burial chamber."

The news encouraged them, and for the next day they tore the wall of the door down. When it was clear they stepped inside, and Josh flashed his light around. "It's full of all sorts of things. I thought it might be empty."

"This may not be the last tunnel. I think whoever made this tomb knew what he was doing."

They began to pick up objects from the floor, and the professor exclaimed, "Look at this!" He held out a clay cylinder with hieroglyphics around it.

"What does it say, Professor?"

The professor held the flashlight in one hand and the cylinder in the other. He examined the writing and said, "It seems to be a record of a trading venture under the authority of the pharaoh, and the pharaoh is—" he paused for a moment and then laughed—"is Mentuhotep II!"

"And Mensah was his chief official."

"That's right. The tomb that archeologists have been looking for, for a long, long time." The professor grew serious as he carefully marked the piece and laid it aside. "We'll have to examine every piece of this. It's going to take a while."

"I'd like to run right down this tunnel and open the next door," Josh cried. "I'm not sure I've got enough patience for this sort of work."

"I feel exactly the same way, my boy, but we might destroy the one piece of evidence that would be most helpful if we did that. But I'll tell you what we can do. We can be very careful as we move. We can go through this material and label it, put it in boxes, and go over it in detail later. I'm anxious to get to the end of this tunnel myself."

★ ★ ★ ★

The labeling of the artifacts took longer than the professor thought. They worked hard at it for a week, and even Kefira grew expert in identifying and labeling assorted pieces.

Finally the job was done, and one morning the three of them stood before another sealed door.

"I think I know what to do," Josh said. "We'll make a hole, and you can take a look."

"That's exactly right, Joshua. We need your strong right arm for this."

Josh had become quite expert at removing stones, and by the light that the other two held for him, he began to pull out a stone. It was no more than eight inches square, and when he had successfully removed it, he stepped back and said, "Take a look, Professor."

Phineas moved forward and shined his light through the opening. He pressed his forehead against the stone, and then he was absolutely still.

Finally Josh could not wait. "Can you see anything, Professor?"

Phineas did not move for a moment, and then he turned, and his face seemed stricken. "Yes," he said, "many wonderful things!" He handed the flashlight to Joshua, saying, "Take a look."

Josh held up the light, and he also grew very still. He turned then and handed the light to Kefira, saying with a smile, "Take a look."

Kefira looked through the hole not knowing what to expect, but she caught her breath. "Why, that looks like gold!" she breathed.

"It probably is, my dear. I've never seen such treasures."

The three of them took turns looking, and finally Josh said, "It's a real find, isn't it, Professor?"

"Yes, it is. God has been good to us." He turned to Kefira and said, "Your dream is responsible for whatever success we have, my dear. I'm so happy that you came to us."

★　★　★

It took less than a day to open the door, and when the way was clear and they stepped inside, Josh exclaimed at the sight. By the light of their flashlights, they saw a gilded throne and vessels made of alabaster. All around on the walls, bizarre paintings seemed to leap out at them, their colors fresh and clear as if they had been painted yesterday. In the center of the room, a royal statue stood like a sentinel, gold-kilted with gold sandals, armed with the traditional mace and staff and the protective sacred cobra upon his forehead. They stood in awe taking it all in, and then the professor went forward and walked around the room. "Here's another sealed door," he said. "It probably leads to the burial chamber."

"Here's another one," Josh said. "I wonder where it leads."

They spent all morning just gazing, and the professor took photograph after photograph of the antechamber.

Finally he said, "Now we will open these two sealed doors. One probably goes to the burial chamber, the other, perhaps, to a treasure room. It's the way many tombs were built, and this one seems to be following the usual pattern."

★　★　★

The work proceeded slowly from that time onward, and the professor gave strict instructions that nothing would be touched. "It's very fragile," he said, "and just introducing the atmosphere could destroy precious things."

The men removed one sealed door and found that it indeed was a treasure room.

"Why, it's packed with gold and treasures!" Kefira breathed. "Why did they want to be buried with all of this?"

"They believe strongly in an afterlife, but it was a rather physical afterlife. You'll notice food is always left with the bodies, and statues of servants to serve them in the afterworld. They were very serious about death."

They then moved to the final sealed door, and when that was down, Josh asked, "What if the mummy's not here?"

"Ordinarily, I would say it might not be, but there have been absolutely no signs of grave robbers. I think we have the mummy we're looking for."

They entered the room, and there on a high platform was what they were seeking. They saw the sarcophagus of a royal person.

The professor moved closer and shined the light on the inscription. He stood absolutely still, then whispered, "The body of Mensah."

"Then we've found it!"

"Yes, we found it, Josh, and soon all the world will know about it." He turned and said, "You'll be a famous man."

"No, you'll be the famous man, Professor."

The professor put one hand on Josh's shoulder and the other on Kefira's. "There's enough glory for all of us, and I've decided to tell the world exactly how we found this tomb—that God gave a dream to a young woman, and the dream came true."

Josh stood speechless, and Kefira could not speak either. The professor laughed suddenly and said, "But this is not the greatest discovery." He waved his hand at the sarcophagus and included the golden treasures heaped in abundance.

"It's not!" Kefira exclaimed. "What is?"

"This is." Professor Welles reached into his pocket and brought out a leather pouch. He carefully undid the drawstring and drew out a small clay cylinder. "This is the greatest treasure of all."

Josh could see the hieroglyphics, and when the professor handed it to him, warning him to be careful, he began to try to read it. "I'm afraid my study of hieroglyphics isn't good enough yet, Professor. You'll have to read it for us."

"All right, I will." Phineas took the clay, holding it as if it were made of very fragile glass, and began to read. "'The pharaoh extends his good will to the strangers in our kingdom. Especially he wishes that the gods will bless—'" here the professor swallowed hard—"'Abraham the Hebrew.'"

Josh too swallowed against the lump in his throat. "I can't believe it, Professor," he whispered.

"I can't believe it either. I've been going over the fragments we found in the first tunnel. Most of them are of little interest, but when I found this one, I think my heart nearly stopped."

He held up the clay cylinder and said, "So Abraham found his way to Egypt and somehow the pharaoh knew of him, and he wished the gods to bless him. Well, not the gods of Egypt, but God himself blessed Abraham, the father of the faithful."

Kefira reached out and touched the cylinder. "Father Abraham," she whispered. "He was here."

"Exactly as the Scripture says," Phineas said, nodding. "Now, this will be what I give to the world, so much more than the mummy of a dead man."

"What will happen now, Professor?"

"Everybody will hear of this tomb. You remember when Carter and Lord Carnarvon found the tomb of Tutankhamen? The news stunned the world. Well, I think this will be equally stunning."

The three stood there in the midst of all the glories of ancient Egypt, but each of them felt that the bit of clay was of more value than all the gold in the tomb of Mensah.

★   ★   ★   ★

For the next two months, life was a whirl for Kefira. The word got out, and as the professor had prophesied, the desert became filled with eager onlookers—Egyptologists, newspaper reporters, government representatives. The professor handled it all well, but it was a hectic time.

Letters poured in from all over the world. Famous scientists offered their aid, countries vied for part of the treasure for their museums, and the story of how the tomb was found was blazoned across the newspapers of the world.

"You're famous, Kefira," Josh said. The two of them had walked out of the camp to get away from the furor and the constant pressure for interviews.

"I wish I weren't sometimes," Kefira said. "They all want to know everything about me, and there's not that much to tell."

"I think there is. You might as well get used to it."

The two reached the tiny spring and stood looking down as it bubbled out of the sand. It was relatively quiet now, for it was late enough that the reporters, who usually stayed awake until the wee hours, had all settled down.

Josh took her hand, and the two stood there silently. "The quiet's so good," Kefira said.

"Yes, it is. I get tired of all the noise, and the people are getting in the way of the work."

"It's going to take a long time, isn't it?"

"Yes, I would say at least a year."

"By then Chaim will be out of prison."

"Yes, and we'll be there waiting for him when he comes out."

"Would you really do that, Josh? Leave the dig and return to America in time for his release?"

"He's my brother. Of course I will."

He turned to face her then and said, "It would be nice if we could get married at my home. My family would love to do that. To fuss over you and welcome you as the newest Winslow."

Kefira had thought of this. "But a year is a long time to wait for a husband."

Josh laughed, pleased. "I don't know what to make of you."

"You can make of me that I'm a woman in love. Do we have to wait a year? Can't people get married in Egypt?"

Josh laughed again. He reached out, threw his arms around her, and lifted her clear off the ground, swinging her around. He put her down and kissed her firmly. "Yes, we'll get married this week, and our honeymoon will be here."

"Oh, Josh, can we really do that?"

"It won't be much of a honeymoon."

"We can go look at the pyramids for a couple of days. A lot

of people come all the way from America just to do that, and we can be there in just a few hours."

"Yes, we can do that." He took her in his arms and held her gently and kissed her. "Then," he said, "we'll go home, and the Winslows will welcome my bride."

Overhead the moon looked down, shedding pale light over the scene. The desert was quiet, and for the moment the only thing that moved was the man and the woman. From the distance, a wild dog of the desert approached silently. He halted abruptly, the silver of the moon reflected in his eyes. He watched the two, then turned and disappeared into the darkness, but the man and the woman did not see him. They looked up at the stars, at the moon, and finally at each other, and then the woman whispered, "Yes, Joshua Winslow. This very week I'll be your bride."

Looking for More Good Books to Read?

You can find out what is new and exciting with pre-views, descriptions, and reviews by signing up for Bethany House newsletters at

www.bethanynewsletters.com

We will send you updates for as many authors or categories as you desire so you get only the information you really want.

Sign up today!